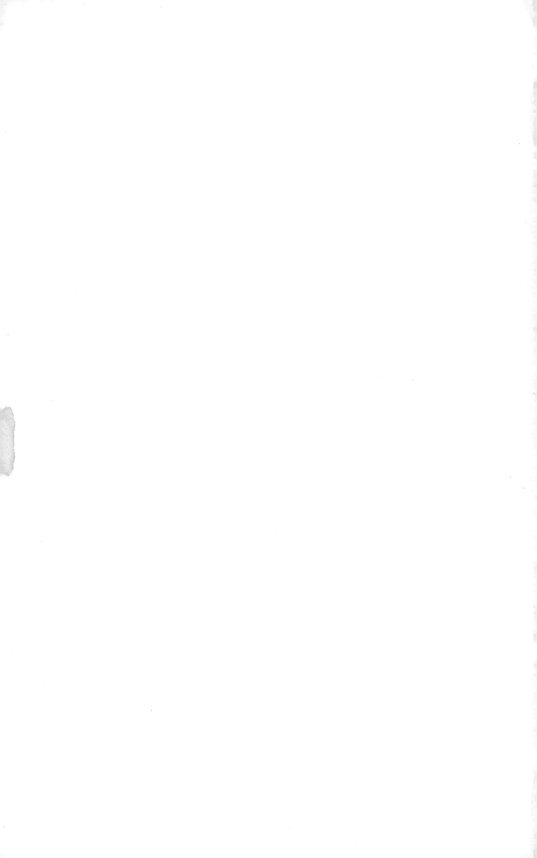

THE RAGE OF INNOCENCE

ALSO BY WILLIAM D. PEASE

Playing the Dozens

THE
RAGE
OF
Innocence

A NOVEL BY

WILLIAM D. PEASE

VIKING

VIKING
Published by the Penguin Group
Penguin Books USA Inc., 375 Hudson Street,
New York, New York 10014, U.S.A.
Penguin Books Ltd, 27 Wrights Lane, London W8 5TZ, England
Penguin Books Australia Ltd, Ringwood, Victoria, Australia
Penguin Books Canada Ltd, 10 Alcorn Avenue,
Toronto, Ontario, Canada M4V 3B2
Penguin Books (N.Z.) Ltd, 182–190 Wairau Road,
Auckland 10, New Zealand

Penguin Books Ltd, Registered Offices:
Harmondsworth, Middlesex, England

First published in 1993 by Viking Penguin,
a division of Penguin Books USA Inc.

10   9   8   7   6   5   4   3   2   1

PUBLISHER'S NOTE
This is a work of fiction. Names, characters, places, and
incidents either are the product of the author's imagination
or are used fictitiously, and any resemblance to actual
persons, living or dead, events, or locales is entirely
coincidental.

Grateful acknowledgment is made for permission to reprint
an excerpt from *Scoundrel Time* by Lillian Hellman.
Copyright © 1976 by Lillian Hellman. By permission of
Little, Brown and Company.

Library of Congress Cataloging-in-Publication Data
Pease, William D.
The rage of innocence: a novel / by William D. Pease.
p.   cm.
ISBN 0-670-83519-6
I. Title.
PS3586.E2425R34   1993
813'.54—dc20   92-50727

Printed in the United States of America
Set in Garamond No. 3

This book is dedicated to my mother,
and to the memory of my father, who in all probability
is still scratching his head in wonderment.

I also want to take this opportunity to express my thanks to those whose encouragement, advice and assistance have contributed so much.

First and foremost, with love and appreciation to Laura Brank, from start to finish an honest critic, a sympathetic ear, an encouraging voice and the one whose good opinion I covet most; to my agent, Kathy Robbins, and my editor, Al Silverman, both for their insights and encouragement and for keeping me on course; to Bob Higdon, for the periodic reality checks and for constantly rescuing my bytes; to my "beta testers," Genie Ford and Cindy Dunn, both literate and insightful readers; to Elliott Newcomb for his legal counsel; to Ford and Jane Davis for reacquainting me with Baltimore; and to Clark Stith, who saved me from exposing just how little I remember of my college French.

AUTHOR'S NOTE

This is a work of fiction. The characters and events described herein are solely the product of my imagination, and any resemblance to any persons living or dead is purely coincidental. In some cases I make reference to historical events, and historical persons appear under their own names. Where such references are made they are made solely in a fictional context. Finally, to those readers who examine fiction for factual anomalies, I alert you first to the fact that the town of Maryville and its environs are imaginary, although in my mind's eye they represent any number of locations both east and west of the Chesapeake Bay; and second, that I have taken the artistic liberty of ignoring the organizational and jurisdictional mire that exists among the various state, county and local law enforcement agencies and have purposely reorganized the Maryland State Police in a manner I thought best suited this story.

From childhood's hour I have not been
as others were—I have not seen
As others saw—I could not bring
My passions from a common spring.
From the same source I have not taken
My sorrow; I could not awaken
My heart to joy at the same tone;
And all I lov'd, I lov'd alone. . . .

—EDGAR ALLAN POE

THE RAGE OF INNOCENCE

PROLOGUE

On May 19, 1952, American playwright Lillian Hellman, in response to a subpoena to appear before the House Committee on Un-American Activities then investigating the threat of Communists infiltrating Hollywood, wrote the following letter to committee chairman John S. Wood:

Dear Mr. Wood:

As you know, I am under subpoena to appear before your Committee on May 21, 1952.

I am most willing to answer all questions about myself. I have nothing to hide from your Committee and there is nothing in my life of which I am ashamed. I have been advised by counsel that under the Fifth Amendment I have a constitutional privilege to decline to answer any questions about my political opinions, activities and associations, on the grounds of self-incrimination. I do not wish to claim this privilege. I am ready and willing to testify before representatives of our Government as to my own opinions and my own actions, regardless of any risks or consequences to myself.

But I am advised by counsel that if I answer the Committee's questions about myself, I must also answer questions about other people and that if I refuse to do so, I can be cited for contempt. My counsel tells me that if I answer questions about myself, I will have waived my rights under the Fifth Amendment and could be forced legally to answer questions about others. This is very difficult for a layman to understand. But there is one principle that I do understand: I am not willing, now or in the future, to bring bad trouble to people who, in my past association with them, were completely innocent of any talk or any action that was disloyal or subversive. I do not like subversion or disloyalty in any form and if I had ever seen any I would have considered it my duty to have reported it to the proper authorities. But to hurt innocent people whom I knew many years ago in order to save myself is, to me, inhuman and indecent and dishonorable. I cannot and will not cut my conscience to fit this year's fashions, even though I long ago came to the conclusion that I was not a political person and could have no comfortable place in any political group.

I was raised in an old-fashioned American tradition and there were certain homely things that were taught to me: to try to tell the truth, not to bear false witness, not to harm my neighbor, to be loyal to my country, and so on. In general, I respected these ideals of Christian honor and did as well with them as I knew how. It is my belief that you will agree with these simple rules of human decency and will not expect me to violate the good American tradition from which they spring. I would, therefore, like to come before you and speak of myself.

I am prepared to waive the privilege against self-incrimination and to tell you anything you wish to know about my views or actions if your Committee will agree to refrain from asking me to name other people. If the Committee is unwilling to give me this assurance, I will be forced to plead the privilege of the Fifth Amendment at the hearing.

A reply to this letter would be appreciated.

Sincerely yours,
Lillian Hellman

On that same day, nervous about her upcoming appearance before the committee and anticipating the financial ruin that was inevitably to come, Ms. Hellman decided that for the moment she would ignore her concerns. She bought a Balmain dress, an expensive hat and a pair of white kid gloves to wear to the hearing two days later. She had lunch at Harvey's Restaurant, then a Washington institution where, it was said, J. Edgar Hoover and his closest associate, Clyde Tolson, had lunch every day.

On the morning of May 21, after a long and sleepless night, Ms. Hellman took a taxi to the offices of her attorney, Joseph Rauh. Rauh greeted her with the news that Thurman Arnold, a former assistant attorney general and a law partner of the future Supreme Court justice Abe Fortas, had called to warn Rauh that Hellman's letter to the committee would almost certainly result in her being jailed for contempt. Although she was upset by the message, even to the point of illness, Lillian Hellman dismissed Thurman Arnold's concerns, determined to follow through on the course she had chosen.

By eleven o'clock that morning, she, Joseph Rauh and Rauh's assistant, Daniel Pollitt, had arrived for the committee hearing in the Old House Office Building. There, she maintained her position set out in the letter of May 19, which letter was made part of the record and distributed to the press. She again expressed her willingness to testify about herself, her own beliefs and activities, but she refused to name others. After some verbal wrangling between the committee and her lawyers, Lillian Hellman was excused from any further testimony or appearance before the committee. She had neither testified about the activities of others nor been cited for contempt for her refusal.

The committee hearing, however, was the least of it. Her life had changed dramatically. Having been added to Hollywood's blacklist of suspected Communists or Communist sympathizers, Lillian Hellman saw the wealth and security of her pre-blacklist days quickly dissipated. "Hardscrabble," the Westchester County farm so dearly loved by her and her longtime companion Dashiell Hammett, was sold. Hammett, who had been jailed in 1951 for refusing to reveal the names of contributors to the Civil Rights Congress bail fund, was to spend the last ten years of his life essentially without any royalty income from books, film, radio or television that was not attached by the Internal Revenue Service. Lillian Hellman, then America's most prominent woman playwright, was for a time reduced to a part-time job under an assumed name in the food section of a New York City department store.

But America enjoys a short and selective memory when it comes to the politics of its personalities. It took some years, but Lillian Hellman reestablished herself, eventually gathering the financial rewards and critical acclaim her art deserved. Even Hollywood returned, offering her the movie scripts she no longer wanted.

But it was never quite the same. In *Scoundrel Time,* Hellman's memoir of the McCarthy era, she concluded:

> I have written here that I have recovered. I mean it only in a worldly sense because I do not believe in recovery. The past, with its pleasures, its rewards, its foolishness, its punishments, is there for each of us forever, and it should be.
>
> As I finish writing about this unpleasant part of my life, I tell myself that was then, and there is now, and the years between then and now, and the then and now are one.

On June 30, 1984, Lillian Hellman died at her home on the island of Martha's Vineyard.

■■■

On the morning of Lillian Hellman's appearance before the House Committee on Un-American Activities, Martin Lessing, a thirty-two-year-old assistant professor of French literature at the University of Maryland, sat in a jail cell barely more than a mile away from the Old House Office Building. Three days before, Lessing had been arrested and charged with trafficking in classified government documents, and he was waiting for friends to find an attorney willing to represent him. Like Ms. Hellman, he had refused to divulge the names of his associates: but unlike the playwright's, his refusal went unnoticed except in the files of the FBI, where it was noted cryptically, "Subject refused cooperation."

On the evening of May 21, 1952, about the time Lillian Hellman was boarding her plane to return to New York, Martin Lessing died of pneumonia, alone in his cell, his request for pen and paper— the only request he had made of his jailers—having been refused.

A reporter for *The Washington Post* prepared a story about Lessing's death as a sidebar to the coverage of Lillian Hellman's appearance before the committee. But for reasons of space, the story was dropped and the event went unreported. For all but those few people who knew him, the event might never have happened.

PART *One*

1 $\mathcal{S}$outh of town, where the river widens
and turns brackish with the tidal reaches of
the bay, a small flock of geese drifts quietly
at the edge of a marsh less than a hundred
yards from Cooper Avery's house. Some
feed, their tails tipping skyward as their
long necks stretch to probe the shallows for the submerged vege-
tation and shellfish that sustain them. Others, their heads held high
and still, listen for the sound of dangers they cannot see. A pink
penciled line of first light creases the horizon, but it will be hours
before the sun is high enough to burn off a heavy mist rising from
the river; and the only sound is that of the river's current lapping
softly against the muddy bank.

Suddenly, from the shore, comes the sound of footsteps. At first
dull and distant, the footsteps turn quick and heavy as they scrabble
down a footpath and onto a short wooden pier reaching out into
the river.

The geese stop their feeding, alert to the intrusion.

At the end of the pier, where a small rubber skiff is tied, the
footsteps halt, and a low, anxious muttering mixes with an awkward
stumble into the skiff and the clunk of something heavy dropped
on its wooden seat. A paddle slaps lightly at the water, and its
handle chafes the hollow rubber hull pushing against the current
of the ebbing tide.

The geese collect themselves and begin moving toward open
water.

At the outer edge of the marsh, a hunting blind stands naked and empty and heavily shrouded by the mist. Goose season is still a month or more away, and the blind has not been dressed with the sheaves of dried salt grasses that will camouflage the men who will huddle on its chilled platform, braced by their shotguns and flasks of whiskey. The skiff slides through the fog until with a light thud it collides with one of the blind's thickly barnacled pilings. There is a startled curse, and the paddle stabs and scrapes at the piling to push the skiff away. The strokes turn quick and incautious, and the small rubber boat waddles toward the middle of the river, where the current is strongest.

The geese continue to move away until they hear the paddling stop. Several moments pass before the silence is again broken, this time by the muffled, metallic grunt of an outboard engine's starter rope. One pull, and then a second, and then a third, and the engine suddenly fires with a hesitant, uneven sputter, catching its breath, filling the morning with a loud, rasping drone that drives the skiff upstream toward a channel marker whose light blinks faintly in the thick gray distance.

The geese wait, and when all they can hear are the sounds of the river and each other, they begin their cautious glide back to the marsh, where again they will feed until it is time to move on.

▬▬▬

Cooper Avery went to settlement on his 217 acres of prime waterfront property on the third of June, 1977, the day before he and Marian Thurston were married. Marian, a product of Guilford, one of Baltimore's more coveted and affluent neighborhoods, was reluctant to start her new life in the wilds of southern Maryland and more than an hour's drive from the city. But her father approved, even encouraged, the purchase, as he did the marriage. Edward Thurston was pleased with his future son-in-law and easily forgave Cooper his lineage. Cooper's father, Albert Vinson Avery, then a fifth-term member of Congress, was in Thurston's eyes little more than an annoyance, a politician whose only talent was for keeping the political winds at his back. The congressman's son, however, avoided the public eye and showed an admirable lack of interest in politics beyond the practical advantages its influence might provide. Edward Thurston liked that, and he saw in Cooper his own aggressive vision of the future and his willingness to take whatever risks necessary to build a future that was his own. And he took pride in the way Cooper had uncovered and seized upon the opportunities presented by the outstanding tax liens and civil judgments that had put on the block the farm that had been in Oliver Johns's family for more than six generations. Before anyone but the attorney for the Johns family's estate quite knew what was happening, Cooper had managed to piece together a network of minority partners and bank financing to purchase all but a single acre of the farm for little more than a third of its market value. He quickly subdivided the land into 112 very expensive homesites, which he christened Fishing Creek Estates, and in the process managed to reserve for himself the Johns family home, an imposing if neglected Georgian mansion nestled in a grove overlooking the mouth of the river.

The deal was settled less than an hour before Cooper and Marian's wedding rehearsal was scheduled to begin at St. Mark's Episcopal Church. Cooper was twenty minutes late, but Edward Thurston, smoothing over the anxious and angry expressions of his wife and daughter, forgave Cooper his tardiness. And later, to the crowd of people gathered for the rehearsal dinner at the Harbor Island Yacht and Country Club—those people whom Thurston counted as friends and whom Congressman Avery counted as contributors—Thurston extolled Cooper's cunning and only half-jokingly warned that they had best watch out for this newest fox in the henhouse. For Cooper Avery, it was an auspicious beginning.

But it was only the beginning. Neither Cooper Avery nor Edward Thurston had seen any good reason for Maryville, the nearest settlement only a few minutes' drive from the then nascent development, to remain forever the sullen, dingy river town that boasted little more than a single boatyard, a hardware and dry goods store, a diner that closed at dusk, two gas stations, and a bar where the local farmers and watermen drank beer from the bottle while their Labrador and Chesapeake Bay retrievers lay curled in the sawdust at their feet. In partnership with Thurston Construction, Cooper began quietly and selectively purchasing certain prime properties along Maryville's waterfront. With the judicious exercise of influence among the directors of the State Department of Natural Resources, the river's narrow channel was widened and deepened to accommodate a proper marina and the deep-draft sailboats that brought with them the disposable income to encourage the opening of restaurants that served imported wines and added sherry to the native crab soup.

Slowly but surely, Maryville was discovered. Soon weekend tourists were browsing for watercolors and polished wooden decoys and the brass wire models of skipjacks and log canoes that filled the shops that had been renovated and leased to the artists and craftsmen and the second-income housewives from the city. Aside from the profits that came with such development, the new Maryville also managed to add some luster to the reputation of Thurston Construction, a reputation that in the past had been tarnished by civic groups and preservationists' objections to what they termed the company's "scorched-earth policy" in creating shopping malls and industrial parks throughout the eastern half of the United States.

Marian, too, had played her part. Armed with the promise of a new and more chic Maryville, and with notebooks filled with clippings from *House Beautiful* and *Southern Living,* Marian had set about to supervise the gutting and renovation of the house Oliver Johns's great-grandfather had built in the 1860s. It was to become the home that had filled her dreams since adolescence.

She was there at every stage, beginning on the day she followed the contractor around the property asking questions and offering suggestions as he pounded brightly painted stakes into the ground to establish the building lines for the additions. She had carefully tied strips of red cloth around the trunks of oak and beech and loblolly pine to guide the bulldozers that were clearing most of the land behind the house to allow a panoramic view of the river emptying into the Chesapeake Bay. Each evening she tacked notes to the foundation or to the framework or to the Sheetrock or millwork to point out errors, to order changes and, on occasion, even to express her satisfaction. It took more than a year and nearly sixty thousand dollars over budget, but when it was finished, Marian was certain that this first estate in Fishing Creek would forever be the queen of the fleet.

But it wasn't enough. In the beginning, friends both social and business would come from the city, not as often as Marian would have liked, but often enough to fill most weekends with cocktail and dinner parties and cookouts by the new gazebo overlooking the water. And on those long midweek days of their first summer, when her feelings of detachment from the old life in Baltimore were most acute, Marian would cajole her closest friends to abandon the city to come and sun themselves on the dock, drink whatever struck their fancy, and compare the reality of their lives to the fantasies that had carried them through the Lowell Academy and Sweet Briar College. With the chill of fall and through that first winter, Marian migrated back to the city almost daily, enjoying long lunches with friends or with her mother, or shopping, or taking in a matinee until it was time to meet Cooper, who by then had been made vice-president of Thurston Construction, and they would begin their long, quiet ride home.

By the following spring, lot sales in Fishing Creek had begun to pick up, and several houses were under construction. Marian had been inducted as the community association's first president, and she was pregnant. It had begun to look as if the promise might be realized.

On February 18, 1980, in the emergency room of the county hospital, Edward Thurston Avery was born, two weeks early and while Cooper was on the West Coast scouting new opportunities for Thurston Construction. Marian never made an issue of Cooper's absence. Indeed she made no comment whatsoever; she had, after all, been raised in her father's house, and like her mother before her, she had learned to temper her expectations. And as had her mother in her own marriage, Marian found the spaces left by Cooper's ambition easily filled by the life of her child. Mother and daughter—each had found her place in the continuum, and Marian felt no need, and perhaps no right, to question it.

Marian doted on Ned, trying, if only half-consciously, to shape her son and his future in the image of her past. But Ned was not so easily molded, except, perhaps, physically. By his tenth birthday, he had begun to mimic the plumpness that Marian had acquired during her second pregnancy and had never lost. Intensely shy— Marian said he was just sensitive—Ned often seemed oblivious to any stimulus but his own, and for the most part, he kept his thoughts to himself. A battery of psychological tests had placed him in the exceptionally bright category, but they had done little to bridge the gap between Ned and his father. Cooper tried, but he could never quite mask his disappointment at Ned's aversion to fishing or to the sight and sound of a shotgun bringing down a goose; nor could Cooper suppress his anger on those winter nights when Ned would sneak Cooper's two gundogs from their pen behind the garage and lead them to his bedroom.

"Damn it, son, they're not lap dogs," Cooper would snap before he'd retreat and leave the boy to Marian, who, with a forgiving smile, would countermand the order to return the dogs to their pen, comb her fingers through the boy's long, sandy hair and kiss him goodnight while the dogs lay curled beside his bed.

Alice was different. Cooper and Marian's second child, born two years after Ned, stood as tall as her brother and was everything he was not, or so it seemed to Cooper. Bone-thin and electric with energy, Alice would squeal with delight whenever she hooked a fish: and while she might utter an occasional "Oh, gross!" as Cooper cleaned and scaled their catch, she never hesitated to reach into the pail to serve up the next victim. And she was constantly asking Cooper when he was going to teach her to shoot.

"Never!" Marian repeated over and over, and in the same determined tone she used in threatening divorce if Cooper acceded to Alice's wish for a football helmet for Christmas.

It wasn't everything Marian had hoped for, but it was far more than she had feared.

■■■

It is Saturday morning, the morning Cooper and Marian usually reserve for their comfortable routines, the morning they arise early to allow themselves a cup of coffee before Alice, now eight, explodes from her bed and fills the kitchen with her chatter while Ned hunkers behind the comics and quietly eats his breakfast. It is the day that Cooper can slip away for an hour or two at the hardware store, looking over tools he does not need, trading gossip and listening to the usual predictions of a harsh winter. It is the time for Marian to sit at the kitchen table, silent and sleepy-eyed, both hands cupped around a warm mug, her head cocked a bit, wondering what to wear that evening and absently inspecting the floor's coat of wax, which no one but she thinks worn and faded.

But this Saturday is different. Cooper has spent the last three days in Boston negotiating with several banks and institutional lenders. He is now the company's president, Edward Thurston having turned the daily operations of his corporation over to his son-in-law and freed himself to spend his days manipulating the computer that manipulates his finances. Cooper is not expected home until late afternoon.

Alice is three houses away, in the home of Charles and Ellen Haley, sound asleep in a third-floor loft, her best friend, Megan, in the bed beside her. Ned, too, was to have slept over, Megan's twin brother being one of Ned's very few friends. But Ned showed signs of a cold, and at the last minute Marian thought it best that he stay home.

The Avery house is quiet. The bedrooms are empty. The kitchen is not filled with the aroma of coffee and the morning paper has not been delivered. In the center of the floor, Marian Avery lies face down and motionless. The first faint rays of light shine on a small gold bracelet on her left wrist. Over her head rests a pillow scarred by a single dark hole and a scattering of feathers. A few wisps of down have fallen to the floor and form a trail to Ned, who sits huddled in the far corner, his right hand locked in a fist that clutches the cloth of his pajama top. He, too, is motionless, except for the shivering that comes from the cold linoleum floor, and the slow rhythmic movement of his left hand, which smears traces of blood and a few tiny feathers onto his pant leg. His eyes are fixed and he makes no sound.

It will be hours before anyone finds them just as they are now.

2 *T*he Maryville bypass loops east of town, cutting through wide, flat fields of corn long past its harvest and lying fallow and undisturbed except by the geese that forage in the dried remains. The noontime sun has cleared the air, leaving a bright, watercolored sky. Beyond the fields and clustered about the clapboard and tin-roofed farmhouses at the ends of narrow dirt drives, the trees are awash with the color of autumn. And for these few moments, Christine Boland's world feels clean and forgiving.

She is in no hurry, although she knows she should be, and she keeps the speedometer's needle just a notch above the posted forty-five-mile-per-hour limit. She lets the wind lift her hand from the car's side-view mirror and watches it plane in the cool rush of air, imagining herself on a flight to some place other than where she is headed. A yellow school bus filled with bright-jerseyed football players on their way to the junior high school championship lumbers along ahead of her. Several of the boys look back at her, then turn to each other and laugh and punch each other on their padded shoulders. Christine blushes a bit but then smiles, and she flutters her fingers in a coquettish wave, which ignites an explosion of hoots and hormonal offerings from the back of the bus. *Thirty-eight years old,* she thinks with a self-conscious shake of her head, *and still drawn by the opportunity to excite a busload of adolescents.* She steps on the accelerator and quickly passes the bus, leaving their laughter and her smile behind.

The bypass stretches on for another mile or so before she turns down a narrow two-lane road that leads straight to an entrance guarded on both sides by a low brick wall. At the center of the entrance there is a small cedar-roofed kiosk bearing a polished brass sign that reads "Fishing Creek Estates." A sheriff's department car is parked in front of the kiosk, and beside it, a uniformed officer looking not much older than the football players she has just left behind stands talking to the driver of a Mercedes-Benz. The driver leans back in his seat, allowing his wife to stretch across him to join the conversation. Christine waits a moment or two before reaching for the emergency light, which she sets conspicuously on the dashboard. The sheriff's deputy looks startled by the sudden blue flashing and quickly waves the Mercedes on.

" 'Morning, Deputy," Christine offers along with the badge identifying her as a detective sergeant with the Maryland State Police.

"Yes, ma'am," the deputy answers, now standing stiff and erect.

Christine takes a moment to look around. "Is there usually a guard on duty here?"

The deputy does not allow himself the informality of leaning down to speak to her as he did with the people in the Mercedes-Benz. "No, ma'am," he says, "it's just 'cause of the homicide. That's pretty unusual around here, and, y'know, who's involved and all. I guess the word's spread real quick. There've been lotsa people coming 'round for a look-see, so the sheriff said to close the road 'cept for residents and such."

Christine nods and watches the deputy's eyes drift down toward the hint of cleavage revealed by the open collar of her white cotton blouse. *It must be the country air,* she muses, and lets the offense pass. "How do I get to the scene?"

"It's Ollie Johns's old house," the deputy says eagerly, his eyes still fixed on her and his hand pointing more to the sky than to the road ahead. "You take this road all the way to where it splits, then follow it to the right until it comes 'round to where you can see the water from the road. Big brick house on the river side. You can't miss it. You'll see all the police cars."

"Thanks." She drives on slowly.

Fishing Creek Estates has none of the rough agricultural feel of the rest of the county. Its roads are a smoothed black composition bordered by rounded curbs and grass berms as carefully tended as the lawns which spread between the widely spaced houses. Even the trees are ordered, the native growth having given way to the developers and been replaced with Bradford pears and Japanese crab apples, with dogwood and red maples and white oak, all carefully positioned to complement the carefully positioned houses.

Christine pulls a brush from her purse and passes a few strokes through the dark brown hair which falls lightly and just barely to her shoulders. She shakes her head to add some fluff and quickly flicks her fingers at the wisps of bangs, which seem a shade or two lighter in the bright sun. A turn to the right, a curve to the left and she can see the police cars gathered in front of the house and the neighbors huddled in quiet conversation across the street. She pulls to the curb and drops the hairbrush into her purse as she notices the neighbors noticing her.

As she steps from the car, she is uncertain whether her sudden discomfort comes from the prospect of her work over the next few hours, or from the immediate stares of the neighbors. She turns her gaze upon them, not long enough for it to be called a stare, but long enough for it to be noticed and to define them as the audience. Violence, especially violence out of context, has its own hold over those who can observe its effects without being touched, and between their open expressions of horror and sorrow are always wedged the secret thoughts that titillate and spike their imaginations. On some level, Christine enjoys their attention, enjoys that elevated sense of being special, of being an integral part of their morbid entertainment, and even, as now, of being the entertainment itself.

She turns toward the Averys' house. O. B. Hardiman, the commander of the homicide branch, is standing on the narrow front porch some fifty yards from the street. He signals her with a quick rolling wave of his hand that does not interrupt his conversation with several crime scene technicians. *Big Daddy,* she thinks with an inward smile, looking at this large man with a solid globe of a belly standing next to one of the four Ionic columns which grace the rounded portico. She tries to imagine the captain in white linens and a Panama but cannot, his preference for dark suits, expensive and finely tailored to minimize his burly physique, being too much a part of his character. Still, there is something almost baronial about this scene. A wide slate walkway bordered by mature boxwoods leads to the house, whose original center structure can easily be distinguished from its two telescoped additions by the new brick-work, which cannot quite match the original century-old masonry.

Captain Hardiman dismisses the technicians as she approaches. "Took you long enough," he says abruptly.

He has this way about him, often seeming to the uninitiated brusque and impersonal. But she knows him too well to be either intimidated or offended. O. B. Hardiman respects intelligence above all else, and while he would deny it, Christine understands how many times he has gone out of his way to make room for her talents in a world of men who seem truly comfortable only with clones of themselves. And but for his constant and annoying habit of calling her "honey," she can say that in her thirteen years with the state police, O. B. Hardiman is the only man who has never treated her as anything but a professional.

"I got here as soon as I could, Captain," she answers without apology. "This is my day off, you know."

He shrugs that he understands but that he is not particularly sympathetic. "Honey," he says, "I've got a problem here that I thought could use your special talents."

"What's the problem—*sweetie?*"

A young trooper standing behind Captain Hardiman smiles, then stiffens as the captain turns on him. "Clear everyone but Detective Wyzanski and the coroner out of the house." The trooper turns away, and Hardiman frowns. "Why do you have to do that?" But before she can give him the answer she has given him so many times before, he shrugs it off. "Never mind. Paul's inside," he says, almost as if it were a question.

She knows he is looking for a reaction, questioning whether there might be any friction in her working with Detective Paul Wyzanski, the man who two years ago was her lover. The affair had lasted only a few months before Paul began to show signs of be-coming far more serious than Christine wanted, and she gently but adamantly sent him back to his wife. Christine allows no reaction at all but to ask, "And?"

"Well, Sergeant, we have sort of a strange one on our hands here. The reason I called for you is that we have a ten-year-old boy who I suspect may have seen his mother's murder."

Christine's expression hardens. "Jesus," she whispers, almost to herself.

"But we can't get him to say anything. He's acting, I don't know, I guess you'd call it catatonic. It's as if he doesn't hear anything anyone says, as if he doesn't even know anyone's there. He doesn't move. He just stares straight ahead like he's in another world."

With master's degrees in forensic science and psychology, Christine Boland has long ago earned the captain's confidence—and some think dependence—whenever a case turns "strange," as he would put it. She takes a moment before answering. "It sounds like severe shock."

"I don't know what it is clinically, but I was hoping you might be able to get through to him. Maybe get some kind of response. Anything."

"He's still here on the scene?"

Hardiman nods but then adds, "Well, not right here. He's at a neighbor's house."

"Has he been seen by a doctor?"

"Yeah, the coroner's seen him. He's fine physically, but the doctor suggested that it'd be helpful to get someone with psychological training to try and talk to him. He doesn't really know whether the boy is in shock or just frightened, or whatever."

She looks at him skeptically. "What about the local hospital?"

Hardiman shakes his head. "Chris, for Christ's sake, down here the closest thing to psychological treatment is a case of beer and a fistfight."

"Captain, I'm hardly qualified to—"

"Look," he interrupts, "I just want you to see if you can get through to him. You know how important time is in these things. It can't hurt to try, can it?"

She takes in a deep breath and lets it go slowly. "Yeah, it could. I just don't know. If the boy's really in a precarious state mentally or emotionally, we don't want to add to the trauma."

"I understand that. That's why I called for you. All I'm asking is that you talk to the boy. See what you think and use your best judgment."

"Has anyone tried to talk to him? Family, neighbors?"

"Not really, at least not since the sheriff got here. The father's out of town. We've been trying to track him down through his office but we haven't found him yet. The grandparents are on their way down from Baltimore. But it's gonna take a while. And I asked

them if it'd be all right for a psychologist to talk to the boy and
they said all right."

"Captain, I'm not licensed for—"

"Sergeant, I'm just asking you to see the boy. This is a murder
scene. And right now, that's a priority."

"The dispatcher said this is Congressman Avery's son. Is that
right?"

"Grandson."

"You talked to the congressman and he said it was all right to
talk to the boy?"

"No, I talked to the Thurstons, the wife's—you know, the victim's side of the family. They're the ones who're on their way down
now. The congressman lives somewhere in Florida now."

"And the father?"

"Like I said, he's been away on business. Boston, the neighbor
said. We just haven't had any luck finding him."

"Don't you think you're playing with fire here? I mean these
people are not your average John Q. Citizen. And for me to start
playing doctor—"

"Chris, I'm not asking you to treat the boy, just try to get through
to him. We're not stepping over any lines here. It's our job. Just
see him. Use your own judgment."

"It's just the one child?"

"There's a younger sister, but apparently she was sleeping over
at a neighbor's last night, the same neighbor where the boy is now.
We're keeping the two apart. She doesn't know what's happened
yet. The little girl, that is."

"What did happen here?"

Captain Hardiman shrugs and lifts his eyebrows with a tilt of
his head. "Well," he says, dragging the word out, "looks like a break-
in. Maybe the woman caught the man in the act and he killed her.
A single shot to the back of the head."

"A burglar? Shot a woman in the back of the head?"

Hardiman again shrugs.

"Any evidence of rape or a fight?"

"Not so far. The house was tossed but there are no marks on
the body except for the bullet wound."

"Close range?"

"Contact wound. Through a pillow."

"What?"

"Through a pillow," he repeats.

She shakes her head. "You got a theory?" She knows he does. She only wonders whether he is ready to share it.

"Look, I'd rather you took your own read on this after you go over the scene, but first I want to try and get through to the boy."

Christine frowns. "Well . . . let me look around first. I may see something that'll help with the boy."

"Okay, let's go," Hardiman says quickly, and he reaches for the front door.

Christine stops him with a hand on his coat sleeve. "Let's slow down a bit here. Before we start I need some background. Tell me about how the boy was found, and where. And who found him? And when?"

Captain Hardiman releases the information in a soft, even staccato. "About a quarter to ten this morning. A neighbor, Ellen Haley, found the body—and the boy. The younger sister, name's Alice, was sleeping over with her friend at the Haleys' house. The boy—"

Christine interrupts him. "How old did you say he was?"

"Ten. His name's Ned. The sister, Alice, is eight. The boy was supposed to have slept over too, but he had a cold or something. This Mrs. Haley, the neighbor? It wasn't easy getting a clear story out of her. She was pretty hysterical, but as far as we can piece it together, she called the house this morning around eight-thirty to tell Mrs. Avery that she was sending Alice home."

"Avery is the victim?"

"Right, Marian Thurston Avery. Husband's name is Cooper. The former congressman's son."

Christine stores the information with a nod.

"Anyway, there's no answer. Mrs. Haley thinks that's strange but waits another half hour or so and calls again. There's still no answer. She tries again around nine-fifteen and when there's still no answer, she decides to walk over to the house. She lives over there," he says, pointing to a large brick colonial three doors away. "She leaves Alice and her daughter, both the same age, watching cartoons and comes over here. She knocks on the side door. She gets no response and then walks around to the back door to the kitchen. She sees a windowpane broken out of the kitchen door and figures something is wrong. For whatever reason she doesn't try the door but goes back around to the garage, where she knows the Averys keep a spare key. She takes the key and goes in through a side door and down a hall to the kitchen. She finds Mrs. Avery on the floor, face down. In her nightgown. There's a pillow over the head, and at first it just doesn't compute. She walks over and lifts the pillow. Then, when she realized what she was looking at, she said she just fell to her knees and threw up on the floor. She didn't even see the boy at first. He was huddled in a corner. He never said a word."

Christine settles back against the door, wincing at the vision.

"Anyway," Hardiman continues, "she uses the kitchen phone to call her husband. It's his reserve weekend." Hardiman flips the pages of his notebook. "Army major. Charles Haley. It takes a while to get him to the phone, but finally he tells her to call the police. She does, and while she's on the phone with the sheriff's department, she sees the boy for the first time. She said he never said a word, never moved. He just sat there on the floor, staring at his mother's body. When the sheriff got here, they found Mrs. Haley and the boy in the living room. She was holding the boy and crying hysterically. The sheriff's deputy said the boy never reacted at all. Not a peep, not a whimper. The only thing he was doing was trying to wipe his hand on his pant leg, his pajama pants. There was a smear of blood on his pant leg and hand and a trace or two of feathers. He obviously had handled the pillow or touched the body."

"Jesus," Christine whispers again. "Any weapon found?"

"No, nothing."

"What about the time of death?"

"Roughly between four and seven this morning. The coroner got here around ten-thirty. Rigor had started to set but he could break it pretty easily."

Christine again shakes her head. "I don't know, Captain. It sounds like the boy's in deep, severe shock. I'm not sure we're the ones who should be talking to him. I mean even if he didn't see the actual killing, if he just woke up and found the body, it could have the same effect on him. It might take a whole team of doctors a long time and a lot of patience to unlock what's in his mind. I just don't know."

Hardiman nods. "Understood. And I don't want you doing any-thing you're not comfortable with. But at least see him. See what you think."

Christine's eyes move away, scanning the expanse of lawn and the small gathering of neighbors, one of whom shouts at a child racing his skateboard down the line of police vehicles. She nods slowly. "I'll give it a try, but let me take the tour first."

The front door opens onto a large foyer whose dark slate flooring leads back to a center hall, which in turn leads to the kitchen at the back of the house. Chalk marks surround several incomplete and dried footprints on the slate. Christine stops and Hardiman says, "The sheriff's deputy who got here first saw the prints and marked them so no one would walk over 'em." Christine smiles and Hardiman says, "Yeah, pretty impressive for a county man. I told him to give me a call if he ever thought of coming over to us. One of the first scenes I've been on in a long time that hasn't been screwed up."

Christine squats for a closer look at the pattern and the few flecks of dirt. "Mud? Work boots, maybe?"

"Or a hunting boot. There're better prints by the back door in the kitchen. More dirt. Looks like that's where he might've come in."

"But where'd the mud come from? This neighborhood looks like a golf course."

"Could be from the riverbank. The lawn stops about fifty feet from the shore, and there's a path leading through the brush to a dock."

"Any prints down there?"

"A few, but they're not clear."

"You think he came from the river?"

Hardiman offers his characteristic shrug, which Christine knows means "Yes, but don't hold me to it."

"Are there enough prints in here to trace his movement?"

"There're a few spots in the living room, and some depressions in the carpet that look the same. A few tracings upstairs in the master bedroom and on the staircase carpeting."

Christine looks at the long Oriental runner climbing the stairs from the foyer to the second floor and then looks back at the footprint on the slate. She takes a small pad from her purse and jots down some notes. "Any chance these were here beforehand? Maybe someone other than the killer?"

"Not much. You'll see this place is kept like a showroom. Even the kids' rooms. It looks more like a magazine layout than a house with young children. Shall we take a look at the body?"

"Not yet. I want to see the rest of the house first."

They start in the living room. It is large and expensively furnished with formal antiques. Christine does not know the period, nor does she particularly care, but she recognizes the style and expense of the furnishings, which set the Averys apart from her life in that quarter of Baltimore where the sounds and smells of small shops and ethnic eateries rise from the street to fill her three-room apartment near the harbor. Even the upholstery and drapery fabrics—bright, almost ceremonial silks contrasting with the snow-white carpeting—seem to mark a life neatly ordered by the expectations of others. Nothing here is out of place or out of balance, except for the few footprints traced by dried specks of dirt and the yellow and red strips of evidence tape—and the sofa, where a single throw pillow sits at one end.

Christine stares at the pillow for a moment until Hardiman picks up her silent question. "The matching sofa pillow was the one he shot through."

The dining room mirrors the condition of the living room, except that the drawers of a large cherry sideboard are opened to display the Averys' collection of monogrammed silverware. A pair of silver candlesticks sits undisturbed on the top of the sideboard, as does a matching pair on the dining room table. "Pretty selective for a burglar," Christine murmurs, and she jots down a few more notes.

Hardiman says nothing.

They move back through the living room and across the hall to a study paneled in oak, with bookshelves reaching from the chair rail to the ceiling. Many of the books have been pulled from the shelves and lie strewn on the floor. The drawers of a large leather-topped desk are pulled out and there are gash marks where the center locking drawer has been forced open. Papers are spread across the top of the desk. Christine takes her time reading some of them, making notes and lifting several with the tip of her pen to see what is underneath. A computer and its video monitor and printer have been pulled from their custom-built shelf behind the desk, and lie on the floor below their still-plugged-in cables. Also on the floor is an oil painting of a Chesapeake Bay skipjack, its canvas torn by a bronze sculpture in the style of Frederic Remington which lies on top of it. Christine frowns and shakes her head. "Looks more like a vandal than a burglar."

Again, Hardiman says nothing.

Behind the study is a family room that shows no sign of having been searched. A television, two VCRs, and an elaborate sound system remain undisturbed. Christine herself takes only a cursory look around the room. She then turns to Hardiman. "In here?" she asks, reaching for the door across the hall from the family room.

"Powder room." He smiles as if she is about to discover something.

The powder room is immaculate except for a cigarette butt which has been stubbed out and left on the narrow counter between the sink and toilet. Christine moves closer and inspects the butt without touching it and then turns to Hardiman with a sharp and curious frown.

"You tell me," he says, echoing her incredulity.

She turns back and stares at the crushed cigarette and the blackened ash and yellowish burn marks on the marble surface. "I haven't seen an ashtray or any signs of a smoker."

"I know. And the neighbor, this guy Major Haley, says that Mrs. Avery was a fanatic about smoking in her house. Absolutely against it. And another thing, just looking at the way this house is kept, can you imagine the wife or anyone else stubbing out a cigarette on that marble counter and leaving it there? I'd say our man is a smoker, and a slob. Maybe he left enough saliva behind for the lab to pick up."

Christine again turns toward the sink and toilet. After a moment or two, she says almost under her breath, "There's something not right about this."

Hardiman steps closer to the door. "What're you talking about?"

"I don't know, Captain, it's just a thought, but if I were a man and I were in here to, you know, relieve myself, and I'm nervous and I'm smoking and I finish, what do I do with the cigarette? Slob or no slob, wouldn't it be a whole lot easier to just toss it in the toilet? I mean, I'm no expert here, but am I right? Wouldn't it be a lot easier to just toss it in the bowl?"

He nods slowly.

Her voice turns contemplative, almost whispering her thoughts. "I don't know, but if I'm a woman and maybe I'm in here to just splash water on my face, I'd toss the butt in the toilet. But maybe . . . Maybe if I'm sitting on the toilet, and if I'm nervous, and I'm smoking and I finish with the cigarette—am I going to lean back and, you know, toss it between my legs? I'm real nervous or maybe I'm scared, and maybe I'm thinking about what has just happened or is about to happen or is happening right now, and I don't give a damn about the house and—maybe I just stub it out on the counter right next to me. You know, without really thinking about it."

Captain Hardiman stands rigid by the door, his eyes moving quickly between the cigarette butt and the toilet, his expression intensely curious. "You think a woman might've been part of this?"

Christine squeezes by him to the hallway. "I don't know, Captain. Like I said, it's just a thought." She pauses. "Can you tell the brand?"

Hardiman remains in the powder room, shaking his head, and says without turning toward her, "No, but maybe the lab'll be able to come up with something."

"I don't know," Christine repeats. "It just looks odd to me. Let's go upstairs." She reaches the bottom of the stairs before Captain Hardiman can pull his attention away from the powder room and the stubbed cigarette.

There are four bedrooms and three baths in the main section of the second floor. A short hallway leads to a separate guest room with its own bath, which appears to have been built as an addition above the garage. That room, like the children's rooms, has not been disturbed. Again, Christine jots a few notes while Captain Hardiman leads her to the master bedroom and bath. There the drawers of both dressers have been rifled and clothing has been tossed about. The drawers of a dressing table have been similarly searched. In the master bath, a mirror held to one wall by concealed hinges has been pulled aside to expose a small wall safe. The safe has been opened, and it is empty.

"A *very* selective burglar," Christine says to Hardiman's continued silence. She looks carefully around the edges of the safe's door and framing. There are no marks of force. She then looks back to the shambles of the bedroom and says, "He ransacks the bedroom, but opens the safe without a mark?" Hardiman smiles, but he says nothing and Christine asks, "Alarm systems?"

Hardiman shakes his head. "You ready for the kitchen?"

Christine hesitates. "What about the basement?"

"There's a workshop and furnace room. Storage area. A locked gun cabinet with a couple of shotguns and a deer rifle. But nothing looks disturbed. There's no sign that he ever went down there." He takes a moment and then says, "C'mon, let's get it over with."

Christine's eyes narrow a bit, and her words come with stifled embarrassment. "You know I hate doing bodies. I'll do it, but you know I hate it."

Hardiman smiles the way he always does when Christine Boland confesses to him what she would never confess to others. It is a silent, sympathetic, but transparently amused smile. "I know."

"No, Captain, I don't think you really do."

Captain Hardiman leads Christine downstairs and into the kitchen, where Paul Wyzanski is leaning over the counter and flipping through his notebook. He looks up. "Hello, Chris."

"Paul." Her quick smile of greeting evaporates over the body of Marian Avery, lying prone on the kitchen floor, a dark mat of dried blood and wisps of feathers clotting the otherwise curled, silver-blond hair at the base of the skull. Mrs. Avery's nightgown, a light, opalescent blue, drapes the body from the neck to midcalf and forms itself to the soft curves of her ample figure. Her face is twisted slightly to the left and lies in the blood that has seeped from her mouth and nose. Her eyes are open. A royal-blue pillow matching the one on the end of the living room sofa, its center torn by a single hole clotted with bloodstained feathers, sits on the counter in a large clear plastic evidence bag.

"Hello, Doc," Christine says to the county coroner, who sits by the kitchen table, a small dictation recorder in his hand.

"Chris," Harold Curling says, smiling. "I haven't seen you since that autoerotic hanging a few years back. But I read that paper you presented at Johns Hopkins last spring. Very impressive."

She smiles. "Thanks, I wish I had more time for academics." Her eyes scan the kitchen, but she makes no move toward the body as the coroner rises from his chair and kneels next to it to begin his lecture. He is quick and to the point.

"A single entrance wound here. The central portion is round with a slight laceration moving up and to the right from the wound. From the size, I'd guess something in the range of a .38. Some evidence of black powder around the margins and in the soft tissue inside. Also portions of feathers consistent with that," he says, pointing to the bagged pillow on the counter.

"No exit wound?"

Dr. Curling shakes his head. "The right eye's bulged and blackened. Bullet's probably lodged behind it, in the frontal lobe. I'm guessing the track is pretty straight from back to front, a little off-center of right and slightly upward." The coroner starts to lift the head to demonstrate.

"That's all right, Doc, I don't need to see it." Her eyes again drift to other portions of the kitchen as she asks, "Anything else?"

"Not really. No other evidence of force, no external evidence of genital or rectal trauma. Looks like a clean hit."

"Thanks, Doc," Captain Hardiman says. "I appreciate your waiting. You can have your boys take the body now." He turns to Wyzanski. "We're finished in here, right?" Wyzanski nods. "Paul, why don't you fill Chris in on the rest while I walk the doc out?"

Detective Wyzanski begins his detailed description of the very little they learned from Mrs. Haley before she broke down completely and her family doctor was called in. As he speaks, Christine moves toward the back door and crouches down on one knee by the broken glass and mud prints on the floor. As if she neither hears nor cares about the information he is offering, Christine says, "Paul, come here and look at this."

Wyzanski steps over the body and comes to her side, leaning over her shoulder. "What is it?"

Christine takes her pen and points to two shards of glass lying over a portion of a muddy footprint. "Let me ask you something. Assume the killer breaks the glass pane in the door, reaches in to unlock it and then steps in. Wouldn't you think he'd either step on the glass and crush it, or if he missed the glass, the footprint wouldn't be covered at all by the glass? But look at this. These two shards are lying on top of the print." Wyzanski stares in silent concentration. "Did anyone see any evidence of glass specks in any of the other bootprints?" He shakes his head. "Neither did I. But think about it. What if the killer comes in the back door without having to break the glass, tracks prints around the house and then after he's finished, he closes the door and *then* breaks the glass to make it look like a break-in?"

Wyzanski stands up straight and shakes his head. "You're right." He chuckles. "Damn it, I hate it when you do that."

She looks up with a smile, but says nothing.

"I'll get the captain."

Captain Hardiman takes his time returning to the kitchen, and when he does he refuses any expression but a pensive nod as Christine again points to the glass shards lying over the bootprint and poses her theory. He does not need to say anything to Christine. It is enough that he calls for the photographer and orders more detailed shots of the evidence by the kitchen door and then of the powder room.

"I'm ready to see the boy now," Christine says as the photographer kneels for his close-ups, and the coroner's assistants collect the remains of Marian Avery.

■■■

Ned Avery sits alone in one corner of the Haleys' guest bedroom, the corner between two lace-curtained windows through which the bright sun streams unimpeded. He looks as antiseptic as his surroundings, as if his pallid complexion and thin, sandy-blond hair had been bleached to match the white walls and white bedspreads and white area rugs that accent the highly polished dark oak floor and the dark mahogany posts of the twin beds. A small, pinched-faced woman from the county health department sits by the door, motionless except for her hand, slowly turning the pages of a paperback novel. Ned, too, is still except for the twitching of his pale blue eyes and his left hand, which rhythmically rubs the thigh of his pressed blue jeans. An oversized sweater hangs loosely on him and diminishes the plumpness of his face, which, with its vacant expression, looks almost gaunt.

Charles Haley, in whose house they are now, stops before he reaches the bedroom door and turns to Christine. He clearly does not want to enter the room.

"Something wrong, Major?" Christine asks.

The man looks down the hall toward the bedroom where his wife, Ellen, lies asleep, heavily sedated by their family doctor. "I . . . I think I should see to my wife. I can't help you with Ned."

Christine looks at him curiously. "Is there something wrong? Something you want to tell me?"

He gently takes Christine's elbow and leads her a few steps down the hall, away from the guest bedroom. He takes a deep breath. "Detective, I don't know why but the boy—Ned, he—I don't know how to describe it, but he just went crazy when he saw me."

Christine frowns. "What do you mean, 'crazy'?"

"When I got to the house, the Averys' house, the sheriff's people were already there, and they told me my wife was inside with Ned. She was hysterical and not making any sense. And they told me Ned wouldn't say anything and was acting like he couldn't hear anything, like he was in a dream world or something. And so I went in. The second he saw me he just started shaking and moaning and, I don't know, it was like he was terrified of me. It didn't make any sense. I mean I've known the boy since he was born. He spends half his time over here with my son. I've taken him to ball games, even when Cooper—the boy's father—when Cooper is out of town or something. I've taken him fishing with us, things like that. We've always gotten along real well. I mean the boy's always been shy— I mean really shy, almost withdrawn, I guess—but we've always gotten along. But, God, the second he saw me he just went crazy." A hint of nervousness shows in the eyes of the blunt, burly man standing stiff in his military camouflage and highly polished boots.

"Interesting," she says, more to herself than to him.

"I've never done a thing to the boy, I swear. I've always been—"

"Don't take it personally, Major," Christine interrupts with a gentle shake of her head, "the boy's in severe shock. There's no way to predict what might have caused him to react that way. Did you say anything to him? Touch him in any way?"

"Not at all. He just started moaning and scrunching up in a ball the second I walked into the room. One of the deputies held onto him while I took my wife out of there, but I never touched him. I might have tried to say something, just to tell him that it was me, that everything was gonna be okay, but he just got more and more upset, so I took my wife and got out of there."

"Did he seem to react at all to the deputy touching him or taking hold of him?"

Haley shakes his head. "No . . . I don't know, he might have. I don't know. Ned just seemed suddenly frightened or crazy or whatever, and so I got out of there in a hurry, you know, with my wife."

"When was the last time you saw the boy before this morning?"

He rubs the back of his hand across his forehead several times. "I don't know. You know, I see those kids so much I don't really pay much attention. Yesterday maybe. I really don't remember."

"Have you had any occasion lately to discipline the boy or yell at him for any reason?"

"He's not my son," Haley answers stiffly. "It's not my job to discipline him."

"I understand that, Major, but with your children's playmates being over here all the time, it wouldn't be unusual to have to discipline them once in a while. Like to tell him not to dip your cat's tail in the paint can or whatever."

"We don't have a cat."

Christine dismisses his comment impatiently. "You know what I mean."

"No, well sure, maybe I've said something to the boy once in a while. Ned can be strange at times. He doesn't always listen. But I've never really disciplined him. It's not my place. Besides . . ." Haley says, then stops himself.

"Besides, what?"

The man looks away, speaking to some other audience. "Look, it's not for me to judge someone else's child. It's just that it doesn't do any good to yell at Ned. He'll just look at you and go on with whatever he's doing or just go to his mother. She pampers that kid too much. She . . ." Again, he stops himself and looks at Christine. "I can't believe something like this could happen here."

"It can happen anywhere, Major. Nobody's immune."

The man squints with annoyance, but before he can speak, she tells him, "I'd appreciate it if you'd wait nearby. I may want to ask you a few more questions." She walks toward the guest room as Haley retreats.

Christine introduces herself to the county nurse and asks if Ned has said anything or made any attempt to leave his chair. The woman, brushing from her forehead the long black hair that hangs in irregular curls, says no. She asks if Christine wants her to leave the room, and Christine shakes her head as she walks over and crouches beside the boy.

She introduces herself to him, speaking in a quiet, even voice while watching his eyes dart about the room in small increments, focusing on nothing. His left hand continues to rub his thigh in short, erratic movements. She begins her questions slowly.

"Can you tell me when your father is coming home?"

There is no reaction.

"Can you tell me where your sister is?"

Again nothing.

Christine allows some time between each question.

"Is your sister's name Alice? Do you know where you are, right now? Where is your mother? Do you know what happened to your mother? Do you want to go home? Would you like to see your sister, Alice? Would you like to talk to Mrs. Haley or Mr. Haley? Is there someplace you would rather be? Is there something on your hand? Is there something on your leg?"

But to each question there is no answer, no indication that the questions are even heard.

Christine reaches over and very gently touches the boy's shoulder. He does not react. She lightly touches the boy's hair and brushes a lock from his forehead as she imagines his mother might have done. Nothing. Then, very slowly, she places her hand between Ned's left hand and his thigh so that his stroking movement will catch the tips of her fingers. His brow furrows a bit and his eyes twitch more violently and his hand rubs even harder. He has the anxious look of a blind child at once trying to identify and remove whatever has caused this sudden and strange sensation.

Christine turns back to the county nurse. "Have you tried to talk to him?"

"Some," she says, "but he hasn't responded at all."

"Who else has been in here to see him?"

"No one really, except for Captain Hardiman and one or two of his people."

"Was there any reaction to any of them?"

"No, none."

"Was anyone wearing a uniform who came in here?"

"No, except for the sheriff's deputies that brought him over here."

"Did he show any reaction to any of them?"

"Not really. He seemed to have more eye movement when they first brought him here. But after they left, a little while passed, and he seemed to settle down to that stare. I mean I can see his eyes looking around, but it's not like he actually sees anything, you know?"

As the woman speaks, Christine watches Ned. He shows no sign that he is aware of their conversation. She turns back to the woman and says, "Would you mind going down the hall and asking Major Haley to come to the door?" Turning back to the child, she says, "Tell him to just come to the doorway and stand there a moment. Not to come in."

The woman leaves the room, and Christine speaks to the child in a low, reassuring tone. "You're safe here, Ned. No one can hurt you. I know all these people are strange to you but they are here to protect you. Do you understand? Can you hear me?" The boy says nothing. "I asked Mr. Haley to come see you. Is that all right? He wants to help you, too. Are you afraid of Mr. Haley?" Again there is no reaction, and Christine can hear Haley's footsteps approaching the door. She turns and kneels beside the boy's chair, keeping her eyes focused on his expression.

As Haley steps into the doorway, Ned's eyes flicker as if he is trying to focus, and suddenly he lets out a low, awful moan. His body begins to shake, and his lungs begin to suck deep, choking breaths, and his mouth contorts in a rictus of fear. "Oh God," Haley moans, as he steps back quickly, and Christine reaches out to put her arms around the boy. Ned's reaction is instant: he buries his head in her chest while his fingers dig into her breast and clutch the material of her blouse and bra and her soft flesh in his tightening fist.

"*Jesus!*" she yelps in pain and pulls his hand from her breast, but Ned's fist grips even tighter the material of her blouse and bra, which he clenches in his teeth, and his lungs strain to draw air through the bunched cotton. Christine draws the boy even closer, speaking softly and rocking him as Haley backs down the hall, voicing his protests.

"Why did she do that? I'd never hurt that boy. I never did anything to hurt that boy. Why did she do that?"

3 _A_lexander Sergeevich Trigorin leans back and cocks his head curiously as he follows the tips of his fingers sliding easily over her dark, oiled skin. The muscles are stretched and tightened by the arching of her back, and her spine rises like a string of beads beneath the flesh. The soft mounds of her buttocks round and converge on the tender valley between her legs, the line of her thigh then opening as one leg strains forward but does not quite lift her from her static, supplicant crawl. Her right arm and hand stretch toward some place she cannot see; her head hangs low between her shoulders. Her body shines in the several spotlights which concentrate on her and leave the rest of the room dark and shadowed.

Alex's eyes travel the length of her arm until they stop to contemplate the hand whose forefinger is lifted in a weak, almost curving point. "Shit," he mutters. "It's just not right. It's just . . ." And with a sharp shake of his head, and a sudden violent twist, Alex crushes her hand in his and breaks it off at the wrist. "I've given this child the hands of a _muzhik!_" He angrily kneads the clay fingers between his own thick hands before throwing the resultant ball against the far wall.

He turns with a deep sigh and reaches for a heavily smudged bottle of lemon vodka, careful not to let it slip from his hand still slick with the wet clay. He pours three fingers into a tall glass and moves to a set of French doors that open onto the wide iron grate he calls a balcony, but which most would call a fire escape. Pulling the doors open, he lets the chilled air brace him while the vodka goes down with a comfortable burn. He looks past the disordered mix of tenements and bars with names like "Tony's" and "Earl's," past the boilermaker's shop to the end of the block and across a single line of railroad tracks to the warehouses and beyond, to the docks where a container ship is berthed. The night is young but winter-dark, and the ship's floodlit superstructure stands like a lonely monument against a thick black sky. A brief shiver passes through him, in part from the cold, in part from the memory of his years at sea on Liberian-registered freighters, and of the long days that had no names and the months that had no meaning beyond the weather that came with them. He does not regret those years, but neither does he yearn for them.

From this high window Alex can look out on a world that cannot see in. Christine envies him that, or so she says. She will stand by the window or sit on the fire escape for long quiet periods, just staring, her gaze carrying over the flat, tarred rooftops and the bramble of TV antennas to the harbor. He can almost see her now, in her apartment across the harbor, amid the lights of Fells Point, where the once grimy seamen's bars have been turned into the fashionable pubs of young professionals, where the shops and markets are more scenic than useful, and where even the old sewage pumping station has been converted to a bright and polished museum. Yes, he can almost see her there, if that's where she is. He doesn't know, and he wonders if he even wants to know. She so often seems a confused collection of his own emotions: the first woman to fire his imagination, the only woman to drag him to the pit of frustration, to spin his hopes, to excite his anger, to match his fantasies, to twist his dreams. She isn't worth it. But there are days when she is everything.

Alex closes the French doors and turns back to the lighted sculpture, its right arm now reaching toward its severed hand, still stuck to the wall. The figure looks particularly alone and vulnerable perched on the small workstand in the center of that portion of the room he calls his studio. The whole apartment—once an open attic atop a narrow building whose first floor houses an Italian bakery, whose second is occupied by the accounting offices of Hiram Sugarman, and whose third encompasses two sparsely furnished apartments in which tenants rarely stay more than a month or two—has the look of a studio. Except for a small kitchen and bathroom, the apartment remains open, partitioned only by the uses to which he puts its various corners. In one, a sofa and several leather-strapped director's chairs border a worn Oriental rug and face a wall of books and stereo and video equipment. In the opposite corner, near a second set of windows and the apartment's only closet, is a large iron bed whose linens have the disheveled look of erratic use. Except for a square wooden table and four straight-backed wooden chairs next to the kitchen, the rest of the large room is given over to the benches and pedestal tables and easels and brushes and the odd-shaped knives and mounds of clay that are the tools of his art. Despite its stark, utilitarian look, or perhaps because of it, it is the first and only place Alex has never had the urge to leave.

Born of Russian parents who had immigrated to the hills of West Virginia a year before his birth, Alex last saw his mother twenty-nine years ago, when he was seven, the night before she escaped the coal fields—and his father—to tend bar in a back-street joint in Pittsburgh. Alex's father died twelve years later, on his forty-sixth birthday, bitter and racked with the pain of black lung disease. He had spent those years teaching Alex that if he expected nothing, he could not be disappointed. Alex has tried to hold on to that lesson, but time and experience are slowly chipping away at what were once hardened principles. He has begun to allow himself some optimism, at times even exuberance, over what could be his future. His job as a loading supervisor on the docks pays well and demands little of him, mentally or physically. And in the past year his sculptures have begun to sell: a banker's wife has commissioned a piece for her garden in Baltimore's Homeland section, and a small midtown gallery has offered him his own show in December. And he finds it oddly satisfying that there have come to be nearly as many collectors who consider it an amusing curiosity that this artist works on the docks as there are dockworkers amused by his sculpting.

From the floor below, he can hear the echoed thump of a door closing and a few heavy footsteps descending the wooden staircase. They stop a moment, and cryptic greetings are passed before they continue downward while other, lighter footsteps move slowly up the last flight of stairs. *Christine!*

He tosses back the last of the vodka and wipes his hands on a worn towel that hangs from the workstand. A mixture of anger and anticipation rolls in his stomach as a key rattles in the lock and the door opens. Christine steps inside, and she stops a moment before slowly leaning back against the door, which thuds shut.

"Are you still angry?" she asks. Her chin is lowered but those large dark eyes are fixed on him. Even in the weak light where she stands, Alex can see that her face, two days ago a smooth oval with the bright, almost ruddy complexion of a Sunday picnic, has paled. Her expression is stiff, and her hair lies flat and sweated on her brow. Beneath her open suede jacket, her blouse is soiled and crumpled.

"Are you all right?" he asks, moving toward her.

Christine's purse, heavy with the weight of her service revolver, drops to the floor with a clunk. She doesn't move and lets him come to her. He slips his hand through her hair and feels the moist heat of the back of her neck. He tries to lean back to look at her expression, but she will not let him, pulling him to her and nuzzling her face between his neck and shoulder. Her arms close about him and hold him tight. He tries again, taking her shoulders and gently pushing her back, and he sees the small, dirty tear on the front of her blouse. "What happened? Are you—"

"No, I'm fine. It's just work."

He takes the torn material in his fingers but she brushes his hand away, shaking her head. "Not now," she whispers with a hint of irritation. "I'm all right." She smiles a bit as if that will answer his concern.

He says nothing, and he stares at her staring at him.

"You're such a jerk sometimes," she says, a sudden, playful smile coming over her, and she reaches over to unbutton his loose, oil-stained shirt.

"Stop it, Christine."

She doesn't, pulling the shirt loose and sliding her hands up his back, pulling him closer while her lips move to his neck. He again takes her shoulders in his hands and separates himself from her. "I'm surprised to see you."

"No you're not."

"Yes I am," he insists. "The way you stormed out of here Thursday night, I—"

"Let's not argue," she interrupts with a light toss of her head, and she moves quickly to the sofa, where she throws her jacket.

"I'm not arguing. I'm just saying I'm surprised . . . and pissed. It's beginning to wear thin, Christine, it really is. These damn moods of yours. I mean, one minute you were asking about how my father died, and then all of a sudden you're up and pacing the room and acting as if somehow I had just insulted you. And then you just announce that you have to go, and I don't see or hear from you for two days? Yeah, I'm still angry, and I still don't have a clue about what set you off."

"Look, it wasn't you. It's just that a lot of things have been building up—work and all that—and I guess when you started talking about your parents, particularly your father, I just couldn't help thinking about my own parents, and losing them."

Alex knows little more of Christine's family than that her father was an Air Force colonel who, with her mother, died in an automobile accident in Germany when Christine was twenty. A year before that, her older brother and only sibling had been killed in Vietnam. Even that small bit of information took months to learn, and until now, she has refused to allow the subject to be spoken of again.

"I . . . I didn't handle it very well. I don't like to think about it, and I guess I just had to get away, to be alone. I'm sorry."

"Why couldn't you have just told me?"

"I don't know why. It's just hard for me to think about, even after all these years."

"Listen—" Alex says softly, but she quickly puts her fingers to his lips.

"Do we really want to go into all this right now?"

He shakes his head slowly. "One of these days we're gonna have to learn how to talk to one another. We can't keep bouncing each other around like this."

"I'm sorry. I really am." She offers an apologetic shrug and again moves close to him and wraps him in her arms. "Let's talk about it later, okay? But not tonight. It's been a real bad day, and I feel like playing." She leans back and again smiles. "Can Alex come out and play?"

He doesn't answer, and her grin widens, and an impish snicker escapes as she kneels slowly before him and pulls him to her, rubbing her cheek like a kitten on the soft hair of his belly. "My brooding *khudozhnik,* always so serious. You need to relax."

"What I need," he says in a voice half frustration and half encouragement, "is for you to stop driving me crazy. What I need—"

But she is not listening and Alex does not finish, his thoughts turning priapic as her hands gently and unobtrusively loosen and strip him of his pants, freeing and exaggerating his excitement, manipulating and teasing him with the tips of her fingers and tongue.

"Christine, please."

He reaches down and slips his hands under her arms, and in a single, easy motion, lifts her to his height so that her toes just touch the floor. Her eyes are full, and she says, "Come to bed with me, please."

Alex studies her, and his expression softens with a barely perceptible shake of his head. "Why do I let you do this to me?"

She doesn't answer. She doesn't need to. She has only to kiss him. He puts her down and looks at his hands. Almost shyly, he holds them up to her, his fingers and nails caked with the dried bits of clay. "Let me wash up."

"You don't need to. I like your dirt."

"But I don't."

When he returns from the bathroom, the studio lights have been turned out and the room is colorless but for the shadowed blacks and shades of gray that come from the reflected lights of the city. Christine is standing by the window at the end of the bed, her back to him. Without acknowledging his presence, or even turning from the window, she begins to unbutton her blouse. Alex moves up behind her and stops her undressing with a light touch of her shoulder and a kiss on the back of her neck. She often looks taller than her five feet six inches, the effect of a thin, athletic body which to the world she holds aggressively erect. But here, alone with him, her posture slackens. Her hands drop to her sides and her head droops forward as he slips off her blouse and gently peels her skirt and undergarments to the floor. She stands against the night, her skin pebbling and her back arching with the sensation of his fingertips slowly tracing the contours of her body until he is filled by her. She turns slowly and then pulls him onto the bed, gathering him to her, capturing him with her arms and legs, engulfing him, moving with him, breathing with him, evenly, then quickly, then urgently, then opening herself and taking him, holding him, until she spends the last of her energy in a violent shudder, and then releasing him to his own finish.

Neither speaks, and in the long silence that follows Alex feels himself drifting off. He does not fight it.

■■■■

It may have been minutes, or even hours, he does not know, but when he awakes, Alex is alone on the bed. He cannot see her in the darkness, but he can hear the muffled sobs from across the room. He gets up quickly and walks to the sofa, where she is curled in his bathrobe, a pillow drawn to her face, her body shaking. He turns on a lamp and kneels beside her, and with his fingers combs the hair from the side of her face. "What's wrong?" She does not respond, and he tries to turn her toward him. "Christine, what's wrong? Tell me."

Suddenly, she whirls on him. Her eyes are wide and her breathing quick and forced. Her voice is as frightened as it is threatening. "Don't touch me! Get away. Get away from me!"

Her violence startles him and pushes him back on the floor, where he sits for a moment, confused.

"Haven't you had enough?" she hisses. "Can't you leave me alone?"

In an awkward, stumbling movement, Alex gets to his feet and backs away from her, his voice on the edge between concern and anger. "What is wrong? Talk to me for God's sake!"

Christine's eyes are fixed. Her hands lift to the sides of her head but do not touch it, shaking with her body as if to ward off any touch, any intrusion. "I just need you to leave me alone—just leave me alone."

Alex turns and paces the floor in fast, irregular circles, unsure of his own reaction, trying to control what is quickly turning to rage. He fixes on the sculpture with its severed hand and slams his fist through its delicate torso. One of the thin metal wires used to support the sculpture pierces his flesh, and he grabs his hand with a sudden howl. "Aoowwww, *fuck!*" He wheels toward Christine, his face drained of color, his breathing heavy and rapid to keep up with the pain.

"Oh, no," she whispers. Her eyes move from his hand to the mashed and twisted sculpture fallen from its pedestal. She sits up and draws her arms tightly across her stomach, her whole body rocking on the edge of the sofa, and again she whispers, "Oh, no, no." Her eyes, deeply reddened, spill over, and soft fluid drains from her nose. He holds his hand out to her, not pleading but showing her his anger. She rushes to him and grabs him, as he tries to back away but cannot. "I'm sorry," she says, weeping. "I'm sorry. I didn't mean that."

Alex stiffens at her touch, and he falls back against a post in the middle of the room, his eyes and lips closed. For several moments they stand together, Christine clutching him to her, muttering her apologies, until she catches herself and takes his wrist in her hands and pulls him to the bathroom. He does not resist but stands silently by the edge of the sink, taking long, deep breaths to suppress the pain as she ministers to his hand, still crying, but silently. She manages to clean and wrap the wound, then lets him go, taking a step back and looking frightened by what she has done. She reaches over to barely touch his bandage. "I'm sorry. I don't mean to hurt you . . . not your hands."

Alex, too, reaches out, and with his uninjured hand he touches her cheek. "What's happening to you?"

It takes a moment before Christine settles herself with the release of a long breath and leans against him. "I don't know. It's just been such an awful day. Can we lie down?"

Alex draws her close and then leads her to the bed, where for a long time they lie in silence, Christine curled tightly against him, one leg coiled across him, holding on. Finally, without lifting her face from the crook of his arm and chest, she begins to describe the scene of Marian Avery's death and the details of her encounter with Ned, and Alex can feel himself tensing with her tale.

Finally, she raises her head. Her eyes are swollen and dark, and her face is white and streaked with tears. "And when the boy saw this man, Major Haley, he seized up with a fear I'd never seen before. And he grabbed me. He just grabbed onto me with his hand . . . and his teeth, and his grip was so tight and painful." She rises a bit and opens her robe.

Alex winces at the sight of her breast and the deep, ugly bruise on its underside, and his words come as a whispered mix of pain and wonderment. *"My God!"*

"I didn't know he'd . . ." she starts, but a sucking sob interrupts her. "I didn't mean that to happen. I just didn't expect it. I should've . . . I should've known."

She collapses against him, and Alex cradles her, offering what he can of his understanding.

4

*I*t was the beginning of summer and already
the ground was hard, and the grass was brittle
and dusted by a month of hot, dry weather.
The old men sitting on the bench had been
clucking about someone named Johansson
knocking out the American Floyd Patterson
before their conversation turned somber and to the south, to some place
near the Riviera, where the Malpasset Dam had burst and people had
died in the floods. She tried to imagine what a flood might look like, but
she couldn't hold the image as she stared at the water in the canal; it
was still, its surface painted with a fine powder of dust and pollen
gathered in sweeping, stagnant designs by brief and intermittent puffs
of air.

From the Rue du Bain-aux-Plantes, the footsteps of a half-dozen or
more children thundered back and forth along the narrow park, dodging
and weaving and ducking the football they kicked at each other, letting
go shouts of surprise and peals of laughter, even anger, as the ball hit
or missed its mark. From behind a lamppost at the opposite end of a
small footbridge arching over the canal, she watched the children play.
She stood silent and unmoving, like a spy, her arms hugging the lamppost's cool metal, her eyes peeking from behind its protection. Her muscles
tightened and her eyes widened at the sight of the ball bouncing off the
side of one boy's head and knocking him to the ground. The other children
stopped, freezing for a moment, until the boy got up and rubbed his head
to the sudden taunting laughter of the others. The oldest boy, or at least
the biggest, grabbed the ball and for a moment began reorganizing the
play before his eyes caught her watching him. He stopped.

The boy said something to his companions, and suddenly their attention was fixed on her. He shouted across the canal, but she could not distinguish whether his call was inviting or threatening. She did not wait to find out. She never allowed others the option of accepting or rejecting her, and so she turned quickly, and ran across the street and to an alley beside the café where her mother sometimes worked.

The alley was short and shaded, as it always seemed to be, the three- and four-story buildings on either side backing closely upon it and guarding it from the sun for all but an hour or so at midday. The sour-milk stench of yesterday's garbage filled the alley, and she ran hard toward the bright sunlight at its end, where she stopped to catch her breath and to peek around the corner. The street was alive with commerce. The shopkeepers mingled with their neighbors and customers in front of their shops, which filled the first floors of these ancient buildings with their gray-tiled roofs and cross-beamed façades. Across the street and partway down the block, she saw the grocer, Roland Michaud, fussing over the fruits and vegetables set out in open stands in front of his shop. She stood for a moment, watching Michaud and thinking.

She was just a month past her seventh birthday, tall for her age, and skinny. Not thin or wiry, not even lanky. Skinny. The kind of skinny that angered Michaud each time he had to yell at her for stealing an occasional apple or banana or her particular favorite, an orange. How many times did he have to tell her? How many times would he have to catch her, snatching her by the arm, then immediately loosening his grip out of fear that he might injure this fragile child with the dark eyes set deep in a sad, hollow face, eyes that stared in a mixture of fright and defiance?

"Don't steal from me," he would tell her, over and over. "You ask and I will let you have an apple. But do not steal from me. I will tell your mother."

But he never did tell her mother. He knew it was useless, as useless, it seemed, as yelling at this child who never spoke to him, who never spoke to anyone as far as he could tell, who would just stare until he let her go, and then fly away, past the butcher shop and around the corner, disappearing until the next time.

She waited for Michaud to turn his back, then crossed the street and walked another block before turning right, down a narrow cobbled street that was not much more than an alley. There were no trees here, and the houses were narrow and for the most part divided into small apart-

ments and rooms to let. There was little to distinguish one from the other but for the variety of flowerpots on the stoops and the different displays of paint on the stucco fronts, pale blues and pinks and yellows, like faded pastel stripes on a long beige wall. She picked up a pebble from the pavement and threw it at a dog sniffing a garbage can. The pebble pinged the top of the can, startling the dog, which trotted off. She picked up another stone but only held it in her hand when she saw that the first throw had drawn the attention of Mme. Pinchot.

"Ah, it's you," Mme. Pinchot said. "What mischief are you up to today?"

The child stopped but did not answer.

"Well, no matter," the old woman said with a slight smile. "Tell your mother that we have work for her. M. Pinchot has some English documents that must be translated. But she must come today. We cannot wait forever. Will you tell her that?"

The child nodded absently and skipped on down the street to the corner, where she took another right, traveled another block, turned right again, and stopped. She peeked around the corner and saw the man her circuitous route had intended to avoid. Michaud looked back at her from the opposite end of the short street, then wiped his hands on his apron and picked up an orange, which he held out to her in a silent offering. She did not acknowledge him.

She wheeled away and broke into a slow run until she turned down another alley and continued to the corner, where she mounted, two at a time, the stone steps leading to a darkened doorway. Inside, she climbed three flights of wooden stairs to a short hallway, where she walked cautiously to a small apartment at the front of the building. Before trying the door, she pressed her face to the jamb. She could smell the perfume and hear the sounds that meant she must be quiet. Opening the door only wide enough to let herself pass through without the hinges creaking, she slipped in and to her room, where for just a moment or two she stood at a narrow window looking out on the street. She then pulled the curtains closed and got down on her hands and knees to retrieve from beneath her bed a stack of worn and faded papers folded and wrapped in several turns of red yarn. She inspected the package, and, satisfying herself that it had not been disturbed, she again placed it in its spot beneath the bed, in the small carton behind the box that held her clothes. She then sat back against the wall and pulled her knees to her chest and wrapped her arms around them.

She reached into the pocket of her smock for the stone she had picked up from the street. She studied it for a moment and then closed her fingers upon it, pressing it into her palm, hard, until the pain stifled the sounds from the room next door, the sharp squeaks of the bedsprings and the rhythmic beating of the iron headboard against the wall.

5 $\mathscr{C}$ooper Avery is a tall man with clean features that seem perfectly engineered for their purpose. He is sitting straight at the dining room table, his spine pressed against the back of his chair, his arms reaching out toward the sympathy cards and letters piled before him. The fingers of one hand move as if they are independent of the rest of him, holding open a small handwritten note. The other hand is poised, ready to write down some notes in the spiral pad before him. Thin, efficient lips above an angular jaw barely move as he speaks. "Funny," he says quietly, "a few years back, this guy tried to cut my throat in a deal that wasn't worth more than seventy, eighty thousand." He sighs. "Just business, I guess."

Christine glances at Paul Wyzanski, who is leaning against the frame of the door leading to the kitchen. Her recent promotion to the rank of detective sergeant means that she has been relieved of individual case assignments and is under consideration for a transfer from Homicide to a supervisor's desk in the Economic Crimes Unit. But O. B. Hardiman has asked her to assist Detective Wyzanski for a few days until Wyzanski's partner is freed from a homicide case in trial before the circuit court. Although neither has said anything to the other, both she and Wyzanski know there is more to it; the captain wants to keep Christine involved in the Avery investigation.

Christine asks Avery, "How is your son doing?"

Still staring at the note in his hand, Avery says, "The same. Still not a word. Still . . ." He hesitates; his eyes, a deep opaque blue looking almost black in the dark puffed circles beneath them, narrow to a squint. "The doctors are talking about a special clinic up in Pennsylvania. Maybe that'll help."

"And your daughter?"

He smiles weakly. "She's with her grandparents. Marian's folks." He looks about the room for a moment. "I guess I'll have to sell this place, if I can even find a buyer after what happened here."

Paul Wyzanski straightens a bit, frowning. By her look, Christine repeats the caution she offered on the ride down to meet with Avery: "Don't try to read too much into his or the boy's reaction. In one way or the other, they're both in shock, and people can do and say some pretty strange things when they're like that."

On the preceding Saturday, after Cooper Avery arrived at his house unannounced and uninformed by anyone of his wife's murder, his outward emotions swept back and forth, like the arm of a metronome, between short spasms of stifled weeping and stoic calm. The detectives asked as many questions as his condition allowed, which wasn't many, until he insisted upon seeing his children. He first spent more than a half hour alone with his daughter, holding Alice in his lap and trying to explain that her mother was gone. The child was then given a sedative and Avery held her until she finally drifted off to sleep. Warned of his son's unstable condition, Avery still insisted on seeing Ned, approaching cautiously the room where his son sat still and silent. Avery stepped into the room quietly, almost hesitantly, until Ned's vacant stare suddenly focused on his father and the child began the rocking and the fearful moaning that he had exhibited at the sight of Charles Haley. Avery rushed toward the boy, reaching out to hold him, to reassure him that everything would be all right, but the boy's reaction turned instantly more violent, almost convulsive, and Detective Wyzanski and the county nurse stopped Avery and gently backed him out of the room, where he fell back against the wall, stiffened by his own fear. It took some time, but Avery eventually arrived at a state of almost fugue-like calm, and he returned to Alice's room, where he lay down on the bed beside her, holding her until Marian's father arrived to take them both to his home in the Guilford section of Baltimore.

Four days have passed, and the detectives have come to Cooper

Avery's home to ask him the questions they were not able to ask him the Saturday before.

"Mr. Avery," Christine says, "I know this is very difficult for you, but I wanted to ask you a few questions about your son's reaction to Mr. Haley, and to you."

Cooper Avery stares intently at Christine. "Charlie told me what happened. He told me what you had done. It really shook him up. And Ned." He shakes his head. "I don't understand why."

She hesitates a moment. "I'm really sorry about that. Truly, I am. But we can't help thinking that there must be some correlation between Ned's reaction to Mr. Haley and his reaction to you. We've talked briefly to the doctors and to some psychologists at Johns Hopkins. Obviously, they can't say what caused the reaction, but they do say that there's clearly something about you and Mr. Haley that triggered it, something common between the two of you that may remind him of whatever he saw when your wife was killed. Or maybe it's something totally unrelated to the murder. It may be that Ned can't handle whatever he actually saw, and he has replaced that with some other fear that he associates with you or Mr. Haley."

"Fear? Of me?"

"Well, not necessarily a fear of you, but something about you and about Mr. Haley. They tell us that it would be very helpful, not only to us but for your son, to figure out if there was anything at all that may have been common to the two of you. Let me ask you first if you know whether there had been any trouble between Ned and Mr. Haley. Even something that otherwise might seem insignificant. For example, something as minor as yelling at him for running through the flower bed or whatever."

"No. There's never been any trouble. Ned can be difficult at times. Marian really spoils him . . ." Avery stops himself. "I mean he's—he's a good kid, he really is. He never really gets into trouble. It's just that he's real quiet and keeps to himself. He's a very sensitive child. Sometimes he just seems to be in a world all his own."

"How had you and Ned been getting along? I mean we all know that there are always some rough spots between parents and kids, but had there been any unusual problems or tension?"

Avery stops at that and simply shakes his head.

"The doctors say that the reaction could have been triggered by something as trivial as an article of clothing, or some physical trait. But we can't think of anything along that line. I mean you and Mr. Haley are very different physically. He's much shorter, and heavier and darker-complected. And your clothing couldn't have been more different. I mean you were in a business suit, and Mr. Haley was wearing that fatigue uniform or whatever it's called. Can you think of anything similar between the two of you that Ned might have fixed on? Even before last Saturday, something he might associate with both of you?"

Again, Avery shakes his head. "No, not at all, except that Charlie and I have been pretty good friends over the years, even before Ned was born. We've spent a lot of time together, you know, at each other's houses, hunting, things like that. Our families are pretty close. But otherwise I can't think of anything."

Christine nods. "Again, we understand how difficult this is for you. But if you could give it some thought and if anything occurs to you, no matter how insignificant or silly it might seem to you, we'd appreciate your letting us know."

Avery responds with a stare, as if he is thinking of something other than their conversation.

Paul Wyzanski moves from the door and sits down at the table opposite Cooper Avery. "Have you had a chance to make an inventory of the things that are missing?"

"Not really. I gave you the list of things that were in the safe. The wills and Marian's jewelry and the five thousand in cash. I haven't been able to inventory everything in the house, particularly not in my office, not the way they tore it to pieces. But as far as I can tell they were just after money and jewels, things like that."

"But there's something about that I don't understand," Wyzanski says. "There was some jewelry left behind that was pretty much out in the open. A few rings and necklaces in the drawer of Mrs. Avery's dressing table. Is there any reason why they weren't in the safe?"

"That was just junk, you know, costume jewelry. I guess they could tell the difference."

"Was it well known among your friends or others that Mrs. Avery had expensive jewelry here in the house? I mean did she often wear expensive jewelry?"

Cooper Avery looks almost offended. "If you mean did we go around bragging about things like that, of course not. But my wife grew up with the finer things. And in our circle of friends, people often have and wear, well, expensive things. Cocktail parties and the theater. Occasions like that. My wife was no different. We didn't flaunt it, but we had no apologies for being successful."

"I'm not suggesting otherwise, Mr. Avery, we're just looking for anything that might help us here."

Avery's nod carries a hint of irritated acquiescence. "All right. I understand."

"What about the safe?" Christine asks. "Who besides yourself and Mrs. Avery would have known that the safe was located in your bathroom?"

"No one except the contractor who installed it and I guess Marian's parents."

"And the combination?"

"No, no one but my wife and I knew the combination."

"How 'bout your children? Did they know?" Avery frowns. "I mean about the safe. I'm just wondering whether the children might have said something to their friends, at school or wherever. You know how kids talk."

"I don't know," Avery says. "I don't think we ever said anything to them about it, but I really don't know."

"There was also that small leather case in Mrs. Avery's dresser," Wyzanski says. "The one that had the diamond ring and pendant. Those appear to be pretty valuable pieces."

"I have no idea what they're worth. They were given to my wife by my grandmother just before she died. They've been in the family for a long time. I expect they're worth quite a bit, but I have no idea how much."

"Why wouldn't they have been in the safe with the other jewelry? The stuff that wasn't costume jewelry."

"I . . . I don't know. I thought they were. Maybe Marian was going to wear them or maybe . . . I don't know. I can't tell you why she would have put them in her drawer."

"Can you think of any reason why the burglar, or burglars, would have left them behind?"

Avery does not move, offers no gesture. Neither does he answer the question. His expression signals that he is offended to be asked to fathom the mind of a burglar. After a moment or two, Wyzanski says, "Well, I guess they just missed them."

"Mr. Avery," Christine says, "you mentioned a moment ago that someone had tried to 'cut your throat'—I think those were the words you used—in a business deal. I know you didn't mean that literally, but can you think of anyone who might have—"

"Hmmph," Avery interjects, to himself and paying no attention to Christine Boland. He is studying a small card he has picked up from the table. "Strange," he murmurs.

"Something wrong?" Christine asks.

Avery's eyes narrow a bit, and he says to no one in particular, "No." He briefly moves his fingers through the pile before him as if looking for an envelope to match the card in his hand. "Where am I supposed to send a thank-you note?" he asks himself and lays the card aside.

Christine looks at the card, trying to read it upside down, studying it. "Is there something about that card?" she asks.

Avery shrugs. "No, it's just that I don't recognize the name. I'll have to check my Rolodex in the office." He quickly jots a few words in his notepad and looks up. "I'm sorry, Detective, you were saying?"

Christine, too, is jotting down a note, and she says, "I was just asking if you or your wife had any enemies."

"No, of course not."

Christine offers a solicitous smile. "Mr. Avery, I don't mean to offend you, but it's pretty difficult to go through life without upsetting someone. I know it's hard to imagine anyone doing something like this, but you just never know. Maybe something that happened a long time ago. An argument, a fight, an insult?"

Cooper Avery looks at her curiously. "Are you saying that this wasn't just a robbery, that someone might have come here specifically to kill Marian . . . or me?"

"I have no idea, Mr. Avery, I really don't. But to be honest, given the way only parts of the house were ransacked, and the valuables that were left behind, it's possible that they were looking for something specific, which would imply some knowledge of you or your family, or maybe the break-in was just a cover for something else. And the manner in which your wife was killed is not what we would expect to see if she had somehow interrupted a burglary in progress."

"What are you saying?"

"I'm not saying anything. It's just that until we have something concrete to go on, we have to examine all the possibilities. And one possibility is that robbery wasn't the primary motive here."

Avery stands up abruptly, and he begins to pace the room. "That's just not possible. You didn't know Marian. She wasn't the kind of person who made enemies. She was always very popular. She put together the community association here practically single-handed. She, she . . ." He turns toward the window and takes a deep breath. Then, very quietly, he says, "You didn't know her. She wasn't the type of person who angered anyone."

"And you?" Christine asks evenly.

Avery turns back with a scowl. "Me?"

Christine nods. "Again, please, I don't mean to be insulting, but could there be anyone in your past, a business competitor, anyone who might harbor a grudge?"

"A grudge?" he asks with a sardonic grin. "You think this happened because of a grudge?"

"I don't know why it happened. That's why I'm asking the question."

"Sure, I suppose that I've angered my share of people. You can't succeed in business without getting someone angry at you at one time or another." His voice has turned insistent. "But I've never cheated anybody. I've gotten the better of a few and a few have gotten the better of me. But that's business. But no one's ever accused me of cheating them. Maybe I'm a little more aggressive than some people like, but no one's *ever* accused me of playing dirty. *No one!*"

Avery turns back toward the window as Christine and Paul Wyzanski exchange glances. After a moment, Wyzanski asks, "What about your father?"

Avery doesn't move and it takes a moment for him to reply, still facing the window so that his expression is hidden. "My father?"

"Yes. Again, there may be no connection, but he's been quite a prominent man in the state. Politics and all that. Are you aware of any problems or grudges involving your father that may be connected to you or your wife?"

Still without turning, Avery answers. "I have no more interest in my father's politics than he has in my business. Other than the family and, I suppose, a few social relationships, we have no mutual interests. Certainly none in a political or business sense. No, I cannot imagine there would be any connection there. None at all."

"Do you have any siblings?" Christine asks.

He turns as if he has decided to rejoin them. "Yes, a sister. She and her family live in Seattle. And, well, I can't imagine any connection there either. We don't see very much of each other. Living so far apart and all. It's been a long time, a couple of years, I guess, since we saw them last . . . until the funeral."

"Is your family still here? Your parents and sister? We'd like to talk to them if possible."

"No. They left yesterday. I thought it best. Alice, my daughter, she needed some quiet, some relief from all the people. And Ned too."

Detective Wyzanski switches directions. "I noticed in your basement that you own quite a few weapons."

Avery stands a bit straighter. "I'm a hunter, Detective. Have been all my life. And they're all registered."

"Yes sir, I understand that. I was just wondering whether you had any other weapons besides the shotguns and rifles that are in the case downstairs?"

"No, I keep everything locked up in the gun cabinet. With the kids, you know."

"No handguns?"

"No."

"I know our people inspected the cabinet and all the guns last Saturday. And you said they were all there. But you were upset and not really focused. Understandably. You're sure there was nothing missing from that cabinet. Not another gun you might have overlooked or forgotten."

"No."

Christine looks at Wyzanski, then back to Cooper Avery. "Mr. Avery, would you mind taking us through the house room by room? There might be something out of place or missing that you might have missed the other day. Something that might help us. Would you mind?"

He agrees with a relenting sigh. "All right."

They start upstairs, Cooper Avery leading the two detectives to the master bedroom, which, but for the addition of the black smudges of fingerprint powder throughout the room, looks just as it did when Christine first inspected it. No effort has been made to clean or straighten the disordered remains of the previous Saturday. The detectives stand back as Cooper Avery moves cautiously and stiffly about the room. He stops a moment, as if gathering the courage to look through the closet where his wife's things are hung. But he does look, as the detectives have asked him to do, and then goes on to the rest of the room, seeming to gather his strength. He falters a bit when he leads them through an inspection of Ned's room, but regains his efficiency as they go through the rest of the house, room by room by room.

In the downstairs powder room, Christine points out the smudge left by the cigarette stub they discovered, which is now being analyzed in the state police forensic lab. She tells Avery what they found and asks, "Did Mrs. Avery smoke?"

He lets go a slight chuckle. "God, no. She didn't allow any smoking in the house. It was one of the few arguments we'd have. I mean she wouldn't even allow guests to smoke. And sometimes it could be a bit embarrassing. You know, when we'd have a cocktail party or something. She'd try to be polite about it, but she was very insistent." He smiled. "Jesus, she'd die if she saw that . . ." He stops himself, suddenly pained and self-conscious. "I'm sorry, I . . ."

Detective Wyzanski nods gently. "That's all right. We understand. Did you ever smoke?"

"No. Well, I used to. A coupla packs a day. But Marian finally wore me down. I gave it up years ago. It wasn't easy, but I did it."

They finally return to the dining room, and Avery turns pensive as he looks at the silver candlesticks and silverware in the open drawer of the sideboard. "She never got used to the dark," he says, almost to himself.

Detective Wyzanski looks at Christine with a frown and then at Avery. "I beg your pardon?"

"The candlesticks. I was just thinking about how Marian never could get used to the nights here. How dark it gets. It never really gets dark in the city. All those lights, all the reflection, it never really gets dark. People who grow up in the city never really know what night is. How complete it gets. Black and clean and how the stars really do shine. She never really got used to it. It always kind of scared her. She kept those little night-lights all around the house, in the hallways and wherever. She always said it was for the kids, but they really were as much for her. Sometimes she'd imagine that strangers had been in the house."

Christine looks up sharply. "What do you mean?"

"Oh, it was nothing. She just never got used to being away from the city. Sometimes her imagination just got the better of her, particularly if she was here alone or with just the kids."

"Did you ever have a problem, a break-in or whatever?"

He shakes his head, dismissing the thought. "No, never. It's just that Marian was very particular about the house. Everything had to be just so. Everything had its place. And every once in a while she'd get up in the morning and she'd think she saw something out of place or moved around or whatever, and she'd start worrying that someone might have crept in during the night. But there was never anything to it. There was never any sign of a door or a window being broken or left open or whatever. And nothing was ever taken. It was just her imagination."

"Do you remember when these incidents might have happened, or your wife thought they happened? Was it recently?"

Again Avery dismisses the question with a shake of his head, seemingly lost in other thoughts. "No," he says, "it was nothing. You know, she spent the last ten years on a campaign to put in high-intensity streetlights. All that time trying to make this development into another Guilford or Roland Park or whatever." He picks up one of the candlesticks. "We bought these in England. Six, maybe seven years ago. The grandparents watched the kids while we took a little vacation. Damned expensive, these were. Even over there." He suddenly looks up at the two detectives. "You know, I have to wonder myself why they wouldn't have taken something like this. These are very valuable. Why wouldn't they have taken something like this?"

"I have no idea," Wyzanski says, as Christine takes out her notebook and scribbles a few words. "Mr. Avery, why do you keep saying 'they'? Is there some reason you think more than one person might have been involved?"

"I . . . I don't know, it's just . . . Jesus, I don't know why."

Avery is clearly unsettled and picks up a few sympathy notes and stares absently at them.

"Just one other thing and then we'll be leaving," Wyzanski says.

"Yes?" he answers, looking up, suddenly composed.

"You told us that you had been in Boston on business and hadn't left until Saturday around noon. Is that correct?"

"Yes."

"Well, we checked the airlines and there seems to be some confusion. Apparently they only have a record of you flying from Boston to New York and that was on Friday. They couldn't find a record of—"

"What are you saying?" Avery cuts in, his face swelling and flushing.

"Well, as I said, the airline records show that you flew to New York on Friday and—"

"You checked on my travel? What is it that you're saying?"

Detective Wyzanski raises his hand slowly. "Calm down, Mr. Avery, we're just trying to determine—"

But Cooper Avery will have none of it. "No, I want to know exactly what it is you're trying to say here."

Christine tries to interject. "Mr. Avery, you have to understand—"

"No, no, I understand. You come into my house . . . My wife has been murdered and you come into my house—and now you tell me that you are investigating *me?* How dare you." His every muscle seems tensed, and a slight quiver comes over his face.

"Mr. Avery, please."

"No, you understand! This interview is over. This interview is over *right now!*"

■

As they back out of the driveway and pull away from the house, Paul Wyzanski turns to Christine, but he does not speak.

Neither does she look over. She stares out the open window of the car, letting the cold air comb through her hair. "I don't know, Paul," she says. "He's almost too easy."

6   *L*ayton, Strange & O'Casey occupies the top three floors of the Seaman's Bank & Trust Building, a thin tower of glass and steel rising like a needle from a wide plaza encircled by the redevelopment of Baltimore's downtown and the inner harbor, a development that itself was the germ of renewal which has spread like a creeping antisepsis to what was once the blight of worn-out factories and dingy offices, idled dock- and railyards, and back-alley bars. The factory workers in steel-toed shoes and the pea-coated dock hands who once called the area their own have abandoned it to the bankers and brokers and lawyers who make and exchange their fortunes in climate-controlled offices only steps away from the marbled and carpeted comfort of upscale shops, pubs and restaurants. Once gray and grimy and, except for the scattering of bars infamous for their freewheeling raunchiness, nearly lifeless, the inner harbor is now a place where spouses and lovers meet for lunch or a stroll along the waterfront; where from April to October tourists paddle about the harbor in their tiny rented boats, snapping pictures of the U.S. Frigate *Constellation* set permanently aground in front of the Pratt Street Pavilion; and where mothers come and perch their children on the railing of the pool outside the National Aquarium to watch the long-snouted gray seals and their dog-eyed cousins, the harbor seals, swim mindless laps or laze on the rocks while their nostrils pulse in search of some hint of the sea on air heavy with colognes and french-fried potatoes. It is all very new and very neat, and Phillip Layton, the founding partner of Layton,

Strange & O'Casey, is very proud of the integral part which he and his partners have played in bringing it all about.

From his corner office on the twenty-seventh floor, Phillip Layton has an expansive and unobstructed view across the harbor to Fort McHenry and beyond, past the Key Bridge where the Chesapeake Bay stretches southward to the sea. But that view holds no interest for him; it is the plaza below and its surrounding structures that fascinate him: the carefully planned and constructed neatness, everything ordered and in its place, especially from this height, where he is not assaulted by the sight of sandwich wrappers and soda cups that occasionally miss the trash cans and scar the brickwork that radiates from the center of the plaza in an elaborate compass-point design.

Layton stands by the window, his back to his audience. "I'm not quite sure I know what it is that you're trying to ask," he says cautiously and without turning.

For a moment Cooper Avery studies Layton's back; the stiffness of Layton's posture signals his discomfort. Cooper's eyes fix on the top of Layton's desk, a large black-lacquered affair which, like the rest of his office—all chrome and rosewood and black leather against a soft gray carpet and matching walls—is adorned with a minimum of furnishings. In contrast to the stark but expensive efficiency of this office are two large paintings which hang on contiguous walls, each done in bold, primary colors, each depicting one-dimensional figures with flat Oriental features. Cooper does not recognize the artist. The paintings are new since he was last in this office some six months ago. But that's not unusual. Phillip Layton routinely replaces the artwork in his office. He is not a sentimental man, and Cooper likes that in a lawyer.

"What I need to know is whether we can talk confidentially," Cooper says.

Layton turns slowly, his hands seemingly pinned to the lapels of his suit coat. "Of course," he says, lowering his narrow chin into the loose folds of his neck and peering over the top of his half-lensed reading glasses.

"Phil, this isn't about the business." Cooper hesitates, then adds, "And this isn't a matter I feel should be shared with my father-in-law. At least not right now."

Layton's voice hints at the offense he has taken. "Cooper, this firm has represented Ed Thurston and your father and both your families and your business for many years. Have you ever known us to violate a confidence?"

"I don't mean to offend you. It's just that I'm faced with a situation that is—well, particularly sensitive."

"Before you say anything more, is there any reason to believe that this, ah, 'situation' could implicate some conflict of interest between you and your father-in-law or the business?"

Cooper frowns ever so slightly, almost imperceptibly, and says, "No, this is a personal matter."

Layton moves back to his desk and sits with a minimum of motion. He then squares a yellow pad with the edge of his desk blotter. "Well, whatever I can do."

"It's about my wife." Layton does not react. They have already spent several minutes exchanging condolences and thank-yous for the law firm's generous contribution to the Marian Avery Memorial Scholarship Fund established at Sweet Briar College within three days of her death. "Two detectives from state police headquarters came by to talk to me yesterday. I, um, really wasn't able to talk to them the first time—you know, last Saturday—after they found Marian."

"Of course."

"And then there was the funeral and trying to deal with Ned and everything."

Layton nods in the silence of Cooper's pause.

"Anyway, these two detectives met me at the house yesterday and were asking all the expected questions. You know, was I aware of any enemies Marian or I might have had, exactly what was missing from the house, who might have known about the safe where we kept our valuables, things like that." Cooper's gaze drifts past the lawyer and to the window, which from his perspective opens only to the sky. "And about the way Ned reacted to me."

Layton's expression turns curious.

"Well, Ned seemed frightened when he first saw me. And he had the same reaction to one of the neighbors who got to the house before I did. I don't know, the doctors seem to think it might have been some kind of associative reaction to something he saw—or thought he saw, you know, when Marian . . ." Cooper stops, and Layton fills the void.

"How's Ned doing?"

"He's better, thanks. The doctors say he's calmed down quite a bit. He still won't talk or try to communicate in any way, but he's doing better. It's going to take time, but I know he'll be fine. He just needs time, I guess."

"And your little girl?"

Cooper smiles. "She's holding up as well as can be expected. Alice is a real trouper. She's staying with Marian's parents. In fact, we both are until I decide what to do with the house. I don't know what I'd do without her. I think she does more to keep me going than I do for her. She's a real trouper, that one."

Layton smiles, barely. "You were saying about the detectives?"

Cooper stands and moves toward the window. "Do you mind if I smoke?"

Layton makes a grudging gesture toward a chrome-and-glass table and a crystal ashtray set in a black leather frame. Cooper remains by the window and lights a cigarette, blowing out the match but keeping it in his hand. "They started asking me about where I was last week. Particularly last Friday and Saturday."

The lawyer slowly swivels his chair toward Cooper's back and folds his hands in his lap. "Did you have any problem answering their questions?"

"I, uh, didn't handle it well. Jesus, the way they asked the question they made it sound as if they thought I might have had something to do with Marian's—you know, her death."

Layton's voice is calm and soothing. "I'm sure that's not so. Of course you're upset, and you probably just misjudged the situation. There's no reason to be concerned, I'm sure."

"Phil, I wasn't able to tell them the truth. I got real upset and practically threw them out of the house. I just didn't handle it well. God knows what they think now."

Layton's brow furrows, and his close-set eyes fix in alarm. Cooper turns and immediately reacts to the lawyer's expression, talking quickly as he moves to the ashtray and violently stabs out the cigarette, on which he has taken only a puff or two. "No, no, no, Phil. Jesus, that's not what I meant."

"Are you sure I'm the one you want to talk to? I could get Stan Rubinow up here. He's had considerable experience with police matters."

"No, Phil, this isn't . . . Listen, I just need advice on how to handle this. I don't need a lawyer to represent me. The problem —the problem is that I was seeing somebody. A woman. A married woman. In New York. I've been seeing her off and on for almost a year now. I, ah, stopped off to see her on my way back from Boston Friday night. We spent the night together and she dropped me off at the airport late Saturday afternoon. That's why no one was able to find me."

"I see." Layton waits a moment and then asks, "What makes you think the police have any suspicion that you might be involved with Marian's death?"

"I don't know. I guess the fact that no one could find me on Saturday and the way Ned acted so frightened of me. I swear to you, Phil, I had nothing to do with it. We may not have had the best of relationships, but I loved her. I could never have done something like that. Never."

"You don't have to say anything, Cooper. I understand. I can also understand why you're upset, but there's nothing here to worry about. No one's going to accuse you of being involved with Marian's death without some hard evidence, and the fact that you may have been having an affair with another woman is not evidence. Did you say anything at all to the police about where you had been?"

"No. I just got angry when they said they had checked with the airlines and found out that I had flown to New York on Friday. I had told them on Saturday that I had come directly from Boston. I guess I panicked a bit, got angry that they were checking up on me. I didn't handle it well at all. I just blew up and ordered them out of the house."

Layton nods pensively. "Yes, I suppose that would make them at least curious."

"Exactly, and what concerns me is not that someone might accuse me of killing my own wife, but that the police will start snooping around about where I was and the whole affair will come out. I couldn't face the children with that. And it would kill Ed. And Marian's mother? *Jesus!*"

"Does anyone else know of your relationship with this woman?"

"No, no one."

"And you can trust her discretion? She's not suddenly going to want to leave her husband for you, is she? I don't mean to be indelicate, but you understand."

"No, no, it's not like that. She has as much reason to keep this quiet as I do. Maybe more."

"You're certain of this."

"Absolutely."

"Well, then, perhaps there won't be any problem."

" 'Perhaps' isn't good enough. I need to be sure there's no problem."

"I don't understand."

"Phil, this isn't just any woman. This is the general counsel for Barth-Sanders."

Cooper watches Layton's face flush instantly and deeply. "You don't mean . . . Not Sydney Lambert?"

Cooper nods and the room fills with the tension of his revelation. For months Thurston Construction has been fighting off a hostile takeover bid by Barth-Sanders Industries. And although Cooper Avery could more than double his personal net worth should Barth-Sanders succeed in its bid, he has joined his father-in-law and the rest of the board of directors in leading the public fight against it, a fight ever more in danger of being lost by Thurston's inability to secure sufficient financing to buy back a controlling share of its outstanding stock. Cooper is the man heading the search for financing.

He studies Phillip Layton's stunned expression. "It's just sex, Phil. Believe me. There's nothing else going on." He turns quickly back to the window with a deep sigh. "Okay, sure I've tried to pump her for information, and once in a while I'd get a tidbit or two. But that's it. I've got no interest in seeing them succeed. I've got more money than I need, and you think I'd want to end up running errands for that bunch of fucking toe-dancers from Harvard Business School? Hell, I know their only interest is in breaking up the company and selling off the pieces. I've got no future in that."

"This is not good news, Cooper. This is not good news at all."

"I understand that. But it'll be even worse if this gets out."

"What is it that you think I can do?"

Cooper lights another cigarette, his motions suddenly slowing as if his confession has calmed him, put him back in control. He moves deliberately toward the window. "My friend, there isn't a man in the statehouse who doesn't owe you a favor. And it seems to me that if someone could talk to the state police, the chief or whoever, if he could explain to someone willing to listen and able to appreciate the delicacy of this situation, then perhaps there wouldn't be any need for the detectives to waste their time snooping after something that's personal and private and has nothing whatever to do with Marian's death. Maybe there wouldn't be any need for some police report ending up in the wrong hands, with someone who might want to hurt me or Ed or the company or whoever." He stops and takes a deep drag on the cigarette. Layton's expression remains stiff and judgmental. "Phil, if not for me, think of what this would do to Ed. He'd never understand. Just think of the pain they're going through now. What good would it do to make it worse?"

"This isn't my area, Cooper. I don't have dealings with the state police. Besides, surely you or your father would have greater access to the appropriate people here."

Cooper cuts him off. "You know I can't bring my father into this. Besides, his involvement might only exacerbate the problem. He didn't lose the election because he had endeared himself to the boys in Annapolis. You know people, Phil," Cooper says, wagging his finger in emphasis. "Probably more than anyone else in this state. And we bring in close to a million a year in legal fees to this firm." Cooper watches Layton's jaw tighten, but he does not retreat. "Something has to be done. I wouldn't have brought this to you otherwise."

Layton sits a long time in silence, rocking gently in his chair and watching Cooper, who remains by the window, his eyes fixed on Layton. The lawyer rises from his chair and moves slowly to Cooper's side, putting his hand on Cooper's shoulder. "I'm not sure what I can do, but I'll give it a try."

Cooper nods briefly, a dark smile barely creasing his face. "I appreciate it. I'm sorry, I had to come to you. There was no one else I could trust with this."

They continue to stand together, spending the next few minutes discussing the details of Cooper's relationship with Sydney Lambert and his travels over the days preceding Marian's death. The conversation ends with a long silence, which Layton breaks with "I'll let you know. In the meantime, find some excuse to avoid the police if they want to talk to you again. And let me know immediately if they do try to contact you or if you hear of any inquiries they might make about you with others. Friends, business associates, anyone. All right?"

"Should I talk to Sydney Lambert about this?"

"Are you certain she won't say anything?"

"Absolutely."

"Then I wouldn't contact her at all. I assume she knows about your wife."

"Yes. We talked briefly. We both agreed that we couldn't see each other anymore. At least not for a while."

"Good. Let's just leave things as they are. Right now I think the quieter we keep things the better. Understood?"

"Yes, I agree. And Phil, I can't tell you how much I appreciate this."

"No problem. We've all been together a long time. I feel we're like family. Now, you just concentrate on taking care of those children. And yourself. Try to get some rest, and let me worry about this."

Phillip Layton walks Cooper out of his office and down the hall to the elevator, where he leaves him with a nod and "We'll work it out somehow." Layton then returns to his office, and for some minutes he stands by the window, looking across the plaza to several office buildings and a hotel, all of which were completed on time and within budget by Thurston Construction. Layton's firm billed over a half-million dollars in fees on the hotel deal alone. He takes a deep breath and moves to his desk, where he pushes the intercom button.

"Harriet, get Ed Thurston on the line for me."

7 *O*. B. Hardiman is settled in that stiff, quiet posture that so often makes those who do not know him uncomfortable. His broad back is set firmly into the cushioned black vinyl of his desk chair, his hands cupped loosely but squarely over the edges of the armrests. His suit coat, a dark blue with just a hint of a pinstripe, is open, but neatly so. His expression is static, but he allows his head to nod and turn a bit with the conversation, his chair rocking ever so slightly in reaction; and it is merely a reaction, for O. B. Hardiman does not rock in his chair, and no one can remember ever seeing him rear back and prop his highly polished shoes on his highly polished desk.

Paul Wyzanski holds both hands around a Styrofoam cup of coffee, careful not to spill anything on the dark blue carpeting that adorns the captain's office. "It's all right, Captain," Wyzanski says, responding to O. B. Hardiman's oblique approach to the subject of his and Christine Boland's relationship, "we get along fine. We can work together."

Wyzanski's partner, Charlie Abbot, nods his agreement with Hardiman's suggestion that Christine be assigned to work alongside the two detectives on the Avery matter, a potentially awkward situation since she outranks them both. "I got no problem, Capt'n, 'cept I wonder if Chris'll be real happy about this. I mean everybody knows she's been trying to get out of Homicide. And I thought she was up for a supervisor's slot in Economic Crimes."

"Maybe," Hardiman says.

Wyzanski waits for more, but when it does not come, he says, "Well, like I said, it's fine with me. I suspect we're gonna need all the help we can get, and I don't know anyone better at picking up details and thinking through a case. I mean, none of us picked up on the glass laying over the bootprints in the kitchen."

The intercom on Hardiman's desk buzzes, and Charlie Abbot shakes his head. Before joining the state police, he spent seven years on the city police force, where he never worked for anyone who had an intercom and carpeting on the floor.

"Send her in," Hardiman says and then turns to the two detectives. "Let's make her welcome, gentlemen."

Christine walks into the office, and Detective Abbot gives her a short salute and a crisp " 'Mornin', *Detective Sergeant* Boland," emphasizing her recent promotion.

She grins. "Hello, Charlie. Paul."

"Have a seat, Chris," Hardiman says, and gestures to the electric percolator on a small table in the corner of his office. "Coffee?"

She shakes her head. "No thanks." Her grin remains but twists slightly with a curious suspicion of the three men whose eyes are upon her. "What's up?"

"Nothing," Hardiman says. "We were just talking about this Avery murder. I wanted to get everybody together to go over what we've got and where we're going with it." He reaches for the only file on his desk and opens it to a checklist he has already prepared. "Okay, let's start with the post. Paul, you got the autopsy report?"

"Yeah, last night. Pretty much what Doc Curling said on the scene." Detective Wyzanski carefully puts his coffee cup on the floor and opens a manila folder, from which he pulls the report and begins skimming it aloud. "Let's see, white female, five feet, five inches, one hundred thirty-eight pounds. Everything normal, no abnormalities, chest, back, upper and lower extremities, genitalia not remarkable, both internal and external, anus the same, no lacerations or signs of force, swabs taken, all negative. Et cetera, et cetera. Okay, major trauma, let's see here. We got, um, 'left posterior occipital area . . . just to the left of the midline . . . center of the wound . . . five feet, one inch above the heels, four inches below the top of the head . . . central portion is round, three-eighths inch in diameter . . . a laceration extends five-eighths of an inch upward and to the right from central area,' et cetera, et cetera.

Okay, we got 'a small amount of black powder observed about the margins of the wound, predominantly along right lateral margin . . . also in the soft tissue within the wound. Also observed were traces of feathers consistent with item eight.' " He looks up. "That's the pillow."

Everyone nods.

"What's the track?" Hardiman asks.

"Okay, we got, let's see, 'entrance wound internally beveled at junction between sagittal and lambdoid sutures . . .' "

"God, he loves this stuff!" Detective Abbot says with a laugh.

"Okay, okay, I'm getting there. It's 'left to right and slightly upward' and it goes through, let's see—'fractures extend anteriorly' and, uh, passes through et cetera, et cetera, until it ends, let's see, ah, 'within the infero-medial portion of the anterior pole of the right frontal lobe.' " Wyzanski points to his temple, just above his right eye. "Y'know, somewhere in here."

"Left to right and slightly upward," Hardiman repeats. "A left-handed shooter?"

"Maybe," Paul says, "but maybe not." He gestures as if he were holding a pillow in his left hand and points his right index finger as if it were the barrel of a gun. "It could just be the way he came up on her. Particularly if he was moving quickly, y'know, to catch her before she realized what was happening."

"And the bullet?"

"Copper-jacketed, .38," Wyzanski answers without reference to the notes. "In reasonable shape. The lab says the rifling marks, particularly the twist, are consistent with a Smith."

"A Smith and Wesson? Nothing else?"

"Well, yeah, a few others, but definitely consistent with a Smith."

Hardiman frowns, questioning why Detective Wyzanski is stuck on that particular manufacturer.

"Tell him, Charlie."

"Well, Captain, I was sitting around last night with nothing else to do but wait for the verdict in that trial—"

"How'd that come out, by the way?"

"Jury's still out. Anyway, I had a lot of time to kill, so I just started running computer checks on the name Cooper Avery. And I finally hit a theft report from a year ago. Actually a little more than a year. Last August. Seems our man Avery reported the theft of a .38 Smith and Wesson. The gun was properly registered and all. He reported it missing to the sheriff's department down in the county. They took a report and entered the info in the computer. There's no update that the gun was ever recovered. I called down for the theft report. They said it'd take a few days to find the original and send it up."

"Any indication where the gun was taken from?"

"No, that'd be in the original report. All we've got is the computer listing for stolen weapons."

Hardiman leans back in his chair and raises one hand to his chin. "As I remember, Avery never mentioned that gun when we talked to him on the scene. Is that right?"

"That's right," Wyzanski answers, "and I asked him again yesterday when Chris and I were down there. I mean, I got real specific with him and he never mentioned it."

"That's right," Christine says, "but to be fair, we were asking about any guns he had in his house. I'm not sure it was all that clear we might've been asking about any gun he ever owned."

"Even so, Chris," Wyzanski says, "you'd think under the circumstances he would have said something about it."

"Well, yeah, I suppose that's right."

"Plus, you start thinking about all the other circumstances and you gotta wonder."

Hardiman leans forward, propping his elbows on his desk. "Okay, let's talk about all these 'circumstances.' We all agree the scene doesn't compute, right? I mean there's every indication that the break-in was a cover. The glass over the bootprints, the way they left a lot of valuables behind—"

"And don't forget," Wyzanski interjects, "the only pieces of valuable jewelry left behind were the diamond ring and pendant Avery said belonged to his grandmother. I've never known a thief yet who had much sentiment for family heirlooms."

"And the way this lady was hit," Abbot adds. "If she had walked in on him, a thief would've just bust and run, or just shot her straight on. He's not gonna bother grabbin' a pillow and sneak up on her from behind. This has got all the odor of a planned hit. I mean it's like the guy went to school on how to do it right. Quick, clean and quiet."

Hardiman sits back in silence for a moment, then turns to Christine. "Chris?"

"I don't know. We may be jumping too fast, here."

Charlie Abbot chimes in. "Yeah, but what about the way his kid freaked out when he saw him?"

"True, but remember that the boy had the same reaction to the neighbor. You know, the major. What's his name, Haley?"

"Anything more from the doctors about how the boy is doing?" Hardiman asks.

Christine shakes her head. "No, I talked to them again last night. They say he's calmed down a lot, but he shows no sign of coming out of his state. In fact, they said they're worried that he's sinking even deeper, that the calmness is more a sign that he's getting farther away from them."

"No hint of why he might've had the same reaction to the neighbor and Avery?"

"Nothing."

"You got any ideas?"

"No, I haven't been able to come up with anything similar between them except that they were real close friends, and the boy might associate one with the other because they were together so much."

Abbot says, "Maybe this guy Haley's involved somehow. Maybe he was doing Avery's wife, or Avery was doing his or they were switching off or—"

"Maybe," Hardiman stops him. "We can explore that when you canvass the neighbors, friends, relatives, all that. But listen, just make sure that whoever does all that is subtle about marital discord and motive or whatever."

"How subtle?" Charlie Abbot asks.

"Very subtle," Hardiman warns. "You've seen how the press is all over this. Society victim. The husband's the ex-congressman's son and president of one of the largest contracting companies on the East Coast, if not the country. We start asking questions like we think there's a problem or like we've targeted Avery, it'll be on the front pages of every rag in the state, and the chief'll be all over us."

Detective Abbot shakes his head. "Well, he may not be a target yet, but it seems to me Avery could stand a real close look-see. Am I right?"

"I guess," Christine says, "but I just can't see him killing his own wife that way. I mean, not with the boy there. Somehow that just doesn't make sense."

Wyzanski poses the question. "Maybe, but wouldn't it make some sense if Avery thought his kid wasn't gonna be at home? What if he talks to his wife sometime on Friday, and she says the kids are gonna sleep over at the Haleys' house, which they were supposed to do. But then the boy starts showing signs of a cold, and the missus keeps him home. Avery comes back to do the deed, not realizing the boy's there, wakes his wife up without a fuss, and they go down to the kitchen for a cup of coffee and a little husband-and-wife chat. And then he does her through the pillow. Not much noise there. Might not wake the boy upstairs. And he leaves. The boy later wakes up and finds his mother and freaks out."

Christine leans forward, relishing as always the debate of theories. "Assume that's true. Assume he thought his kids were at the neighbors'. Avery wouldn't take the chance that they'd find the body, would he? I mean, don't you think he would have come up with some pretense to call the Haleys early in the morning? Some reason for them to go over and look in on his wife before his kids go home to find her? And we don't have anything like that here. And, I don't know about the boy, but just looking at the way Avery was with his little girl, I can't imagine him letting her walk in and see her mother like that. Plus, Avery impresses me as someone who would never soil his own hands. He may be a cold fish, but he wouldn't have what it takes to kill his wife like that." She turns to Wyzanski. "You saw him, you talked to him. Don't you think that's true?"

Before Paul Wyzanski can answer, Captain Hardiman asks, "What if he hired someone? That would go a long way to explain why the scene was a little sloppy for a really good cover. I mean, the man's there for a hit. That's his main objective. He has the key to the house, does a professional job on the wife, but doesn't care to spend all that much time following through on the burglary cover. That would also explain the safe being opened without having to blow it. Avery would have given him the combination. And the fact that only certain things were missing—and Avery's absence. By the way, anything more from the airlines?"

"Not yet," Wyzanski answers.

"But," Christine interrupts, "that still doesn't answer my point that Avery wouldn't have let his kids walk in on that. Even if he had hired a hitter to do his dirty work, he would have done something to make sure someone else besides his kids found the body."

Paul Wyzanski leans forward. "Maybe Chris is right. But what if he tried to call someone and didn't get through? Maybe the Haleys disconnect their phone when they go to sleep at night. Or maybe he did get through to Mrs. Haley but she just forgot. I mean that lady was a basket case when we talked to her."

Hardiman nods. "Maybe. Let's check with her again. And all the other neighbors if we have to. And another thing, let's see if we can't find out where Avery was staying in Boston. The hotel will have a record of any phone calls. And if he used a credit card, we can get that. Let's see if we can't track down everyone he talked to while he was away. And Charlie, you're gonna follow up with the county on that gun report, right?"

"Yeah, but I still got a question. I wanna hear more about this lady-sitting-on-the-can theory. Y'know, the cigarette thing?"

Christine smiles broadly. "Charlie, if I know you, you've probably spent more than your share of time peeping through keyholes."

Detective Abbot laughs.

"What do *you* think?" she asks him. "I mean it's just a theory, but what do you think?"

"Well, I gotta admit, it's got me wondering. I asked my wife about it, and she said she thought you might be right. But a woman shooter? I don't know."

"We've been liberated, Charlie. Remember?" and Charlie again laughs. "Anyway," Christine says, "maybe she wasn't the shooter. Maybe she was just along for the ride. Who knows, maybe the shooter's some guy who sits instead of stands. Maybe . . . Hell, I don't know, it's just a thought. I wouldn't waste any time on it. It's just something to keep in the back of your mind if you happen to run across some involvement with a woman."

"You mean if *we* run across some woman."

Christine stops and stares at Detectives Wyzanski and Abbot. "Well, yeah, if either of you—"

"No, no, Sergeant"—Charlie Abbot smiles—"if *we*, like if any of the three of us—"

Hardiman sits forward quickly as Christine's eyes snap toward him. The captain holds up one hand. "Charlie, please. Gentlemen, how about excusing us for a few minutes."

The two detectives rise and leave the office, both chuckling as Christine's expression turns questioning.

"Captain, please, tell me you're not going to do this. You promised."

"Honey, listen to me—"

Her eyes roll, and the captain immediately retreats with his hands up. "I'm sorry, I know, I apologize, it's just an old man's habit. But just listen to me a minute."

Christine is insistent. "Captain, this isn't personal. I owe you a lot, and you know I appreciate it. But you know I've never really been comfortable in Homicide. And you've got a dozen good men dying to get in, and I've got a good shot at regular hours sitting behind a desk in Economic Crimes, and that'll give me the time to start my doctorate and—"

"Sergeant, I understand that, and I'm not going to stand in your way if that's what you really want. It's just that I think I might have a better offer."

Christine cocks her head. "Is this a bribe?"

"Absolutely. Look, I can't guarantee a thing. But in the next few months there's gonna be some reshuffling around here."

"And?"

"And maybe that'll open up a few opportunities."

"Like?"

"Well, like developing our own psychological profiling unit. What you've been pushing for years."

"Really?" she asks, both her voice and her eyes brightening.

"It's possible. The chief sounds like he's finally interested in giving it a try."

Christine hesitates, studying the captain's expression. "So, what's the bottom line here? I'm still waiting to hear the bribe."

"Simple. If you go to Economic Crimes, you step out of the loop. No one's gonna make you a supervisor and then three, four months later have to reshuffle all over again. You stick it out here and I think it'll happen. I think you'll get your unit. It'll probably just be you for a while, but that's what you've been wanting. Right?"

She nods slowly.

"Plus, you'll be helping me out and keeping the chief happy. This Avery thing has really got his attention. He doesn't want any screw-ups. Too many important people are watching. I've got a lotta confidence in Paul and Charlie, but the fact of the matter is, I think you and I probably agree there's a lot of strangeness attached to this one. And that stuff's right up your alley. I've already talked to the chief about it. He won't say it officially, but if you step out of the running for Economic Crimes supervisor to help us out on Avery, he knows he'll owe you one."

Christine keeps her eyes focused on O. B. Hardiman. They do not stare so much as question. "And in the meantime?"

"You'll work directly for me. No other cases. I want you concentrating on Avery. And when it's slow you can help me out with the administrative stuff. Any problem with that?"

"No, that'd be fine. But is the chief gonna let you have two detective sergeants in Homicide?"

"For the time being he will. At least until we close the Avery murder and he decides on this profiling unit."

She smiles. "And if he does go along with it and I get the nod, the profiling unit'll be under your command."

"You see? That's why I want to keep you around. You understand the nuances."

She shakes her head and turns to peer out the window.

"One thing, though," he adds. "Ah, forgive me if this is too personal, but is there going to be any problem with you and Paul working together?" Despite his long career in a field where social deviance is as common as not, O. B. Hardiman holds firmly to his sentimental view of friends, treating what he may think a moral misstep with the same delicacy one might use in approaching the subject of an idiot child or a deformed limb.

Christine answers with a patient and forgiving smile. "No, we get along fine. And if you'd ask him, I'm sure he'd say the same thing."

Hardiman nods. "Yeah, he did. So, whaddaya say?"

"You think this profiling unit's a real possibility?"

He smiles. "You know I can't promise anything. It all depends on the chief. But I'd say it's as close to a sure thing as you can get without a signed contract. But not if you go to Economic Crimes."

"How much time do I have to think about it?"

"None. I've got a meeting in fifteen minutes. They're making a decision this morning. You'll get the job if you want it." He stares at her for a moment. "Well, what'll I tell them?"

Christine turns and again looks out the window. For a moment her fingers tug gently at a thin lock of hair. Without turning back to Captain Hardiman, she says, "Okay. I'll take my chances and stick it out here."

His nod signals his pleasure. "It's the smart move. You'd have been bored to death in Economic Crimes."

She turns back from the window with an almost stiff expression. "Captain, the way things have been going lately, I was looking forward to a little boredom."

8

At the corner of West Tenth and Bleecker streets, Paul Wyzanski and Charlie Abbot shuffle their feet against the cold and argue about which way to turn. They have just spent an hour "making their manners" with the New York City Police Department, letting the Sixth Precinct know that they will be working its turf.

"No, man," Charlie protests, "it's back the other way."

"Charlie, the sergeant said it was just a coupla blocks south."

"Yeah, but we're going east. We gotta head back toward the river and . . . Shit, it's too cold to fuck around. Let's just ask Jungle Jim over there." He tilts his head toward a tall blond man in heavily studded black leathers leaning against a lamppost and holding a leash attached to a sequined collar around the thin neck of his companion, who Charlie assumes is another man, but he's not quite sure.

Paul rolls his eyes as Charlie walks up to the man in leather and says, "We're looking for Barrow Street, between Hudson"—turning back to Wyzanski—"and what was it?"

"Bedford," Paul says.

"Yeah, between Hudson and Bedford."

Neither the man in leather nor his companion says a word or offers a gesture.

Charlie remains still while the man inspects him, keeping his hands stuffed in the pockets of his rumpled trench coat, his shoulders hunched forward and minimizing his short but bulky physique.

"Look, friend, I already got a date," Charlie says, gesturing toward Paul Wyzanski standing straight in his pressed and buttoned topcoat, "all I want is directions."

Again there is no response, and Paul sees the swelling of Charlie's impatience, which at times interferes with the exercise of his better judgment. At six feet, two inches, Paul Wyzanski can and does look down on the man in leather. He reaches into his breast pocket and produces a black leather folder opened to his gold detective's badge. "Excuse me," he says. "Perhaps you didn't hear Detective Abbot. We're looking for Barrow Street, between Hudson and Bedford."

The man in leather furrows his brow, hesitant and confused by the idea of two detectives asking street directions. After a moment he nods to his companion, who says, "Go back one block and take a left. It's a coupla blocks down that way."

"Thank you," Paul says politely, and begins to walk away.

Charlie Abbot remains in place, looking the man in leather up and down with exaggerated curiosity. The man asks, "Is there something else?"

"Nah, just wondering—"

"Charlie!" Paul interrupts quickly, unsure of his partner's intent. "Let's go."

It takes Charlie a moment to break his stare, but then he turns, and they start off in the direction given.

It has taken six weeks of endless phone calls and their gathering and reviewing and cross-checking telephone and credit card and airline and hotel records to bring the two detectives to Manhattan's West Village, and still they are uncertain where the trail is leading them. Captain Hardiman's insistence that they keep a low profile in tracing Cooper Avery's activities over the few weeks before his wife's murder has not made the trace any easier. Christine Boland's efforts to arrange another interview of Cooper Avery were not successful. Avery apologized for the outburst that had cut short their last conversation, explaining that the pressures of that first week after his wife's death had been enormous. Christine said that she understood, and Avery assured her that he wanted to cooperate fully. However, his business was at a particularly critical point and his schedule inordinately demanding. To the suggestion that they meet anytime or anywhere convenient for him, Avery said that he was reserving what little free time he had to be with his daughter during this difficult period. Avery made no mention of his son. Christine was referred to Avery's attorney, Phillip Layton, who in turn repeated both his and his client's sincere interest in cooperating fully. But after the exchange of several phone calls, a convenient time just never could be found in Avery's schedule. Of course, if Christine had any specific questions, Phillip Layton offered to gather what information she needed and get back to her. She declined the offer.

The stall only hardened Detectives Wyzanski and Abbot's suspicion and their resolve. They immersed themselves in the gathering of records and either put off or left to others all but a few of the standard canvassing interviews of friends and neighbors. With the help of Captain Hardiman, the detectives called in more than a few favors from the police departments in Boston and New York, and from airline, bank, credit card, hotel and telephone security departments. Albert Chasen, the state's attorney who would be in charge of any prosecution that came of their investigation, obliged them with subpoenas for the records of companies that would not release information otherwise. Although the trail was by no means complete, and they knew little more today than they had six weeks before, what little they had learned intrigued them.

Cooper Avery was indeed a busy man, spending more than half his time flying about the country, staying in five-star hotels and dining at the best restaurants. He also spent an inordinate amount of time on the telephone, charging the calls to two credit cards, one corporate, one personal. The billings to his corporate card were enormous, and although the detectives had so far succeeded in getting subscriber information on less than half of the numbers listed, they revealed nothing more than what would be expected: calls to banks, insurance companies, investment houses, branch offices of Thurston Construction, its clients, suppliers and competitors, and the various hotels where Avery routinely stayed. There were also calls to his home, to his parents' home on Sanibel Island on the west coast of Florida, to his sister in Seattle and to his in-laws in Guilford, all of which made Charlie Abbot pose the thought, "You know, you gotta wonder why he'd even bother using, or even having, a personal card. I mean, the man's the president of the company and obviously he's got no problem charging personal calls to the business."

It was a good question. When they began to look more closely at the charges on Cooper's personal card, which were minor compared to those on his corporate card, they found several calls that further excited their curiosity. Once or twice a week over the past three months, Avery had made calls to certain businesses that never showed up on his corporate card, to an insurance group in Hartford, to a law firm in Boston and to the headquarters of Barth-Sanders Industries in New York City. Christine had sat up when she heard "Barth-Sanders," and left Paul and Charlie in their office for a few minutes before returning with a copy of *The Wall Street Journal.*

"Look at this," she had said, showing them a short article about the takeover fight between Barth-Sanders and Thurston Construction.

Paul had sat back and lifted both hands in the air. "Yeah, but what's it mean?"

"I don't know," she answered, "but doesn't it seem a little strange that if they're in the middle of this stock fight, Avery would be calling the other side?"

"I don't know squat about business," Charlie said, "but what makes me wonder is why use his personal card? Unless maybe he doesn't want anyone at Thurston to know about it. And if not, why not?"

They spent an hour or more looking through what they had of the listed charges to Avery's corporate card and found several calls to both the insurance company and the law firm, but none to Barth-Sanders. Paul and Charlie thought they smelled blood, but Christine, as she seemed to be doing more and more, urged caution.

"What's your problem, Chris?" Paul had asked. "Why're you so sure this guy's clean?"

"I'm not sure. It's just that I think we've got to be real careful about jumping to conclusions here. It's almost as if you guys have already decided that he did it, and so anytime you find something that looks even remotely unusual, you're off and running. We may be overlooking the obvious here."

"What's the obvious we're overlooking?" Charlie asked.

"I don't know, Charlie. All I'm saying is let's not get carried away because Avery's a socially prominent businessman."

Charlie was offended. "That's bullshit! It's got nothing to do with that. Everyone on that scene knew it didn't smell right, including you. Hell, you more'n anyone else. You know it whudn't no burglary."

"Yeah, I agree. But I'm telling you, I can't see Avery killing his wife like that. I just keep thinking about the way it was done. I mean doesn't this look like a classic assassination? It just seems to me there's more to this than a man wanting to get rid of his wife."

"Yeah, okay," Charlie agreed, "I can see that. But if there is more to this, wouldn't you think it'd have something to do with Avery and not his wife? Not to speak ill of the dead or nothin', but shit, Marian Avery was hardly important enough to make someone's hit list. I mean, you think someone at the Junior League'd off her for wearing the same gown to the charity ball?"

Christine laughed. "No. All I'm saying is let's not get stuck on a theory too soon here. And what about his father? Or the wife's father. Why not some connection there?"

"What? Some guy's got a grudge against the congressman so he hits the daughter-in-law?"

Paul agreed with Charlie Abbot. "Yeah, too remote. Let's not look for shadows to chase here."

"I'm not chasing shadows," Christine protested. "I'm just suggesting we keep an open mind."

Both Charlie and Paul dismissed the caution and turned back to their search, and to their theory that Cooper Avery, or at least someone directly related to him or his business, was responsible for the murder of Marian Avery.

It was the receipt of telephone subscriber information listing the Albemarle House, a small hotel on Manhattan's Upper East Side, that caught everyone's attention, including Christine's. Avery's usual residence in New York was the Plaza on Central Park South. Going back and cross-checking the records, Paul Wyzanski established that on at least five occasions during the past three months, Cooper Avery had called the Albemarle House using his personal telephone credit card. Each one of the calls had preceded by a day the date that Cooper had arrived and checked in at the Plaza. A call to the Albemarle House established that although it had a small room where the guests were served a Continental breakfast and afternoon tea, compliments of the house, it had no dining room or bar. Nor did it serve anyone other than guests of the hotel. The call also established that the manager knew no one by the name of Cooper Avery. Captain Hardiman agreed that Detectives Wyzanski and Abbot should check it out.

Paul and Charlie had nosed out of the Holland Tunnel shortly after one o'clock, but it had taken them another hour and fifteen minutes and several quarrels to find the Albemarle House nestled on East Eighty-ninth between Park and Madison avenues. The hotel's front was plain, and they had walked past it twice before spying the small brass plaque on the gray brick façade next to the double glass-and-wooden doors. Inside, the Albemarle's small lobby gave off an air of expensive elegance, its deep red carpeting setting off the wood-paneled walls and plush leather chairs. From behind the desk, a small man in a black blazer peered skeptically over round glasses rimmed in thin black plastic. Paul Wyzanski did most of the talking, quietly explaining their purpose and showing a subpoena with which he said Henri Foulard could comply by simply answering a few questions.

Henri—the gentleman pronounced his name to rhyme with "ennui," which was his manner, *On-ree Foo-larr*—came as close as he could to conceding their authority by saying, "Well, if this is really necessary."

Charlie Abbot smiled. He enjoyed dealing with foreign nationals, who seemed less inclined to question his authority or, as in this case, his lack of authority. Neither he nor Paul felt any need to explain to Foulard that unlike federal subpoenas, a subpoena issued by a state or county is without effect in another jurisdiction unless it first goes through the legally cumbersome process of being reissued under the authority of the state in which it is to be served.

Henri Foulard opened his palms, suggesting that they were wasting their time. "I spoke to someone about this a week or more ago."

Paul nodded. "Yes, I was the one who called."

"Well, as I told you, I know of no one by the name of Cooper Avery. We have a small but steady clientele, and I would know of that name if he were one of our regular guests."

"Well, is it possible that this man used a different name?"

"Oh, no, no, no. Our guests are not of that sort. They are all very respectable. We do not have persons who need to use a false name."

"I understand. But perhaps this person would have some private reason for using another name. Or perhaps—"

"I cannot speak to that. No, no, we do not cater to such people. Of course our clients enjoy their privacy"—he emphasized the very English pronunciation of the word, *priv'asee*—"which is their right. But I know of no one who would need to disguise himself."

Wyzanski shook his head impatiently. "What I was about to say was that perhaps the gentleman we are looking for was calling for one of your regular clients. Maybe just to arrange a dinner or business meeting. We're simply curious why this man Cooper Avery would call here each time he comes to New York but never stay here, particularly since you don't have a restaurant or bar or anything."

"But how would I know something like that? We certainly do not listen in on our clients' phone calls."

"No, but maybe we could look through the guest list for the days on or before these calls and see if there is one guest who was always here on those days."

"May I ask what this is all about? I am the manager, but the owners would be very upset if I were simply to open our guest lists to you."

"Well, I don't think it would be appropriate for us to discuss that. You understand that if we find that Mr. Avery has done no wrong, it would be unfair to make known the facts of this investigation."

Foulard nodded vigorously. "Of course."

"That's why we have come here personally. To try and keep this matter as quiet and confidential as we can. And I'm sure that the owners would understand your having to comply with a subpoena."

"Ah, yes, I see. Well, I suppose we could look through the records. It will take some time, of course, and I have no one who can cover the desk right now." Paul raised his eyebrows, signaling that he did not intend to be put off. "What does this man Avery look like?" Foulard asked.

"He's quite tall, about six foot three. Thin, pale complexion with blond—well, more graying—hair. Short, very neat hair, combed straight back. He's very wealthy, dresses in very expensive suits, but not at all flashy."

Foulard frowned a hint of recognition, then cocked his head a bit and said, "This man sounds very much like our Mr. Belkindas."

"Belkindas?"

"Yes, yes. Mr. George Belkindas. He has been coming here several times a month for the past year or so. Maybe longer."

"Do you know what type of business this Mr. Belkindas is in?"

"No. Not at all. He is, ah, a very quiet and private gentleman. Very polite, but he does not discuss his business with me."

"Well, when he comes here, does his office make reservations for him or does he pay with a company credit card or something like that?"

Foulard pursed his lips, his indifferent air dissipating, his brow furrowing just a bit as if he were forcing himself to pass on a secret. "Well, no," he said hesitantly, "he—well, when I take the reservation, it is always Mr. Belkindas who calls himself. And he always pays in cash. In advance actually. He is a very valued client. A very elegant and quiet man."

"He pays in cash?" Paul and Charlie Abbot exchanged a curious look. "In advance? Isn't that a bit unusual?"

"Well, no, not really. It is perfectly normal."

"How many of your other clients pay in cash and in advance?"

Foulard took a half-step back from the desk, his outstretched fingers lightly drumming the counter like an imaginary piano. "Well, I couldn't really say how many. You know, to remember such a thing over the years."

"How many in the past three months?"

"Well, I do not remember anyone. But, of course, that does not mean, you know, that it does not happen—on occasion, perhaps."

"How many regularly pay cash in advance like this Mr. Belkindas?"

"Yes, well, I see your point." Foulard suddenly leaned forward, speaking very quietly over the desk. "Gentlemen, please, the guests will soon begin checking in or coming for tea." It was just after three o'clock. "Can we go into my office?"

Paul nodded and Foulard picked up a dark red phone and punched in two digits. Within a minute, a young woman with black hair pulled back in a severe bun walked through a rear door and joined Foulard at the desk. "I need to talk with these gentlemen in the office," he said to her. "Can you watch the desk until I return?"

It took only a minute on the computer for Foulard to pull the room records of George Belkindas. Over the past year Belkindas had visited the hotel an average of two or three times a month, no visit extending beyond a single night. Checking through a thick spiral notebook that he pulled from his vinyl portfolio, Paul Wyzanski verified that each of the visits over the past few months had come within a day or two after Cooper Avery had called the hotel using his personal credit card, and each visit matched precisely the days on which Avery had been checked in at the Plaza Hotel some thirty blocks away. The records also showed that Mr. Belkindas had last checked into the Albemarle on the Friday before Marian Avery's body had been discovered and that he had not returned since.

Charlie Abbot squinted and drew out the manager's name in an attempt to be polite, but the effort sounded almost mocking. "Mr. *Fooolarr,* does this Belkindas ever have, you know, *guests?*"

Foulard was obviously embarrassed, and one hand picked imaginary lint from the sleeve of his jacket. "Well, I guess sometimes, yes."

"How often is sometimes?" Charlie pressed.

"Well, you must understand that I am not always here. And of course I do not watch the comings and goings of our guests. Beyond seeing to their comfort, what our guests do is their own affair."

"How often does she meet him here?" Charlie pressed even harder.

Foulard seemed frozen and uncomfortable in his silence.

"It's the same woman every time, isn't it?"

"Gentlemen," he said a touch nervously, "please understand. I do not want to say something I cannot be sure of because I am not always on duty, and I do not question our guests. And Mr. Belkindas has always been a very proper gentleman."

"Please, Mr. Foulard," Paul said, "just answer Detective Abbot's question. We're not asking you to pass judgment. But this is very important."

With an exaggerated sigh, Henri Foulard reported that each and every time George Belkindas had stayed at the hotel, a woman had met and stayed with him. Foulard had never been introduced, nor had he ever heard a name mentioned, either first or last. "She is, I would say, perhaps in her early to mid-forties. Very elegant. Blond hair," and he swept his hands back along his head to indicate the style, "and quite tall. Quite striking, I must say. Yes, she and Mr. Belkindas make a *very* elegant couple."

"And this woman always stays with him?"

"Yes, well, except the last time. It was a bit strange, I admit."

"What was?"

"Well, the last time Mr. Belkindas was here he checked in and paid in advance as usual. He went to his room and made a call and then left. He was here no more than a half hour or so and then he left. He did not say anything. He just left and did not return."

"He took his bags with him?"

Again Foulard looked uneasy. "Well, you understand, Mr. Belkindas never has luggage. Oh, perhaps a shaving kit or something. But he never has luggage."

Detectives Wyzanski and Abbot smiled broadly at each other while Henri Foulard sat in the corner of the office, one knee bouncing in a short, nervous rhythm.

They asked Foulard how he knew about the phone call Belkindas had made, and Foulard explained that the hotel charged its guests seventy-five cents for each local call. While the bill itself only listed the fact of the call, a computer printout kept track of the number called and that number appeared on a slip of paper stapled to the hotel's copy of the bill. They went to a file room behind the office and found a dozen or more of Belkindas's billings. Among other calls, they found one local number that was called at least once during each visit. Charlie asked permission to use the office telephone and Foulard nodded, although he stiffened a bit when he noticed Charlie punching in a long-distance number.

It took some time, all three men sitting in silence, for Charlie to reach Christine at headquarters. He asked her to check the number Belkindas routinely called against their list of calls charged to Avery's personal card. Forty-five minutes passed before Christine called back to verify that she had found a match. The subscriber information attached to that number listed an address on Barrow Street in Greenwich Village and the name Victor Rais.

The detectives asked Foulard to make copies of Belkindas's hotel and phone records, which he did. They thanked him and left.

And so the trail has led them here, to the West Village, searching for the home of Victor Rais. It is almost seven-thirty, and the night is overcast and threatens snow. Charlie Abbot is again complaining, this time about the fact that they have left their car near the Sixth Precinct station and are conducting their search on foot. "Man, whaddaya got against using the car? It's too damn cold to be hoofin' it all over the city."

"Look around, Charlie. Where ya gonna park?"

"That's whatja got cabs for. Ya know what I'm sayin'?"

"There it is." Paul points, happy to cut off the discussion.

The Barrow Street address they have been looking for is a tall, narrow town house. A short flight of brick stairs leads to a highly polished wooden door guarded by an ornate iron gate. Lights shine through the first-floor windows and highlight the equally ornate iron bars that enclose them. The second-, third- and fourth-floor windows are barless and dark. Paul looks at his watch and shrugs. "Maybe we'll catch him at dinner, and they'll offer us a bite."

"Yeah, count on it," Charlie sneers. He has also been complaining about his hunger.

They begin to cross the street as a black limousine pulls to a stop in front of the house. The driver gets out and circles the car to the right rear door, where he stands almost at attention. A woman appears from the rear of the car and stops a moment, speaking to the driver, who nods in return. Charlie and Paul look at each other with surprise, and they mimic in silence the description they received from Foulard. *Tall, blond and elegant.* In unison they sweep their hands back along the sides of their heads.

They cross the street quickly and approach the woman. The driver looks alarmed, and he moves between her and the detectives.

Paul Wyzanski smiles and pulls his badge from his pocket. "Please, don't be alarmed. We're police officers. There's no reason to be concerned."

The woman steps back a bit and peers around the chauffeur. Paul maintains his smile and asks, "Mrs. Rais?"

She looks at both detectives with a sudden, curious frown and Paul repeats, "Excuse me, are you Mrs. Rais? My name is Detective

Wyzanski and this is Detective Abbot. We've just come from the Albemarle House."

The woman's back straightens, and she turns to the chauffeur. "It's all right, Peter, you can go. But if you would, please put me down for an eight o'clock pickup tomorrow?"

"Yes, ma'am," the driver says, and takes more than one glance over his shoulder as he moves toward the driver's door.

"You are Mrs. Rais, aren't you?" Paul asks.

Her frown remains, and her eyes dart back and forth between the two detectives. "Well . . . yes. I'm sorry, it's just that I, ah, rarely use that name. It's my husband's name."

Charlie leans forward a bit, his expression mildly inquisitive. "Excuse me, I'm not sure—"

"Yes, well, I am Mrs. Rais, I suppose. It's just that I don't use that name professionally."

"Oh, I understand." Charlie nods. "Do you mind if I ask what name you use professionally?"

"Well . . . Do you mind telling me what this is all about?"

Paul nods. "It's about George Belkindas," and he allows a brief moment for this to be absorbed, "and Cooper Avery."

Her mouth shows the strain of someone who is trying to smile agreeably, but who cannot. "I'm sorry," Paul continues, "what name did you say you used professionally?"

Again, it takes a moment while the woman's eyes continue to sweep back and forth. But finally she takes a breath to smooth her edge and fixes a soft, even stare on Paul Wyzanski. "My name is Sydney Lambert. Won't you come in?"

■■■■

The detectives are led down a long center hall to a large den whose walls are covered with fully stacked bookshelves and autographed pictures of people neither man recognizes. A large mahogany desk sits in one corner, its top covered with the accoutrements of business: a telephone with three separate lines, a fax machine, a leather-framed blotter on which sit several expensive fountain pens, and a neat stack of typed memoranda, one corner of which is billowed like an accordion by the handwritten notes which are paper-clipped to each document. Charlie has moved to the desk and is fingering through the stack and reading the notes while Sydney Lambert is in the kitchen next door. She has offered the detectives coffee and something to eat, but Paul Wyzanski—to Charlie's displeasure—has said that just coffee will be fine.

Paul, his ear cocked toward the kitchen, suddenly but softly warns his partner, "Charlie!" and flips his thumb toward the swinging door. Charlie moves quickly from the desk and feigns interest in the titles of several books as Sydney Lambert enters the room carrying a tray loaded with a silver pot and its matching sugar bowl and creamer, and cups and saucers.

Paul rises quickly from his silk-upholstered armchair. "Can I give you a hand?"

"No, I'm fine," Sydney Lambert says. "If you'll just move those papers on the desk."

Charlie moves the papers he has been reading to one side, and Sydney Lambert sets the tray in the middle of the desk. "I'll let you gentlemen pour your own," she says, as she fills a cup for herself. "I don't take cream or sugar."

Charlie seems unsure just how to fit his thick fingers around the handle of the china cup, which to him looks more like a part of the dollhouse set he bought for his six-year-old daughter last Christmas. But he succeeds in pouring his coffee without a spill, leaving almost half the cup for the heavy load of cream and sugar he requires. Paul pours his own cup, taking no cream and just a half-spoon of sugar, and returns to his chair.

Sydney Lambert settles in a straight-backed wing chair in front of the desk while Charlie looks about, uncertain whether he wants to sit in the matching wing chair. There being no alternative but the high-backed leather chair behind the desk—which even he knows would be bad form—he takes the wing chair, sitting stiffly and holding the cup and saucer in front of him as though they might break if he made any sudden move.

"Well, gentlemen," Sydney Lambert begins with a smile, "what can I do for you?"

Paul leans forward. "Ms. Lambert, I take it you know Cooper Avery."

"Yes."

"And you're aware that his wife, Marian, was murdered almost two months ago."

"Yes, I heard about it. What a horrible thing."

Paul nods. "Well, Detective Abbot and myself are in charge of the investigation, and in doing some background checks we came upon your name, that is, your married name."

"Background checks? I'm not sure what you mean by that."

"Of Mr. Avery," Paul says. "Of his activities over the past few months."

"Of Mr. Avery? Is he under suspicion?"

"Well, not necessarily. It's just that in a case such as this we have to, I guess you'd say, cover all the possibilities."

"I understand. But what does any of this have to do with me?"

"If I might, let me ask you something first. You said that Sydney Lambert is your professional name. What exactly is your profession?"

"Well, when I say that it's my professional name, it's my maiden name. It's just that I use my maiden name in my business. I'm an attorney."

"Oh, really? Are you with a law firm here in New York?"

"No, I'm not. I'm general counsel for Barth-Sanders Industries."

"What does that mean, exactly, to be general counsel?"

Sydney Lambert offers a smile of suffering patience. "It just means that I supervise the legal affairs of the corporation. We have many law firms representing our various interests. I supervise those matters and advise the president and board of directors."

Charlie Abbot shows the scrunched facial expression of someone trying to remember a connection, and Paul stumbles a bit trying to do the same. "Barth-Sanders? That's, ah, a pretty large outfit, isn't it?"

"Yes, quite."

"It doesn't . . . Oh, wait, I just recalled. Isn't your company somehow involved with Cooper Avery's business? Thurston Construction?"

Charlie sits back with a sudden knowing smile that is tinged with curiosity.

Sydney Lambert studies his expression and then turns back to Paul. She shows no sign of discomfort. "Well, no, not really. Barth-Sanders has offered to buy a controlling interest in Thurston Construction, but other than that we have no involvement with them."

Charlie cuts to the chase. "But you are involved with Cooper Avery. Isn't that right?"

The offense Sydney Lambert takes is palpable. Her silence is complete and extends almost too long, as if she is conscious of just how long it would take to have its maximum effect. Neither detective blinks. Finally, she extends her cup and saucer toward the desk and sets them down without a sound. She then pulls her arm back and folds her long, thin fingers in her lap and says, "No, I am not involved with Cooper Avery."

"Ms. Lambert, we—"

"I know Cooper, of course. He's a very prominent businessman. Thurston Construction is one of the five or six largest contractors and developers in the country. Of course I know him. I know a great many people. But I am not, as you say, *involved* with him."

Paul takes a moment. "Ms. Lambert, as I was about to say, we've spent some time looking into a lot of records, including hotel and telephone records. As I told you outside, we just spent the afternoon at the Albemarle House. We've seen the records of visits and telephone calls to your phone here. We've talked to the manager about the woman who visits the man registered as George Belkindas. We've—"

"But—" She interrupts sharply, then hesitates, trying to reconstruct her façade of calm. "But what does Mr. Belkindas have to do with Cooper Avery?"

"Ms. Lambert, please," Paul says, suddenly doubtful of his assumption that Belkindas and Avery are the same man and hoping Sydney Lambert will, by his tone, assume he already knows the answer and thus will supply it herself. "We understand that this might be a bit delicate."

"No, you gentlemen understand nothing. You look at a few pieces of paper, and suddenly you jump to all kinds of conclusions with no regard for the people you may hurt. You should be very careful about the accusations you make. Aside from hurting innocent people, you could gather some serious trouble for yourselves."

Charlie Abbot does what he always does when challenged. He smiles, broadly, and says nothing. Sydney Lambert remains silent as if contemplating her next move, but all she can muster is a stiffening of her back and the statement, "I don't appreciate your accusations."

Charlie lets his smile subside and leans forward to place his own cup and saucer on the desk. "Ma'am, I don't recall our accusing you of anything. What is it that you're so concerned about?"

Sydney Lambert glances at the phone on her desk and Charlie asks, "Is there someone you want to call? We'd be happy to excuse ourselves for a few moments, if you'd like. A lawyer maybe?"

"No, that's not necessary." She stands abruptly and circles her chair to the back of the desk, and from the top drawer she pulls a leather cigarette case and lighter. She lights a cigarette and takes a long drag, letting the smoke out in several short puffs. She looks about the room and then moves to the opposite corner, where she finds an ashtray. She takes one more puff and grinds the long remainder into the crystal bottom before turning toward the detectives. "You have to understand. I'm neither proud nor ashamed of what I've done. It's just that this could be disastrous to my career. Can you understand that?"

"Yes, but—" Paul tries.

"My husband and I have been married almost twenty years. And after all that time we have come to an understanding."

Both detectives sit back. Both know this woman no longer needs to be asked any questions.

"I suppose there are those who would gladly cluck their disapproval, but it is an understanding that works for us. He travels all the time. In his business. He's gone probably nine months of the year. And I'm busy myself. With work. Traveling. My husband and I are lucky if we get to see each other three or four days a month. Sometimes we have to arrange to meet in other cities, or I'll go to Brussels, even for just a few days. He has an office there and we have an apartment, and a house in Grindelwald. Do you know it? Grindelwald?" Both detectives shake their heads. "Switzerland? Near Interlaken? It was beautiful once. Still is, I suppose. It's just in the past few years it's been so overrun with tourists. We keep talking about selling, but somehow we just can't do it. We were always very happy there." A hint of moisture glistens at the edges of her eyes, and she moves quickly back to the desk. "I'm sorry," she says as she reaches for and lights another cigarette. "This is very hard—very hard. We don't—haven't had, well, a *relationship* for years. He's . . ." She stops to take another puff of the cigarette. Her hand shows a barely perceptible shake. "That's not an excuse.

It's simply a fact. But we understand one another. We don't question each other. But neither would we ever want to embarrass the other, *and,*" she emphasizes, "I have no intention or desire to leave him. Nor he me. You may not be able to understand this, but our marriage is a solid one."

Paul stands and retrieves the ashtray from the other side of the room and takes it to Sydney Lambert. He places it on the front of the desk as she returns to her chair and sits down.

"Thank you," she says, then turns silent for a moment.

The detectives wait.

Her smile is strained. "I suppose in your line of work none of this is surprising, is it?"

"No, not really," Paul says.

"I'm just concerned about what my husband would think if this all came out. And my job. I'd lose my job. This could ruin me. And I just don't see how any of this relates to Cooper's wife's murder. I just don't understand this."

Charlie makes a motion as if to speak, but she cuts him off. "I stopped it. As soon as I got wind of the takeover bid, I stopped it. That's the truth, but they'd never understand that. The people at Barth-Sanders, I mean. They wouldn't believe it."

"Why don't we go back to the beginning," Paul urges. "Back to when you first met Cooper Avery."

"Oh, God," she whispers aloud, and then, with a slow release of breath, "All right."

It takes Sydney Lambert another forty-five minutes and several cigarettes to tell the tale, often halting, often jumbling her story, while the detectives sit quietly and take few notes and ask few questions.

She met Cooper Avery several years ago, at a cocktail party here in New York. She doesn't remember where, but over the years she would occasionally run into him through mutual business acquaintances. About a year before, they found themselves stranded at the same hotel in Chicago, a snowstorm having canceled their flights until the next morning. After a long dinner and too many drinks, she returned to his room. She makes it clear, without saying so directly, that Cooper Avery was neither her first nor her only lover, making the point as well that neither she nor Cooper considered their affair anything more than that; it was simply an affair of convenience. Yes, they routinely went to the Albemarle House when he was in New York, neither she nor Cooper wanting to be seen at the Plaza, where it was likely they might run into a friend or business associate. And her own loyalty forbade her ever taking Cooper into her and her husband's bed. She also emphasizes that she never allowed Cooper to speak of his wife or of their relationship, nor would she ever speak of her own marriage, although Cooper often pressed her to do so. She has no idea whether George Belkindas is the name of a real person or simply one that Avery made up. She has never asked, nor does she care.

She claims that she ended the relationship several months before Marian Avery's death, within days of first hearing that her company was considering a hostile takeover of Thurston Construction. Cooper objected, and for some time pestered her with phone calls trying to rekindle the affair. But she was adamant and refused to see him again.

"That Friday before Mrs. Avery's body was found. What was it, Charlie?"

"The twenty-sixth."

"Yes, the twenty-sixth of October. Avery checked into the Albemarle House, called your number here, and then left. He was only there a half hour or so and he never returned. Did he come here?"

"No."

"Did you see him that day—or evening?"

"No. And I don't remember him calling me. As far as I can remember, I would have been at work. Maybe Gretchen took the call, I don't know."

"Gretchen?"

"Yes, she's our housekeeper."

"Do you remember her giving you any message from Avery?"

"No. He wouldn't have left his name anyway. I was very strict about that. And Cooper was very cautious about that as well. He wouldn't have left his name even if he had called."

"You don't have an answering machine?"

"Yes, but Gretchen has standing orders to answer the phone while she's here. You know, to let people—strangers, you know —to let them know that someone is home and all that."

"She's here every day?"

"Yes, during the week, up to about three o'clock."

"That's a lot of cleaning for only one person living here most of the time," Charlie says.

"Well, she prepares a meal for me and puts it in the refrigerator so all I have to do is toss it in the microwave." She glances at Charlie and says, "I haven't looked to see what she's made, but there's always plenty. Would either of you like something to eat?"

"No. Thank you, but we're fine," Paul says as Charlie scowls. "But you're sure that you neither saw nor heard from Avery that day."

"I am absolutely positive."

The conversation ends several minutes later with the detectives assuring Sydney Lambert that they will make every reasonable effort to ensure that her affair with Avery will not be reported except in their own confidential files. "Of course," Paul cautions, "we can't predict where this investigation might lead. You just never know."

"Do you people really believe Cooper would be capable of such a thing? I mean killing his wife?"

"No, please, Ms. Lambert, understand that we're not accusing Mr. Avery of anything. At this time it looks like someone broke into his house and killed his wife. What we are trying to discover is whether there might have been someone besides just a random burglar who might have had some reason to kill her or him. We just don't know. That's why we have to track down every possibility."

"I understand. I don't know," she says in a soft, almost whispered aside, "Mr. Avery may be a lot of things, but a murderer he is not."

"I'm sure you're right," Paul says, and Charlie chirps in, "Ma'am, could you point us to a real good restaurant around here?"

She does and they leave.

▬

It is nearly ten o'clock when they arrive at the corner of West Tenth Street, just a short distance from the Sixth Precinct. They have decided to drop their notebooks in the trunk of the car and then check out one of the restaurants Sydney Lambert suggested. Paul judges her credible, but Charlie is more than skeptical.

"Man, I just don't buy that act. I mean she only comes off what she thought we already knew, and she only did that when she figured her lawyer's Mau Mau routine wasn't gonna put us off. Then alla sudden she's this weepy, sentimental broad worried about her husband's feelings that she's been fucking around on for years? Give me a break. Besides, what the fuck's Avery doing checking into the Albemarle if not to see her?"

"Maybe he was setting up an alibi."

"Nah, if he's lookin' for an alibi, he'd use his own name."

"Maybe not. Maybe he just wants a backup if he absolutely needs it. He keeps the affair quiet, but it's there if push comes to shove."

"You think? Maybe. Maybe for both of them. You see the way she was lightin' up?"

"Yeah, you got the stub?" Paul asks. Midway through their conversation, as Sydney Lambert's attention was focused on Paul, Charlie reached over and took one of the longer butts she had left and slipped it into his pocket.

Charlie nods with a grin and pulls the butt from his pocket. "Marlboro Lights. Too bad the lab hasn't come up with a brand for the one left on the sink."

"I don't know that they've tried that hard. Maybe this'll give them some incentive. But I can't see this lady being involved. No, I just don't see it. By the way, where'd we leave the car?"

Charlie looks around. "Wasn't it right along here? That's the precinct house down there, isn't it?"

They spend another twenty minutes wandering up and down the streets surrounding the Sixth Precinct until reality hits them.

"Motherfucker!" Charlie shouts.

"Ah shit," Paul moans. "The captain's gonna kill us. Sonofabitch, the captain's gonna kill us."

"Us? Goddamnit, didn't I tell ya to stick it inna garage and take a cab? Didn't I tell ya?"

"He's gonna kill us. I swear to God he's gonna kill us."

"Motherfucker! I mean stealing a cop car? Shit, this is one tough burg!"

The desk sergeant at the Sixth Precinct agrees, with a broad smile he cannot suppress. "Yep, what's it been? A few hours? My man, your ride's already chopped inna hun'red pieces and gracing the shelves of half the parts stores in Jersey."

"Motherfucker," Charlie repeats, although the word has been reduced to a groan.

The desk sergeant is now surrounded by several detectives and patrol officers, whose communal laughter drowns out Charlie's epithets. "Welcome to the Big Apple, gentlemen. Wanna see a bus schedule?"

9 $\mathcal{O}$utside the narrow-paned window at the end of the hall, the glow of Christmas lights softens the night. Alex stands a moment, considering his reflection in the window and the appearance he is about to make. His hands still feel the sting of the scrubbing he has given them, and a flesh-colored bandage covers the end of one finger, where his effort to remove all evidence of the gritty clay caused the cuticle to bleed. The white silk scarf is smooth and cool against his neck, and his black cashmere topcoat is heavy and confining. They are new, the scarf and topcoat, as is everything he is wearing, and were far more expensive than anything he ever thought of buying for himself. But Christine said that you only get one first night, and he should do or spend whatever it took to feel good about it. It is the night of his first gallery showing, and he does feel good, except for his nerves, which have infected him with almost childlike insecurity.

He has stopped in the hallway just outside Christine's apartment to prepare himself. He buttons the topcoat, packaging himself in neatness: but no, that's wrong. Too formal, too uptight. He unbuttons the coat and sweeps one flap back to put his hand in the pocket of his purchased—not rented, *purchased*—tuxedo pants. Better. He unbuttons the tuxedo jacket with his other hand and affects a certain jaunty stance. Perfect, he decides, or at least as good as it's going to get.

"Perfect!" he hears from over his shoulder, and he turns to see

Christine's neighbor, Mrs. Braverman, smiling at him from the end of the hall, her day's trash neatly bundled in a small plastic bag held in one hand, while with the other she forms a circle with her thumb and forefinger to signal her approval. "That's just the look you want."

He smiles with embarrassment. "So, whaddaya think?"

"Besides my husband when he was your age, and maybe Paul Newman, I think you're the handsomest man I ever saw." She tilts her head toward Christine's apartment. "Don't keep her waiting, now. Go ahead."

Alex knocks lightly on the door and waits, his hand still in his pocket, maintaining the pose he affected for the window. He doesn't hear any movement from within, and he is about to knock again when the door opens and his reaction spills forth in a slow whisper. *"Whooaaa!"*

He does not move, his lips still formed for the words that do not come, and Christine's smile is as shy as he suddenly feels. He has never seen her like this. Her hair is swept back and gathered in soft, rounded swirls held by a small diamond clip. Her dress is black and forms to her body, and the neckline is scooped just enough to hint at the swell of her breasts. He does not notice her reaction to him until she teases, "Whoa, yourself. You look wonderful." She leans forward to kiss his cheek lightly, and he notices her lipstick, just a hint of pale coloring he has never seen before. He cannot quite describe it, and it makes him wonder if he has ever seen her wear lipstick.

Christine steps back with an admiring nod. "Who would have thought that this *muzhik* image of yours was just a cover? Obviously you've long been a frequenter of posh bistros and swank supper clubs." She reaches out and takes his one hand, the other still stuck in his pants pocket. "Come in," she says, and gently pulls him forward and closes the door.

As often as he has visited Christine's apartment, it has the sudden appearance of a place he has never been. There is the faint scent of incense and fresh wood, and the light from the porcelain lamps at either end of the couch is mellowed by the steady flame of the candles on the mantel and a low fire in the fireplace. On the butler's table in front of the couch, a silver tray is adorned with black bread and caviar and slivers of salmon. Beside the tray, an ice bucket holds a bottle of Russian champagne.

"Christine," is all he can say, and she lets out a chuckle and asks, "Is your hand cold?"

"Oh, no," he stammers, pulling his hand from his pocket. He takes off his coat and looks about until she takes the coat and scarf from him and lays them over a chair in the corner. She leads him to the couch, where he sits and feels his expression lighten to an almost silly grin.

"I thought you might need a little private celebration to calm your nerves."

"Christine, this is, I don't know, this is . . ."

"Honey," she mocks gently, "you just sit here and gather your thoughts while I go put on the finishing touches. I'll be right back." She starts toward the bedroom, and Alex looks nervously at his steel watch with its cracked crystal. "Relax, we have plenty of time," she says. "The gallery's only ten minutes away, and besides, you want to be a little late so that you can make a grand entrance. Open the champagne. I'll only be a minute."

He pops the cork but places the open bottle back in the ice bucket to await her return. He takes a piece of black bread, however, and with it scoops up a dollop of caviar, which he eats quickly, as if otherwise she might catch him.

Christine returns to the room, her head tilted as she fits the post of a diamond earring through one ear and attaches the backing. She cocks her head to the other side to don the second earring and then runs her fingers over a thin diamond necklace. "There," she says, moving to the couch and sitting down.

Alex reaches over and barely touches the tip of one ear and the necklace. "They're beautiful," he says.

Christine touches the necklace herself, dipping her face shyly. "They belonged to my mother."

Alex nods. "She would have loved to see you like this. You look gorgeous." Alex sits still, staring at Christine, until she nods toward the ice bucket. "Time for a toast."

"Oh, yes, of course." He reaches for the champagne and pours two tall glasses. "To us!" he says.

"No, not tonight. This is your night," and she raises her glass.

"To you. To your success. To your gift, your talent, and your courage."

He does not, cannot, take his eyes off her as he sips the champagne and says in a whisper, "Thank you."

"A little nervous?"

"Oh, no, not really, I mean, I've done everything I can, you know. I mean there's nothing else I can do but show up. I mean there's nothing to be nervous about except to show up, right? Well, maybe a little."

She laughs lightly and reaches over to just touch his cheek with her fingertips. "Were you at the gallery all day?"

"No . . . well, all morning. I had to get out of there, though. I was getting edgy. I just went home and worked most of the afternoon to kinda calm down. I think everything's okay. I like the way Nicky set up the room. I mean he's arranged it so that each piece really has its own space. And that's not easy in a small gallery like that. I'm just a little worried about so many people being in there at once. I mean how that many people are gonna be able to fit into that room and still see anything, I don't know. He says he's expecting up to a hundred, hundred fifty people. Of course most of them are gonna be there to see Parker Randolph. I mean he's the draw. But I keep thinking—"

Christine reaches over and touches her fingers to his lips. "Sweetheart, they're coming to see you. Sure, Randolph's got the name and he's established. But he's also old news. You see his stuff on postcards in every tourist shop in town. What's exciting about that? You're new, the one everyone's going to want to talk about at their next cocktail party. 'I've just discovered the most *maaarvelous* new sculptor' and all that. And Nicholas Kane would not have gone to as much trouble as he has, including engraved invitations and personally calling all those critics he was talking about, if he didn't believe in you. Was he there today?"

"Nicky?"

"No, Randolph."

"For about ten minutes."

"And?"

"He's all right. He's got a touch of that overly polite arrogance about him, but I suppose he's entitled."

"I'll bet he's a lot more nervous than you are right now."

Alex frowns his skepticism.

"Think about it. The mighty Parker Randolph deigns to allow his new paintings to be shown along with the works of this newly discovered sculptor from the docks. What if everyone likes your work and ignores his? Imagine it."

Alex smiles a moment, then dismisses the thought. "What do you think?" he asks, sitting back and drawing attention to his tuxedo. "You think this is too much? I mean I asked Nicky and he just said, 'A loincloth, if you please, Alex.' You know Nicky. But the invitation did say 'black tie optional,' right? And I . . . Hell, I don't know what I'm talking about." He shakes his head and takes another long sip of champagne. He looks nervously at his watch.

"Sweetheart, it's your show, and you look wonderful, but that's all wrong."

"What? What's wrong?"

"The watch."

"The watch? You think I should take it off? Yeah, I guess it's a little rough. You think I should take it off? I just feel naked without a watch. I don't know why."

She nods. "Take it off."

"Really?"

"Take it off."

Alex fumbles with the steel clasp that months ago he bent with a small hammer to ensure that it would hold, and Christine leans back to open the drawer of one end table. As he lays his watch on the butler's table, Christine hands him a small box wrapped in shiny black paper and a blue felt ribbon.

"What's this?"

"It's a box wrapped in a ribbon."

"I know, but—"

"Just open it."

He does so, slowly, his eyes constantly moving from the box to Christine. Inside the box is a round gold watch with a single diamond set at twelve o'clock and a black alligator wristband. Alex holds it in the palm of one hand while his fingers trace the gold case. He turns it over and reads the engraved inscription. "To Alex, with love on opening night."

He is stunned, and he holds the watch out to Christine as if there's been some mistake. Only his eyes speak as he leans toward her.

"Careful of the lipstick," she whispers.

■■■■

Nicholas Kane insinuates his thin angular body between Alex and Christine and takes her by the arm. "Please, my dear, you must come talk with me alone. Alex, you entertain all your admirers while I steal this woman for a little chat."

The room is crowded with people in formal dress drinking white wine and champagne. As he moves Christine toward a far corner, Nicky presses close to her and speaks softly in her ear. "Isn't it wonderful, nobody's even bothering to look at Alex's work. They're simply buying. He's a hit and they don't even know why."

"Really, you've sold something?"

"Something? My dear, we've sold four pieces already. Parker Randolph's beside himself."

"Did you expect such a reaction?"

"Well, of course I did. I'm a genius."

Christine leans back with a broad smile.

"Well, maybe not four pieces, at least not so quickly. But I did manage to stack the deck a bit. Mrs. Carstairs? You know, the woman who commissioned that silly little piece for her garden? Well, I simply told her that she could not have it until I had a chance to show it here. She loved the idea. Anyway, she brought several of her friends and, you know, the competition started and by the time you and Alex arrived—and you both were very naughty to be so late—anyway, by the time you got here the whispering was rampant, and before you know it, a feeding frenzy. Genius, I say!"

"Nicky, I agree, you are a genius. Thank you for all this." Christine gives him a hug and a light kiss on the cheek.

"My dear, I owe you my life."

Sixteen months before, Christine forgave Nicky Kane his possession of several grams of cocaine and turned him into a snitch informing on his and his associates' suppliers. Several warrants and arrests later, she turned him loose. Nicky never had to testify, and his activities never came to light. His only obligation was to look at Alex's work without ever divulging his and Christine's relationship.

"Yes," he says, "for all that nasty business last year, but for Alex too. He is only beginning to use his talent and look how they love him. The poor man just doesn't know it yet." He shakes his head at Alex and then turns to her accusingly. "And what, may I ask, have you got planned for him?"

"What do you mean?"

"He keeps looking at his watch. Every five minutes he's looking at his silly watch. Do you two have to catch a bus or something? I mean these people are all here to see him and they are *buying!* And he acts like he can't wait to escape."

She laughs. "No, he's just a little nervous. We do have dinner reservations later. A little celebration."

"Oh no, no, no, no."

"No?"

"No. Absolutely not. We are all going out together. We have an entire corner at Danielle's reserved. Absolutely. Ralph will be very angry if you disturb his plans."

"Ralph?"

"Yes, it does seem a silly name for a lover, doesn't it? It sounds more like something you'd name your golden retriever. Maybe if he would spell it with a W. Wralph. What do you think? Well, never mind. He's arranged everything, ordered the entire meal. You and Alex. Everyone fun. And Parker Randolph. I must say I've never understood his popularity. But he always draws. I rather think of him like bait in a trap. But, anyway, we are going to party. Didn't Alex tell you?"

"No. Like I said, he's been a little preoccupied."

"It'll be grand. We can only hope Parker decides to bow out. He usually does. That's why I made such a point of inviting him." Nicky turns quickly toward a woman who has stepped up to his side and lightly touches his elbow. "Yes? Oh, Mrs. Haley, how nice of you to come. Isn't this exciting?"

The woman is short, and her weight is accentuated by a cocktail dress that hangs loosely about the bodice but smooths out like a stretched balloon over her belly and hips. Her light brown hair is permed and sprayed and moves in precise increments with each tic of her head.

"I'm sorry to interrupt," she says. "I just had to say hello. We have to be going soon. A dinner party. But I did want to stop and say thank you for inviting us. It's been wonderful."

Nicky looks seriously at her. "You cannot leave without buying at least one of these sculptures. You'll never forgive yourself if you don't."

Mrs. Haley laughs. "Yes, they are interesting. Is it true that this Alex Trigorin works on the docks?"

"I'm sorry," Nicky says, ignoring her question, "I've completely forgotten my manners. Mrs. Charles Haley, this is Christine Boland."

"Ah, yes." Mrs. Haley nods with a smile, both hands cupped around her champagne glass, offering neither to Christine. "You're the young lady with the sculptor. This must be very exciting for you."

Christine's smile hardens a bit, but she nods agreeably and says, "Yes, we're all very proud of Alex's work."

A white-jacketed waiter moves up to Nicky and whispers in his ear. Nicky turns back to the two women and says, "I'm sorry, ladies, apparently someone wants to make a purchase. Will you excuse me?" As he starts to turn away, he winks at Mrs. Haley. "I told you, Ellen, these sculptures will all disappear on you." He nods toward a spotlighted figure in the corner. "Just imagine that young girl with her flowers in the corner of your sunroom. Hmmm?"

"That's a little girl?"

Nicky smiles. "True art is never literal."

"Yes, well, thank you, Nicky. I'll consider it." She turns back to Christine as Nicky moves away, her expression becoming mildly inquisitive. "I'm sorry. I confess I'm often terrible with names, but haven't we met?"

"Yes, but only briefly. I was one of the detectives on the scene of Mrs. Avery's murder."

Ellen Haley tenses visibly, and her voice turns quiet and pained. "Oh, God, yes. I'm sorry. I wasn't . . . What an awful, awful thing. I still can't sleep. The nightmares. I'm sorry. I guess this is not something we should be talking about."

"No, that's all right. I understand. These matters are traumatic for everyone."

"I can't imagine what it must be like to do your kind of work. It must be, I don't know, draining. And for a woman."

Christine looks away. She sees Alex again looking at his watch, and she smiles. Mrs. Haley follows Christine's gaze and hesitates before saying, "Forgive me if this is the wrong time to be asking you something. Obviously it is, but there has been something bothering me for weeks and I just don't know what to do. Do you mind?"

Christine pauses before shaking her head. "No, go ahead."

"Well, I know it's just a little thing, and it doesn't seem to be important at all, but the detectives who came to speak to me, I don't know, a week or maybe two or so after—you know, after . . ."

Christine nods.

"They kept asking me about whether Cooper had called our house on that morning. And several neighbors said they had asked them the same question. I know at the time I was so upset that I didn't really answer their questions. I don't know whether I was really focusing or not. It was such a horrible experience. Everything." She stopped and took a deep breath. "Anyway, since then, I've been thinking about that. You know, it didn't seem all that important at the time, but the detectives seemed so insistent on that point that I began to think back as best I could. And well, I talked to my husband, and he said he was certain Cooper hadn't called. But he left the house very early. My husband, that is. He always does on his reserve weekends. Before six. And I would have still been asleep. And I've begun to think that Cooper must have called me, because why else would I have been so worried to start calling over there in the morning? I mean Marian and I often baby-sat each other's children just to let each other sleep late, you know? And now I think Cooper must have called me that morning. I'm just not sure what to do. Is that something the other detectives should know? I mean, if it would help, shouldn't I tell them?"

"Do you remember which detectives questioned you about that?"

"Again, I'm terrible with names but I remember one gentleman was tall and quite good-looking. I think he had a Polish name or something."

"Wyzanski? Detective Wyzanski?"

"Yes, I believe that's right. Do you think I should call him?"

"Are you really certain that Mr. Avery called you?"

"Well, I think I am, yes. I mean, the detectives were so insistent that I try to remember that one small thing, and so I've really given it quite a bit of thought. I am pretty certain that Cooper would have called. He was like that. Very concerned about his family. Very devoted. If he had called Marian in the morning and no one answered the phone, I know he would have called us. Our families have been very close for years. Do you think I should call this Detective Walinsky?"

"Well, Mrs. Haley, I am working with Detective Wyzanski—"

"Yes, I'm sorry, Wyzanski."

"Anyway, why don't I save you the trouble and report what you've said to Detective Wyzanski, and if he feels it is still important, he will call you."

"Thank you. That's very kind of you. That takes a real burden off my mind. I'm sorry to have brought this up now. It's just that I've been so concerned."

"I understand."

"Thank you. Now, if you'll excuse me, I'll go rescue my husband. And by the way, I, ah, do want to tell you that as upset as my husband was at the time about—well, you know, that little incident with Ned, we really do understand that you were just doing your job."

"Thank you. It isn't always easy."

"Yes, I'm sure. And won't he be surprised to know that you're the same woman. I shouldn't tell you this but he and several of the other men have been remarking all evening about how lovely you are. Won't he be surprised?"

Christine smiles evenly. "Enjoy your dinner party."

■

The party of eight is pleasant but subdued until Parker Randolph, midway through his second drink, grows tired of listening to the repeated tales of Alex's success, the response to Alex's work having been unexpectedly exuberant. Parker thanks Nicky, explains that he has an early plane to catch in the morning, and leaves.

"Probably has an important meeting with Hallmark Cards," Nicky jokes, and the mood lightens considerably, allowing Christine to keep her distracted mood in check.

By eleven o'clock, filled with a four-course dinner, two desserts, too many drinks and the relief that his first show has not been a disaster, Alex nods off at the table. Halfway home, in the back of the cab, he comes alive and turns to Christine, who is staring absently at the harbor they are passing.

"God," he sighs, "everyone should have just one night like this."

She turns toward him with a smile and slides closer, leaning against his shoulder.

"Just one thing."

"What's that?" she asks.

"The watch."

She sits up. "You don't like it?"

"Christine, no one's ever done anything like this for me. Not ever. I love you for it. For everything." He pauses. "I know it was you who somehow conned Nicky into giving me the show."

"What makes you—?"

"Sweetheart, I know. Let's just leave it at that. The point is, I love you for what you've done. I love you—and I love this watch. But why didn't you put your name in the engraving?"

"It's for you, not me. Besides, you don't want your next girlfriend asking you a lot of stupid questions about who I was. This way you can always say it was from your aunt or someone."

"Would you mind if I had your name put on it?"

She looks away and says, "Let's not talk about it now."

A few moments pass, and Alex asks, "Did something happen to upset you tonight?"

"Why, did I seem upset? I'm sorry."

"No, no, it's just that at the dinner, you seemed a little distracted. Are you okay?"

She looks at him and shakes her head. "You know I get nervous when you start reading my moods."

"What happened?"

"Nothing really. It's just that I ran into one of the witnesses in that Avery murder. It's got me a little worried, that's all."

"Worried? Why?"

Christine repeats most of her conversation with Ellen Haley and Alex says, "I'm not sure I understand what has you worried. You report what she said and let Wyzanski deal with it."

"But don't you see? I don't believe for a minute that Cooper Avery really called that woman. It's just that Paul and Charlie Abbot got so intent on their theory that they ended up putting ideas in the woman's head. She thinks she's trying to help. She thinks that somehow it must be really important that Cooper Avery called and so now she thinks that he did."

"And?"

"And, if I tell Paul and Charlie about this, it'll only confirm what they think. They'll push her some more and all of a sudden everyone'll be convinced beyond all doubt that Cooper Avery called, and that'll stick another nail in his coffin."

"You're not thinking of keeping this to yourself, are you?"

"I don't know. I suppose not. I'm just worried that everyone's just looking for what they want to see."

"What do you mean? I'm not sure I understand why this phone call is so important, why it puts the final nail in this guy's coffin."

"Not the final nail. Just another one. You see, the theory is that if Cooper Avery killed his wife or had her killed believing that his children were over at the Haleys' house, he would have done something to make sure the children didn't find the body. Like call the Haleys to say that he was worried about his wife. You know, he called home but no one answered. Then he calls the Haleys or someone to have them check the house first to make sure that Mrs. Haley wouldn't just send the kids home and they'd walk in and find their mother's body. It's just a theory but like everything else that seems to be going on here, they start bending over backwards to prove that theory instead of just looking at the facts that are there."

"You don't think he did it, do you?"

"Not on what we've got. It doesn't make sense. I think it's more likely that Avery himself was the target and maybe something went wrong. He wasn't there or whatever. I don't know. But that's not what I'm worried about. I mean, sure, I don't want to see us end up with the wrong man for the wrong reason. But the real question here is why. Why this happened. And no one seems to give a damn about that."

"You think why's more important than who?"

"Right now, yes, I do. I think the why is everything. It's the only thing that will lead us to who really did it. But everyone seems to have closed his mind to everything but the obvious and easiest target. They're not really looking. They're just trying to squeeze what few facts they have into a theory they've already settled on. And this thing with Ellen Haley is just going to fuel the fire."

"Do you think you know where to look?"

"I don't know. Maybe. I just don't know."

Alex softly strokes Christine's hair with the back of his fingers. Not knowing quite what to say, he says nothing. They ride on in silence for a minute or two until Christine again nestles against him. "Tomorrow," she says. "I'll worry about this tomorrow."

10

*C*harles "Don't call me Chuck" Waddells, like most of his neighbors, has lived in the county all his life, as did his parents, and his parents' parents, and generations of parents long forgotten. Time and the elements have hardened him. His hands are thick and callused, and his face is weathered and worn like an old boot from too many winters working the oyster dredge on his uncle's skipjack, the *Anne B.* Hunched over the bar of the Blue Point Tavern, a half-dozen beers into this Sunday afternoon, he wears the expression of a man who knows where he stands in life and is not altogether happy about it. They call him "Doan," short for "Doancawmechuk," the sobriquet with which he has been forever tagged by the locals, who find his peckish insistence on being called Charles reason enough not to.

The owner of the local hardware, Enoch Beall, looks to him with a sour frown. "Doan, that's an awful hard thing to say."

"Look, I ain't said nothin' 'bout the lady deserving to get killed. All I'm sayin' is whatever happened up there got nothin' to do with us."

"Hell it don't," Enoch Beall argues. "You got some crazy man out there'll walk into another man's home and shoot a lady in the back of the head, and you don't think it could happen to one of us?"

"What I'm sayin' is that weren't no one local doin' a thing like that. What it is, is that whatever trouble those people got, they brought with them. Ain't been a murder around here since I can remember, 'cept a knife fight or two around Muddy Bottom, but you can't really call them murders. Y'know? Idn't that right, Ollie?"

Oliver Johns, who spent thirty years and three marriages squandering his inheritance until forced to sell his land and home to Cooper Avery and the developers of Fishing Creek Estates, nods from the corner table where he sits alone. "Doan's right," he says in a low growl that speaks of the warm whiskey he nurses from a glass with no ice. "Avery and all his lawyers . . ." He stops himself, and the room falls quiet. The Blue Point Tavern has played host to Oliver Johns's speeches before. But no one wants to listen anymore. Once the closest thing the county had to landed gentry, Ollie Johns now lives alone in a sparsely remodeled tenant house on a spit of land unmarked on the maps and maritime charts, but which the local watermen call Point No Point. No more than they would begrudge a rich man his wealth will they waste their sympathy on a man who throws his away. "Doesn't matter," Johns says, shrugging, and periods his thought with a small, slow sip of his whiskey.

Doan looks down the bar, hinting his apology for almost drawing Oliver Johns into their conversation. Enoch Beall tosses a quarter on the bar and reaches for the bowl of hard-boiled eggs. He takes one and begins to peel away the shell. "All I know," he says, "is that it just gives me the creeps thinkin' about someone who could do a thing like that still walkin' around among us." He heavily salts and peppers the shelled egg, bites off a third and washes it down with his beer. "And as far as I hear, the police ain't got pea turkey jackass. Not a clue." He turns to a young man standing at the bar a few feet away. " 'S'that right, Simon? You were up to the house that day."

Deputy Sheriff Simon Neavitt could easily pass for several years younger than his twenty-three years. It isn't his close-cropped blond hair or the lack of any noticeable beard so much as a certain diffidence that is his way. He shrugs. "I dunno. I suspect there's more known than you might think," he says without looking up.

"Like what?"

"We're not s'posed to talk about it, y'know?"

The bar erupts in a chiding groan. "That's police talk for 'we don't know dick,' " Doan laughs.

Enoch Beall shakes his head. "Shit, Simon, like we're only the people sittin' around wonderin' if some crazy man's gonna be comin' through our back door tonight."

"Hey, Simon," Doan calls out. "Idn't it true that nobody owns the water?"

"Doan, what the hell's that got to do with anything?" Enoch Beall complains.

"Nothin'. I'm just asking. Idn't that right, though? Nobody owns the water?"

Simon Neavitt looks over with an impatient shake of his head. "Whaddaya talkin' about?"

"Like the river. Or out on the bay. Nobody owns that, right?"

"The state does, I guess."

"Yeah, but like the water. Nobody can own that. Right?"

"Yeah, right, so?"

"So, like nobody can just sorta stake a claim on some place out on the water and it's his."

From the far corner, a large bearded man rears back and says, "What's that, Doan? You workin' up a defense for all them crab pots yer allus raidin'?"

The room erupts with laughter, and Doan spins on his stool. "Goddamnit, Earl, don't say that shit. I ain't never touched another man's lines. I run more lines and get more crabs than any man in this county."

"Man, the only crabs you get on yer own is from your ol' lady."

Doan tries to leap off his stool but is caught by the bartender, Harley Winn, who grabs the shoulder of Doan's shirt and pulls him back. "Back off that shit, Earl," Harley calls across the room. "I told you any more fights in here and I'd throw you out for good."

Earl Barkin shrugs and throws a piece of crab cake to the husky red retriever lying at his feet, and Harley says to Doan, "Whaddaya gettin' all worked up? Earl's just runnin' his mouth. Have a beer fer Chrissakes."

The chorus then goes up, a half-dozen or more men calling out to Earl and asking him to insult them so they too can get a free beer.

Enoch Beall calls down the bar. "So, Doan, whaddaya worryin' 'bout who owns the water?"

"I dunno, just thinkin' 'bout that blind sittin' there in the marsh off Fishing Creek. Nobody's usin' it. Not even brushed out. Seems this year there's been awful lotta geese 'round there. Me 'n' my brothers thought maybe if that Avery fella weren't gonna be usin' it, we'd might brush it out and use it ourselves. That ain't illegal, is it? I mean if the man's moved away and ain't gonna use it? It's not like the marsh is his property, y'know?"

Earl Barkin shows an immediate interest and steps over his dog to move quickly to the bar. "Is that right, Simon? That blind don't belong to no one if the man moved away?"

"You boys better not get all fired up about that blind," Enoch Beall cuts in. "Mr. Avery was in this week and bought three boxes of shells and some new camouflage."

Earl turns to Doan. "I thought you was sayin' the man moved away."

"That's what I heard, and when we came upriver yesterday that blind still wasn't brushed out."

"Look, I don't know whether the man's moved or not," Enoch Beall says, "but I'm tellin' ya he came in this week and bought the shells and huntin' clothes. Now what does that tell ya?"

Doan leans around Earl. "Hey Simon, what's the story? Did the man move out or what?"

Simon Neavitt looks up from his beer. "I don't know. The place is up for sale, but whether he's livin' there right now, I don't know. But that blind's still his as far as I can see."

"Hey, Ollie," Doan calls over his shoulder, "wudn't that blind yours at one time?" But Oliver Johns does not answer, may not even have heard the question. He is sitting with both hands cupped around his glass, his eyelids heavy, his head drooped and nodding.

Harley Winn leans over the bar and speaks quietly to Doan. "What's the matter with you, Doan? Why don't you leave the man alone?"

Doan lifts his hands in innocence. "Shit, I'se just askin' the man a question."

"Gimme 'nother beer," Earl Barkin says and turns to Doan. "Man, when was the last time you got through a day without doin' somethin' stupid?"

"Yeah, well . . ."

Harley Winn interrupts them. "Shit, why don't you guys take it outside? You're giving me a headache."

Earl moves back to his table, Doan sulks over his beer, and the bar falls quiet but for the jukebox playing in the background. Simon Neavitt steps off his bar stool and moves next to Enoch Beall, where he leans in with a quiet question. "You say Mr. Avery was in this week?"

"Yeah, why?"

"Just wondering. What were the clothes like? The stuff he bought."

"Huntin' clothes. You know, the camouflage, jacket, pants and hat. Why?"

"He ever buy stuff from you before?"

"Yeah, sure, he used to come in and browse around almost every Saturday. And sometimes he'd come in for shells or fishin' gear or whatever. Tools and such once in a while."

"No, I mean did he ever buy a huntin' suit from you before?"

Enoch pauses in thought, staring at Simon curiously. "Yeah, well, seems like he did a year or two ago."

"You know many people wear that kinda stuff out in a year or two?"

Enoch frowns and shakes his head slowly. "You mind telling me why you're askin'?"

"I don't know, Enoch. I just had a funny thought. Prob'ly don't mean a thing."

Enoch glances over his shoulder as if he has just been made privy to something important. "Whaddaya thinkin'?"

"I got no idea. Really. It's just somethin' that made me think, that's all. Ain't nothin', okay?"

Enoch nods. "Yeah, sure. But you thinkin' that's got something to do with what happened up there?"

Simon Neavitt looks away. "Nah, just thinkin' was all."

■■■

Christine pours herself a cup of coffee and then turns to Captain Hardiman, who is half-seated on the edge of his desk. This casual pose does not fit him, and the silence makes her uncomfortable. "Can I pour you one?" she asks.

Hardiman shakes his head.

She takes her time measuring out a half-spoon of sugar and

stirring it into the coffee before moving to the corner chair and sitting down. "What can I do for you, Captain?"

"Something's just come up on this Avery matter, and I wanted to talk to you about it."

"You want to wait for Paul and Charlie?"

"No, I asked them to go back down and talk to that neighbor —what's her name? The woman who spoke to you at the gallery?"

"Mrs. Haley?"

"Yeah, Haley. Odd, isn't it, where you'll pick up bits and pieces of information?"

Christine cocks her head and averts her eyes with obvious skepticism. "I'm not so sure that information isn't something we planted in her mind. I don't mean on purpose, it's just—you know."

"I understand what you're saying. Paul told me about the little speech you gave him."

"It wasn't a speech, Captain."

"Sorry, poor choice of words."

"Why, was Paul upset?"

"No, not at all. He was just telling me about your skepticism. And I don't necessarily disagree with you. I just think we've got to cover the field."

"And Charlie?"

"Well, you know Charlie. He's great at digging up the information, but analysis isn't exactly his long suit."

"Well, all I was saying is that we've got to be careful that we're actually digging it up, not planting the seed."

"I know. But that's not what I wanted to talk to you about. About an hour ago I got a call from one of the deputies that was on the Avery scene. Remember, I was telling you about the guy who chalked the footprints right away so they wouldn't be walked over?"

Christine smiles. "Yeah. I thought you'd have him in the academy by now."

"Yeah, well, maybe. But listen to this. Yesterday, he was sitting around one of the local joints down in Maryville, and there's some talk about the Avery killing and whether or not Avery's moved or whatever. Apparently the local hunters want to use Avery's hunting blind. Anyway, this kid overhears the owner of the local hardware say that Avery had been in sometime in the last week or so and bought some new hunting gear. And part of what he bought was a new suit of camouflage. You know, the kind of clothes that look like the military stuff?"

Christine sits up with sudden curiosity.

"And so he asked the man a few questions and it turns out that he sold Avery the same kind of hunting clothes before, maybe within the last two years. And the kid thinks that's a little strange. You know, since like he said, most hunters'll keep their gear longer than they will their wives." Christine offers a slight smile as Captain Hardiman walks around his desk and sits down. "And then he says that he remembered the boy's reaction when that major first showed up in his fatigues and he wondered if there might've been some connection there."

Christine leans forward. "And you think it was the camouflage Ned was reacting to and not the major?"

"That's what I wanted to talk to you about. You think that's possible? And if so, what does it mean?" Captain Hardiman smiles broadly and with a shake of his head says, "You know, the deputy got all nervous and embarrassed like it was a stupid idea, and he was sorry to be bothering me and all. But I think he may be on to something. I think there may be a connection here. What do you think?"

Christine stands up and starts to pace the office, holding her coffee cup just below her lips as if it is part of her thought process. "Somehow I think I'm going to regret saying this, but I suppose it could explain some things." She runs through her thoughts, debating the point with herself. "The boy has the same reaction to the major and Avery. The major is wearing camouflage but Avery isn't. But Avery's a hunter, and Ned might easily associate him with wearing the same kind of clothes, particularly when he would be carrying a gun, a shotgun or whatever for hunting. He associates the clothes with shooting . . . with *the* shooting maybe. He sees his mother being shot, or maybe just heard the shot and came down to find his mother. If . . . I don't know, maybe if it's true that Avery was having this affair with the woman in New York, maybe there had been some fights or arguments between Avery and his wife. The boy's super-sensitive to all that, and maybe just a little frightened of his father. I mean there's plenty of indications that the relationship there was at least strained. Maybe whatever the boy saw, he thought for whatever reason that his father had done it, and he associates the camouflage with Avery and guns."

"Maybe it's a whole lot simpler than that," Captain Hardiman says. "Maybe Avery *did* do it. And he was wearing his hunting camouflage at the time. He gets some blood on the clothes and has to get rid of them. Burn them, toss them in a Dumpster somewhere. Whatever."

"I've got two problems with that," Christine says. "First, I still can't buy that he'd kill his wife with his son in the house. Second, why would he bother dressing up in hunting gear?"

"The answer to the first thing is this Mrs. Haley. Avery thinks his kids are over at the Haleys' house. That's why he calls in the morning. Just like you said a long time ago. He'd want someone like Mrs. Haley to check the house first so the kids wouldn't walk in and find their mother. Second, he's supposed to be out of town. Everyone in the neighborhood knows him. So he wants to sneak up on the house just like any burglar. And he wears the camouflage and maybe a ski mask so that if anyone does see him going in or out, they won't recognize him." He pauses a moment, tapping the end of his pen to his temple. "Let me ask you something. When you and Paul went back through the house with Avery, did you see any hunting clothes?"

She thinks for a moment. "No, I don't think so. But I wasn't looking for anything like that at the time. I could have seen it, and it just didn't register."

"I doubt it. But Paul said the same thing. I raised him on the radio. He doesn't remember seeing any hunting clothes either."

"What does he think of your theory? I know Charlie'd love it."

"I didn't lay it out for him. I just asked the question. Told him we'd talk after he and Charlie got back."

"Maybe while they're down there they ought to check with this deputy and the hardware store owner. See if the man has copies of the sales slips. You know, both for the stuff Avery just bought and maybe slips from when he bought the hunting outfit before."

Captain Hardiman snaps his fingers and says, "You're right!"

It takes some time for Captain Hardiman to again raise Paul Wyzanski on the police radio and give him the instructions while trying to ward off the long explanation Wyzanski is obviously pushing for. For a moment or two, Christine continues to pace restlessly in front of Hardiman's desk, until she plops down in her chair and stares at the tip of a large icicle rhythmically dropping beads of water released by the bright morning sun. "Paul, I just don't have the time to go over everything now," Hardiman says. "Just contact this Deputy Neavitt and tell him to take you to the hardware store. We're looking for any copies of any receipts for hunting clothes Avery might have bought over say the last three or four years. And let me know what you find. . . . No, just come on back to the office. We'll talk then." He turns to Christine. "Where were we?"

"You're ready to indict Avery."

"Not yet, but I got a feeling that's where we may be headed."

Christine's gaze moves back to the icicle, and for a moment or two she says nothing. Then, turning only her eyes toward Captain Hardiman, she says, "This clothes thing makes a nice theory. But that's all it is. Theory. How are you going to prove it?"

Hardiman stands up and again moves to the front of his desk. "That's what I want you to do. Prove it or disprove it. One way or the other. I want you to contact the boy's doctors and see if we can't run some kind of controlled experiment. See if we're right or wrong."

"I don't imagine they'll be all that anxious to run experiments on that child."

"Well, not an experiment. You know what I mean. You said yourself that it'd help the boy if the doctors could unlock whatever it was that caused the reaction."

"What if the doctors want Avery's permission?"

"That's covered. I talked to the D.A. He says he'll get a court order if necessary."

"You've already presented this case to the D.A.?"

"No, I just called to ask whether there were any legal problems. But I can tell you he's damn anxious to get his hands on this."

Christine shakes her head slowly, and Hardiman frowns.

"Chris, you want to tell me why you're so hung up on this?"

"I don't know, Captain, I just keep coming back to the same question. What's the man's motive? A hit like this takes a damn strong motive and I can't see one here. It just doesn't compute. Avery's affair? No, no way. First, according to Paul and Charlie, the woman in New York had already broken things off. Plus, Avery can have all the women he wants, and nobody'd be the wiser. The way he travels and with his money he could have women stashed in half the states across the country. He doesn't need to kill his wife for another woman. Second, the way this woman was killed. This was planned. This was a hit. And if Avery planned it, he was damn sloppy about it. It's almost as if someone was trying to make a point here. Almost setting it up to make it look like Avery did it. It just seems to me we keep jumping on a lot of coincidences because they make an easy fit."

"Well, at some point all these things that fit stop being coincidences. I mean why'd the man check into a hotel in New York, pay in advance, and leave without a word a half hour later? Setting up an alibi, maybe? And now the hunting clothes and the ballistics?"

"See?" Christine says. "That's what I mean. You're stretching the ballistics to fit a preordained conclusion."

"What do you mean by that?"

"Look, Avery reports his Smith and Wesson .38 stolen a year ago. And Charlie does a bang-up job of tracking down ATF records of the purchase to find the serial number. So we know when the gun was manufactured and we run ballistics and find what? That the bullet that killed Marian Avery has rifling marks that're consistent with .38s manufactured in the same job lot as Avery's missing gun. Captain, I understand that'll sound good to a jury, but hell, you could run the same tests on my gun or yours or any one of a thousand Smith and Wesson .38s and probably come up with the same conclusion. And that brings me back to my original point. Can you really imagine Avery planning to kill his wife with his own gun and reporting it stolen and then hiding it away for a whole year just waiting for the right opportunity? And then picking as his perfect opportunity a time when his kids were going to be around? No, I don't buy it. I don't buy it at all."

"And what's your theory?"

"What I've been saying almost from the beginning. Everything about that scene reeks with motive. A very specific motive. There was a point being made here. We just don't know what it is and we're not really looking for it. Sure, it's easy to come up with the obvious. Maybe Marian Avery found out about his affair. Maybe since her father holds the purse strings on Avery's company she uses that to threaten him. So he kills her. But with his own gun that he reported stolen a year ago? And with his son around? Not a chance."

"Isn't that the whole point of what this Mrs. Haley is saying? That Avery called her to make sure the kids wouldn't find the body?"

"No, Captain, that's not the point!" Christine's voice has turned almost angry. "I keep telling you that Mrs. Haley doesn't know whether Avery called or not. She just thinks he did because Paul and Charlie kept pushing the point and now she thinks she remembers it because that'll help. She doesn't know who it'll help, she just thinks it will. Besides, that doesn't make any sense either. Look at all the telephone charges on Avery's credit card. It shows him calling home every other day. Why wouldn't he have used his card to make that call? If he was looking for an alibi, wouldn't he have wanted to show that he called from New York or wherever? But there was no call. No charges. Nothing."

"But there was the call the night before. Around five o'clock, before Marian Avery called Mrs. Haley to tell her that she had decided to keep the boy home because he had a cold or whatever. She probably told Avery at that time that the kids were going to be staying over at the Haleys'. There's your opportunity."

"Opportunity for what? On the sudden spur of the moment to sneak down from New York, get out the gun he had hidden away a year before, jump into his hunting clothes and blow his wife's brains out? Then sneak back to New York?"

"Yeah, maybe that's exactly what he did."

Christine shakes her head slowly and says nothing while the captain studies her hardened expression. "I understand your point," he says, finally. "And understand that I'm not suggesting that we're about to go out and arrest the man. All I'm asking you to do is to try and set up something with the boy's doctors to see if these hunting clothes mean what we think they might. Okay?"

Christine rises slowly from her chair. "I'll take care of it," she says coolly. "Anything else?"

He makes no gesture and keeps his eyes fixed on hers. "No, that's it."

Without another word, Christine leaves the room.

■■■

The William T. Packard Clinic sits on fifty-one acres of rolling Pennsylvania countryside overlooking the Susquehanna River nine miles south of Lancaster. The entrance road winds through a thick stand of trees until it reaches the crest of a hill and a wide, open pasture from which they can see the river and four gray stone buildings which nest on a bluff near the river's edge. A tall spired cupola sits atop the four-story main administration building and lends to the complex an aesthetic air reminiscent of a small New England prep school. It is only when they come close enough to notice the webs of rubber-coated steel wire that guard the windows of the top two floors that the scene appears suddenly Dickensian.

The drive from state police headquarters has taken an hour and a half, and in that time Christine has barely spoken, fending off Paul Wyzanski's attempts at casual conversation with an occasional nod or a shrug or a short answer if a question is pushed. There is no hint of anger, only the message that she has been captured by her own thoughts and has little interest in being rescued. To Paul it has the familiar sound and feel of the day she ended their affair. It came without buildup or warning, without argument or tears. She simply ended it, quietly, quickly, as one might put to sleep a sick dog. It rained that day as well.

Paul slows the car to a crawl as it reaches the circular drive in front of the administration building. Christine points her finger to the right, and her words follow. "The visitors' lot is over there, behind the main building."

"You've been here before?"

"Once."

Paul wants to ask whether her visit was business or personal but decides that she is in no mood for jokes. "I don't know what I was expecting," he says, "but it sure wasn't this. This looks more like an English manor house than a hospital."

Christine's nod is barely perceptible, just enough to acknowledge him. As they step out into the cold, oily drizzle and begin walking toward the main building, Paul stoops to crowd under her umbrella. The scent of her perfume mixed with her closeness feels warm against the chilled damp, and the sound of her body moving within her coat and dress reminds him of all that he has tried to put aside. It is the first time that he has felt alone and truly uncomfortable in her presence.

The receptionist is expecting them, and after offering to bring them coffee and a pastry, she ushers them down a hall whose floor is a highly polished wood accented by long Oriental runners. At the end of the hall they enter a large wood-paneled office where two men and a woman are waiting. The introductions are handled by the man who steps immediately from behind his desk with an open, enthusiastic smile. He is short and thin; his hair is snow-white and his complexion a winter pallor edged with redness, as if he had just faced a raw wind. He has all the appearance of an aging leprechaun. "How do you do, Detectives, I'm Dr. Eckert, the medical director here at the clinic." He reaches first for Christine's hand, which she offers.

"Good morning. Christine Boland," she says. "And this is Detective Wyzanski."

"Yes, yes, it's good to meet you both. And this is Dr. Storrs, who is in charge of the Avery boy's treatment. June Storrs."

"Yes, nice to see you again," Dr. Storrs says to Christine.

Paul looks curiously at Christine as Dr. Eckert continues the introductions.

"Curtis Graham, the attorney for the clinic."

Dr. Eckert motions for everyone to be seated as he returns to his desk. The receptionist returns to the room with a silver tray holding the coffee Christine and Paul asked for and the pastries they did not. "Dr. Eckert? Anyone else need some fresh coffee?" she asks brightly.

Dr. Eckert waits for his companions to shake their heads and then announces, "No, I guess not. Thank you, Polly. That will be all." Polly retreats and Dr. Eckert begins, leaning over his hands, which are folded on his desk, "Well, Detectives, we have an interesting situation here."

Paul leans forward abruptly and tilts his head toward the lawyer, Graham. "Excuse me, Doctor, but is there some problem, legally?"

"No, Detective, there's no problem. We just need to make our position clear in this matter."

"George, perhaps I should explain," lawyer Graham interjects, and turns to Paul. "We've reviewed this matter both medically and legally, and we want you to know and clearly understand that your presence here today must be as observers only. What we're about to do here is not to assist you in your investigation, although if in fact it has that side effect, so be it. What we are doing today has been determined to be medically appropriate. That is to say that the medical staff here has reviewed the Avery boy's case in great detail and has determined independently that it is in the boy's best interest to try to unlock whatever might be causing his condition. This—well, this persistent state he is in. George? Dr. Storrs? Is that correct?"

Both nod, and Christine asks Dr. Storrs, "Do I understand that the boy's condition has not changed significantly in the past two months?"

"Well, he shows less evidence of overt distress, but frankly that concerns me." Dr. Storrs turns to the lawyer. "Is there any problem discussing the specifics here?"

"No," the lawyer says.

She turns back to Christine, who appears for a moment to be studying this woman. Dr. Storrs is within a year or two of Christine in age, attractive, with light reddish hair pulled back in a loose fall. Her eyes are a deep green and look at Christine directly, and with intent, through a large pair of glasses framed in tortoiseshell that softens the clinical stiffness of her starched lab jacket. She leans forward a bit, and addresses Christine with an almost shy, familiar smile. It is as if no one else in the room matters, and as she speaks her right thumb and middle finger absently roll the wedding and engagement rings on her left hand.

"Detective, first I wanted to thank you for your report and coming up here earlier to discuss this matter." Paul looks to Christine, his heightened curiosity showing in a quick frown. "Your observations of the boy on that first day have been very helpful."

Christine allows herself a brief smile.

"The boy's father, unfortunately, has not been able to help us a great deal. I don't mean purposefully. But he does seem to be having trouble accepting the severity of the boy's condition. He hasn't really been able to focus on aspects of Ned's past that might be pertinent."

"He hasn't spoken at all? Ned, that is?"

"No. All we know is what we have observed. At first he was very agitated. Unable to sleep and when he did sleep, we would observe what appeared to be the expected nightmares. Again, it is difficult to tell much since he has been completely nonverbal, even in sleep, and the agitation was brief and spasmodic, almost as if he were able to suppress quickly whatever dreams or nightmares he was having. Given the mutism it's hard to tell whether there's a formal thought disorder. His actions appear to indicate at least some loosening of associations. There's no true psychomotor dysfunction in the sense of say a catatonic rigidity or posturing or negativism, but he often seems unaware of his environment. He shows a marked volitional disturbance at times, and at other times not. For example, he appears to like to read, but we can't always tell, even by observing eye movements, whether he's truly focused on what he's seeing or just scanning the page over and over with no purpose. Often he'll start reading, or at least appear to be reading, and then suddenly he'll just stop for long periods with no apparent change of focus onto something else. He simply stops. And the response doesn't seem to change with the subject matter of what we give him. He shows no raised or lowered interest whether it's a children's book or a newspaper."

Christine asks, "The hand movements, the rubbing of his leg, has that stopped?"

"Yes, very early on, except when he was particularly agitated, but that seemed to fade pretty quickly and we haven't observed that or any other ritualistic behavior in weeks."

"It sounds as if you believe you're dealing with more than post-traumatic stress."

"Well, frankly, we've been treating it, or trying to treat it, as a stress disorder. But there are signs in the boy's past of at least some, if not significant, emotional problems. There's a history of withdrawal and dependence and hints at some phobic reactions. But he never was really evaluated except for intelligence, which is quite high. And the father's and grandparents' observations have been— well, shall we say more hopeful than clinical. I have no doubt we're dealing with posttraumatic syndrome, but the unusual severity of the reaction indicates other aggravating factors."

Paul Wyzanski leans forward. "Doctor, do you think he'll ever be able to testify?"

Dr. Storrs looks surprised at the question. "I seriously doubt it," she says stiffly and moves her eyes back to Christine. "I think our primary problem now is that Ned has been too successful in suppressing the stressful stimuli. He has literally gone away. I think he's either there or at the edge of total psychogenic amnesia. And every day he seems to show fewer and fewer signs of any affective response. I think his mind is strong enough to create a total barrier and I'm afraid we're going to lose him behind that wall. That, quite frankly, is why I am recommending that we go ahead and see if he has any reaction to these hunting clothes. Maybe if that was the source of the reaction you observed, it could bring him back to a point where we might begin to deal with it." She looks over to Dr. Eckert. "I don't know, but I hope."

Dr. Eckert presses forward in his chair and rests his elbows on his desk. "Obviously we considered the possible downside of further stress, but we feel that we need to find some key to opening the boy up. And his father agrees."

Christine sits forward. "Mr. Avery knows we're here?"

Curtis Graham speaks up. "Medically speaking, you aren't here."

"I'm not sure I understand what that means," Paul says.

"What it means, Detective, is that the procedure this clinic is following is dictated by medical and not legal considerations. And it is important that you understand that. We are not here to assist your investigation in any way, and whatever reports you choose to make of today's activities might well reflect that. You are here as observers only."

"Okay"—Paul nods—"I understand that, but I take it Mr. Avery knows what's happening here today. Did he have any reaction—"

Curtis Graham raises his hand to interrupt Paul. "Well, to be precise, Mr. Avery is not aware that you are here as observers. Is that true, Doctor?" he asks Dr. Storrs.

She nods. "I discussed with Mr. Avery what we intended to do this morning. I explained that we were looking for some key to bring Ned back from his, shall we say, self-imposed mental exile, and that we thought there might be some connection between Ned's association of the camouflage or hunting clothes his neighbor was wearing and Mr. Avery's being a hunter. I explained the risks and what we hoped to accomplish."

"And he had no problem with that?" Christine asks.

"No. He simply said that we should do whatever we thought might help Ned."

"He didn't voice any other reaction or hesitancy?"

"No, not at all. Except, of course, he was again anxious about his son, about whether Ned will ever regain what he considers a normal state. But that's standard. Parents in these situations always have trouble dealing with the reality of what their children might be facing."

"Has he visited Ned often?"

Dr. Storrs hesitates. "Well, after a fashion. Very early on, while Ned was still in a fairly agitated state, we wanted to see if the reaction to his father you described in your report was unique to that situation or still a problem. And so we had Mr. Avery come into the playroom with us. Ned's reaction was not so severe as it apparently had been before, but there was a noticeable fear, a physical withdrawal and curling up and a low groaning. Since then Mr. Avery has refused to let us reintroduce him, although we have suggested it several times. It's going to take some time for him, that is Mr. Avery, to get control over his own fears. Rejection, not wanting to cause the boy further trauma. But he does come here at least once every week or ten days and he'll sit for hours watching Ned in the playroom through the one-way glass. And there really isn't much to see. As I've told you, Ned's affect is for the most part almost totally flat. Even in the presence of other children who will try to stimulate him, touch him or whatever. At most you'll see Ned's eyes occasionally pick up and follow another child or one of the nurses or orderlies whom he's used to. But it'll only be for a few seconds." Dr. Storrs sits back, and her eyes pass back and forth between the detectives. "Now I'd like to ask you a question, if I may. It is very important to me in trying to help Ned to know whether there is any evidence to suggest that Mr. Avery killed his wife. If in fact that's what Ned saw, I need to know about it."

Christine looks to Paul, who stares back. Neither speaks for a moment. Finally Christine says, "Doctor, I wish we could answer that for you. I really do. And I'm not being coy here or claiming confidentiality. The truth of the matter is there's a strong difference of opinion among the investigators. There are some convinced that Avery did it. There are some, including myself, who think not, or at least think there's not enough evidence to come to that conclusion. That's about the best I can tell you. I'm sorry."

"But would you say at least that until you find proof one way or the other, that for Ned's sake I should assume there's a possibility that Mr. Avery killed his wife?"

Christine shakes her head slowly, more in hesitation than in answer. Paul shows no such reserve. "I think that would be a safe assumption."

A long silence precedes Dr. Eckert's saying, "Well, I guess we'd best get on with it."

Dr. Storrs leads the procession out of the office and down one flight of stairs to an underground tunnel, which in turn leads to Building 2, otherwise known as the Alma Packard Children's Center. On the center's second floor Ned waits in a large, brightly lit room filled with plastic furniture with rounded corners, shelves of books and soft toys, and a one-way glass that stretches along one wall from waist level to the ceiling. As Dr. Storrs opens the curtain that covers the glass in the observation room, Christine can see the green hills and blue skies and white clouds of a pastoral scene, complete with brightly colored hot-air balloons, applied to the side of the glass facing Ned with special paints that allow them to observe without being observed.

Ned is alone but for a young nurse who sits across a low table from him reading aloud from a *People* magazine. Ned seems intent on his own magazine. Which one it is Christine cannot tell, except that the pages are composed primarily of type set around a single small black-and-white photograph. Ned's eyes do not move, and his hands show no interest in turning the page. His plumpness is gone. His face is pale and drawn and expressionless, and his hands barely poke out from the long sleeves of a bright blue sweater. He is more mannequin than real.

Christine stands at the glass peering intently at Ned as Dr. Storrs explains what she is about to do. At first, she says, to minimize any possible trauma, they thought to simply show Ned a set of hunting clothes. But after some discussion, they decided that might be unwise; Ned might assume the clothes are those the police theorize may have been worn by the killer. Therefore, it has been decided that they will introduce an orderly who is known to Ned and who will be wearing his usual white uniform. As the orderly and Dr. Storrs carry on a conversation with Ned, the orderly will slip the hunting camouflage over his clothes in full view of the boy. The entire procedure will be recorded by a concealed video camera.

"Any questions?" Dr. Storrs asks.

Neither Paul nor Christine answers beyond a shake of the head.

As Dr. Storrs leaves the room, Christine backs a few steps away from the glass, into the darkness behind the three men.

It takes a minute before the door to the playroom opens, and Dr. Eckert turns up the volume of the speaker in the observation room. Dr. Storrs and the orderly, a young man with a ready smile carrying a large plastic bag, enter the room. There is an easy, almost playful exchange of words between Dr. Storrs and the orderly. How well they think Ned looks, and they wonder aloud whether Ned will allow them to join him. The young nurse, too, joins the speculation, but Ned shows no response at all to the conversation around him. Indeed, his eyes and posture show no recognition that anyone new has entered the room until Dr. Storrs sits down next to him and gently takes his hand while she invites the orderly to join them at the table. For a moment, Ned's eyes lift from the magazine to the orderly's face, but his expression does not change. He then looks at Dr. Storrs and as he does, pulls the left sleeve of his sweater down over his hand. Again, his expression does not change except that his attention slowly turns to the plastic bag the orderly has placed on the table. He does not reach for the bag or show any other reaction but to stare at it. For several minutes Dr. Storrs, the orderly and the nurse carry on a light conversation about Ned, repeatedly asking questions as if the boy has joined their talk.

"Is your hand cold? Is that why you pulled your sleeve down?"

"It is cold today."

"Yes, I guess we won't be able to go outside, what with the rain and all."

"Ned doesn't like to go outside anyway."

"Oh, sometimes he does, don't you, Ned?"

Dr. Storrs nods at the orderly. "Well, if you've got to go outside, you ought to have something warm on. Like Ned's sweater, maybe."

"Well, I got some new hunting clothes. They're pretty warm."

"Why don't you show Ned your new clothes?"

The orderly picks up his plastic bag as the conversation goes on in the same unemphasized tone. From the bag he pulls a green camouflage hunting jacket, which he lays on the table. Ned shows no reaction at all. The orderly does the same with the pair of pants, and again, there is no reaction.

Paul Wyzanski leans against the glass with a sigh and looks back at Christine, who is barely visible in the darkness. He cannot see her expression.

The chatter in the playroom goes on for several minutes until it is suggested that the orderly try on his new hunting clothes to see if they fit. The orderly stands, and as he carries on his conversation with Dr. Storrs, he begins to put on the hunting pants. Ned continues to stare without expression. The orderly puts on the hunting jacket and for a moment stands before Ned in silence. Dr. Storrs lightly puts her hand on Ned's back, and she asks if he thinks the orderly's hunting clothes fit. Ned looks first to Dr. Storrs and then back to the orderly, and it happens.

At first, there is a rapid increase in his breathing, and a low, almost weeping moan escapes. He is rocking in his chair, and his hands begin to claw at his chest, pulling at the sweater. Dr. Storrs is trying to soothe Ned and at the same time tell the orderly to quickly take off the clothes. She has leaned close to the boy and is talking quietly. But the sudden movements of the orderly taking off the jacket startle him, and Ned lets go a howl as he swings to his right and grabs Dr. Storrs by her hair. He pulls her head to him and tries to cover it with his body, clawing and reaching, howling and weeping. The orderly tries to extricate Dr. Storrs from the boy's grip, but Ned reacts even more violently. Dr. Storrs yells at the orderly to leave, while Dr. Eckert races from the observation room to help the nurse help Dr. Storrs.

"*Jesus God Almighty,*" Paul Wyzanski whispers, frozen to the scene, reluctantly obeying the doctor's instructions that under no circumstances is he or Christine to come into that room. He turns to Christine, who is now lit by the light from the hall sneaking through the open door. Her expression matches Ned's, before the break.

■■■

They remain just long enough to talk briefly with Dr. Storrs as she is being treated for the cuts and abrasions caused by her glasses' being crushed against her cheek and the bridge of her nose. She is not anxious to discuss the implications of Ned's reaction beyond debating with Dr. Eckert whether it is best for her immediately to join the team now working with Ned or to wait until he has been calmed. She is insistent that she deal with Ned directly and immediately.

Neither Paul nor Christine speaks of what they have witnessed until they pull into a diner about five miles down the road from the clinic. After giving their order, Paul asks with a shake of his head, "Do you think they'll ever be able to cure him?"

"Cure?"

"I mean, I don't know, keep him from going back into that state he was in? I mean do you think what happened might help him out of that, that—what? That vegetative state?"

Christine raises her eyes to Paul and says, "I don't know. But maybe he was better off in whatever little world he had found for himself."

11

*T*uesday, May 21, 1963. Her eleventh
birthday, which she suspected Monsieur knew,
although there was no reason that he would.
She had never said anything. He had never
asked. It was just that this afternoon he seemed
different. Both of them, in fact, Monsieur and
Madame. They were almost conspiratorial; a concept she understood, if
she could not put a word to it. When she had come from school, as she
had done almost every afternoon for the past two years to earn a few
francs for herself and her mother, Madame was upstairs in the living
quarters, not at the counter by the front door counting out the customers'
change from the worn wooden drawer, nor helping her husband restack
the bins with fruits and vegetables for the early-evening shoppers. No,
something was definitely different about this afternoon. Maybe they knew
it was her birthday. Maybe she only hoped they knew. Maybe she hoped
they did not know.

No, no one knew it was her birthday. Except her mother. And M.
Roth, of course. His card had come almost a week ago. Like always. All
the way from America and always early, with the small check her mother
had to take to the bank and she would have to wait for what seemed like
forever before she would receive the few francs for whatever she wanted.
This year, if there was enough—her mother had not said how much M.
Roth had sent—it would be the large atlas in M. Gagnon's bookshop
across the street, the one with the color photographs and maps of all the
places she would one day go, the one M. Gagnon let her leaf through,
sometimes for as long as she liked if she swept out his shop and ran to

the small café at the corner to get him a fresh coffee and a brioche. But she could not think about all that. She had work to do.

She took the broom and swept her way to the front door and then out onto the sidewalk, which she made as clean as the floor inside. It was not always easy. The customers were so often careless about the bits of paper and straw that dropped from the bins where they pushed and pulled and poked and squeezed the fruit as if M. Michaud might try to slip something past them. She swept around Michaud, who was standing back a moment, inspecting his display. He was very particular about how his produce was displayed.

"Do you want me to spray the bins, Monsieur?" She liked the job of taking the hose with its small, nozzled end and lightly spraying water over the bins to make the produce shine.

"No, I will do that," Michaud said, and he signaled with his eyes that two women had just gone inside the shop. "Why don't you stay at the counter. You know how much everything is, do you not? And how to make change?"

She could not believe her ears. "Monsieur?"

"You do know your arithmetic, don't you, how to add and subtract?"

Of course she did. Better than anyone in her class. Better even than anyone in the class ahead of her, she thought. They were all so stupid, her classmates. And the sisters sometimes didn't seem so bright either. She had caught them in mistakes. But she was too smart to ever say so. She knew that to avoid notice was to avoid trouble. And so she would parrot back whatever answers they wanted. It was easier that way. But M. Michaud asking her to stand at the counter and to take the customers' money and to give change? He must be testing her. That had to be it. But why? What had she done? It had been nearly two years since she had stolen from him. Two years!

She remembered that the day had been hot, just before the shop closed for lunch. It must have been summer. She had not seen Michaud standing just inside the door when she slipped up and reached for an orange. He caught her as he had done a few times before, but this time it no longer seemed the game she thought they had been playing. He was angry, he said, and he acted as if he were. He did not let go of her arm. He took her inside and called Madame from the back of the shop.

"There is only one way to stop our little thief from bankrupting me. We will stuff her like a goose until she will never again think of food. What do we have to stuff her with?"

It did not take long for Mme. Michaud to produce a large pot of stew. Beef she thought, but she was not sure.

"There," Monsieur had barked. "Eat!"

She remembered looking to Madame to see if they were serious. It was a strange punishment to be sure. "You'd best do as you are told, child," Madame had said. "You don't want my husband to call the police."

And so she ate. The stew was tasty enough, but it soon lost its flavor. She ate until she could eat no more. Even pride and stubbornness could not force more down. Her throat felt as if it had swollen shut and her stomach was bloated and heavy.

"Please, Monsieur," she begged, the first words she had ever spoken to him, "I am sorry. I cannot eat any more."

"Good," he had said. "Now you will stop stealing from me. And to make up for all you have taken before you will come here each morning for a week, and you will sweep out my shop."

She had not said anything, trying to judge his seriousness.

"And if you do not, I will take you to the river and feed your toes to the fishes."

She remembered wanting very much to laugh. It was such a foolish thing for him to say. But she did not laugh because his face was stern, and he seemed so intent. And so for the next week, she came each morning and swept out his shop, and by the fourth day she asked if there was anything else Monsieur wanted her to do, and at the end of the week he gave her some change for the extra work she had done, and he told her that if she would come to help out for an hour each day he would pay her for her labors.

And so she did; and after she learned the price of the fruits and calculated how many times and what she had stolen from him, she had gathered together the money and had paid him, together with an apology, for her crimes. He was very pleased, she remembered, and she had not spoiled his pleasure by telling him how she had spent almost a month stealing trinkets from the shops around the Place Kléber and the Rue des Grandes-Arcades and fencing them to the children whose pockets always rattled with coins. She had since come to the shop nearly every day, and the only quarrel, if indeed it could be called that, had been between her and Madame, who often fussed that she should spend more time playing with the other children and less time working. Madame was kind, but not very bright, and, well, not very attractive either. Madame was much too heavy and never allowed herself the bright clothes and the makeup and the perfumes and colognes that could so easily lift her mother out of her moods. She often tried to picture Monsieur and Madame together, alone, in bed. But she could not. Perhaps that was why they had no children, or at least none that they spoke of. She had never asked, nor would she. It was not her concern. And she understood. She would never have children.

. . . "Well, do you?"

"Monsieur?"

"Do you know your arithmetic? Can you make change for the customers?"

"Yes, of course, I can do that." She stood staring at him.

"Well, go ahead. Those ladies will not wait forever."

"I am being tested," she told herself again. "I must be very careful." And she was, meticulously adding the figures Michaud had written on the paper bags and then marking the prices of the few items the two women had picked up inside, adding them together and announcing what was owed. She made change very, very carefully, opening the drawer only far enough to barely be able to slip her fingers inside for the bills and coins. She knew all too well how easy it might be for someone to reach over to a drawer opened too wide and snatch the money away. That would not happen to her. She was much too clever for that.

For the next half hour, she stood behind the counter, taking money and making change, both proud and nervous. Not once did she open the drawer wide enough to allow some thieving hand to enter, and not once—although she was tempted—did she open the drawer just to look inside and count the money.

She was just beginning to feel comfortable at her post when she saw M. Gagnon walk across the street carrying a package wrapped in bright red paper. He stopped in front of the shop to speak with Monsieur, and after a moment or so the two men came inside.

"So." M. Gagnon smiled at her. "I see that you are taking over the shop."

She blushed and looked about shyly while Monsieur went to the stairs at the back of the shop and called out, "Anise? Are you ready?"

She looked back at M. Gagnon, and asked apprehensively, "Did you sell the book? The atlas with all the pictures?"

Gagnon smiled. "No, not today."

She could hear Mme. Michaud descending the back stairs and suddenly she realized why Madame had been upstairs, why M. Gagnon was here, and what was in the bright red wrapping. The next few moments were filled with her blood racing, and her senses were consumed by the bright white cake flecked with shavings of orange peel and ablaze with candles. They all seemed to be talking to her at once, but all she could hear was a distant chatter. It was all sight and sound and smell and nothing else.

And then M. Gagnon put the package on the counter, and Madame told her to open it. Her hands felt weak and tremulous as she carefully pulled the wrapping apart to reveal the book of dreams she knew was inside. She did not want to look up and see the faces of these people. She did not know what was expected of her. She wanted to run. But Madame said that she should make a wish and blow out the candles. She blew out the candles, but she did not bother with a wish. She knew all about wishes. But she could not say that to Madame.

There was a moment of silence and M. Gagnon said, "Perhaps you should save that beautiful cake for you and your mother. Yes?"

She saw Monsieur look suddenly uncomfortable, and she blurted out, "Oh, no, we must all have some now. My mother . . . My mother and I won't be eating until much later, not until nine o'clock at least."

Their understanding smiles told her that there must be more. And so the story just fell out, like the contents of a valise whose clasp has come undone suddenly, and before she could catch them, the words were spread before everyone.

No, they would not be eating until much later. You see, Signor Ligure was coming by to pick them up. He was a distant cousin of her father. Well, actually, he wasn't coming himself. He was having a car come around, with a driver. He was very rich, Signor Ligure. She had never met him, but her mother spoke of him quite a bit. She said he was very handsome. He didn't live here in Strasbourg. No, he was Italian. He had been away for many years, in the Far East, she thought. But now he was coming to see them, and when he had heard that it was her birthday, he insisted that they join him for dinner on his boat. The one he was traveling on. He was going to have dinner served while they cruised up the river. Not on the Ill, of course, but on the Rhine. That was why they would not be eating until late, it being so much farther to the Rhine. She hoped that the moon would be full.

"Well," Mme. Michaud said, "that is good fortune for all of us. We can all have some cake together and it will not spoil your dinner."

So they each had a piece of cake, and she and Monsieur shared a second piece. And while they ate, she could not stop talking. She opened the book and turned to page after page of maps and photographs and pointed out interesting facts about all the places she was sure they did not know and were glad to hear about. Soon customers began to come in, and M. Gagnon said that he must get back to his shop. Madame wondered that she must have much to do to get ready for her wonderful evening on Signor Ligure's yacht, and so, she said, it would be all right if she left a bit early tonight. She thanked Madame with a smile, but she was sorry that she had made up the lie that now forced her to leave.

Monsieur was standing by the bins with a customer, the old woman who lived by the canal who always smelled of garlic. She approached Monsieur shyly, her book clutched tightly under her arm, the remains of her cake packed carefully in a box tied with string and held in the other hand. She wasn't quite sure what to do, feeling more confused than anything. As the old woman poked about the lettuces, she walked up to Monsieur and tried to think of what to say. When nothing came, she felt a sudden panic and awkwardly tried to reach out her hand without dropping the book. Monsieur's face turned curious, if a little shy itself, and he helped her by gently taking the tips of her fingers in his hand. But for those few times so long ago when his hand would arrest her arm, she had never touched him, nor he her. His hand was large and rough and very warm and it seemed to swallow her.

"Thank you, Monsieur," she said in a rush, and she then turned and ran down the street toward home.

There was a small package wrapped in Christmas paper sitting in the center of the small table in the center of the small kitchen. She could hear her mother's heavy sleep and smell the alcohol and she understood. It wasn't her mother's fault. The anniversary of her birth was the anniversary of his death. It was better that her mother sleep. It had been a good day and she did not want to cry. She carefully took her cake from its box and placed it on the table next to the package she would open later when her mother awoke. She cut a small slice and took it with her to her room, where she sat on the bed, her legs crossed in front of her.

The book in her lap, she turned to the map of the United States and found the home of M. Roth. She wondered if he was as rich as she imagined, and whether she would ever meet him. She took a bite or two of the cake, but she could not finish it. She carefully wrapped the remains in a napkin, and then lay down and held her book close to her.

It did not take long for her to slide off the edge, to that other world where she and Signor Ligure sat on the deck of his yacht, at a table set with exotic foods lit by candles whose light danced off the silver service, and he told her tales of his travels while his servants poured her wine, and into the night they sailed, under a full moon, following the Rhine to the sea, and across the sea to America, to a place called Baltimore.

12 ifteen minutes north of Fishing Creek
Estates lies the county seat. Except for the
cluster of strip malls and fast-food restaurants which lines the highway just outside
of town, it looks and feels just about as it
did when tobacco was king. Though the
times and an ever-evolving economy have brought their changes,
still, each spring, the tobacco buyers come to walk among the heavily laden baskets, rolling the cured golden leaves between their
fingers and holding each sample to their noses as if it were a fine
wine, and, having assayed its value, nod their bids to an auctioneer,
whose distinctive, lyrical songs only they can understand. This year's
sales have not yet begun, and the auction warehouses are not yet
filled with last year's crop, but still the old wooden structures with
their long tin roofs sit like enormous containers of potpourri giving
off their sharp, sweet scent.

Coming into town from the north, just past the Big Four and
Bright Leaf warehouses, the road narrows and dips sharply under
a concrete bridge with "Southern Railway" lettered across its face.
Just as quickly the road rises again and flows onto a wide avenue
pointing straight to the center of town and to the red-brick courthouse, where, in an office on the first floor rear, Cooper Avery's
fate is being debated.

Christine squeezes her eyes closed while the fingers and thumb
of one hand massage her brow. She is beginning to feel as pained
as her expression and more than a little irritated. Her words start

low and build almost to a shout. "Charlie, how many times have we got to go over this? *The sonofabitch never called!*" She stops, feeling embarrassed in the long silence that follows. Finally, she mumbles, "Sorry."

Two days after she and Paul had returned from the William T. Packard Clinic, State's Attorney Albert Chasen received a call from Phillip Layton, Cooper Avery's lawyer, who suggested that it might be helpful if he and his client could sit down and discuss the investigation. Chasen agreed and then called Captain Hardiman, who in turn sent Christine, Paul and Charlie Abbot to brief the prosecutor before his meeting. Christine wonders why the captain did not come himself; whether he thought his presence might stifle the debate that was growing stronger and at times more acrimonious, particularly between her and Charlie Abbot, or whether he simply wanted to distance himself from whatever decision was reached. She suspects it is a bit of both, and it disappoints her.

Albert Chasen steps in. "I don't understand, Detective," he says to Christine. "If we're talking about Mrs. Haley, she testified before the grand jury last week that Avery *did* call that morning. Is there something else that I oughta know about?"

Christine stares at Chasen. He is as nondescript a man as she has ever met. He is somewhere between his late thirties and early forties, she guesses, five-nine or -ten, and afflicted with a kind of pudginess that makes it difficult to tell whether he is truly overweight or simply softened by a physical nature that seems as subdued as his thoughts. His hair is combed back and held to its neatness by some form of stiffening spray that darkens its color almost to brown. His eyes fall somewhere between brown and hazel and seem constantly caught in an expression that is curious or confused, it is hard to tell which.

He is, however, not without distinction. Six years before, he became the first person—and to anyone's knowledge, the only person—ever elected to a countywide office as an independent. And while he scored no front-page victories, neither did he suffer any front-page defeats. He is just what the people of the county like in their public servants, steady and reliable and, most of all, unobtrusive.

But Christine is certain he wants more. She can hear it in his voice, like a man whose hunger lies dormant until the steak is put before him. It seems to her that for Albert Chasen, Cooper Avery is fresh meat.

"Look, Mr. Chasen," she says with what calm she can muster, "this phone call to Mrs. Haley is a red herring." Charlie Abbot lurches forward in his chair, and Christine quickly raises her hand to stop him. "Charlie, this isn't personal, it's just business. Okay?" Charlie sits back, and she continues, looking at Chasen. "Here's what I think happened. Fact. Mrs. Haley said nothing at all about a call from Cooper Avery on the day Marian Avery's body was found. All right, she was hysterical and all that. But!" she emphasizes, "she was able to help us locate and contact members of the family. She was able to help us deal with the children, and she told us that she thought Avery was in Boston and where he might have been staying. If she was able to do that, plus describe in some detail how she found the body and what she did, don't you think she would have remembered a phone call from Avery that morning? Particularly if the call alerted her to some problem at Avery's house?" No one answers. "Second, the idea of the phone call came from me, not Mrs. Haley. We—me and Charlie and Paul were sitting in Captain Hardiman's office throwing theories around, and I was saying that if Avery had killed his wife or had someone else kill her, he would have done something to make sure that the kids wouldn't walk in and find the body. That's when Charlie and Paul go back and press Mrs. Haley about whether there was a call and still she's not sure. Two months later I run into her up in Baltimore and she says she's been thinking about it and maybe, just maybe there was a call. I mean it is so clear that the idea was planted in her brain. She wants to help. The police keep telling her how important it is for her to remember whether Avery called to express any concern for his family. She thinks it would help if there was a call. She has no idea who or how it would help, just that it would, and so now she's convinced herself that the call happened."

Charlie edges forward on his chair, and again Christine reaches out, her hand poised like a traffic cop's to stop him. "One last thing, Charlie. Avery's telephone records show a call from New York to his house late in the afternoon the day before the body was found. But there's no record of a call to the Haleys' house the next morning. Think about it. If Avery wanted to establish his alibi, why wouldn't he have used his credit card for that call? He'd want the whole world to know he called the Haleys' house from New York or wherever. But he didn't use his card. He didn't leave the trail. Because he never made that call. It never happened."

Charlie leans forward, scratching his forehead. "You're wrong," he says softly, "and I'm gonna tell ya why. The fact there was no credit card call seems to me to be even more proof that Avery himself killed his wife. He didn't have it done. He did it himself."

Christine looks startled. "Come again?"

Charlie's jaw tightens at Christine's expression, but he maintains the quiet tone of his voice. "Okay, first we've got Avery in New York checking into the Plaza Hotel and calling home on his credit card. The old lady tells him the kids are gonna stay over at a neighbor's that night. An hour later he checks into the Albemarle House under an assumed name. He pays in advance but leaves there within a half hour or so and doesn't return. Why? Who the fuck knows?" Charlie looks at Albert Chasen with a sudden embarrassment, wondering whether his language might have offended this quiet man. Chasen does not respond, and Charlie goes on. "Anyway, nobody's with him. His lady friend says she didn't see or talk to him that day. I don't know, maybe he rents a car, takes the train, pays cash, no names. Whatever, he makes his way back here and kills his wife.

"Now, what's important here is timing. The coroner puts the time of death somewhere between four and seven in the morning. He thinks it's probably closer to six or seven, but let's assume it's as early as four in the morning. Avery does the deed and now has to get back to New York. Driving or a train—hell, even if he flies—by the time he gets to an airport and all that, it's gotta take him at least four, four and a half hours. That puts him back in New York at say eight-thirty at the earliest. I mean absolute earliest. Probably closer to nine-thirty, ten, even eleven o'clock." He turns to Christine and lifts his finger in a point of emphasis. "Think about it. Like you always said, he'd never want his kids to find the body so he'd call the Haleys. And he knows how early his kids wake up so he can't wait to get back to New York before he makes the call. He's gotta stop along the way. He's gotta make sure he calls early enough that the kids aren't sent home for breakfast or whatever. So he stops somewhere along the turnpike maybe and makes the call. But he can't use his credit card because if anyone ever checks, how's he ever gonna explain being in a phone booth somewhere along Route 95? He can't. So he drops a few coins in a pay phone." Charlie sits back with a satisfied smile. "That, little lady, is why there's no credit card record."

Christine bristles. *"Little lady?"*

Albert Chasen cuts the tension with a question. "Can't we check the phone company records to see what if any long-distance calls came in to the Haleys' phone that morning?"

"We've been checking, but doing a fish-eye search takes a lotta time. I mean stop and think about all the possible area codes and whatever. Plus, he could very well have been within this area code. I mean with all the phone booths, a diner somewhere between here and Baltimore. Maybe it'll turn up, maybe not."

Christine sits forward and speaks slowly. "Gentlemen, I'm sorry, but it seems to me that we're building a case out of thin air here. We're not looking at facts."

"What facts are you suggesting that we haven't looked at?" Chasen asks.

"Well, there's one thing everyone seems to have forgotten, and that is the possibility that we're dealing with a stalker."

Chasen looks up with sharp surprise. "A stalker?"

"Yes, Mr. Chasen, that's right. A stalker. One fact we've ignored is that when Paul and I interviewed Avery, he said that there were several occasions when his wife thought someone had been in her house."

Detective Wyzanski leans forward, sounding the tone of a mediator in the escalating debate. "Yeah, that's right," he says quietly, "but Avery also said there was nothing to it. Remember? He said there was never any sign of a break-in, nothing was ever missing or left behind. He thought she was just nervous about living out in the country. She was afraid of the dark or whatever."

"Maybe. But maybe she was right. Avery said she was very particular about her house. Maybe she noticed things that she just couldn't put her finger on. Maybe Avery wasn't really listening to her."

"What are you saying, Detective?" Chasen asks.

"Look, a stalker isn't going to break down a door or smash a window. And the signs they leave behind are usually pretty subtle. Little things. Something out of place. An otherwise innocent item that wasn't there before. Some small knickknack that's taken. Whatever it might be, it was probably something that might not otherwise be noticed except by a woman like Marian Avery, a woman who was very particular about keeping her house just so. And when you really look back on that scene and the way the woman was killed, doesn't it seem like we're dealing with a whole different set of motives? Bad blood, revenge, who knows? Maybe someone was even trying to set it up to make it look like Avery killed his wife. To me that makes a heck of a lot more sense than Avery doing the deed himself."

Chasen nods silently and rocks in his chair for a moment before turning back to Christine. "Detective, I'm curious why you're so adamant that Avery did not kill his wife. This stalker business seems even more speculative than all the other things that concern you. Besides that, the circumstances here just keep building to where I don't see how we can just toss it off as coincidence. Everything about the scene, what was stolen, what was left behind, the glass shards over the footprints you so cleverly spotted, the fact that the safe was not damaged and that Avery was the only other person with the combination, even the fact that the slug from Marian's head matches the gun he reported stolen."

Christine's eyes are lowered and her head shakes in frustration. "With all due respect, that gun business is even weaker than the phone call." She hesitates, then reaches for her purse and from it takes her service revolver. She stretches forward and lets the gun drop with a clunk on Chasen's desk. "Run the same tests on that gun. And on Charlie's and Paul's here. I'll wager you'll come up with pretty much the same conclusion on all of them."

Chasen barely looks at the Smith and Wesson .38 and does not change his expression. "I thought you had all changed over to nine millimeters?"

Paul smiles and shakes his head. "Next month, maybe. The first ones went to the troopers. They figure detectives need pencils more than guns."

Christine is insulted, and her voice hints at it. "My point, sir, is that up to a few months ago, a .38 Smith was standard issue. And all your ballistics show is that the rifling marks on that slug match *a* Smith .38. But the only way to come up with real proof is to either find Avery's gun or run elimination tests on every other .38 sold out of that lot until you do find an actual match."

Chasen shakes his head. "All I am saying, Detective, is that it's a very compelling coincidence when you add up everything else."

"No! It's not," she blurts back, causing Chasen to straighten his back and frown deeply. "Does anyone here really believe that a man would hide away his gun and report it stolen and then wait for a year or more just hoping that one day his wife will send the kids off for the evening while he's out of town but still close enough so he can sneak home and kill her and then sneak back to wherever? That's crazy. You want to indict the man so you're making facts out of theory and assumptions. But those assumptions defy logic."

Chasen's annoyance is apparent as his hands grasp the wooden arms of his chair and he pushes himself firmly against its back. "I don't *want* to indict anyone, Detective. I have a duty to indict if that's what the evidence dictates. Are we clear on that?"

Before Christine can respond, Paul interjects himself. "Chris, you're right. The way you put it, it wouldn't make any sense. But put another twist to it. For example, a year, a year 'n' a half ago, Avery starts having this affair. Maybe he thinks he's in love with the woman. He and his wife have a fight. Maybe they're not getting along at all. Maybe in the middle of this fight he gets so angry he thinks of killing her. Maybe he gets so angry he goes to the basement to get his .38. But the kids are around, and he thinks, no, he can't do it. The blood cools a bit, and he thinks if he ever did want to kill her he wouldn't want to use his own gun. He'd have to plan and all that. So he hides the gun away somewhere, maybe just to avoid the temptation, and reports it stolen. Doing all that gets it out of his system. It doesn't patch up the marriage, but it lets him blow off the rage or whatever. A year later, something happens. Another fight. Another woman. Maybe even the same woman. But something happens to make him think this is the time he has to act. The gun's available and been reported stolen for over a year. Circumstances click, his wife says the kids are gonna be out of the house, and he snaps. It's now or never. And he does it. That would explain the scene. You know, like you always said. Half-baked. I know you think someone may have been trying to set him up. But the sloppiness could just as easily have been a plan not fully thought out. He took the opportunity that was suddenly presented to him and then tried to cover as best he could." He hesitates and tilts his head with raised eyebrows. "Possible?"

She stares a moment, then relaxes her posture. "Yes, it's possible. But what suddenly makes him snap? Why then? What's the sudden need or motive?"

Albert Chasen leans forward and plants his elbows on his desk, folding his fingers together. "The stock."

All three detectives' eyes snap toward Chasen, and Paul asks, "The what?"

"The stock!" Chasen repeats.

"What stock?"

Chasen looks at all three curiously. "His wife's eleven percent interest in Thurston Construction."

"I don't understand," Christine says. "Are you saying Avery killed his wife for stock in the company where he's already president?"

"Not the stock so much as the voting power. I thought you all knew about this."

"About what, specifically?"

"You know about Barth-Sanders trying to take over Thurston, right?"

The detectives all nod.

"Well, old man Thurston had over the years given stock to his daughter, a big chunk as a wedding gift and all that, but all that stock amounted to a little more than eleven percent interest in the company. Basically avoiding future inheritance taxes. There had never been a problem since Marian had always voted the stock however her father wanted her to. Until a few years ago when Cooper got his wife to sign an agreement giving all her voting rights over to him. Again, that wasn't a problem until this takeover bid started. Avery had always voted along with his father-in-law. Anyway, when Barth-Sanders started to make its bid, the old man went to Marian and tried to make her rescind the agreement, to take back her proxy as it were, to make sure he had control. Apparently that eleven percent is more than enough to make the difference."

"Did she?" Paul asks.

"No. There were some arguments about it. She hadn't agreed

and she hadn't refused. Essentially she was caught between her father and her husband."

"But what's in it for Avery if he doesn't have his company anymore?" Christine asks.

"Something in the neighborhood of thirty-five to forty million after taxes."

Charlie Abbot lets out a soft whistle.

"Plus there are rumors that Barth-Sanders may have an offer out to sweeten the deal if Avery can deliver the stock, a piece of the action or whatever. Maybe Sydney Lambert will tell us what the deal is. And by the way, I want to make sure that she and Avery don't run into each other today."

Sydney Lambert has been called to testify before the grand jury, and her appearance is set for early afternoon. Albert Chasen relishes the idea of questioning her before the grand jury fresh on the heels of his interview of Avery.

Charlie nods and says, "We'll take care of it."

Christine's forefinger is tapping lightly on her lip, and her eyes narrow before she asks, "Mr. Chasen, do you mind telling us where this information came from? All this stuff about the stock and the arguments over who gets to vote it or not?"

Albert Chasen sits motionless for a moment. "Well, it comes directly from Edward Thurston."

"Christ," she says softly with a light shake of her head, "the sharks are gathering." She cocks her head. "Did he come to you or did you go to him?"

"Does it matter?"

"Yes, I think it might. Maybe Thurston has his own motives."

Albert Chasen leans forward and shows the first sign that he is capable of aggression. "Detective, I asked you before and you never really answered me. Why is it that you're so sure Avery didn't kill his wife? Give me facts. Why is it that you're so willing to question everyone's motives but his—or yours, for that matter?"

Paul watches Christine's body turn rigid. Before he can stop her, she says to Chasen, "I'm just trying to do my job here. And I thought my job was to find the truth. And maybe I'm wrong, but I thought that was your job, too."

Chasen's face puffs and reddens but he says nothing. Christine stands and lifts her gun from the desk top and slips it into her purse.

"You'll have to excuse me," she mumbles, "I have work to do." She turns and walks out of the office.

Paul excuses himself and quickly follows, catching Christine in the outer hallway. He stops her with a hand on her arm. She falls back against the wall and lets her head flop back, resigned.

"Chris, what the hell are you doing?"

Her eyes narrow, and her words come in a hiss. "I don't have to take that shit from him. And you tell your partner he'd better start watching his mouth. That 'little lady' crack—"

"Hold on a minute," Paul interrupts. "Look, I'm not here to defend either one of them. I don't care about that. But this isn't like you. Chris, you're taking this crap personally. It's just business, remember? And like it or not, the man's the D.A. You can't come up in his face like that. Charlie doesn't matter. Okay, he was way outta line, but you know he doesn't mean to be insulting. It's just his way. And so he forgets you've got rank. You can cut him off at the knees anytime you want. But so what? That petty bullshit never bothered you before. So what's going on here?"

Her eyes soften, and she says, "You're convinced he did it, aren't you?"

He nods slowly. "I think it sure is beginning to look that way. But that doesn't mean that I don't think you should be asking all the questions that you've been asking. I just think you oughta be more willing to listen to the answers." He lets the silence go on a moment, and then says, "Look, you know I'll do anything you want me to do on this. Follow any leads you've got. You just tell me what you want, and I'll take care of it. Just don't walk out on us."

Her eyes settle on his. "He didn't do it, Paul."

He shakes his head a bit, then looks away and takes a deep breath. He turns back to her, staring, studying. "Who's telling me this? Detective Sergeant Boland or the woman who gives the best back rubs known to man?"

She releases a smile. "Both."

He smiles too. "You just tell me what you want me to do, and I'll do it. Whatever you say. All I'm asking is what you keep telling us—keep an open mind. Okay?"

She nods. "Okay. It's a deal." Her smile widens and her eyes drift shyly to the floor. "Were my back rubs really the best?"

"No question."

13 *S*econd thoughts are crowding Cooper Avery's mind as he listens to his heels click along the linoleum-floored hallways of the county courthouse. He is no stranger to courthouses, but this one is beyond his experience. It has none of the quiet solemnity of the federal courthouses where corporate litigants and their lawyers in fresh, starched shirts and crisp, expensive suits exchange polite nods and wage their wars on printed pages neatly bound in colored bindings, the contents all tabbed and indexed and speaking the King's English. Here the halls are lined with wooden benches piled with people who sit stunned and sorry, angry and apprehensive, bored and boastful: witnesses, defendants, wives and lovers, mothers, children, friends and enemies, mixing by chance, debating their causes, protesting their fate, warning those who cannot hear —*"The man lied on me. You tell that sorry muthafucka he best be watchin' his back. You hear me, muthafucka? You tell 'im!"*—crying and laughing, silently waiting, looking for answers no one can give them. To Cooper, the noise is all one, like a night filled with crickets to a man raised on a treeless street in a treeless city, an abstract annoyance, something removed from him but somehow still ominous.

Light fixtures hang from the tall, vaulted ceilings like dull yellow mushrooms, adding little to the light that squeezes through the translucent widows of the office doors stenciled with names and functions: "Recorder of Deeds—Blanche C. Armstrong, Deputy Clerk"; "Civil Division—Domestic Relations Branch—Harold J.

McIntyre, Chief Deputy Clerk"; "Criminal Division—Warrant Section"; and finally, at the end of the hall, facing him, "Office of the State's Attorney—Albert W. Chasen, State's Attorney," and in much smaller letters, "All visitors must sign in at reception desk." A small arrow neatly drawn in Magic Marker on a piece of cardboard taped below the sign directs those visitors to an open doorway on the right.

An electric typewriter is clacking at the desk just inside the door, and beyond the desk, the room opens wide enough to accommodate a sofa and four side chairs, all covered in a dark, mustard-colored vinyl. A long coffee table veneered with an amorphous wood grain is stacked with magazines splayed like a poker hand just laid down. In the corner, a metal coat rack the color of dirty nickels holds a dozen metal hangers. Sunlight comes through the window in columns, accentuating the dust dancing in the fusty air. But for the receptionist who stops her typing to have Cooper Avery and his lawyer, Phillip Layton, sign the register, the room is empty. It shouldn't be, Cooper thinks. Sydney Greenstreet and Mary Astor and Peter Lorre should be here. Ward Bond should be leaning in the doorway, and Humphrey Bogart should be flirting with this girl whose smile is strained through boredom. Cooper wonders when the last time a man wearing a twelve-hundred-dollar suit sat here, and that thought leads him to suspect that his nerves may well be justified. He has seen the resentment that wealth and power can sometimes draw from those who have less or none of either. He has just never been in a position to be held hostage by it.

Phillip Layton smiles, but his discomfort is apparent. He inspects all the furnishings as if it is of some moment which seat he chooses. Cooper wonders if Layton has given as much thought to the decision to have this meeting. "I suppose it couldn't hurt," was as far out on a limb as he allowed himself. But Cooper insisted. Something had to be done.

He was busy when Dr. Storrs called from the clinic. He didn't really focus. *Of course, do whatever you think best.* And later—the next day, actually—when he thought about it, he called Dr. Storrs back. Ned had suffered a strong reaction to seeing the clothing, but she was encouraged that he had come out of his trance. They believed that the "presentation," as she called it, had opened a certain window of opportunity. Ned was verbalizing. He was not coherent, mind you, not focused, but at least verbal, at least for the present. But somehow Cooper knew there was more to it. It was something in Dr. Storrs's voice. He pressed her for details, and he could hear her reluctance. And then she said that the state police had been there to observe the presentation, and he pictured what the police might have seen in Ned's reaction to the hunting clothes, much as he had pictured Ned's reaction to seeing Charles Haley in his fatigues, much as he remembered Ned's reaction to him. The thought of that day still turns his stomach. *Don't think about it. Deal with today.*

And he remembers the cool strain in Dr. Storrs's voice. Yes, there is more to it; it doesn't take much imagination to realize where this investigation is headed. Something has to be done. It's obvious Phillip Layton's quiet approach has accomplished nothing. It seems obvious, too, that the problem has to be addressed head-on. And so he insisted. He directed Layton to make the arrangements. But now that he is here, he wonders if it was a mistake.

Albert Chasen's secretary steps into the reception area and invites him and Layton to follow her. *Stay calm, stay firm, stay humble.* No, he didn't care for coffee, but thank you anyway. He watches her walk in front of him, trailing a whiff of her perfume, a body much younger than her face compacted by a straight skirt and sweater. Phillip Layton walks behind him, and Cooper is glad of that. If only for a moment he can enjoy the security of no one seeing his expression, of no one seeing his nerves. It is like awakening in that still-warm spot in a cold bed in a cold room, knowing that when you move, as inevitably you must, you will suffer the cold. But for those few brief moments, that warmth is all you need.

The secretary—Cynthia, he thinks she said—stops and knocks on a door, but she does not wait for an answer before opening it and standing aside to let them pass. He hears the door close behind him. *Stay calm, stay firm, stay humble.*

Phillip Layton steps forward to shake Albert Chasen's hand. They smile and address each other by their first names as if they have known each other for some time. Layton has said that they have never met. The game's the same, no matter the players. He is introduced.

"Mr. Avery." Chasen nods. He is neither cheerful nor unpleasant.

"Good morning." Cooper smiles as his eyes take in the unexpected. He recognizes the tall, quiet-voiced detective and the woman with the dark eyes that now seem fixed on him. *Christine Boland, wasn't it?*

"This is Detective Wyzanski and Detective Sergeant Boland." They shake hands.

"Yes, we've met. How are you," he says. It is not a question.

"And . . ."

A short, stocky man stands quickly and shakes his hand firmly. The man mumbles his name, and Cooper cocks his head. "I'm sorry?"

"Abbot," the man announces. "Charlie Abbot."

Cooper nods. "Cooper Avery." He looks to Phillip Layton with a question he knows not to voice.

Layton smiles as he sits, and makes light of it. "Well, I didn't realize we'd have such an audience."

"I thought we could all save some time by having the investigators here," Chasen answers. "Perhaps get all our questions and concerns out on the table at one time."

Layton's lips pinch uncomfortably, and he looks unsure where or how to start. "Well, I assumed something a little less formal. I—"

Cooper cuts him off. "No, Phil, it's okay," he says, as he sits and crosses one leg over the other. "I'd like to get these things resolved." He opens himself with the spread of his hands, and speaks softly but directly. "Well, Mr. Chasen, let's just be direct. I, ah, asked Phil to set up this meeting because there are some things I think you and the investigators ought to know. As you can imagine, this business is quite foreign to me and it has been, well, it's been very difficult for me and my children."

Chasen's head bows slightly. "Yes, I understand."

"And to be quite honest, when I heard that the detectives had been at the clinic to observe this demonstration or whatever it was with my son, I . . . Well, to be honest, I was very angry."

"Do you mind if I ask why you were angry?"

"Because, Mr. Chasen, it very much felt as if my son were being used for investigative purposes without regard to his condition." He hesitates and looks at Detective Boland. She does not flinch and her eyes do not move. "He is in a very fragile state, emotionally." Chasen draws a deep breath as if he is about to launch some defense, but Cooper stops him with a shake of his head. "No, I understand. Or at least I think I do. You have a job to do, and as far as I understand things from Dr. Storrs—"

"Who?" Chasen asks.

"The child's doctor," Paul explains.

"Yes," Cooper continues. "Anyway, Dr. Storrs explained that the demonstration was for diagnostic purposes. She did say that there had been some suggestion from the police of a possible connection Ned might have made between the hunting clothes and whatever he saw when his mother died, but that the doctors had determined to run this demonstration for medical purposes. Whether or not that's true doesn't really matter. I gave my permission because I was told they wanted to do this to try and help my son. I just wish I had been told beforehand that the state police would be there."

"Would that have made a difference in your decision?"

Cooper plants both feet on the floor. His hands are clasped in front of him, and he leans forward until his silk tie brushes against them. His posture is aggressive but his words are not. "No, it would not have. Ned is my son, and the doctors at the Packard Clinic are reputed to be among the best in the country for children with severe emotional problems. I just wish they had been more candid with me. It just soured a bit the confidence I had in them. My relationship with them. But I have put that aside, for Ned's sake."

"I must tell you, Mr. Chasen," Phillip Layton says, "we question the propriety of what was done there. Legally."

Layton does not explain further. From their conversation the day before, Cooper is not sure Layton has a further explanation. Cooper lets the sound of the challenge sit a moment before saying, "Well, that's another matter. The point is that it seems to me that if you have any questions that concern me, you should come to me and ask them. You don't need to involve Ned. Again, you have to understand how serious his condition is. I'll answer any questions you have, but I'm asking you to leave my children alone."

Cooper watches Chasen lean forward and plant his elbows on

his desk. He takes his time speaking, as if to give his words more import. It seems so obviously a pose, something he himself might do if he were nervous. But why should he be nervous?

"Mr. Avery, let me assure you that we have no intention of bothering your children. You, and Mr. Layton, of course, are certainly welcome to discuss any of this with the doctors, but I can assure you that showing your son the hunting clothes was a decision they made. The detectives took no part whatsoever. They were simply allowed to observe the, ah, well, demonstration, I guess you called it. But I am curious about something. Why is it that you assume that the showing of these hunting clothes has anything to do with you?"

It was the first question Phillip Layton had asked Cooper. He gives Albert Chasen the same answer. "Because, Mr. Chasen, I assume if it had nothing to do with me, you or the detectives or the doctors would not have made such a point of not telling me that the police were interested in this *'demonstration.'*" He enunciates the word carefully, almost sourly. "We are talking about my wife who was murdered here, and you are conducting your demonstrations with my son. I would think that unless there was some investigative or police purpose for not telling me, the honorable thing would have been to inform me of what you were doing. And I assume I am dealing with honorable people here."

Stay calm. Layton warned you of this. Stay calm, be humble.

He shakes his head. "I'm sorry. I hope you can appreciate how upsetting this whole business is. It's just that it's very hard." He sits back and very briefly massages his forehead. "Do you mind if I smoke?"

"No," Chasen says, "I'll get you an ashtray." He picks up the phone and pushes the intercom button. "Cynthia, would you mind bringing an ashtray in here for Mr. Avery? Thank you."

Cooper takes his time lifting a pack of cigarettes from his coat pocket and shaking one loose. Cynthia appears with a large ashtray, which she sets down on the edge of Chasen's desk nearest Cooper. "Thank you," Cooper says, and she acknowledges him with a smile and leaves.

"Anyway—" Cooper touches the flame to the end of his cigarette and draws a long puff, which he lets out with relief. "I, ah, couldn't help thinking about all this and what significance these hunting clothes could possibly have. I mean, I assume that you people must have some evidence or theory or whatever that maybe whoever killed my wife was wearing clothes like that, and that's what Ned saw. And I called Charlie Haley. I asked him if any of this made sense to him because we had talked about Ned's reaction to him, and he said that he had been wearing his cammies that day—"

"His what?" Chasen asks.

Cooper hesitates. Chasen obviously had never been in the military. "His camouflage fatigues. Charlie's a major in the reserves. Anyway, the more we talked about it, the more we thought it made sense that Ned might have seen the killer wearing hunting or military camouflage, and when he saw Charlie, it terrified him."

Chasen remains silent and motionless for a moment. Then he asks, "But why do you think this has anything to do with you?"

"Are you telling me that it doesn't?"

"Mr. Avery, I'm simply trying to understand the connection that you've made."

"As I told you a moment ago," he says, stubbing out the cigarette from which he has taken only a puff or two, "I assume there is a reason I was not told that the state police were interested in this clothing business. And when Charlie and I were talking, he asked whether I thought Ned might have made some association with my hunting and this killer. Maybe that was why he had the reaction he did to me."

"Your hunting?"

"Yes, Mr. Chasen, my hunting."

The smug sonofabitch is enjoying this cat-and-mouse.

Cooper glances at Detective Boland. She still has not moved, and her eyes remain fixed on him. "I've been a hunter all my life, or at least since I was about fourteen. Ned never liked it. I mean he is still too young to really hunt or learn to shoot, but he didn't even like the idea of it. He was frightened of guns. But he'd see me in hunting clothes every season. I had a duck blind in the marsh just off my property. Maybe if this killer had worn camouflage or something like it, in his terror, in this awful mental state . . ." He draws a deep breath. "Maybe he associates the hunting with what he saw. I don't know." Cooper feels a tremor in his stomach; he can see Ned on the floor, he can see him clutching at this detective with the still, dark eyes. His face flushes with a prickly heat, and a sudden, short wave of dizziness passes over him. "I'm sorry, but could I get a cup of coffee or water or something? This is, ah, this is very hard to talk about."

"I'll get it," Detective Wyzanski says, standing up. "How do you take it?"

"Cream and sugar, please. Thank you."

"Anyone else?"

Everyone shakes his or her head but Detective Boland. "I'll go with you," she says to Wyzanski, and they leave the room.

Chasen smiles weakly and says, "Why don't we just take a break while they're getting the coffee."

Layton leans close to his client and whispers, "Are you all right?"

Cooper's eyes begin to burn with moisture, and he catches himself with another deep breath. "Yeah, I'm all right. It's just harder to talk about than I thought it would be."

"We can stop anytime."

He shakes his head.

The short, stocky one, Detective Abbot, sits forward in his chair, his elbows resting on his knees, absently working on his fingernails with a small penknife. Curious, Cooper thinks, no one, at least not the detectives, has a notebook or a case file. Chasen's desk is piled with papers but he makes no reference to them. And no one is taking notes. Layton said to assume that they would be recorded, if only to remain conscious of the fact that whatever he said could come back to haunt him.

Cooper's pulse has not slowed a bit. He cannot relax. It is like nothing he has ever experienced. No matter what the situation, he has always felt equal to it. But this isn't an equal setting. None of this matters to these people. They collect their paychecks no matter what. Save a life, destroy a life, it is all the same. The only thing at stake for them is ego. His life versus their egos. At this moment he envies them, imagines them after this meeting, going to lunch and talking of other things. And later, tonight, taking in a movie, sitting in a bar, bedding their wives or lovers, whatever, wherever, their own lives unaffected by what happens here.

Stay calm, stay firm, stay humble.

The detectives return. The woman, Boland, hands him his coffee. Her expression is neutral, not exactly smiling, not exactly hard. It's the eyes that bother him. It's not a stare so much as a concentration. "Thank you." She nods and returns to her seat with her own cup of coffee.

Chasen begins. "Mr. Avery, we were talking about how these hunting clothes may have affected your son. I take it you own some hunting clothes, camouflage or whatever they're called."

"Yes."

"When did you purchase those clothes?"

"I beg your pardon?"

"When did you purchase the camouflage suit you now own?"

"Well, I bought a new set a few weeks ago."

"Did you have a set of these clothes before?"

He hesitates. "Yes."

"Why the need for the new set?"

Phillip Layton leans over to him, but Cooper puts his hand up. "No, that's all right," he says quietly to Layton and turns back to Chasen. "I bought a new set because I was planning to go hunting. I couldn't find my old set of clothes. I don't know where they went. Whether they were lost in the move, I don't know. Maybe they're still packed in boxes somewhere."

"You've moved from the Fishing Creek house then?"

"Oh yes, shortly after my wife died. I couldn't stay there. Alice, my daughter, was having awful nightmares. I rented a house in the city, near Marian's parents, until—I don't know, until things are a little more settled."

"You don't remember packing your hunting clothes?"

"I didn't pack anything. I had professional movers go in and pack everything. I just told them what things to put in storage and what things to move to the house we're in now."

"I see." Chasen looks at the detectives, but none of them responds. "I'm sorry, we got a little sidetracked about these hunting clothes. You said earlier that there was something you thought we should know. Is that right?"

"Well, yes, there is. I, ah, recall when Detectives Wyzanski and Boland came to see me at the house, I became quite upset when I realized they were looking at my travel at the time my wife was killed." He is talking to Chasen but looking at the detectives. "And I cut off the discussion and ordered them out of the house. I'm sorry," he says to the detectives, but neither makes any gesture in return. "Anyway, it is true that I was devastated by what had happened, not only to my wife, of course, but to our children. Ned ... Well, you know that. But Alice, too. She's in many ways stronger and more outgoing than Ned, and tougher, but she's—she's suffered terribly. Awful, awful nightmares." He takes a handkerchief from his pocket and dabs his eyes. "I'm sorry. Anyway, I was terribly upset. But, in truth, there was more to it than just what had happened. You see, the fact of the matter is that I was seeing another woman in New York. It was an affair that is over. I won't insult you by going on about the guilt I feel, given the circumstances, but that is why I became so agitated with the detectives. If that had come out at the time—even now—the thought of facing my children, Marian's family, I couldn't have handled it. In any event, that's why I stopped over in New York on my way back from Boston and why no one could find me that Saturday. I was with this woman."

"How long had you been seeing Sydney Lambert?" Chasen asks.

The words come like a punch in the chest. The sensations fill him, almost blocking out the sound. *Sydney Lambert! They know? They've known all along? How?* He looks to Phillip Layton, whose only gesture is to meet Cooper's eyes with his own. Thoughts race and twist and confuse until he stops them. *Stay calm. You're alone here. Just stay calm.* "For about a year. But as I said, it's over. It was over the instant I got home."

The questions begin to pour forth, from Chasen, from each of the detectives except her. Except Detective Boland. She never utters a word. She never averts her eyes. He takes the questions one at a time, answering each but volunteering no more than he must.

"Why the name Belkindas?"

"I don't remember, actually. I may have just seen the name somewhere. I just made it up."

"Why did you check in at the Albemarle House and leave almost immediately thereafter?"

"Look, we—Ms. Lambert and I—we almost always met at the Albemarle. For obvious reasons, we really couldn't be seen together. And so when I got to New York I did what I usually did. I checked into the Plaza and then went to the Albemarle. I called Sydney and she said to come over to her house. So I did. Her husband was in Europe. We stayed there that night."

"At her house?"

"Yes, at her house."

"But you had already paid for the room at the Albemarle, and at the Plaza."

He shrugs. "The money doesn't mean anything." *Stupid! You shouldn't have said that. Be careful.*

"Did you call your wife that evening?"

"Yes, but not from Sydney's—ah, Ms. Lambert's house. I called from the Plaza."

"What did you talk about?"

"The normal things husbands and wives talk about. How were the kids and all that."

"Did she tell you the children were going to be staying at the Haleys' that night?"

"I . . . I don't remember specifically. She may have. I just don't remember that."

"Did you call her the next morning?"

"No."

"Why not?"

"There was no reason to. She knew I would be home that afternoon."

"Did she know you were in New York?"

"Yes."

"What reason had you given her for being in New York?"

"Business, of course."

"What if she had an emergency?"

"You mean how did I deal with the possibility of her trying to get in touch with me?"

"Yes."

"I would call the Plaza to get my messages just before going to sleep and as soon as I woke up. And, well, I know the regular night clerks, and I give them a little something to call me if there is an important message or an emergency."

"Were there any?"

"Messages?"

"Yes."

"No."

"Did you call anyone that morning? That Saturday morning?"

"You mean home?"

"No, I mean did you call anyone at all?"

"No, not that I recall."

"You're certain?"

"Not absolutely. I could have made some business calls or whatever. But I don't think so. I was with Sydney Lambert. I wasn't thinking about business."

"How did you get home?"

"From New York?" They nod. "I took the shuttle."

"Into National?"

"Yes, of course."

Detective Boland releases her first smile as her eyes switch to Detective Abbot, who asks, "Why didn't you fly into BWI?"

"I don't understand. What difference does it make which airport I flew into?"

"Didn't your itinerary say you were flying in and out of Baltimore?"

"Yes, I suppose it did. But itineraries often change. I'd had a last-minute meeting scheduled in Washington the morning I left. The meeting had been at the Mayflower Hotel, and so I left my car there, in the garage next door. After the meeting I took the shuttle out of National to Boston. So, naturally, I flew back into National, and took a cab to the Mayflower to pick up my car."

Detective Abbot looks skeptical. Detective Boland looks as if she is trying to suppress a smile. Cooper opens his hands in question. "All you need to do is check the finance office of my company. I'm sure they'll be able to show you the ticket receipts."

Chasen moves on. "I understand that your wife had signed over her voting rights to the stock she owned in Thurston Construction."

Cooper pauses to light another cigarette. *Jesus Christ. What is he thinking?* "Yes, many years ago."

"Why was that?"

"I beg your pardon?"

"Why did she sign over her voting rights?"

"Well, I don't understand what possible relevance that has to anything, but if you must know . . ." He hesitates and looks at Layton.

Layton whispers, "Do you want to step outside and talk?"

"No, I'll answer the question."

Layton looks disturbed.

Cooper goes on. "Well, the truth of the matter is that Marian's father could be quite—well, not to mince words, he could be a real pain in the ass. He wanted to believe that Marian was interested in and knowledgeable about the business. He was always calling her and telling her what to do, how to vote and all that. But the truth was she just couldn't be bothered. It didn't interest her at all. And it got to the point that she'd get very annoyed about being reminded about the simplest matters, even to just sign a proxy or whatever. So some years back—I don't remember how long it's been—but anyway, she signed all her voting rights over to me. That's all. I know Ed, her father, was probably upset about that, but he never said anything. At least not to me."

"Did she ever rescind that power?"

"No." Again, he looks to Layton, who does not respond by word or gesture.

"Did she ever suggest that she was going to or that her father wanted her to?"

Cooper's jaw tightens. "No. Absolutely not. If that's what she had wanted, that's what would have happened."

"Did you and this Sydney Lambert ever discuss the Barth-Sanders bid to take over Thurston?"

The question stops him, and for an instant freezes all thought. But it takes only an instant before he is awakened to the obvious. Marian's signing over the voting rights to him was not a matter of public record. And he had hardly flaunted his relationship with Sydney Lambert. Quite the opposite. No, the pieces are coming together. Layton must have gone to Edward Thurston about the affair, and Thurston must have gone to the police with his suspicions about the stock and the fight with Barth-Sanders. It is the only explanation. These detectives aren't that good.

Cooper draws on his cigarette, slowing the pace. He can feel the tension begin to drain from his muscles. He is somehow comforted by the thought that he can now see his enemy, as if that begins to even the odds.

"No," Cooper answers Chasen, "except to talk about not talking about it. It's true that when I first heard about the takeover bid, I tried to pump Sydney for information. But at that time she wasn't really involved and didn't know anything. Or at least that's what she said. We agreed not to talk about it and we didn't."

The rest of the meeting is just noise. Cooper's mind focuses more on analyzing his situation, developing his alternatives, one of

the first and most immediately attractive of which is to fire Phillip
Layton on the spot and tell him to find his own way home.

*No, not yet. Don't panic. Maybe Layton can be turned to my own
use. Can these detectives be that good?*

How to handle his father-in-law? And Sydney Lambert, he needs
to talk to her immediately. It shouldn't have ended the way it did.
He shouldn't have gotten angry. He has to move quickly, he has
to end this meeting. He listens carefully for the right moment, the
right question on which to make his stand, developing in his mind
the stance he is to take and the impression he is to leave. The
question comes quickly and in the tone of voice he now expects
from this Albert Chasen, this pasty little man in his drab little office,
the almost too snide tone of a weakling emboldened by the gun he
holds to your head.

"Isn't it a fact—?"

Cooper raises his hand quickly, startling Chasen and stopping
the question. Cooper sits back and begins to shake his head, allowing a hint of a smile to come over him. He speaks very slowly. "Mr.
Chasen, if it's a fact you assume you know, why are you bothering
to ask me?" He stubs out his cigarette. "Gentlemen, Sergeant Boland, once again, I understand that you have a job to do. But
unfortunately, it seems that you are not so interested in hearing
what I have to say as you are insistent that I give you answers that
will confirm whatever suspicions you have. There's nothing I can
do about that. I can only tell you that if you think I had anything
whatsoever to do with my wife's death, you are wrong. I would
have thought that it was your obligation to let the facts and not
your predisposition dictate the course of this . . . this investigation,
I guess you call it. The facts are that I was in New York from late
that Friday afternoon to midafternoon that Saturday; that for reasons not one of you here can fully appreciate, I was with Sydney
Lambert during that entire time; that on Saturday afternoon she
drove me to La Guardia, where I took the three-thirty shuttle back
to Washington. Check the airline records and you will see that I
am telling the truth. And yes, I have a selfish reason for coming
here. As much as I want whoever murdered my wife to be caught
and suffer the consequences—and I *do* want that very much"—his
jaw is visibly tightened, and his eyes scan each person there before
he goes on—"at the same time, I do not want my children or anyone

else, for that matter, hurt further because you people may be rushing to easy conclusions. And you must know what effect my affair would have on my children. And on Sydney Lambert, for that matter. For it to become known publicly that she and I had a personal relationship in the midst of this takeover bid by Barth-Sanders could destroy her career. Unnecessarily. We had no deals and we passed no confidential information between us. I hate to sound crass, but the fact of the matter is that the relationship was a purely sexual one for both of us. We were simply two people whose marriages for different reasons were, shall we say, incomplete. And so I came here to answer your questions and to ask that you consider very carefully before letting any of these matters become public. That's all I have to say other than to tell you once again," and he points his finger at Chasen while his words come out with a slow, angry emphasis, *"I did not kill my wife!"*

■■■

Just as her secretary is telling Cooper Avery, "I'm sorry, she's out of town today. Would you care to leave a message?" Sydney Lambert is being seated in the grand jury room on the third floor of the courthouse. She has never thought about it before. She has never had occasion to. The grand jury: it is something she associates with lurid headlines, little more than a couple of words spoken by a reporter appearing "live from the federal courthouse." It is something you hire other people to deal with. But she thinks it best that she deal with this situation herself. She wants to keep as low a profile as possible, and keeping a low profile means not contesting the grand jury's "invitation." In his telephone call, the one in which he invited her to appear or be subpoenaed, this prosecutor said she would appear as a witness only, not as a "subject" or a "target" of the investigation. "For background," she thinks he said.

She is not sure what she was expecting, but this is not it. The inquisitional aura of it all. There is no judge, no bailiff, no bench. No windows! The room is configured like a tiny amphitheater, with three tiered rows of desk-like seats—twenty-three of them, she counts—all facing her, looking down on her as she is seated in a chair next to a long table behind which the prosecutor sits. He is staring down at his papers and looks neither at her nor at his audience. A court reporter sits next to him, her face covered by a mask into which she speaks inaudibly. The mask moves up and down with the movements of her mouth, which are reflected in the pulsing of her temples.

Only fifteen of the grand jurors' seats have been filled, predominantly by women: women who she guesses are all in their forties or older. The men must have found excuses not to serve. There are only three on the jury. They are all older. Retired, probably. Two blacks and a white man who nods on the edge of sleep. The rest watch her without expression. One or two actually seem to be keeping notes. Several whisper to each other. One woman gets up and leaves the room for a few minutes. Sydney does not blame her. The room is hot and heavy with the scent of people tired of being stuffed together in a closed space for a long time. A large fan hums in the background, pointing toward the ceiling, circulating and mixing the bad air with itself. It is a room designed for stale, dark secrets.

The prosecutor seems anxious to get through it all, somewhere between nervous and indifferent. He had spoken with her in his office, but only briefly. She had been late, he said, and the grand jury was waiting. He really could not be any more specific than to tell her that the investigation involved the death of Cooper Avery's wife. No, she was here simply as a witness. He was obligated to advise her of her rights, but that did not imply that she was in any way suspect. It was simply something he was required to do. A formality. And now, here, he does advise her. And it is a formality. It's as if her rights bore him. Like the words of a tour guide describing some obscure curiosity at the end of a long shift at the end of a long season, her rights spill forth in a single, rambling drone, uninterrupted by pause or emphasis.

"You have been called as a witness to give information in a matter now under consideration by this grand jury as such you have certain rights you have the right to an attorney if you cannot afford an attorney you have the right to apply to the court for the appointment of an attorney if you choose to hire an attorney or have the court appoint one for you you may seek the advice of that attorney at any time however you may not have the attorney present with you in the grand jury room but if you wish to consult with your attorney you may stop the proceedings at any time to consult with him you also have the right to refuse to answer any question the truthful answer to which might incriminate you do you understand these rights and are you willing to answer the questions asked of you in these proceedings?"

Curious, she thinks, to have the right to an attorney but not here in the room. But it does not matter. She is only a witness, after all. She can handle this.

The prosecutor's questions seem as perfunctory as his advice.

"Please state your name for the record."

"Sydney Lambert."

"Are you employed?"

"Yes."

"By whom?"

"Barth-Sanders Industries."

"How long have you been with that company?"

"Seven years."

"And what do you do?"

"My title?"

"Yes."

"General Counsel."

"Do you know a man by the name of Cooper Avery?"

"Yes."

"How long have you known him?"

"For several years."

"In what capacity?"

"Business."

"And?"

"And personal."

And then, just as she is girding herself, the most curious thing happens. The prosecutor takes out a report and starts talking to himself, although in the official transcript, she is sure, it will appear as if he were addressing her.

"On the thirteenth of December last, you were visited by Detectives Wyzanski and Abbot, in New York. At that time you gave a statement. Isn't that correct?"

"Well, I don't recall the date. It was a Thursday, I believe."

"But you did meet with them?"

"Yes."

"And that was in New York City?"

"Yes."

"And at that time you gave them a statement."

"I spoke with them."

"For some time, isn't that correct?"

"Yes, I suppose it is."

"I am now going to read to the members of the grand jury the detectives' report summarizing your conversation with them. I would ask you to listen carefully to this report."

And without looking up, assuming that she will do as she is asked, he proceeds to read the report. For the next twenty minutes he drones on in the stilted, semigrammatical language of whichever detective typed the report. "The subject was asked . . . The subject reported . . . The subject asserted to have no knowledge of . . ." It is not inaccurate so much as it is incomplete. And it makes her sound as if she succumbed to their interrogation, rather than voluntarily answering their questions. It concentrates primarily on her relationship with Cooper Avery, when it began, when it ended, why it ended, that she had not seen him for two months before his wife's death, that she had not seen or talked to him on Friday, October 26. And it embarrasses and angers her by taking care to note her lack of a "*relationship*" with her husband, the apparent typed quotation marks being emphasized by this squalid creature, this prosecutor, who raises to each side of his head two fluttered fingered signals. That's not necessary. It is a cheap and classless thing to do. And to note how much she smokes? For what possible reason?

But she learns quickly. Answer precisely and only what is required. Offer nothing. Explain nothing.

When he finishes the statement, Albert Chasen looks up for the first time and says, "Ms. Lambert, that was the statement you gave to the detectives, was it not?"

"No."

"No?"

"No."

"I don't understand."

She shrugs.

"Ms. Lambert, are you saying that you did not talk to Detectives Wyzanski and Abbot?"

"No."

He stops a moment, showing his confusion. "You did talk to the detectives."

"Yes."

"Well, what is it that you're saying about your statement here?"

"I'm saying that it is not my statement. It is the detectives' statement."

He pauses a moment, collecting his thoughts. "Well, ah, the question is does that report accurately summarize what you told the detectives on December thirteenth?"

"I told you that I did not remember the date."

"Does that report accurately summarize what you told the detectives on the one and only occasion that those detectives visited your home in New York City?"

"We talked of many things."

"I'm sure. The question is, of the things that you spoke of during that meeting which are summarized in this report, is the report accurate as to what you told the detectives?"

"It's a summary."

"Is it an accurate summary?"

"Of what I told them at the time?"

"Yes."

"As far as it goes."

"That's a yes?"

"As far as I recall."

"Thank you," he huffs and pushes the report aside gingerly, glad to be done with it, she supposes. "Now, Ms. Lambert, are you aware of any special arrangements or agreements between Barth-Sanders Industries and Cooper Avery?"

"No."

"There are no agreements or offers outstanding?"

"That wasn't your question."

He sighs deeply and his face begins to flush. "Ms. Lambert, I understand this is uncomfortable for you. But please, just answer the question."

"I am answering your questions."

"Have there been any special offers, agreements, arrangements or inducements made by Barth-Sanders Industries to Cooper Avery in return for his assisting in your company's acquiring control of Thurston Construction?"

"No."

"No?"

"Not as you phrase it."

He stops and thinks, tapping his pen impatiently on the table. "Has Barth-Sanders made any special offers to Cooper Avery relating to its bid to acquire a controlling interest in Thurston Construction?"

"No."

"No offers whatsoever?"

"Your question was whether there were any 'special' offers." She takes some pleasure in raising her fingers to emphasize the quotation marks as he did. A woman in the last row giggles. "Mr. Chasen," she says, tiring of the game and recognizing an opportunity to end it, "why don't we just get to the point. Barth-Sanders has made a public bid to buy a controlling interest in Thurston Construction's stock at sixty-four dollars a share. In addition, it has offered certain financial guarantees to the executives of Thurston. I don't know the specifics of those offers off the top of my head. But I am sure if you contact my assistant in New York, that information will be made available to the grand jury. Suffice to say that yes, if Barth-Sanders acquires Thurston Construction, the officers and major stockholders of Thurston would stand to make a considerable profit. Is that what you wanted to know?"

"Is Cooper Avery among the officers and major stockholders who would make this profit?"

"He is an officer. How many shares of stock he owns, I do not know."

"And what is the nature of the financial guarantees Barth-Sanders has made to Mr. Avery if it acquires Thurston?"

"I don't know."

"You never talked about it?"

"No."

"You weren't involved in putting together the offer?"

"Not the figures, no."

"As general counsel you weren't involved?"

"I worked with many lawyers on the various legal aspects. As to the specifics of the financial incentives, no, I was not involved."

Chasen looks a bit flustered and purses his lips as if trying to think of another question. He asks if any of the grand jurors have any questions and seems relieved when a woman in the last row raises her hand. It is the woman who had giggled a few moments earlier.

"Ms. Lambert, I don't mean to embarrass you"—Sydney smiles that it is all right and the woman smiles in return—"but you know this man Avery real well, I guess, and I'd like to hear what you think, you know, about whether he's the kinda man that could shoot his own wife?"

"One moment." Chasen jumps in. "Ms. Lambert, would you please step outside while I discuss a matter with the grand jury?"

"Am I not allowed to answer that question?"

"If you would step outside for just a moment."

She shakes her head and steps out into the hall, where she rummages through her purse until she finds a pack of cigarettes. Detective Abbot suddenly appears in front of her holding a match.

"Everything okay in there?" he asks.

She ignores the question and his match, retrieving her lighter from her purse. He shrugs and moves away. A few moments later, Chasen sticks his head outside the door and calls, "Ms. Lambert, we're ready."

She drops the cigarette to the tile floor and mashes it with her shoe. She returns to the room only to hear Chasen say, "The grand jury has no further questions for you at this time. You are, however, subject to being recalled should there be other matters we would need to ask you. In the meantime, we would ask that you keep the matters discussed here confidential."

"What do you mean by 'ask'? Are you saying that I am not allowed to speak to anyone about my own testimony?"

"Well, no, it's just that the grand jury is—well, it's just that we like to maintain the confidentiality of our investigation."

"My question is whether or not I am legally prohibited from speaking to anyone about my own testimony."

"Well, no."

"Am I excused?"

"Yes."

"Thank you." She stands, and as she does, she looks to the woman in the back row. "I guess Mr. Chasen doesn't want you to hear it, but the answer to your question is no. I don't think Cooper Avery could ever have shot his own wife."

14 $\mathcal{T}$he night and the rain, black and slick, absorb what little light there is, and the wetness clings to the windshield like an oil the wipers can only smear. In front of the house, a half block away, a Cadillac sits with its lights out. No cloudy gray vapors spill from the exhaust, and so she assumes there is no driver. The night is too cold for anyone to be sitting without the engine and heater running. Christine does not want to come any closer, but she must. She cannot read the license plate from where she is parked. She slips the car into gear and begins to roll forward. Just ease by and then circle the block, she tells herself. It is better to keep moving. The streets here in Guilford have long been emptied of people who have somewhere to go and something to do: in Guilford, people who belong do not sit alone in their cars with the motor running and the lights out on a night that can only be described as miserable.

She is almost upon the Cadillac before she can read the three-letter, three-digit Maryland license plate. She commits it to memory and debates calling it in. She is about to step over the line, and that thought causes her to mistrust everything and everyone. She knows too well how small coincidences can lead to grand disasters.

Relax. You're letting your imagination run away with you. So what if it gets back to Hardiman. You were curious. You were just checking him out. They used to call it initiative.

She picks up the microphone and radios the dispatcher, mumbling her car number but clearly stating the color code for the day.

"Say again?" the dispatcher answers.

"Cruiser one fifty-seven," she says clearly. "Calling for a license check. The code is orange."

"Go ahead, one fifty-seven."

"Roger. Checking the registration on a late-model Cadillac De Ville, black. Maryland tag Papa Mike Echo three zero three."

She turns left and up the hill, feeling the tires struggle a bit for traction as the rain caught in the rapidly falling temperatures begins to coat the street's surface with a slick gel. In the few minutes it takes for the dispatcher to call back, she listens to the distant, crackling voices radioing for and receiving information, or instructions, or just talk, most of it official, some of it not, some of it mixed—like the detectives tracking a trailer truck they think is filled with cartons of untaxed cigarettes, engaged in their coded argument with the backup team about where they will meet for a beer after the bust. To her the sounds are calming: they are the comfortable routine of her world. Just as these houses must be for *them:* all neatly spaced side by side. All a little different, all much the same. Brick or wood or stucco, Dutch colonials or Capes, Victorians or Tudors, bits and pieces of each, they are all the same. Neighbors huddled together. Warm light, like soft yellow eyes, peeks out between barren trees and ice-laden shrubs to empty, blackened streets. Behind the light appear the occasional shadows of movement, the sweep of a drape, the corner of a chair, a lampshade, nothing more. She imagines the smell of their kitchens, the sounds of their children, the feel of their carpets. Cats and dogs and homework. Their world.

She turns left again.

"Cruiser one fifty-seven?"

She stops at the corner and reaches for the microphone. "One fifty-seven."

"One fifty-seven, your Papa Mike Echo three zero three is a 1990 Cadillac registered to Edward, S as in Sam, Thurston, one seven two three Wendover, Baltimore. No outstandings. Over."

She nods to herself and pauses before acknowledging the information and signing off. Another left and she is again heading toward the house. For a moment she is confused, and she slows the car to look around, thinking she must have made a wrong turn. But she quickly realizes that in the short time it has taken her to circle the block, Edward Thurston's Cadillac has left.

The time for second thoughts has passed, and she drives directly to the walk leading to the front of the house and parks. She does not bother with her umbrella but walks quickly to the front door, which is adorned by a small rounded portico whose roof is supported by two narrow columns. She rings the bell and waits.

She hears the click of the lock and the rough sounds of someone struggling to open the large wooden door. There are a couple of short tugs, and the door jerks open. A little girl looks at her, more curious than shy. Christine recognizes Cooper Avery's daughter immediately.

"Hi. My name's Christine Boland. Is your father at home?"

Alice looks skeptical or maybe disturbed. Her eyes seem darker than Christine remembers, a much deeper blue, and she is thinner, almost skinny. Her light blue bibbed overalls hang loosely on her, even over a thick sweater. Alice doesn't answer, but turns from the open door and walks down a center hall and calls out, "Daddy?"

Cooper Avery appears at the end of the hall, walking toward the front door. His eyes squint for a curious moment until he recognizes Christine, and instantly he slows his pace. His clothes surprise her. The rumpled khaki pants and plaid wool shirt soften the hardness of his expression. Alice walks up behind Cooper and leans against him, peeking around him to stare at Christine. Cooper reaches down and gently pats the child's forearm, which hugs his hip. He does not speak.

Neither does Christine. She smiles at the child and looks directly at Cooper, silently offering the suggestion which Cooper takes.

"Sweetheart, why don't you go in and finish fixing us that hot chocolate while I speak to Ms. Boland?"

The child looks at her father and then at Christine, but she does not move.

"It's all right, honey, you go ahead. I'll be right there."

Alice slowly releases her grip on her father and walks down the hall, looking over her shoulder several times. She stops at the end of the hall and crowds against the jamb, staring back at her father and Christine, who still have not spoken to each other.

Christine begins, her voice purposefully quiet. "Mr. Avery, I know that you have absolutely no reason to trust me. But I'm taking a chance on trusting you. I'm here on my own because I believe that you had nothing to do with your wife's murder. But I'm here also to tell you that unless I miss my guess, you will be indicted." She reaches into her purse and takes out a pen and one of her business cards. As she writes on the back of the card, she says, "This obviously is not a good time to talk. This is my telephone number at home. I'm willing to help you if I can, but in order to prove you did not kill your wife, I'm going to need your help. Think it over and give me a call." She hands him the card, and a sudden frown covers his face. Still he says nothing.

Christine turns to leave, but she stops on the edge of the porch, standing in the open, the cold rain flattening her hair against her forehead. She looks back. "Just two things. First, I could probably be fired for this. Second, I'm sure Mr. Layton's a fine corporate lawyer, but today he led you like a lamb to the slaughter. Ask yourself if you'd want a lawyer specializing in traffic cases or divorces restructuring the finances or handling a stock issue for your corporation. Do yourself a favor, Mr. Avery, hire the best criminal lawyer you can find. I suspect you're going to need it."

Avery does not move, does not speak. Confusion fills his eyes, and he looks as if he is about to speak. Christine pauses to give him his opportunity, but he does not take it. She turns and walks to her car. Opening the door, she looks back to the house. Cooper Avery remains in the open doorway, the light and warmth to his back, a cold, black night facing him.

15 "*I'm sorry, Anise, I cannot feel sad. I cannot help thinking that it is a good thing—*"

"*Stop! I cannot believe I am hearing these things from you. If the child heard you.*"

"*It is the child I am thinking of. Tell her, Gagnon. I know you agree with me.*"

M. Gagnon lowered the small coffee cup from his lips, and his face twisted with the discomfort of saying out loud what most were thinking to themselves. "Yes, sad to say, Roland is right." It was the Friday before Bastille Day, and they had all gathered in the apartment above Michaud's produce market, Gagnon and the half-dozen other merchants along this block of the street who had closed their shops just long enough to attend the funeral. "I know it is an awful thing to say, but she may be better off now that her mother is dead."

Mme. Michaud stopped in mid-slice the cutting of the cake she had baked, and she dropped the knife to the table. "I cannot listen to this," she said, moving to a chair, into which she dropped heavily and dabbed a handkerchief to her eyes.

Mme. Watteau, the butcher's wife, moved over and sat on the arm of the chair, taking Mme. Michaud's hand. "Anise, it is not a reflection on the child that Nicole was—well, what she was."

"She was a drunk and a tart," M. Michaud said, almost angrily, "and if you ask me, she was crazy as well. Filling that girl's head with all that nonsense about her father. I don't think Nicole even knew who the father was. No child should spend her life having to make up fantasies because she is ashamed of her own mother."

"Stop it! All of you. What if she were to walk in here and hear you talking like this?"

"I am sorry, Anise," M. Michaud said, "it just makes me angry."

"Well, it does her no good for you to be angry at her mother."

"Where is she, by the way?" Gagnon asked.

Mme. Michaud again dabbed her eyes. "She said she needed to be alone for a while. I think she wanted to go back to the apartment. She'll be along when she's ready."

"Where will she stay?" Mme. Watteau asked. "Has that been settled?"

Mme. Michaud looked to her husband. "Did you talk to her?"

His eyes dropped a bit. "Not yet. I will today—this afternoon—when she comes back."

"Roland, I told you you have to talk to her. She must hear it from you. She will never ask herself. You know how stubborn and proud she is." She turned to Mme. Watteau. "I told her she should stay with us. We have the extra room, and you know she has been like a daughter to us. But she cannot ask. She has to hear it from Roland." She looked toward her husband with a frozen scowl. "But my husband cannot bring himself to deal with a child. He might actually have to admit to her that he wants her to stay, or even worse, admit that he loves her like she was his own."

Michaud said nothing, hiding behind another sip of coffee.

"I was just surprised," said Mme. Watteau, "to hear Father Fagen talking to her about living with the sisters at the convent."

"What?" Mme. Michaud said, alarmed.

"Yes, today, at the gravesite, he was saying that she could not live alone, her being just sixteen and all, and saying that the sisters would take her in and that would be better than an orphanage. I was really surprised, since I thought, like we had talked about, that she'd be with you."

Mme. Michaud's whisper comes like a viperous oath. "That meddlesome bastard!" And then out loud, as much to herself as to the others. "Oh my God! What does she think? Did she say anything to the Father?"

"No, not that I heard."

Mme. Michaud struggled to rise from her chair. She moved directly to her husband and took the coffee cup and saucer from his hands. "You must go to her right away. Now. You must tell her that she will stay

with us. You must tell her that we will not have her going to any convent
or orphanage."

"Anise . . ."

Gagnon interjected. "Surely, she would not take the Father seriously."

"Gagnon's right," Michaud argued. "Besides, you already told her
to come stay with us."

Mme. Michaud's voice turned harsh. "She has not heard it from you.
She does not know whether you want her here or not."

"Anise . . ."

"No! You must go to her now. Gagnon, you go with him. The two
of you. And don't you come back without her. I won't have her thinking
that we would abandon her to the convent. Now go, both of you!"

▬

She stood in the hall, looking back at her room. The two small suitcases
that had not been out of her mother's closet in years were stuffed with
all they could hold and rested by the door. She reached into the closet and
took out the long lined leather coat whose wide fur collar her mother
pulled about her face in winter so that only her eyes and her dark, curly
hair would show. It was hot, even for July, but she slipped the coat on;
it would be easier than carrying it, and in a few months she would
need it.

She looked about the small sitting room and kitchen and wondered
who, if anyone, would claim these few furnishings in payment for debts
that were owed. She walked into her mother's bedroom and satisfied herself
that everything was as clean and as neat as she could make it. She would
leave those who would come no cause for tattled tales: the rooms had all
been swept of their secrets. She checked the large leather pouch that hung
from her shoulder. The letters and photographs were there, tied together
as they had always been with the same red yarn, the bundle now protected
by a thick manila envelope which took up almost a third of the pouch.

She started to back out of the room, but stopped, her eyes focusing
suddenly on a small bottle of her mother's perfume sitting on the top of
the dresser. She walked over and picked up the bottle, opening the top
and slowly passing it beneath her nose. Again and again the scent swept
past her, as her eyes closed and her imagination played scenes of the past
and scenes of the future as if they were one. She opened her eyes slowly
and tipped the bottle against her finger, and as so often she had watched

her mother do, she transferred the scent behind each ear, and to that warm and now sensitive spot between her breasts. She touched the end of her finger to her tongue and wondered that she did not sense its taste. She replaced the top and dropped the bottle into her bag.

The rooms were dark behind the drawn curtains, and for a moment she thought of opening them. But she decided to leave them closed. She did not want to be there when the light first came through the window. There was nothing more to do but leave.

■■■

Only moments before Michaud and Gagnon turned into the alley from the east, she turned the corner at the opposite end, heading west. They did not see her, nor she them, ever again.

PART  Two

16

When he first brought it up on his
tongs, Earl weren't even curious. He almost tossed it back in the water, being all
covered with slime and half-rotted out like
it was. But he didn't. Maybe he thought
he'd just snag it again. Maybe he didn't
think about it one way or 'nother. Worryin' more 'bout his oysters,
prob'ly. Whatever, he just slung it to the back of the boat. He'd
been down to the beds near the mouth of the river. No way to
make a living, tongin'. And one man workin' off a fourteen-foot
skiff can't hardly pull up enough oysters to make it worthwhile. But
what can he do? The bank took his boat. The *Adelina*? Yeah, they
took it. And still what, three weeks to the end of the season? You
know that don't make no sense. Put Earl and three other men outta
work. Now how's a man to make his payments if you take his boat
from him? That's the trouble borrowing money from a bank that
don't know nothin' 'bout the work a man does.

Anyway, so Earl just tossed it in the back of the skiff till he got
however many bushels, and after he sold that he come by to get
some gas and have a beer. He said he was gonna throw it in the
trash can there on the dock. If he'da done that, you know it woulda
been the end of it. Nobody'd ever know. But when he picked the
bag up, I guess 'cause it had some weight to it, and like I said, it
was startin' to rot, he kinda pulled it open and there they was. Well,
you know, there was all this crud all over 'em, but he could see
enough to make him curious. So he took it over to the hose and
washed 'em off, and damn if they weren't there right in front of

him. 'Course, he didn't know what he was lookin' at. You imagine Earl Barkin knowin' bout things like that? But he knew 'nuff to ask, knew they was probably worth more'n them bushels o' oysters.

So anyway, he brought 'em in and asked me. Weren't anybody here but me and Ollie. And Ollie was out of it already. There in the back booth. I swear the man's wearin' me out. Even the regulars're gettin' tired of seeing him drunk and sleepin' back there all the time. I mean I know he's had some hard times but still, 'nuff's enough.

Anyway, so what was I sayin'? Oh, yeah, so anyway Earl brings 'em in here and lays 'em out on the bar and asks what I think. And, Jesus, I'm tellin' ya, they were somethin'. I mean I don't know nothin' 'bout stuff like that neither, but they damn sure looked real to me. So we talked about it awhile. Arguing 'bout what to do. You know, Earl was sayin' he might take 'em up to Bal'mer and have 'em looked at, you know, to see what he might get for 'em. Neither one of us thought nothin' about it at the time. 'Cept I kept tellin' him he oughta call the sheriff 'cause what if they were stolen, and he sold 'em, and then someone thought he was the one who did it. I mean who'd believe he pulled 'em up from an oyster bed, you know? But he kept sayin' that it weren't any business of the sheriff what he found in the water. So we kept arguin' back 'n' forth. Well, not arguin' really. You know, we were talkin' 'bout it. So I said why don't we ask Miz Dahlgren, you know, the lady that has that art shop or whatever down the next block, next to Dawson's? You know she comes down here every day from Bal'mer for that little shop, and all she sells is paintings and stuff. Don't make no sense to me, but what do I know?

Anyway, I went down to get her while Earl watched the bar and so we come back and damn! I mean you shoulda seen her eyes when Earl showed her. Miz Dahlgren? I mean she looked like she was gonna drop over. Right there. Right where I'm pointin'. I mean she said she weren't an expert or nothin' but if she weren't missin' her guess, what Earl found could prob'ly buy this bar and her shop and half a dozen other shops and still have somethin' left over. I thought Earl'd drop his teeth. And alla sudden he weren't too happy that we got this lady in here 'cause then it looked like he didn't have much choice but to call the sheriff. What with this lady knowin' about it. I mean he weren't happy, but Earl knew what he had to do. So we called. And damn if today we don't hear that they think that stuff might've come out the Avery house when that woman was shot and killed. Idn't that somethin'? Anyway, Earl may get somethin' out of it. I guess the lady's father, the one who was killed? The sheriff said that if it turns out the jewels really was hers, he's gonna pay Earl a reward for turnin' 'em in. That's fair.

But you know, you gotta wonder. I mean why would anybody kill a woman like that to steal her jewelry and then just dump it in the river? Ya gotta wonder, don'tja?

■■■

Christine reaches impatiently for the phone. It is Paul Wyzanski, and her voice echoes her disappointment.

If he hears it, he ignores it. He is too excited. His voice is emphatically soft. "Chris, he did it!"

"What?"

"Avery. He did it."

"Did what? What're you talking about? What's happened?"

"The smoking gun we've been looking for? I think we have it. Listen to this. A coupla days ago, some oysterman down in Maryville pulls this old canvas bag out of the water. The thing was hung up on whatever he was using to fish for oysters. Tongs of some kind. Anyway, he pulls up this bag, and inside are all these jewels. He and a coupla his buddies spend the afternoon debating what to do with them, but eventually they call the sheriff's office. Nice to know there's still an honest soul or two around. But anyway, even the sheriff knows this isn't costume stuff and the first thing he thinks about is the Avery murder 'cause of what had been reported stolen, you know, from the insurance list. So he calls us and today he brings the stuff up here and we have Marian Avery's mother come in along with the guy who had done the original insurance appraisal. There's no doubt, Chris. It's Marian Avery's jewelry."

"Jesus."

"That's right!"

"All of it? I mean it matches the insurance inventory?"

"Well, what was recovered matches perfectly. It isn't everything. But it's about two-thirds of the stuff on the list. Worth more than three-fifty to four hundred thousand, the man said, just the stuff they found. The bag was starting to rot, and the rest could have fallen out or been thrown somewhere else. They've got some divers down there looking to see what they can find. But the point is, there's no doubt it's Marian Avery's jewelry."

There is a long pause before Christine says, "This is unbelievable. Where was it found?"

"In an oyster bed out in the bay, 'bout a quarter mile from the mouth of the river."

"How far's that from Avery's house?"

"I don't know, exactly, probably less than a half mile or so."

"Hmmm."

"What's that mean?"

"Nothing. I was just thinking, I don't know, maybe—"

"Chris, c'mon now. Even you gotta admit, no burglar's gonna walk away with that kinda haul and throw it in the river."

"I don't know. It's possible," she says hesitantly.

"What?"

"I mean what if the man is just a thief, not a killer? She interrupts him, he does something stupid and now he's panicked. He's got a murder on his hands, and he knows that kind of jewelry is gonna be on every pawn sheet in the country."

There is a long silence before Wyzanski answers. "Chris, listen to me. I'm talking as a friend now. That's nonsense. I know this may blow your theory about Avery, but don't let your ego get caught in this. Think about it. There was no burglary. You've been saying so right from the beginning. And you were right. This just proves it."

Her sigh is audible, apologetic. "No, I know, you're right. And I admit this doesn't look good for Avery, but still it bothers me."

"What? What bothers you?"

"I don't know, it just seems to me that this is equally consistent with some other motive. Maybe to set Avery up, to make it look like he did it. I just keep coming back to the fact that Avery wouldn't have killed his own wife that way. Not himself. And not with the kids anywhere around. I mean why wouldn't he arrange a car accident, or stage a kidnapping or something? But not that way."

"Not if he had time to plan, I agree. But he didn't. The timing was bad. You know, the stock deal and all that. He had to do it, and he saw an opportunity. And this wasn't a professional hit. I mean a pro wouldn't have any problem finding the right person to fence those stones. He wouldn't toss that kind of money in the river."

Christine moves to the window, cradling the phone between her shoulder and ear and stretching the cord to its full length. Outside, the sun is bright and the air clear and warm. It is one of those early March days when spring steps over winter, and the street is filled with people stretching their lunch long into the afternoon. But she has not taken advantage of the day. She has been by the phone. Waiting.

"Have you told Avery?"

"Not yet. We're waiting to see him in person."

"What do you mean? What're you gonna do?"

"We called him, or actually, his lawyer, Layton. We asked if Avery could come in tomorrow. We just said we had a few questions about what was stolen."

"And he didn't ask for specifics?"

"Oddly enough, he didn't. He just said he'd try to get a hold of Avery and let us know. He didn't seem surprised or even curious."

"Well, I suppose he'd know about it if you've shown the stuff to Marian Avery's mother."

"I don't think so. We asked them not to say anything until we had a chance to show the stuff to Avery."

"Jesus, Paul, are you trying to signal everyone that you think Avery did it?"

"No," he said, but without conviction. "But I don't think it matters what we say or don't say. From the way Mrs. Thurston was acting—Mr. Thurston, too—I'd say they're convinced Avery at least had something to do with it. I mean no one said anything directly, but their attitude showed. If anything, they were pushing us to say what we thought." Paul waits a moment and then says, "Anyway, you're coming in tomorrow, right?"

Christine hesitates and then says, "Yeah, I'll be there."

"It should be interesting."

"Paul?"

"Yeah."

"I'm still not convinced."

"I know," he says, "but admit that you're a little closer than you were ten minutes ago. I'll get you. It may take a while, but I'll get you."

She smiles to herself. "Maybe you will. I suppose if anyone could, it'd be you." She can almost hear his smile as he rings off with, "I'll see you in the morning."

■■■

She has no sense of the time she has spent pacing about her apartment, flipping through the magazines she does not read, turning on the television she does not watch, turning it off, then on again, through the channels, then off again. She shouldn't have gone to Avery. It was a mistake. But maybe not. But if it was a mistake, it was a *big* mistake. It went beyond a matter of poor judgment. She had stepped over the line. With both feet. That is how they would see it. She knew it at the time. But what else could she do?

Her phone rings again. This time it is the call she has been waiting for.

"Sergeant Boland?" he asks. "This is Cooper Avery."

He sounds nervous, almost shy.

"Yes?"

"Ms. Boland, I, ah, I don't know why I'm doing this. Calling you, I mean. But, well, the truth is I just got a call from Phillip Layton, and, well, I've been thinking about what you said the other night, and I . . . I don't know what else to do. I was wondering if we could meet somewhere tonight. To talk. I've already made arrangements for someone to look after my daughter, so I really hope we can do this . . . you know, meet tonight. Would that be possible?"

"Yes."

"Wherever you say."

She tells him where and when and nothing else.

She then calls Alex at the shipyard. It takes a long time for him to come to the phone. Too long. Long enough for an unreasoned and unfocused irritability to come over her. To have to call him at all seems an imposition, and she begins to feel angry that whoever answered the phone did not stay on the line so that she could escape with only a message. When Alex does pick up, she is ready to end their conversation.

"Sweetheart, I haven't got time to explain things, but I can't make it tonight."

"What's going on?"

"It's just work. Look, I'm really rushed—" It's a lie: her meeting

with Cooper Avery is hours away and only a few minutes' walk
from her apartment. "I just don't have the time to go into it all
right now. I'm sorry, I'll give you a call tomorrow."

"Tomorrow?"

"I'm probably going to be late."

"Wait a minute, Chris. What's going on here? What about the
tickets—"

She cuts him off as if she were addressing a fussy child. "Alex,
I don't have time for this. I'll call you tomorrow."

There is a long silence before he says simply, "Sure. Tomorrow,"
and hangs up.

Her chin drops and she lets out a sigh. She regrets cutting him
off. She regrets the tone of her voice. And she resents having those
regrets. She should call him back, but she does not. She has other
things to think about, or so she tells herself. That too is a lie, but
a harmless one, a lie of convenience to get through the next few
hours. She has nothing else to think about. It is clear what she needs
from Cooper Avery. Alex Trigorin is another matter. But that can
wait, for tomorrow or whenever.

■■■

She is late by a few minutes. She has made sure of that by arriving
early and waiting in the shadow of the large brick building with its
tall, arched entrance to the city pier. She is leaning against the wall,
a single figure lost in the background of the tugboat *Grace Moran*
and the people still milling about Fells Point to enjoy the dying
warmth of early evening. She watches Cooper Avery arrive on time
and alone and enter the bar on the first floor of the old hotel across
the street. Whatever doubts or suspicions he might be entertaining
are well concealed by his quick and willful stride. She waits, giving
him time to search for her inside the bar and, not finding her, to
select a table and order something for himself. She is certain that
he will not wait for her before ordering: he would not want to sit
there alone, without even a drink for company.

She is right, she finds, entering the bar and seeing Avery sitting
at a table in the far corner, his back to the wall. A tall drink—
scotch, she suspects—rests on the table in front of him. His fingertips run slowly up and down the sides of the glass, not nervously,
but almost affectionately, the way one might absently stroke a child's

back or scratch a dog's ear. He does not see her until she is almost upon him, and for the briefest instant, he looks startled. He stands to greet her.

"Mr. Avery."

"Thank you for coming," he says, extending his hand to her.

She takes it. Her grip is polite but no more. For Avery it is the same, a gesture, not what you would call a handshake, as if they are both unsure just how familiar they can or should be. He signals the waiter with raised eyebrows and the barest tilt of his head, and the waiter is there almost before she can sit.

"White wine," she says to the waiter.

Avery leans forward ever so slightly, solicitously. "Would you care for something to eat? Dinner?"

Christine shakes her head. "No. Thank you, but I'm fine."

He dismisses the waiter with a nod and then looks a bit lost. He is searching for a place to start.

She knows he is out of his element, understanding neither the rules nor the players. She lets the silence go on until it is clear that he is prepared to mimic her show of confidence. She smiles and cocks her head toward the briefcase sitting on the chair between them. "Is it on?"

"I beg your pardon?"

"The tape recorder. Have you made sure it's on?"

He cannot help blushing, but he disarms her with a shake of his head and a brief smile of his own. "Am I that obvious?"

"Well, it's just a guess. But am I right?" He nods, and her smile widens. "It's your clothes," she says. He is wearing a tweed sport coat, slacks and an open-collared shirt.

"My clothes?"

She nods slowly. "Yes, your clothes. I'd guess that you didn't come here straight from work. Even though you had to leave earlier than normal to make it, you probably went home to change clothes and to see your daughter. You thought maybe you'd put on one of your casual, just-one-of-the-guys outfits, not the thousand-dollar power suit you wore to the office. You wanted this meeting to be a little more personal, less formal. But you brought your briefcase. You see, just one of the guys wouldn't have brought his briefcase to a bar. Also, you put the briefcase on the chair. I assume you're worried that if you put it on the floor like most people would the recorder might not pick up our voices, particularly in a bar like this that can get pretty noisy." She hesitates a moment.

He does not respond, his expression more bemused than offended.

"Am I close?" He nods again. "You should have stopped by Sentry Electronics. They have some very nice equipment that can fit easily in your coat pocket, like here." Her right hand motions to the breast pocket of her blazer, which holds the recorder she turned on just before entering the bar. "They're very thin and compact. You'd never notice it unless you patted someone down. And very sensitive. Even over the noise in here they'd record our conversation very clearly."

Avery reaches over and pulls the briefcase to his lap. He opens it and takes out the recorder, which he turns off and lays on the table. He ejects the microcassette and hands it to Christine. "I'm sorry. I constantly seem to be underestimating you people."

"That's all right. That's what usually gives us an advantage." She waits a moment. "Did Mr. Layton suggest that? The recorder?"

"No. Actually, he doesn't know anything about this meeting, or, for that matter, your coming by the house the other night. I've thought a lot about what you said. I think you're right about him. He did put me in harm's way. In the meeting with Chasen, I mean. Maybe because he has no experience in these matters, maybe because he has his own agenda. I don't know. But that's done. I can't do anything about it now. But I don't understand why you came to me. And as much as I want to believe you—hell, as much as I'm beginning to think I need to believe you—I don't understand why I should. Why you're doing this. *If* you're doing this. If this isn't some other game."

"Mr. Avery—"

"Wait," he says, raising his hand to stop her. "Before we go any further, there's one thing I want to say. I did not kill my wife. I did not have anyone kill her. I did not want her dead or otherwise out of my life. And whatever I can do to prove that to you and your people, whatever test you might come up with, I'll take. Just as long as I can be assured that you're interested in being fair, that you're really looking for the truth and not that you're just looking for bits and pieces of information to fit into some preconceived notion of my guilt. I . . . I don't understand any of this. I don't understand how this could have happened. I mean all you have to do is talk to Sydney Lambert. She'll tell you I was with her that night. I mean, I can understand that you might think she'd lie for me, but if you'd talk to her and with the airline records and all that . . . And, well, if you want me to take a lie detector . . ." He stops himself, suddenly looking very uncomfortable. He takes a sip of his drink before going on. "If you want me to take a lie detector, I will. I mean I understand they're not all that reliable, you know, that the results are subject to interpretation and all that. But I'll do it. If that's what it takes, I'll do it. I'd want to hire my own expert to make sure—"

Christine stops him abruptly. "Mr. Avery, please. I understand you're upset. Maybe even a little panicked right now. But before we go any further you have to understand a few things. First, I'm not even here."

"I beg your pardon?"

"Listen to me. Officially, I'm not even here. No one knows I'm here, and if they did, I'm sure they'd seriously consider taking my badge. Second, I'm not the one you have to convince, and I'm certainly not the one to advise you about taking a polygraph or whatever. My only advice to you on that score is to hire the best criminal lawyer you can find. Third, I'm not here to question you about your affair, or about your relationship with your wife or your business or whatever, except that there might be something in there to help me figure out the motive for your wife's murder. Do you understand?"

He shakes his head slowly, looking even more confused. "No, I don't." He looks away, and his shoulders drop, and for the first time Christine sees in him a hint of defeat. It makes her uncomfortable, as he begins to speak without turning his eyes back toward her. "It may sound stupid to you, but I have no idea what's going on here. Okay, I understand why eyebrows are raised over my having had an affair with Sydney Lambert, and the fact that she is general counsel to the company trying to buy out Thurston. But to think I'd kill my wife over that? No, it doesn't make any sense. Or hurt my son? For what? Money? Hell, if I never worked another day . . ." Again, he stops himself, and he draws a deep breath which puffs his cheeks as he lets it out slowly. "But how do I prove it to you people? How do you prove a negative? I mean I would think the fact that I was with Sydney . . . I mean what does it take? What do you people want?"

"Mr. Avery, when was the last time you spoke to Sydney Lambert?"

"I don't remember. No, that's not true. It was a few weeks, maybe a month, after my wife died. I've tried several times since to call her, including after that meeting with the D.A." He shakes his head, then goes on. "Anyway, she won't take my calls. I can't really blame her. She tried to be kind, I suppose. I mean after my wife and everything."

Christine sits back, curious at the sudden ease of Cooper Avery's conversation. She wonders at the sound of his voice, the almost distant but confiding tone. Sincerity is an elusive commodity in a world of masks, and her intellect and instincts are tugging at her from opposite directions.

"I called her that night, the night I got home and found, you know, that Marian had been murdered. Anyway, I called her that night, and we agreed that we just couldn't see each other. But she called a few times after that and I guess I got angry. Said a few things I regret. I wasn't handling things very well then." He shrugs. "Even now, I suppose. Anyway, I've tried to reach her several times, but like I said, she won't take my calls." He takes a slow sip of his drink and looks directly at Christine. "But she wouldn't lie to protect me. Just call her. She'll tell you the truth."

"We did. An hour after you left Albert Chasen's office, Sydney Lambert testified in the grand jury that she did not see you on that Friday, that you were not with her that night, and that long before that night—a few months I think she said—she had broken off the affair."

Avery's face freezes, and his breathing becomes labored as his reaction sinks into fear. "But that's not true. I was there. I swear to God I was there. I can describe every detail of her bedroom. I can tell you—I can tell you anything you want to know. Jesus! How can this be happening?" Christine is studying him, and he fixes his eyes upon hers and holds the stare for a moment. "I'm telling you the truth."

She nods just once, keeping her eyes on him. "I believe you," she says.

"But you're telling me that doesn't mean anything, aren't you?"

Again she nods.

"And you're telling me I'm going to be indicted, aren't you?"

"Yes."

"But why?"

"Why you're going to be indicted, or why am I telling you?"

"Both."

Christine leans back and twists toward the bar, signaling for the waiter. "I'm suddenly very hungry."

The waiter comes, and Christine waves off the menu, ordering a hamburger, medium rare, with grilled onions and Swiss cheese, a side of fries, and, holding up her empty wine glass, says, "And I'm going to switch to beer. Heineken, please."

Cooper Avery looks perplexed, and he waves his hand back and forth as if that will help him decide. "I'll have the same, I guess, but not beer. I'll have another," he says, holding up his glass. "But make it a double, no soda, lots of ice and a twist. Thanks."

The waiter retreats, and Christine leans forward. "Look, basically, here's the government's case." She outlines the accumulation of circumstances that have led the detectives and the state's attorney, and, she supposes, the grand jury to believe that Cooper Avery murdered his wife. At first, he interrupts her, claiming not to understand the implications of such items as the shards of glass overlaying the muddy footprints. Or he voices his objections to the conclusions drawn. "You mean to tell me they think I reported that old gun stolen and then hid it away for what, a year or more, and then got it out to kill my wife? That's crazy! And there must be thousands of Smith .38s out there. I mean, Jesus!"

But he soon understands that his objections do not matter, that the grand jury is essentially a captive of the prosecutor, that except under rare circumstances, the grand jury will never hear the defense's theories or evidence and will vote only on what the government presents to it. As it all begins to sink in, Cooper Avery settles back in stolid silence, while Christine's words pass over him.

Their meals come, and as the waiter lays the food before them, Christine says, "And of course, today was the final jewel in the crown. No pun intended."

Avery waits for the waiter to withdraw. He then leans forward. "Today? Why, what happened today?"

"Didn't Mr. Layton call you about having to look at some items out at state police headquarters?"

"Yes, he did. He said he didn't know what the police wanted to show me, but he didn't sound all that concerned."

"Mr. Avery, they found quite a bit of the jewelry that was taken the night of your wife's murder."

He sits up, his eyes suddenly wide and hopeful. "But—but that's good, isn't it? I mean, where did they find it? Have they caught someone?"

"No, Mr. Avery, they haven't caught anyone. They found it in the river, or in the bay near the river. Anyway, whoever took the jewels tossed them in the water near your house."

His expression darkens. "I don't understand."

She takes a bite of her hamburger, delicately slipping a loose strand of grilled onion into her mouth with the tip of her little finger. She takes the time to dab her mouth with her napkin and to sip her beer before looking straight at him. "Yes you do," she says. "It means that whoever killed your wife and ransacked your house was not after money or jewels or whatever." She sits back, her stare questioning.

It takes a moment or two before he turns his face away. "I see," he says. "It just confirms their every suspicion, doesn't it. If whoever killed my wife wasn't interested in the jewels or whatever else was taken, then there must have been some other motive. And the gun, and the affair with Sydney and her saying I lied about being with her . . . And the safe, and Ned and the hunting clothes . . . And the stock." He shakes his head slowly and rubs the backs of his fingers on his cheek while his gaze reaches out to some distance beyond them. "My God, they really do think I did it."

Christine continues to study him, but she offers no comment.

He turns back toward her suddenly. "You know, I don't understand this thing about Ellen Haley. I know I didn't call her that morning. But why would she say that? I mean, my phone bills ought to prove I didn't call her."

"Mr. Avery," Christine says quietly.

"I know, I know. That's something I need to deal with with my lawyer. God, I can't believe this."

"Have you hired a lawyer yet?"

"No. I've been making a few inquiries, but it's not easy. I don't want to go through Phil Layton and, well, this is out of my field. I've never had to deal with any kind of criminal matter before. I've gotten a couple of names. A Bill Ramey and I think the other one is a John or Jack Gabriel. Do you know either of them?"

"Yes."

"Would you recommend either of them?"

"Wait a minute. Let's understand something here. I'm not here as part of the defense team. Okay? Let's be real clear about that. I'm not about to recommend anyone."

"Which leads me to the original question, why *are* you doing this?"

She takes another sip of her beer, and waits a long time before answering. "Well, it's not because I believe you're innocent. It's because I think someone else is guilty, if that makes any sense to you."

Cooper's brow furrows slightly. "I'm not sure it does, but I'm not sure either that it matters." He pauses. "Do you think you know who that someone else is?"

"No, I don't. But I think you can tell me, or at least can provide the leads that will tell me."

"Me?"

"Yes, you, or your father or your father-in-law or someone. Look, everything about the scene, the particular way your wife was murdered, it all leads me to believe that the motive behind all this was personal. I don't know, revenge, a vendetta, it could be any number of reasons, but I do think that whoever did this was making a point—with you, with your wife, with your family. The fact that your wife's jewelry was tossed in the river would seem to confirm that."

"And your colleagues believe that proves I did it."

"Yes."

"And you disagree. Why?"

"I don't know. Call it instinct. Does it really matter?"

He nods. "Yes, it does. It matters to me. Look, I understand that I'm in no position to bargain anything here. You're here because you say you're willing to help me, and I've got no right to look a gift horse in the mouth. I understand that. But you must understand how I might be a little gun-shy. I haven't been making the most informed choices lately and—well, you understand. I just want to know why."

She has turned away from him, casting a stare across the room. She is uncomfortable with his confession of need, of weakness. Can't he understand that he is not the issue, that she will not be responsible for him?

Christine turns back to face the man who a few months ago had dismissed her, and who is now looking to her for reassurance. And she is looking to him for the key.

"All right," she says, "I'll tell you this. I saw you with your children that day, the way you were with them. With Alice, and with your son, how you reacted to his condition—and his fear, I guess. I don't think you could have faked that. I believe anyone is capable of murder, Mr. Avery, including you. And given the right set of circumstances you'd even be capable of killing your wife. But I also think that you would never have done it that way. You have the money and the resources and the brains to have accomplished the same thing without it coming that close to your children. That and all the circumstances at the scene convince me that the truth lies somewhere else. That's why."

Christine's eyes narrow, and her expression hardens as she points a finger at him. "But if I'm wrong, and I find that you really did do it, believe me, you will wish you never saw me, never came to meet me here, never spoke to me."

Avery does not flinch. He nods and allows himself a pensive smile. "I believe you. Tell me what I can do."

Christine leans forward. "When I interviewed you at the house, a few days after the funeral, I asked you whether you or your wife had any enemies. You blew the question off. We'll start there."

For the next hour Cooper Avery is drawn into naming names, anyone who may have had some cause to hold a grudge against him or his wife. But it is difficult for Avery, he is so firm in his belief that those people he may have outmaneuvered in a business deal, or even people who were driven out of business by the superior skills and often voracious appetites of Thurston Construction, would think as he thought. Business is competition, and in competition there are winners and losers. It is nothing personal.

Christine asks him to focus on Marian, and she is surprised at the offense she takes to the manner in which he speaks of his deceased wife. Not that Avery intends any insult; no, just the opposite. Christine knows that he means to compliment. That's what offends her. Marian was "sweet." Everyone liked her. She was invited to join and organize and socialize with dozens of social organizations and charities. She was known for her dinner parties, for her skills as a hostess, for making her guests comfortable. Even those things about which she was adamant and could show even a temper—like anyone smoking in her house—he considered "cute." He even used the word. "She was so *cute* the night she took the cigarette right out of the governor's hand and took it to the powder room and flushed it away. I thought my father would kill her. But everyone else took it well, including the governor. He laughed. He really did."

Christine isn't sure what offends her most, Avery's description of his wife or the woman herself. She wonders if Marian Avery could possibly have been as inconsequential as he describes her. She wonders, too, whether the memories are too personal to be accurate. Christine has given little thought to the person of the victim. Like most victims of homicide, she was of little consequence, little more than a name on a report, a case title, a reason for the wheels of justice to start rolling. It is the living, not the dead, around whom, and often over whom, the wheels roll.

"What about your father-in-law?"

Avery describes Edward Thurston much as Christine thinks he might describe himself. Marian's father is consumed, nearly obsessed with his business and his finances. He is political only insofar as politics might help the business. Otherwise, he thinks it beneath him. He is as devoted to his family as he is to the business, and in much the same way. They are objects of love and of pride, as if both are something he accomplished. He can be rigid and unbending once his mind is set, but still he is a fair man and honest, a man to whom it is simply a matter of good business to avoid making enemies.

"Besides," Avery says, "it wouldn't make sense even if someone did have a grudge against Ed Thurston. They'd go after him, not Marian or me."

·Christine shrugs. "Not necessarily. We could be dealing with an entirely different logic. Assume the motive was to strike back at your father-in-law. Wouldn't killing his daughter make some sense? It certainly would inflict a greater and more long-lasting pain, and whatever point the killer wanted to make would be made even more forcefully."

Avery shook his head. "Jesus. And you think that's what we're dealing with?"

"I don't know. Maybe. But whatever, I do believe that we are dealing with a motive no one is looking for. And I believe that motive is either personal to you or your family or is somehow related to your business. I'm starting with your family first because it seems more probable, and second, it presents a smaller universe of possibilities to check out. Plus, the way this murder was carried out—I'm sorry, I don't mean to be so clinical."

"No, that's all right," he says eagerly.

"Anyway, the method here just doesn't compute with a business-related motive. Not to me at least. I'm not eliminating that possibility, I just give it a lower ranking."

He stares at her for a moment, then shakes his head.

She lets the gesture pass. "Now, what about your father?"

Avery lets go a sigh and dismisses his father or anything having to do with him as having any possible connection to Marian's death—or even, if Christine judges the tone of his voice correctly, to Marian's life. He tries to dismiss his father completely, but Christine pushes him.

"Look," Avery says, "I'm neither ashamed nor proud of it, but my father and I have never really gotten along all that well. It's not that we dislike each other, it's just that we're not close. Never have been. I don't agree with his politics or his philosophy, if in fact he could really be said to have one."

"That's a bit harsh, don't you think?"

"Maybe."

"My point, Mr. Avery, is that politics can sometimes get rough, and your father was a congressman for many years. Maybe there's a connection there. I know it sounds remote, but still, it's a possibility."

Avery shakes his head. "No. This may sound unkind, but the truth is my father was too inept to make enemies."

Christine sits back, unable to mask her surprise at Avery's comment. He, having stepped over the line, looks anxious to go on. His father, he says, is a man who trusts equally in divine guidance and public-opinion polls, which to him are much the same. Charles Vinson Avery had spent his first ten years out of college as an FBI agent until late 1952, when he was hired away from the Bureau to be lead investigator for some congressional committee—Avery can't remember which one. Shortly thereafter, Oren Whittaker, the then senior senator from Maryland, hired him as his administrative assistant. When he retired in 1968, and for reasons Avery claims not to understand, the senator pledged his support for his father's congressional aspirations. "Chuck" Avery managed to upset the political machine of Anne Arundel County by running against and defeating Carlton Mayo in the Democratic congressional primary. There had been rumors of Carlton Mayo's involvement with gambling interests and with the manipulation of race-meet dates at several of the state's thoroughbred tracks.

Avery raises his eyebrows and shrugs as he says, "No one ever knew where the rumors of Mayo's involvement—none of which were true, by the way—but no one ever knew where they started. No one cared. All my father had to do to win was to run on a platform of truth and decency. Which really wasn't a platform at all," he says, taking a last sip of his drink and raising his hand for another. "But he didn't need one. Hell, I don't know that anyone does anymore. Every so often the electorate just starts casting about for someone who is just too stupid to screw them over. All they want is an occasional homily, someone to tell them that the government's going to take care of them while guaranteeing peace and a paycheck. But eventually they figure out that incompetence is never outweighed by good intentions. With my father, it took a while. He finally got swamped by the Reagan tide in 'eighty. You must remember that. My father lost in the primary? To a former football player? And by the largest margin ever recorded in the state. Can you imagine that? Unthinkable."

He stops, alert to the almost stunned expression on Christine's face. She remains still and staring, and she wonders who was more embarrassed by the loss, the congressman or his son.

"I'm sorry," Avery says, twisting uncomfortably in his chair. "We just never could see eye to eye. My father was a man who could sit in his office eating a catered lunch paid for by the taxpayers and proceed to tell you how morally depraved you were because you weren't out running a soup kitchen somewhere. And then, as if you'd be insulted if he didn't, he'd ask you for a campaign contribution."

Again, he stops, as if all at once he recalls why the subject of his father has been brought up in the first place. "No, I can't see Marian's death having anything to do with my father or his politics. He really didn't make enemies, he made people feel sorry for him."

An uneasy stillness settles over both until the waiter comes with Avery's scotch and another Heineken, which Christine did not order, but which she does not refuse. She wants to move on.

She reaches around for the large leather bag hanging from the back of her chair, and she rummages through it as she speaks. "I was looking over my notes this afternoon and there was something that caught my eye. I'm trying to remember now." She pulls two spiral notebooks from the bag, each of which has various pages marked with paper clips.

Avery allows himself a slight smile. "Is my whole life in those notebooks?"

She looks up, distracted, almost annoyed that her search has been interrupted. "No, just this investigation. These and a half-dozen other notebooks." She returns to her inspection, flipping quickly through the paper-clipped pages of both until suddenly she says, "Oh, yes, the sympathy notes."

"The what?"

"The sympathy cards. Remember when Detective Wyzanski and I were interviewing you at the house?"

He nods.

"You were going over a pile of sympathy cards and notes and whatever."

"Yes."

"Well, when I was going through this stuff this afternoon I saw that I had made a notation about one of them. I'm looking for it now," she says to herself as she flips through the pages. "I thought it was in here. Anyway, I remember that there was one I think that had you a little confused or whatever. You didn't know who . . . Ah, here it is," she says, and lays the notebook down so that Avery can see what she is referring to. "See here? I wrote down 'Sympathy note from unknown. No return address.' And then I put in quotes, 'From the friends of Martin Lessing.' Do you remember that?"

He shakes his head.

"You said you didn't know who the card was from, you didn't know the name or something?"

"Yes, there were a number of cards from people whose names I didn't know. I had my secretary go through my Rolodex and through Marian's Christmas card list." He looks a bit sheepish and adds, "Marian had my secretary handle the Christmas cards for everyone but family and close friends. But I don't understand. What do these cards have to do with anything?"

"I don't know that they do. But if someone was trying to send a message by killing your wife, I'd guess they'd want you to know it. Maybe it's in the cards. I just remembered that there was this one card that you said you had no idea who it came from, and there was no return address. And then this note. 'From the friends of Martin Lessing.' I mean it strikes me as a pretty strange thing to say in a sympathy card. I mean I had to read it upside down, so I'm not sure I got it right, but still . . ."

"You were reading the cards on the table?"

"As many as I could, absolutely."

"They teach you that in police training?"

"Oh, sure, we get a six-week course in reading upside down." Avery looks mystified, her sarcasm completely lost on him. She shakes her head. "No, Mr. Avery, no one teaches us to read upside down. It's just a trick of the trade. Cops, reporters, lawyers. Anything we can see is fair game. Anyway, back to this card. Do you remember anything about it or any other card or note that might have seemed strange or from someone you never heard of?"

"No. Not really. I know there was at least one, maybe more, but at least one card that we never knew who it was from. That could be it. The name doesn't mean anything to me." His eyes flit back and forth in thought, and he shakes his head as he looks again at the note Christine had written. "Lessing? No, it doesn't ring any bells, but I can check again." He hesitates. "That *is* a little odd, isn't it? 'The friends of Martin Lessing.' "

"You still have a list of who sent you cards?"

"Actually, I have the cards and notes themselves. It gave Alice, my daughter, some comfort to read all those sympathy cards. You know, all the nice things people said about her mother. Even now, every so often, she'll go back and read them again, over and over. She keeps them in a box. All very neatly stacked."

"How is she doing?"

"The doctor—she's in counseling. Just once a week now. Anyway, the doctor says she's doing well. She's strong, a wonderful kid. In some ways, I think she's handled all this better than any of us. She's much quieter, much shyer than she used to be, but the nightmares seem to come less often, and she's been able to make friends at her new school so she's starting to come out a bit."

They fall silent. The specter of Ned hangs over them, and neither seems to want the fact of him to sever this new and very fragile thread between them.

Christine breaks the silence. "I'd like you to go back through your list and the cards themselves. First look for any card from someone you don't know or who wasn't on any Christmas card list or business list or whatever."

"I understand."

"Also, look through them for any strange or inappropriate notes or references. Like this Lessing thing. Start there, for example. Let me know exactly what the note says and if you have any way of telling me who it is. The same with any other out-of-the-ordinary cards. All right?"

"All right."

"Now, let me ask you something else. You recall when Paul—Detective Wyzanski—when he and I interviewed you at the house?"

"Yes."

"You said something about Marian thinking there were times when a stranger might have been in the house. Remember?"

"Yes, but I told you there was nothing to it. It was just that—"

"No, don't answer so quickly. Think about it. How many times did that happen? When? How long before she died?"

"Oh, I don't know. It may have been three, four, maybe five times over the past few years. But as I told you, there was never anything broken or stolen—except that damn pistol. But you have the reports. That gun was stolen from the trunk of my car. I never even told Marian about it. Marian just worried a lot. She let her imagination get the best of her sometimes. Too much TV, I guess."

"But what if she was right? What if there had been someone in your house? What if you were the victim of a stalker?"

"A what?"

"A stalker. Sometimes we run across people who are obsessed.

They'll stalk their victims, sometimes for days or weeks or months before they decide what they're gonna do. Sometimes they'll leave little hints behind, sometimes not, but they're there for a reason. Maybe it's revenge or some other motive that just keeps building until it gets out of control. Something snaps and they'll kill. Maybe it's over something that happened years before. Maybe something connected to you or your family that you've never thought about. That's why you've got to start being much more expansive about your potential enemies list. You've got to be more realistic about the possibility that what was insignificant to you or your wife could have had a significant impact on someone else. I mean, even something like evicting a tenant to build a shopping center or drumming someone out of the Junior League for some gross social infraction."

Avery stiffens, and Christine raises her hands quickly. "I'm sorry, I didn't mean that the way it sounded. But I'm trying to make a point here. You have to think back: consider carefully how something you or Marian or your father or whoever—how someone in your family might have done something that completely changed someone else's life, and not for the better. Again, check out this Martin Lessing thing. It's as good a place as any to start. All right?"

"I understand. At least, I'm beginning to."

"And remember, time is important here. You haven't got much of it."

"Understood. Should I call you at the number you gave me?"

"Yes. If I'm not there, which is most often the case, just leave a message. And remember," she says as she slips her notebooks back into her bag and slides her chair back, "this has to stay just between us. If what I'm doing gets back to my people, I won't be able to help you at all. Understand?"

Avery stands as she rises from her chair. "Ms. Boland, I find myself as much in the dark as to why you're doing this as I was before I got here. And maybe again I'm being the fool, but for whatever reason, I trust you. Thank you."

She smiles, barely. "Don't get comfortable, Mr. Avery. Get to work."

██

Cooper watches her walk through the bar toward the front door. He watches several men watch her passing. He sees what they see, and for an instant he feels a bit taller in their eyes. She conjures up visions of Marian, of Sydney, and of the others, not because of any similarities, but by the very lack of them. This woman is self-contained, attractive in a way that seems to require no effort. Indeed, he thinks, if any effort is made, it seems directed at minimizing the impact of her looks. Her lips may have been glossed, they may not have been. A hint of eye shadow? He does not remember, the eyes themselves having so held his attention: a deep moist brown, steady and expressive, reflecting a stream of thought he could not read. Her fingers were slender and long, unlike her nails, which were neither long nor short but finely rounded and finished with clear polish. Hands that are useful.

He sees himself in her.

He nods to himself, thinking that it went well. No, he doesn't think, he *knows!* Indeed, it went very, very well.

17 *I*t went well, she thinks.

Cooper Avery did not disappoint her. He even amused her, the way his eyes took her measure while he spoke of other things. But he was so obviously unsure of what he was measuring, so obviously in the middle of a game the point of which still eluded him, a game he wanted to play, might even enjoy playing, if only he understood the rules. She had expected as much of him. She had seen it in the meeting in Albert Chasen's office. The businessman, the negotiator, the manipulator, the man in control suddenly struggling for it, and fearing he had lost it.

But he surprised her, too. The way he spoke as if there were no other dimension to his relationship with his father than that of an intimate observer of a public figure. His almost sneering dismissal of him. *"My father was too inept to make enemies."* Christine thinks how much more there must be to the former congressman, and wonders how much more there must be to the relationship between him and his son. She wonders, too, about the bitter seeds the father must have planted, that the son could say as if of a stranger, *"He made people feel sorry for him."* She imagines that for Cooper Avery, hardly anything could be more damning than that people felt sorry for his father. But there was something more. It was the way he said it, as if he implied something unholy, as if his father's ineptitude were simply a shroud under which was hidden some other, darker offense.

But that is another matter. Cooper Avery's relationship with his father is at best a curiosity. It's of no consequence. Like Avery himself. He is not the point. The point is to uncover the truth, to expose it, to prove it, to prove her point. Avery is merely the key needed to open the doors that need opening. She is sure of it.

She turns off Light Street and onto Key Highway heading south, smiling suddenly. It amuses her to think of Cooper Avery smiling to himself, certain that he has turned her to his own purpose. It is a habit with him, she thinks, the need to win: one of those habits affixed to him as a child, like a brand, an invisible but indelible scar. She imagines Avery growing up with the wealth and power and prominence that must have surrounded him, and how he came to wear his advantages as comfortably and with as little thought as he wore an old shirt; how he grew into other people's expectations as if they were his own; what he thought was his rebellion when he took a path different from that of his father, but to the same end, to the world to which he was born; and how he grew up with a father perhaps known less to him than to the public—or perhaps more to him than his father would want the public to know.

She thinks of her own father, and she wonders, if he had lived, whether time or circumstances could ever have led him to so hurt her, so disappoint her that she could have come to look down on him. The vision of him comes suddenly, floating there above the thought, as he was in her favorite photograph, in his uniform with his arm around her mother, his dark, curly hair above a thin face with an almost too cocky smile, and the way her mother looked at him.

Stop it!

She rolls her car's window down quickly and lets the night wash over her. The day's warmth hangs on like a hint of perfume, but still the air is cool enough to give the harbor's scent a certain freshness. Passing along the foot of Federal Hill Park, Christine looks across Rash Field to the marina, now nearly vacant of the sail- and powerboats that in another month will crowd its finger piers, and to the restaurant whose entrance is jammed with people who are about to enjoy—or already have enjoyed—a drink or two with dinner while they look across the harbor to the lights of downtown. She knows it is false, but somehow she cannot help the feeling that they are all without fears, neither troubled by today nor worried about tomorrow, that at least for tonight, for a few hours, their world is clean, their lives simple. They are all content. Some, even, may be in love. And at this moment, she envies them.

The thought passes with the scene, as the highway curves sharply to the right and heads south past the old Baltimore trolley works toward Locust Point and Alex's loft. Quickly, she is off the highway and onto the cobblestone pavement leading to Alex's street. The wheels bounce hard off the rough stones, the shocks exaggerated by absorbers long past their usefulness. Alex had been promising for a month to contact a friend who could replace them for less than half what it would cost at a shop, but somehow he just never gets around to it. She wants to be angry with him, but she cannot. Not tonight.

He's going to be angry. Okay, he's got a right to be. Don't be cute. Not tonight.

Since the opening at Nicky Kane's gallery, since she gave him the watch and they spent Christmas week on the island of Nevis, she has begun to feel Alex's itch for more, his need to pull her closer. It is not that she is opposed so much as that she is unsure, maybe not of him so much as of herself. It doesn't matter. Until she is sure, she needs the distance.

Alex does not make demands, he makes decisions. For him it is not a question of whether she will change or of whether he would ever expect her to. For him, it is a matter of whether he can live with who she is, and how long and how much effort it will take to find out. She wonders if he knows more than she suspects. It's this Avery thing. How can she explain to him the hold it has taken of her? How can she explain the tug-of-war within her? Does she even understand it herself?

Alex seems to understand without question or complaint the demands of her job, the long and irregular hours, the unpredictability. She loves him for that. And she loves her job. It is always there when she needs it, when she needs the excuse to provide the distance, which she so often does, and has over so many years and so many relationships. But she knows that the past few months have tested his limits, and that for the first time in a long time, that matters to her. That, in and of itself, gives her pause.

She turns off the cobblestones onto the smooth pavement of Alex's street, and she slows the car to ponder the mood he will be in and how she will respond to it, how he will respond to her, and suddenly a smile comes over her. Sometimes men can be so easy.

Stop it!

She pulls to the curb in front of Alex's building and notices that the door to the bakery on the first floor is open. It is nearly nine-thirty, long after closing. Two men stand inside next to the counter where the register sits. The only light comes from a dim fluorescent bulb behind the display case and all she can tell of the men in the shadows is that they are standing very still and that suddenly their attention has turned to her. "Shit," she murmurs, and she slips her hand into her purse and around her revolver. "Not tonight."

She looks around for a phone booth but knows there are none on this block. She thinks of Alex's apartment but knows they'll be gone before she can get to his phone. She thinks seriously of just walking away from it. In all her years with the state police, she has only twice pulled her gun in the field, never once fired it, and has never faced a situation alone. She readily concedes her fear. She slides out of the car, which she keeps between her and the open doorway of the bakery. She is about to stretch across the roof of her car and display both her badge and gun when the owner, Mrs. Ferrante, emerges from behind the counter and calls to her. Christine releases her breath and a nervous laugh, and she slides the gun back into her purse. "Mrs. Ferrante," she answers as the old woman comes to the doorway, "I was just about to arrest you. I thought you were all burglars."

The woman laughs and waves her hand at Christine's foolishness. "In this neighborhood? To steal from me what, a piece of bread?"

The old woman is right. This is an ethnic, working-class neighborhood which the wealthier residents of Guilford or Homeland or Roland Park might describe as "lower-income." This is a place of proud people who take care of their own, and where strangers of a criminal bent know they have more to fear from the locals than they do from the police.

"Christina," the old woman calls, "come here a moment. I have something for you."

Christine walks to the doorway, and Mrs. Ferrante's two sons, Ciro, who only recently has stopped trying to proposition her every time she comes by, and Eddie, stand with their hands up, mocking her.

"Ciro!" the mother scolds, "show some respect." She moves

slowly behind the display case and from it takes a small dish of assorted pastries, which she slides into a paper bag and hands to Christine.

"Oh, thank you, Mrs. Ferrante, but I can't—"

"Don't argue with me. Of course you can. With your figure? *Sempre bellissima.*" The old woman tilts her head and raises an eyebrow, and her words come in a soft, lilting tone, while one finger wags slowly at Christine. "Oh, when I was a young girl . . ." She lets the words hang there a moment, and then with a shrug says, "Now, you take those to Alex. Enjoy yourselves. The night is still young. Yes?"

Christine smiles, and she rolls her eyes a bit. "I don't know. I think Alex may be a little upset with me."

Mrs. Ferrante nods once, but with conviction. "Yes, he is. But let him pout. It is good for them once in a while." She then laughs, again raising a wagging finger at Christine. "I know you have your ways. And the *dolci.* He will not be able to resist. Now go!"

They exchange goodbyes, and Christine promises that in the morning she will stop by for *caffè latte* and a chat. She watches the two sons escort their mother to the old gray Cadillac waiting at the corner before turning to the second doorway.

By the time she reaches the fourth floor and Alex's apartment, she has set her expression for him. She does not use her key, but knocks.

He does not look surprised, but his voice is uncompromising. "Did you forget your key?"

She winces slightly, as if from embarrassment. Music is playing in the background, loudly. Alex's moods show as much in the volume as in the variable styles of his music. Tonight it is some country song, the kind to which she rarely listens. But she does now, for a moment. Something about a bus stop in Texas?

"No, I just thought you might . . . I don't know, I just thought I should knock." He does not move away from the door. "Can I come in?" she asks softly. "I have an offering from Mrs. Ferrante. She told me you were angry."

He stares at her for a moment before moving to the stereo, which he turns off. She steps inside, and he turns back to her. "You needed Mrs. Ferrante to tell you that?"

"Look, I'm sorry. I really am. I just didn't have time to explain things. It was an emergency. I had a problem with work, you know. It doesn't matter. I know I was rude. I just didn't have time to go into things."

She moves closer to kiss him, but he stiffens and Christine stops herself. "I thought you weren't gonna make it tonight," he says. "You were gonna be late or whatever."

"I am late. Just not as late as I thought."

Alex turns and walks back toward the long bench, where he has been molding a mound of clay into something as yet formless and undefined. Christine marvels at what so often evolves from such strange beginnings. What Alex's mind envisions appears slowly, and in small increments; a full figure might start with the tip of an elbow, as if he wants to keep her guessing. He will not talk of them or of what they may become, like an expectant parent who when asked whether he prefers a boy or a girl will answer only that he wants the child to be healthy. For weeks—for he always has a half-dozen or more pieces in progress; some he views seriously, some not, and all take days, sometimes weeks, sometimes months, to complete— she will watch these smoothed, half-formed appendages emerge bit by bit, like some creature struggling with its birth, slowly stretching to break the bonds of its gnarled earthen egg. And then, suddenly, she will see it, and it will capture her, and she will wonder at it and at him and how he could have drawn such beauty from such a formless mass.

"Alex, listen, please, I know the past couple of months have been—"

"Not tonight, all right?"

She moves over and sits on the arm of the couch and takes a moment, watching him concentrate on the unformed clay. She speaks softly. "Can't we talk about it?"

He does not look back, and his voice remains even and uninvolved. "We have talked about it, over and over, but it doesn't change anything. What's the point?"

She nods to herself. "I know, you're right." She takes a deep breath. "Do you want me to leave?"

His hands stop working the clay, and he looks at her a long time before answering. "I don't know. I wish I could say yes and mean it."

She dips her chin to hide the sudden hint of a smile. "Do you mind if I stay?"

"I tried to reach you at the office, around five."

Christine raises her head quickly. "Oh?"

"No one seemed to know where you were. They said it was your day off."

She does not react.

"Somebody finally put me in touch with Paul Wyzanski. I got the impression they thought if anyone would know how to reach you, he would."

"I suppose that's right."

"He seemed a little puzzled when I told him you had said you had an emergency at work. He was very pleasant, though. Almost chatty."

"He knows who you are."

"He said he wasn't sure what you were working on, but he'd try to get a message to you. I take it you didn't get it."

"No, I didn't."

She watches his eyes watch his hands working the clay. Large, strong hands making short, rough movements with a sculpting blade. His face is passive but for his eyes, which squint and widen and narrow again as they follow his hands, focusing and refocusing on what only he can see. If she did not know him better, he'd look as if he were actually concentrating on his work.

"Look, why don't you just ask me whatever it is you want to know?" Her voice carries the rough edges of impatience.

He turns toward her. "I don't want to ask you anything. I never have. I've never asked you where you go or what you do. And I've never asked you to account to me. Not once."

"I'm sorry, I'm not trying to challenge you. I guess I just don't understand why suddenly tonight you're so upset."

"It's not just tonight. It's everything. I don't know what's been going on with you, but—"

"Nothing's going on. I was working. It's this Avery case. It's—"

"No, just listen to me for a minute. We're not joined at the hip here. You come and go as you please. But tonight was your idea, remember? It was you who asked me to change my plans, remember? It was you who asked me—'cause you were too busy—it was you who asked me to take my lunch hour to go buy the tickets to a play you wanted to see, remember? I can understand an emergency coming up, and I'm not questioning it. I've never questioned it. But yeah, it pisses me off to be treated as if I'm some goddamn stone around your neck. Like it was such a burden for you to call to cancel the plans that you made. It's not just tonight. And it's not this Avery case, either. It started before that. These moods of yours. I don't know, they take you over, and when they do it's like you don't even know there's anyone else around."

She looks up to see him studying her, and she drops her eyes again.

"You pull away. You just disappear. And then suddenly, you resurface and wonder what all the fuss is about. It's not like you, Chris. It's just not like you."

She speaks without looking up. "Are you sure?"

Alex reaches for a rag and carefully wipes the blade clean. He then leans back against the edge of the workbench and wipes his hands with the same rag. He, too, speaks without looking up. "Quit playing word games with me. I'm not one of your witnesses or snitches or suspects or whatever."

"I'm not playing games," she says, sliding from the sofa's arm to curl more comfortably on its cushions. "I'm just wondering what makes you so certain what I should be like."

Alex straightens up a bit, still leaning against the bench, and folds his arms across his chest. He reminds her suddenly of a teacher she once had and of the crush she thought she would never get over, until she did a week or two later. "You're right," he says with a crisp nod. "Why should I know anything about you? We've only been seeing each other, what? Almost a year and a half? How could I possibly know anything about you? Why should I have any expectations?"

"That's not what I meant. I . . ." Her voice trails off with the slight shake of her head.

"What? What did you mean? Or am I supposed to guess at that too? Or maybe I'm not even supposed to guess. That's the object of the game, isn't it? Don't ask questions, don't draw inferences or make any assumptions, have no expectations. Is that it?"

Christine winces.

"That's really what you love about your job, isn't it? You're the only one who gets to ask questions. No one gets to ask you anything.

And these people you deal with. You don't really have to deal with them, do you? *They* have to deal with *you,* and you get to walk away whenever you want. You get to choose when and if and how much or how close. Right? And you get to poke around in their lives and investigate them and analyze them and sometimes even play with them, play with their minds, like a kitten batting some helpless bug around before it decides whether to eat it or not. But they can't touch you, can they? They can't ever know you."

Christine's expression is fixed, as are her eyes upon him. She is all at once very, very tired. *Not now. Not tonight.*

Alex pauses, and his voice turns quiet. "Am I getting too close?"

Again, she lowers her eyes.

"That's what's happened to us, hasn't it. Everything was fine as long as we both went along pretending that none of it really mattered. We could walk away anytime we wanted. We were someone to eat dinner with. Sleep with. Play with. And then I screwed up and started acting as if I thought this might have been something more than an extended weekend fling. Imagine it. I actually started talking to you as if I expected you to be there when I woke up in the morning. And even worse, I asked questions as if I might give a damn about the answers, as if I really wanted to know something about you. I mean what was I thinking? How fucking presumptuous of me."

Christine looks up and speaks in a troubled, nearly inaudible voice. "Please stop."

It takes a moment before he shakes his head, and he slips his hands into his trouser pockets as if he is putting away his anger, as if he recognizes that his complaints are futile. "I don't know, Chris, you're just wearing me out."

Christine stands and moves slowly across the room to lean against him, folding her arms around his waist and resting her head on his chest. "Have I really been that awful?"

He strains to lean back and raises his chin to peer down over his nose. He closes his arms around her, and she can feel herself let go. The tension, like an old injury she has learned to ignore, seems more acute now that she can feel it easing.

"Yes," he says with a puff of breath that tickles her hair.

"I'm sorry." They stand there holding one another for several moments before she looks up at him like a chastened child who knows she has already been forgiven. "Does that mean I'll have to be punished?"

"Yes."

She hugs him closer. "Can I have my chocolate-covered cannoli first?"

"No."

"Ooo, you are angry. I'll share?"

He nods with a relenting smile, and she leads him across the room to the bed, snatching up Mrs. Ferrante's bag of pastries on the way. She sits on the bed and draws her feet under her while she opens the bag and inspects its offerings. Alex lies back against the pillows and watches her pull a cannoli from the bag and hold it up with an impish grin. But she quickly loses interest in the pastry, and she frowns, her eyes turning pained and uncertain. She returns his stare and says, "I'm sorry, Alex. I really am. You're right in a lot of ways. Maybe it's been too many years of too many extended weekends. And maybe it does scare me a little to think of it being more than that, to think that I might want it or need it to be more than that. But—but I'm glad you want me to be here when you wake up in the morning."

Alex remains still while his eyes signal curiosity, as if he wonders how she could have any doubt. "Christine, I'm in love with you."

She looks down shyly. "I know." A brief shiver passes over her. "You know, sometimes you make it too easy for me."

He nods his agreement. "I'll try to make it harder from now on."

"And I'll try to make it easier."

■■

It is nearly four in the morning, and Christine is sitting on the edge of the bed, her arms hugging a pillow, her stare carrying out the window and over the rooftops, across the harbor to the few lights of the city that backlight a dark mist over the water. She can hear the heavy rhythmic breathing of Alex's sleep being interrupted, and she feels the brief tremors of the bed as he rolls awake. She does not need to look to see his eyes strain open to no more than a squint, and his fingers out of habit scratch the stubble on his cheek for an itch that may or may not be there. She speaks softly so as not to wake him if she is wrong. "Are you awake?"

His voice is thick with sleep, his words sounding like a swollen tongue. " 'S'matter? Y'awright?"

"I don't know. Can we talk?"

It takes a few moments for Alex to awaken to the task, but he does, signaling his attention by sliding over to gently massage her neck and shoulders.

"Tonight. I, ah—I was with Cooper Avery."

His fingers hesitate at the base of her neck, but only for a second. He says nothing and waits.

Her words come in a slow, even stream, her control emphasizing her concern, sparing the details but fleshing out the context, her context. She describes the meeting in the state's attorney's office, the blind predisposition to indict Avery, the reshaping of facts to fit the theory, the theories like random flakes of snow that are massaged and compacted and shaped into what is assumed to be a cold, hard fact; how she felt compelled to go to Avery's house, to warn him, to offer her help. And then, Marian Avery's jewelry turning up in the river near Avery's house, the call from Paul Wyzanski. The call from Avery.

"That's when I called you. I'm sorry I blew you off. I didn't mean it." She laughs a soft, sour laugh. "That's not true. I did mean it. But not that way. Not you. I was just on edge. Avery's call right after Paul telling me about the jewelry."

"It's okay," he says simply, still massaging, responding to the occasional twist and roll she makes with her back and shoulders to offer the sore spots to his touch.

She turns toward him for the first time. "I told Avery virtually everything. All about our case. What we think, what we found. I even told him what Sydney Lambert, you know, his mistress—or ex-mistress, or whatever—I told him what she said in the grand jury."

"Watch your eyes," he says as he reaches over to turn on the lamp on the bedside table, then arranges the pillows, which he settles against like an old dog arranging his bed. She is constantly reminded of how physical a man Alex is, even in small ways, how much his thoughts seemed geared to his movements, as if to excite one is to excite the other; how much his intellect and his art both stimulate and feed on his need to touch and to feel, to see and to hear, the music he'll play too loud, the lights he'll level to his mood.

He reaches for the water glass he keeps by the bed and takes a sip, then rolls the glass between the palms of his hands while he says, "I'm not sure I understand all of this, or even if I'm equipped to understand it, but why are you so fixated on this case? I mean I've never seen you bring your work home like you have this one. I know I haven't been around to watch your career or anything, but this, I don't know, this one seems to have more of a hold over you than you have over it. You know what I mean?"

She frowns. "Maybe you're right. I haven't really thought about it that way."

"Why? What is it about this case?"

"I'm not sure I know. Maybe it's been all these years watching the system and all the people in it just grind along. You know, where the ultimate goal is to close the case, and however the case is closed, that's the end of it. And you accept that because you have no choice. I mean, who ever really knows what happened and why unless they were there? The only truth is what's wrapped in some neat little package of evidence. Not facts, but evidence. And once it's wrapped, it's forgotten. Am I making any sense?"

"Yeah. At least I think so. But are you just tired of the system, the job and all that comes with it, or is there something about this case?"

"I don't know." She looks away a moment, again staring out the window.

"Are you afraid you've made a mistake, you know, with Avery?"

She turns back. "A mistake?"

"Yeah. Are you afraid that you're wrong, that he really might have done it?"

She takes some time before answering. "No. I'm certain he didn't do it."

"Do you think what you've done so far is right? I don't mean following the rules. I mean, do you think you've done the right thing so far? For the right reasons?"

Again, she takes some time. "Yes."

"Have you done anything illegal?"

She does not answer him.

Again he asks, "Christine, have you done anything that's actually illegal?"

"No. Well, the grand jury thing's kind of touchy. You know,

revealing what went on before the grand jury. But I never quoted anything to Avery. Hell, I really don't know what the woman said in the grand jury. I only know what she said she would say."

"So the worst we're talking about is maybe losing your job over something you believe in?"

Christine does not answer.

"Well, babe, I've never been much of a believer in moral stands. They usually turn out to be so heavily infected with personal interest." He reaches over and takes her hand. "But you've never impressed me as someone who'd go over the edge on some personal crusade. I think you've got to trust your instincts here. I know that doesn't help much, but I'm not in your shoes. I can't judge the alternatives. I can only tell you that I'll be here with a warm bed and a hot meal and a promise that they'll never take us alive."

She lets go a laugh as she blinks at the moisture in her eyes and collapses against him. "Promise?"

"I promise."

18 *H*ans Grassl crossed the Marienplatz and turned up the street toward the soaring gray tower of "Old Peter." But Hans had neither time for nor interest in Munich's oldest parish church, or in its history, which stretched back to the eleventh century. His concern was for the future, and at that moment the future meant only the next few hours, which were closing in on him with an urgency that shortened his breath and lengthened his stride.

Past the church he turned down the alley toward the Viktualienmarkt, where nearly every evening on the way home from his civil servant's desk at city hall he would stop at one of the open-air food stalls for something that would serve as dinner. But food was the last thing on his mind, and the thick and inviting mix of aromas escaped his attention entirely as he hurried past the stalls to the florist shop to buy a single large bouquet of flowers. He had given the matter considerable thought. It was better that he buy just one bouquet. He would give her the flowers before his parents arrived, as atonement for his sins. That would please her, he hoped, calm her, at least for the evening. And she would put the flowers in a vase and put the vase in the center of the table, and his parents would be pleased that she had made an effort in honor of their visit.

Hans had felt caught between them ever since he had returned from Strasbourg. It had been almost a year, and he had spent it first trying to keep his parents and her apart, then trying to get them together, and always, it seemed, at cross-purposes. In less than an hour, they were to meet for the first time.

Hans was the youngest of four sons: a mistake, he suspected, being nearly twelve years younger than Willy, the third son, who was two years younger than Peter, who was two years younger than Ernst. Hans's father, an engineer-businessman-politician, disliked surprises, which none of his first three sons had given him. Ernst, the engineer, now ran the family's international electronics firm. Peter was an oncologist in Stuttgart and Willy a lawyer in Bonn with a hunger for politics. Hans, now twenty-three, had found university life boring and dropped out long before he was even within sight of a degree. And for the last four years he had bounced from place to place and from job to job while his parents kept telling themselves that it was just a phase he was going through.

But there were limits to his father's patience and understanding. It had taken some effort—even for a man of Herr Grassl's reputation and influence—to secure for Hans a clerk's position at the Council of Europe's headquarters in Strasbourg. It was a minor position to be sure, but one that could have led somewhere, even for someone without a university degree. But Hans had found more interesting Strasbourg's café life, when he could afford it, and when he couldn't, the groups of young people who gathered in garrets in the old quarter of the city, sharing their dope and the latest slogans of their radical politics. He had been there only ten months before he resigned as a favor to his father—although his father would never know it—Hans having been told it would be embarrassing to all concerned if they had to fire him, which they were prepared to do.

It had not upset him. Strasbourg, too, had begun to bore him, and he had looked forward to his return to Munich. At the time, he supposed, his only regret was the prospect of leaving her: but his regret was not so strong that he ever thought seriously of asking her to come with him, not that she would have done so had he asked, or so he thought. But then, nothing with her was ever certain.

He had seen her first among a group of young people gathered in a corner of a small café to debate one of the more popular subjects of the day: America as the evil empire. The group's discussion had focused on the assassination of Martin Luther King, Jr., which had occurred only a few days before, and the political resurgence of Richard Nixon, as if the two events were related. There were eight or ten people joined in the debate, only a few of whom Hans knew. He ordered a beer and took a chair on the periphery.

He had noticed her immediately. She was younger than the others, or so she looked, sitting quietly and appearing more a spectator than a part of the debate. The talk flew in bits and pieces, mostly in French, some in German, and all of it heated by exaggerated tones and emphatic gestures. He had barely caught the gist of the argument when someone in the corner made a comment he could not hear. The group fell silent for a moment until this young girl spoke up in a quiet voice, speaking German far better than his French, and associating Nixon with someone named Whittaker Chambers. Someone asked "Who?" while someone else dismissed Whittaker Chambers as ancient history, and someone else dismissed all history as irrelevant, and someone else made some comment in English that sounded derisive—Hans couldn't be sure, his command of English being little better than the typical English tourist's command of German. But the last comment, whatever it was, took effect like no other. This young girl turned on the speaker with English of her own, and her words flowed in a venomous stream that stunned her attacker, and the group as well. He did not know why, but he had half expected the girl to rise and leave, such was the sudden and silent discomfort that had fallen over everyone, and particularly the young man who had drawn the attack. But she did not rise and she did not leave. She held her ground, sitting still and defiant until the man apologized, after which the girl allowed herself a brief smile, and someone made a joke, and the group's conversation rolled back across the Atlantic to more familiar ground.

Hans asked his friends about her. They knew nothing. He asked them to ask their friends, but that proved fruitless. It was a week or two later when he saw her again, at a friend's loft where some of the same café crowd had gathered. He introduced himself in German, and she responded with silence as if she did not understand. She asked him to speak French, shaking her head to mean that she understood no German. He tested her by trying a few halting phrases in English, and again she acted as if she did not understand. He was irritated. He was fascinated.

They talked and drank wine and smoked marijuana until his mind was numbed by a conversation he no longer heard, and his eyes burned, and he found trouble focusing in a room swirling with the unsteady, liquid light of too many candles. He had no recollection of their conversation and very little of their walk home: but she was there when he opened the door to his single room with a washbasin, a small icebox and hot plate, and a bath down the hall which he shared with two students. He recalled that he had offered her wine but not whether she had accepted. The rest of the night was lost to him but for a vivid and perhaps exaggerated memory of the moments inside her, and of her moving against him, and of her digging her fingers into the small of his back, and of the warmth of her breath against his neck, and of the sweet, heavy scent of smoke and sweat and wine and perfume.

It must have been morning, he wasn't sure since it was still dark, but he did remember waking in time to see her at the door, about to leave. "Wait, please, I want to see you again."

"Meet me tonight. Around nine. Pied du Cochon," was all she had said.

He spent the entire day asking everyone he thought might know her what her name was so that neither would be embarrassed when they met that night. They did meet, and neither was embarrassed. And so they met again the next night, and the next, and nearly every night for the next two months.

She was twenty, she said, and he believed her, the way she spoke, the way she carried herself, the maturity of her body and the way she used it, and used him. But still, there were those times when he'd first see her across the street and he'd rush to meet her, or when she'd run ahead of him across the park, or when she'd sit quietly, focused entirely upon some book she was reading—she was always reading—there were those times when he would see a little girl. But it would only be for a moment, until he'd get close, until he could see her eyes. She did not have the eyes of a little girl.

He told her things that surprised him, about himself, about his family. He even told her once that he loved her. It had been only the second or third time that they had been together, after they had made love and he was lying beside her, watching her as she looked away, staring out the window to an empty night. He did not know why he said it. He just did. She laughed at him, suddenly, almost mockingly, and he felt foolish and blushed deeply. But he supposed that she was right. He really had not meant it.

She did not like to talk about herself, and she would become annoyed almost to the point of anger when he asked too many questions. She lived with her parents, she said, in a separate set of rooms on the third floor of their house. But he could not meet her there or call her. It was her parents. Both her mother and father had been in the resistance during the war and had suffered in ways they still would not talk about. Nearly a quarter century since the end of the war and still they viewed all Germans with suspicion, if not open contempt. She made no apology for them. It was simply that they would not understand how she felt, which she never did make clear.

And so when they met, it was at the cafés or at a friend's apartment or at his room, where they would spend a long but never a full night. He never once awoke to find her there, never once saw her asleep in the light of a new morning, and she would not allow him to ask why.

When the ax fell on his job, he recalled feeling almost relieved. His two months with her had exhausted both his reserves of energy and what little money he had managed to save. Except for finding an excuse his father would accept, he looked forward to his return to Munich. But, of course, there was the problem of telling her. He imagined a painful, tearful scene, promises to write, promises to visit. It never happened.

She showed no surprise, and she showed no tears; neither did she show any bitterness or anger. She simply said that she understood, and she wished him well. She smiled and said that she knew he felt compelled to say that he would write and that they would see each other again. He felt challenged and all the more intent on fulfilling what had started out as the empty promises she had so clearly recognized.

He did write, within a few days after returning to Munich and settling into a two-room apartment over a jewelry shop only a few blocks from the Viktualienmarkt. He asked her to come for a weekend. She did not write back, which disappointed but did not surprise him. What did surprise him—indeed, unsettled him—was her appearing at his door unannounced late one night in the middle of July. There she was, standing in the thick heat of the hallway, perspiration streaking her face, two bags resting at her feet, a large leather pouch slung over one shoulder, a long leather coat slung over one arm.

"I was supposed to meet some friends at the train station," she said. "I don't know what happened. I waited for hours but they never showed up. They told me I could stay with them, but I don't know where they are. Could I just stay the night? I'm sure I'll find them in the morning."

Somehow Hans knew that her friends had never existed, but he said nothing. And so she had stayed the night and every night since. It had been almost a year, and she had never been a bother. In fact, once he stopped worrying about what it all meant—a question she would not answer anyway, but for an impatient roll of her eyes—he found the arrangement entirely to his liking.

Her command of English served her well. She quickly found a secretarial job in the registrar's office at the Munich campus of the Uni-

versity of Maryland, which catered to American soldiers and to the children of American diplomats and servicemen throughout Europe. She shared in the rent equally and made few if any demands upon him. She never once complained when he spent time with his friends without her. If anything, it bothered him that she did not. She allowed him more freedom than he needed, perhaps even more than he wanted, and she made it clear that she expected the same freedom in return. Nor did she complain or even hint that she took offense when for months it was obvious that he had not acknowledged her existence to his parents. It was when he did that their problems began.

It had been almost six months since he had gone alone for Sunday dinner at the villa to which his parents had retired along the northeast shore of the Starnberger See, a twelve-mile-long lake south of Munich that had once been the playground of Bavaria's aristocracy. It had taken no time at all for his parents' questions to start. Why had he not come to see them? Why did he always make some excuse when they came to town? Why did he not want them to see where he lived? And so, finally, he told them about her. They were not surprised, which surprised him. His mother said that she wanted to meet her. His father said he wanted to meet the first thing he could remember Hans had ever taken seriously.

When he told her this she fell silent. She did not refuse, she simply avoided the issue, time after time. His mother wrote a note personally inviting her to visit them at the lake. She did not respond, and Hans made some excuse for her. But finally, ten days ago, it had been arranged. Tonight his parents were coming to town. They would meet at the apartment for a glass of wine before going to dinner. Herr Grassl had reserved a table at the Spatenhaus overlooking the royal palace and opera house.

She had been on edge all week, as had he. She had become angry both times he had asked her if she was going to buy a new dress for the dinner, and even angrier when he had offered to pay for one himself. Last night he had crossed the line. He had not let her finish eating dinner before he started complaining about the condition of the apartment and began cleaning around her. She left her food and stalked out, not saying where she was going.

It was late, around midnight, as he was finishing up and hanging her robe in her closet, when he noticed a box about the size of a large dictionary in the corner, under several pairs of shoes. He leaned down and lifted the lid to see inside a manila envelope, and inside the envelope *a collection of papers and smaller envelopes all tied together with several turns of red yarn. He could not resist.*

The papers were old and many were discolored, their creases worn as if they had been folded and unfolded over and over again. They were letters, mostly, and for the most part in English, although some were in French. The handwriting was small and hurried and hard to read, but he could recognize many of them as love letters addressed to a woman named Nicole. The French seemed written in a florid, highly descriptive prose that was beyond his vocabulary, and the English, but for a few words here and there, escaped him completely. There were also papers typed in English, and some newspaper articles that had each been carefully pressed between sheets of bond stationery. There were several small envelopes, which he opened just wide enough to see that they contained old black-and-white photographs; but he got no further before he heard her come through the door.

She froze at the sight of him sitting on the edge of the bed, the letters and papers spread on his lap and on the bed beside him. He tried to apologize, over and over again, but she would not, perhaps could not, speak. She stood rigid and shaking, her hands clenched in tight white fists pressed against her temples. Her breath seemed caught in her throat until she released it in a whisper of rage. "How could you?"

Hans couldn't remember all that he had said or tried to say in the short time it took her to gather up the papers and the yarn and place them back in the manila envelope. It was all she took when she left. She did not say where she was going, and she was not there when he awoke that morning. He had called her office twice, but both times he was told she was away from her desk. He left her messages. She did not return his calls. His only hope was that he would have time to talk to her, to soothe her, before his parents arrived. He would promise her anything to get through this night.

Hans paid for the bouquet of flowers and turned toward home, quickening his pace to a run for the last two blocks. He took the stairs to his apartment two at a time and rushed through the door completely out of breath. The apartment was quiet. He took a moment to look about the room before calling her name.

"Marielle?"

There was no answer, and he could feel everything beginning to close in on him. The sitting room looked different. He could not tell why at first. Nothing was out of place. It just looked different. He carefully laid the flowers on the table and walked slowly to the bedroom. It was there that he suddenly recognized the difference. Everything had been cleaned. Not just picked up and dusted as he had done. The rooms had been scrubbed clean. Even the wood molding around the closet doors looked shined and smelled of fresh oil. He opened the door to her closet. That, too, had been cleaned. Not a cobweb anywhere, not a trace of dust on the floor, not a blouse, not a dress, not a coat or a pair of shoes.

She was gone.

19 From the inner harbor, around which Baltimore's renaissance can be seen in the sharp-angled steel and glass buildings that have no need for addresses beyond the names they have been given—like the World Trade Center or the Gallery or the Aquarium—Calvert Street climbs an easy grade until it crests at the Battle Monument, which separates the city and federal courthouses. From here, and to the north, there remains the old Baltimore, the Baltimore of buildings whose names, if they ever had any, have been wiped from the memories of all but the leasing agents, and whose renovations sometimes mask but can never quite erase the scents and sounds and sights of their age: the fresh paints and varnishes that cover old wood, the waxed tiles and sheets of linoleum that echo the voices and footsteps of people who pass in the halls unseen, and the ceilings high enough to have once cooled the buildings when only fans conditioned the air. The law offices of Gabriel, King & Paretti occupy the southern half of the tenth floor in just such a building.

Jack Gabriel likes it here, and even though his partners occasionally lobby to move to one of the new and more upscale addresses, he doubts that they ever will. What's the point? he argues. There is no one left to impress. The partners all agree that they don't want to expand the firm much beyond the current roster of twenty-two lawyers equally divided between partners and associates, and that their primary concern over the past five or six years has not been finding clients, but deciding which among the many who seek their services to accept. And even though he has never met Cooper Avery, whose arrival his secretary has just announced over the intercom, Jack Gabriel is inclined to believe that this is one client he might turn away. As he does every year at this time, just before the spring that never comes too early for him, Jack Gabriel is thinking he needs a rest.

"He's early," he grumbles, as if Vivian, who has been with him for almost eleven years now, would not otherwise have known that. "How 'bout getting him a cup of coffee or whatever. I'll be with him in a few minutes."

Gabriel presses back in the thickly padded black leather chair he had specially designed and constructed to accommodate the pain from a lower-back injury he suffered while marlin fishing last year. He is going again this year, or so his appointment calendar says, to the little fishing village and resort on the west coast of Costa Rica where for some time he and three friends have been gathering each spring to drink and to fish and to tell tales of their past and future adventures, as if it had not been thirty years since they had graduated from college and the course of their lives had not yet been cut in stone. He will not fish this year, his back won't allow it, but he will spend his days lounging on the deck of the boat and his nights lounging in some small restaurant or bar where the proprietor will pretend to remember him from last year and the year before that and the year before that. And some nights he will spend quietly on the veranda of the hotel overlooking the Pacific until it is late enough to be certain his wife is home and in bed. He will call, and she will tell him about her day, and he will tell her about his, just as they do when they aren't two thousand miles apart.

He takes the file of newspaper clippings one of his associates compiled after Avery called to make an appointment and slips it into his desk drawer. He has read each of the articles carefully, and he suspects that Cooper Avery is about to be charged with the murder of his wife. Not that there is any hint of that in the papers; no, it is simply a matter of logic. The early articles all reported the theory that Mrs. Avery had been killed by a burglar while her husband was out of town. But they also reported that she had been shot once in the back of the head. That, Gabriel suspects, was not the work of a thief. There was also a spate of articles filled with the gossip the papers liked to call human interest: the wealthy daughter from a prominent family, married to the self-made son of the self-made former congressman, and all the fluff and speculation that went with it. Then, for a month or two, the papers went silent, there apparently being nothing more of interest to report, until a week ago when State's Attorney Albert Chasen made an offhand comment to a young reporter for the county paper. There was a suspect in the case, the paper reported, and suddenly television stations and newspapers throughout the state and from Washington to Wall Street were speculating that an arrest would be made soon. Perhaps surprised, perhaps even pleased, by the attention his off-the-cuff remark had drawn, Albert Chasen called a press conference to clarify the situation. The official pronouncement was that the matter "was actively under investigation by the state police and the grand jury, which expects to conclude its work soon."

And now Cooper Avery is here. He told Vivian when calling for an appointment that it was important that he see Mr. Gabriel as soon as possible. It concerned the grand jury investigation into his wife's death, he said, and then added that Mr. Gabriel had been recommended to him by a Larry Falls. That, in and of itself, is a clue.

Larry Falls has never been a client, but he is well known to Jack Gabriel. The former executive vice-president of a major defense contractor, Larry Falls spent two years in federal prison after pleading guilty to conspiring with three named codefendants "and others known and unknown to the grand jury" to illegally obtain and use classified Defense Department documents specifying budget and cost projections for several "black" or top secret programs. Jack Gabriel's client, the man in the Pentagon who had actually stolen the documents and turned them over to Falls and his cohorts for a price, was one of those coconspirators technically "unknown" to the grand jury. Although hounded for more than three years by the Department of Justice, the FBI and the Naval Investigative Service as one of the prime targets—if not *the* prime target—of the investigation, Gabriel's client was never charged and his name never appeared in any of the press accounts that tracked the investigation and court proceedings. However odd it seems to Gabriel that Cooper Avery is coming to him on the recommendation of Larry Falls, it clearly signals that whatever problem Avery has is criminal and not civil in nature.

Gabriel looks again at his calendar and the red ink circling April 15, the day tradition dictates that he and his friends meet in the Costa Rican capital of San José and rent a car for the hour-and-twenty-minute drive up the coast. *I am going. No matter what, I will be there.* Thus assuring himself, Gabriel takes a deep breath and rises from his chair to walk slowly to the reception area and Cooper Avery.

He is not sure what, if anything, the newspaper articles and Avery's reputation have led him to expect, but the man who stands stiffly to greet him is not it. In the few moments it takes to offer Avery a fresh cup of coffee, which he declines, and to lead him back to his office, Gabriel is struck by the immediate and conflicting images Avery presents. His height and a trim physique clothed in a finely tailored gray suit lend an air of almost youthful athleticism; yet his face has the pallid, loose-fleshed look of age exaggerated by tired eyes shaded by puffed and heavy lids. His handshake is firm, even assertive, but his voice and manner seem hesitant, as if he is having trouble matching his instincts to his situation; a man, perhaps, accustomed to order suddenly caught in a whirlwind.

"I'm curious," Gabriel says, resuming his seat behind his desk as Avery takes a moment to choose the wine-red leather side chair over the matching leather couch, "why Larry Falls would have suggested that you see me. I've only met him on one or two occasions and he's never been a client." Larry Falls was represented by William Ramey, a founding partner of Ramey, Ford, Duchoissois, Mayer & Oliver, one the largest firms in the state, and a man with a national reputation for representing prominent people in high-profile cases.

"Well," Avery says quietly, "I've known Larry for a long time. In fact, we were in college together. Anyway, when it became apparent that I needed to get some legal advice I went to him. Because . . . well, to be honest, my first thought was to hire Bill Ramey, because of his reputation. But Larry suggested that I see you." Avery smiles a bit. "He pointed out something I guess like most people I wouldn't have thought about. He said that the problem with lawyers who enjoy the big reputations and the front-page headlines is that they're usually the ones whose clients get indicted, tried and usually convicted. What people should really be looking for are the lawyers you never hear much about, because they're the ones who keep their clients from ever getting indicted in the first place and keep them from having their names plastered all over the front pages of the papers. That's why he recommended you. He said that all the while Bill Ramey was holding press conferences, you were hiding in the background, and your client was never charged. He didn't know how you pulled it off, but apparently you did."

"Well, maybe I just had an innocent client."

"Not the way Larry tells it."

Gabriel allows himself a brief smile. "Well, in any event, I take it from the message you left with my secretary that you're concerned with this grand jury investigation into your wife's death. Is that correct? Forgive me, I hope I'm not being too abrupt."

Avery shakes his head. "I think I'm about to be indicted for killing my wife."

Gabriel sits back, startled not by the information but by the directness of Avery's delivery. "You've been told this?"

Avery nods.

"By whom?"

"Well, first I met with the state's attorney and some detectives last week and—"

Gabriel cuts in. "You met with the prosecutor? Did you have counsel with you?"

"Well, yes, Phil Layton was there." Gabriel's instant frown says everything, and Avery responds, "Yes, I know. It was a mistake."

"Well, Phil's a fine lawyer. It's just that this isn't his area, usually."

"That's what the detective said a couple of nights ago. I think her exact words were that Layton 'had led me like a lamb to the slaughter.'"

Gabriel leans forward and raises both hands as if trying to ward off a loud and unpleasant noise. "Wait a minute, wait a minute. You talked with one of the detectives? Was this at that same meeting?"

"No."

"Was Layton with you?"

"No."

"You met with this detective alone?"

"Yes, but let me explain."

"Wait just a moment," Gabriel says, and he swivels around in his chair to inspect the desk calendar on the credenza behind him. He then picks up the phone. "Vivian, cancel my eleven o'clock, would you please?" He turns back to Avery. "I'm sorry, but whether or not you decide to hire me or I decide to accept your case, I think we need to spend a little time talking here."

Avery nods, looking almost embarrassed. "Yes, I agree."

"Now, let's start with these meetings. Exactly what have you been told that leads you to believe that you are going to be indicted?"

For the next hour and a half Gabriel extracts the details of Avery's meeting in Albert Chasen's office and the more curious meetings with Christine Boland, her coming unannounced to his home and the long conversation at the bar in Fells Point. He pushes Avery to recall exactly what questions were asked and even more to recall the precise wording of his answers.

"No, excuse me, Mr. Avery. Let's not talk yet about what really happened. What I need to know is what you told them happened. Your exact words if you can remember."

Gabriel listens intently, only occasionally jotting down a note. He listens to Avery's words, how he phrases his answers, how he moves with his subject, how the eyes that remain focused while questions are asked stray when he answers, to one or another of the watercolors on Gabriel's walls, to some distant object beyond the window, to his own hands, hands which take an obvious exercise of will to keep from gesturing expressively. He watches Avery swing back and forth, in small but perceptible stages, from the controlled businessman who speaks with precision and who intellectually can piece together the elements of the accusation and understand the conclusions drawn, to a man whose emotional skin has been shaved paper-thin, a man unbalanced not so much by the possibility that he could be convicted of murder and jailed—that seems barely a concern—as by the notion that he could be *accused,* that anyone actually could think that he, Cooper Avery, is capable of such an act. Gabriel supposes this is the reason Avery so easily succumbed to this Detective Boland. She claimed not to believe what the circumstances so clearly implied.

Avery tells him of Christine Boland's inquiries about possible enemies and about the condolences from strangers. Gabriel asks, "Have you checked the sympathy cards as she suggested? What was the name?"

"Lessing. Martin Lessing. Yes, I did. The card says just what she had written down. 'From the friends of Martin Lessing.' I've checked every source I have. I have no idea who this Lessing could be."

"Was that the only card from someone who was a complete unknown?"

"Yes, to my knowledge."

"Did you call and tell Detective Boland what you found, or didn't find?"

"Yes."

"Did she say anything about it? Anything to suggest that she had more information?"

"No, she just said that she would try to check the name out."

"Did you discuss anything further?"

"No."

"She didn't ask you whether you had thought of anyone else who might be a potential enemy, as it were?"

"Yes, she did, but I hadn't thought of anyone, at least not at the time."

"But you have since?"

"I don't know. Not really. It's just that I was thinking about this fella Oliver Johns, the man whose farm I bought and developed into Fishing Creek. Over the years he's turned into a bit of a drunk. Really down on his luck, they say. Anyway, he lives on a small bit of land that his lawyers reserved for him out of the estate. It's not really part of Fishing Creek, but you access his property through our development. Anyway, he has this little house over there that's turned into a bit of an eyesore. Marian, my wife, kept trying to get him to clean the place up, you know, complaining about an old truck body and some outboard engines he had lying around the property. She was right, but to me it was much ado about nothing. After all, it was his property. It wasn't part of our community and it's set off enough that even from the lots nearest his property, you can't see much. It's pretty much blocked off by a stand of pine trees.

"Anyway, a couple of the neighbors started griping and Marian decided to make it her cause, and once she went so far as to call in the county, alleging local code violations or whatever. There were a few months of nasty letters and such, but as far as I know, nothing ever came of it. It all just died out. I guess he cleaned up his yard, I don't know. Anyway, that was four or five, hell, maybe even six years ago. I don't remember. I didn't pay much attention to it all. And I really don't think there's any connection there."

"So you haven't said anything to Detective Boland about this Oliver Johns."

"No."

"Did she say anything about meeting with you again?"

"No."

Jack Gabriel nods slowly, his eyes fixed on Avery. "Interesting," is all that he can say after a long pause, and Avery's attention again drifts out the window. It is, Gabriel thinks, *very* interesting. He turns again to his calendar and flips the page to April and the red circle around the fifteenth. He has to decide.

He calculates quickly the expected range of hours the defense of this case would take. He multiplies that by his billing rate, adds fifty percent of that sum for overhead, fifty percent of that for taxes, arrives at a total, and then, considering Avery's reputed wealth, doubles it. He thinks of Punta Las Marias, and of the late afternoons on the veranda, and of the cocktails that would carry him through the sunset to a long dinner under a sky filled with stars he has never seen here in Baltimore. He adds another seventy-five thousand dollars and says, "Well, Mr. Avery, if we can come to an agreement, I am prepared to represent you. But, whether it's me or someone else, I would urge you to secure counsel as quickly as possible."

Avery nods and asks what the fee would be.

Gabriel goes through the charade of taking out his calculator and a notepad and punching out some numbers as if he had not already decided on a figure. He scrunches his expression a bit, jots down a few meaningless notes, punches in a few more imaginary figures and says, "Seven hundred fifty-five thousand dollars." He enjoys the odd figure he has quoted, as if his calculations were studied and precise.

Avery does not flinch, but neither does he say anything in response.

"Plus expenses," Gabriel adds. "That is a flat fee that will take you through any trial and appeals in the state courts. Beyond that we would have to come to a separate agreement. We would require a third now, and for the rest we can work out some schedule. But in any event, we would require that it all be paid before trial."

"If there is a trial," Avery offers.

"Yes," Gabriel agrees, "if there is a trial."

"Would you be handling this personally?"

"Yes, except that I will have some associates working with me. Research, some legwork, things like that."

Avery nods.

"And my partner, Lisa Paretti. I would want her to be involved."

Avery doesn't respond for a moment. Then, with a cock of his head, he says, "You know, we've been talking about this for almost two hours now, and you haven't once asked me whether or not I did this thing."

Gabriel waits without a word or an expression.

"It's important to me that you know that I didn't do it. I want the truth to come out. I want justice."

Jack Gabriel for the first time allows his own gaze to drift out the window. A moment passes before he turns back to Avery. "I appreciate what you're saying, Mr. Avery, but the truth of the matter is that the last thing you want is justice."

Avery looks startled.

"Listen to me," Gabriel begins, "when you walk into a courthouse you have to suspend reality. Truth and justice are not things, they are illusions, they don't really exist. At most, they are vague concepts that can be and regularly are molded and twisted and formed like Silly Putty into whatever one wants them to be. In practical terms, a trial is nothing more than a competition, and in almost every case, one man's justice is another man's outrage. In your case, if you were to be convicted of killing your wife, you and I would be outraged. The prosecutor would say justice was done. If you were to be acquitted, we would hail the result as the only just one, and the prosecutor would be outraged. And from each of our perspectives, I suppose, we would each be correct.

"As for truth? It's whatever a jury decides it to be. And it doesn't matter whether they decide the matter unanimously and thoughtfully and with a firm belief in the evidence and their judgment, or whether they compromise because maybe they're tired and worn out, and the jury room's too stuffy, or the chairs are too hard, or their boss is complaining about the time they're spending away from work, or their husbands're bitching because they're late getting supper on the table, or they're reacting to some bigotry or prejudice we'll never know about because they'll never admit to it, or whether they decide on some gut-level notion of sympathy or outrage we or the prosecutor plants in their brain, or even if they actually decide on basis of the law, which only a few ever really comprehend except on the most elementary level. The point is, however they do it, the jury will decide, and that decision alone defines the truth. From that point on, as far as the system is concerned, whatever they say happened did happen. And that, my friend, is what everyone calls truth and justice.

"You see, you, like most everyone except lawyers and judges, define justice in terms of right and wrong, good and evil, truth and falsity. The good guy wins and the bad guy loses. But as far as the law is concerned, that has nothing to do with it. The law doesn't care who wins or loses, it's not even concerned with right and wrong, except in a lot of sophomoric speeches that are trotted out for Law Day or the Fourth of July or whatever. The law only cares that the game is played by its rules. No, Mr. Avery, we don't want justice, we want to win. That's the only truth we're looking for. And it's my job to make sure that we take every advantage we can in order to see to it that that's the truth we get. A flat-out, unequivocal win."

Avery allows himself a smile and reaches into his jacket for a checkbook. "Mr. Gabriel, I think you and I are going to get along just fine. I'll have the money to cover this check transferred within the hour."

"Please, call me Jack," Gabriel says, and he turns back to his calendar and writes a note to himself. *"Cancel Costa Rica."*

20 He is thinking about Alice and trusting that she will not see in his face the waves of change that had picked him up from the trough and for a few hours let him see a horizon, before suddenly folding over him and drowning him with an inevitability he had never considered: that she could be taken from him. But now she would, although it will be hours before she knows it, and years before she understands.

The day had started out well. The pressure that almost every night over the past few months had constricted his breathing until the early-morning hours, when only exhaustion allowed him a brief and fitful sleep, had suddenly been lifted by the simple act of writing out a check for just over two hundred fifty thousand dollars. And with that check, he had handed over the need to worry and to figure and to speculate and to plan. He had paid others to take care of all that. And he had been encouraged to watch how quickly they had leapt to their task, how Jack Gabriel had called in Lisa Paretti, a woman who but for her medium height and uncertain age seemed a collection of specifics needing adjectives: bright black hair, smooth, tight skin, large eyes as dark as her hair, a trim figure crisply clothed and held straight in her chair, almost aggressively. She had listened to the story he told again, this time as Gabriel took copious notes while she asked the questions—direct, probing questions that, like her partner's before, never asked what he had done, but only what he had said, what he had heard, what he thought others thought he had done, and why he thought they thought it

—all in a smooth, controlled voice that never hesitated. And then there had been a long, late lunch, the first he had enjoyed in a long time, listening to them plan, listening to them debate, listening to them assign tasks to associates he was told he would meet later.

But then that wave of hope collapsed beneath him. There was a call to Albert Chasen's office to inform the prosecutor that Gabriel, King & Paretti now represented Cooper Avery and that any and all contact sought by the authorities for any purpose whatever should be made exclusively through Jack Gabriel or Lisa Paretti. He watched Gabriel's eyes narrow as he pressed for details of the case that Chasen apparently was hesitant to share. He watched Gabriel's jaw tighten as he instructed Chasen that there would be no need for that, that he would personally guarantee a voluntary surrender. There were sharp looks between Gabriel and Paretti as Gabriel hung up the phone and repeated Chasen's remarks, the last described as being a cynical repetition of Chasen's official statement to the press.

"Cooper," Gabriel said, "I plan to go see Chasen tomorrow. But you should prepare yourself. This crap about him not speaking for the grand jury is just that. Crap. If Chasen wants it to happen, you'll be indicted. Maybe as early as next week. You should quickly do whatever you feel you have to in the event that he does indict. My guess is that he will. And if that happens you can be assured that the press will have a field day. Whatever publicity there has been so far will pale in comparison. And it will last all the way through the trial. It can be a nightmare. You must prepare your family. Especially your children. I don't like to be pessimistic, but you must be prepared."

■■■

Alice has only to see her father pull up in the long gray Mercedes and she knows.

Alice has learned much in the past few months, and she can sense trouble the way one senses a strange odor in a familiar room. Her father was grouchy this morning, but she knew that before he had said a word. She can always tell by the thin, powder-white residue that sometimes lines his lip after he drinks that awful mush to keep him from suddenly holding his stomach and his breath until his face turns red and little beads of sweat pop out on his upper lip and he takes a few deep gulps of air and says no, everything is fine, it must have been something he ate.

But then he has always been a little grouchy in the morning, even before her mother died and Ned had to go to the hospital, where she is not allowed to see him, and they had to move to the house which she knows her father does not like much. She never saw him drink that mush before they moved here. She doesn't much like the house either. There is nothing wrong with it, she supposes, it just isn't *their* house. And she knows it never will be. It's as if they are waiting to go somewhere, only they don't know where or when: as if they are waiting for a phone call to let them know when they can go home.

She knows it is bad news, though, his coming to find her like this.

She is in the Conighams' back yard. Her friend Mary Elizabeth invited her over after school. But Mary Elizabeth got angry the minute she showed up with her football helmet. Mary Elizabeth can be so boring. All she ever wants to do is sit inside and giggle over boys and call girlfriends on the phone. But Alice doesn't care. Mary Elizabeth can sit and pout all she wants. She really came to see Mary Elizabeth's older brother and his two friends anyway. They are ten and just about her height, and even though it is almost baseball season, she always finds it easy to talk them into playing football. They seem to like tackling her as much as she likes being tackled. And tackling boys is one heck of a lot better than talking about them.

But time is called as she and Bobby Conigham and Davey Wheeler and Earl "the Pearl" Mahoney stand still and silent at the sudden sight of her father leaning against the edge of the Conighams' back porch, his features darkened by the shadows of late afternoon, his hands in his topcoat pockets, just watching them, they don't know for how long.

She runs over to him, but before she can say anything, he just smiles and says, "It's okay, Blossom, go ahead and finish your game. We've got plenty of time. I'll just watch, okay?"

So, maybe it isn't trouble after all. He never calls her that when she's in trouble or when he is in one of his quiet moods. Little Alice Apple Blossom is reserved for those times when he jokes around, when he is happy, when she can talk him into almost anything, which since her mother died is the way he tries to be almost every night. Sometimes he tries so hard it makes her sad. She supposes he misses her mother even more than she does. And Ned, too, maybe.

"You all kick off to Earl 'n' me," she orders to impress her father, tossing the ball to Bobby Conigham, who looks peeved since it is their turn. But she knows she can get away with it since her father is right there, and Bobby knows it too. So he takes the ball and walks off his distance while she tightens the chin strap of her helmet and turns to Earl the Pearl and says, "I gotta go after this, so how 'bout lettin' me take it."

"Sure," he says.

Aside from the fact that Earl the Pearl has just about the biggest ears she has ever seen on anyone, she likes him the best. Last fall, when they moved here from Fishing Creek, he was the first one to talk to her. It was in the park, where she stood by a tree one Saturday, watching a group of boys trying to organize a game. She remembers how he just walked right up to her, like he had known her all his life, and said, "We gotta have someone to hold the ball for kickoffs. It won't hurt none to just hold the ball, so if you ain't too chicken . . ." And when she half-nodded and half-shrugged her okay, he said, "So, what's your name?" Earl can be pretty cool.

The ball comes tumbling toward them, wobbling along its erratic course until Earl traps it and tosses it back to her. Earl runs ahead to block but trips before he gets more than a step or two, and Bobby Conigham is closing in fast. She swings to her right, away from Bobby and toward Davey Wheeler. Davey might weigh twice what she does, but he's slow and soft, and even if he does get his hands on her, he never does much but try to hold on while he falls. But Davey moves to the side—for an instant it looks like he is trying to get out of her way—and she finds herself pinched between him and Bobby. The only choice, if she is to show her father what she is made of, is to go straight through Davey. She does, full tilt, with her helmet down, spearing Davey in his soft belly. *Whoompf!*

Suddenly, amid the tangle of bodies, Bobby's and hers and Davey's, which is squirming and gasping but can find no voice, unlike Earl the Pearl, who is pulling at her and saying, "Jesus, Alice!", she understands for the first time the term "having your bell rung." Her eyes are crossed, and her skin tingles all the way down to the tips of her fingers, and when she is suddenly lifted straight into the air she feels dizzy and isn't sure whether that is fear on her father's face or she just can't see straight.

"Jesus, Alice!" she hears again, and then, "Sorry, Mr. Avery."

"Are you all right?" her father asks quickly, and when she nods, he puts her down and reaches for the still squirming Davey Wheeler's belt, which he takes in his hand and lifts him slightly several times, pumping the air back into him.

The tears come without warning, and she says she is sorry, and Earl just keeps saying, "Jesus, Alice!" while Davey looks at her, a little pale and more embarrassed than hurt, probably, and says, "That's okay." But what else can he say with her father right there? And for a moment she wishes her father would go away so she can tell Davey she really is sorry. And Earl and Bobby, too.

And he does. He asks her again, "Are you sure you're okay?" She says yes, and he turns to Davey. "How 'bout you, son? You got your wind back?" Davey nods, taking a couple of deep breaths and holding his stomach, and her father just nods too and says, "Well, okay. If you guys want to finish the last set of downs, I'll go wait in the car. Alice, don't be too long, now."

No one feels like playing anymore, and Earl tells Davey to quit griping because he knows she didn't mean it. She was just being Crazy Alice and besides, he stopped her cold and cleaned her clock, and she says he did not, and Davey says he did too, and Bobby bounces the football off the top of her helmet, and everything is okay again.

It is okay, too, when she gets into the car. She knows she isn't in trouble when she sees his face. It's like the times when the two of them would come back from the boat, and she'd be all dirty and smelling of fish and her father would have that look in his eye like he knew he'd be in trouble, too, if her mother saw her like that, and he'd wink and tell her to sneak upstairs in a hurry and wash up. Even now, even since her mother died, he'll get that look a lot. And she wonders if what they say about her mother being in heaven and looking down on them is true, whether he knows he'll be in trouble for letting her have the football helmet and her playing tackle like that, and how he doesn't make her wear dresses all the time like her mother wanted, and her grandmother wants still.

"How about you and me going down to Luigi's for a pizza?"

Her favorite place? And she doesn't even have to wash up and put on a dress? On a school night? In fact, he wants to go home and change out of his suit. Pizza's no fun in a suit, he says. She says sure, but she wonders. Something is definitely wrong, and so she just up and asks him.

"Well, I've got a little surprise for you. But let's wait until we get to Luigi's. Okay?"

It's a special night, for sure. She gets to order whatever she wants on the pizza; well, everything except anchovies. She has never had an anchovy and for the umpteenth time, he tells her that it's a junk fish and she will hate it and it will ruin the whole pizza and she guesses he must be right, but still, one day she will get a pizza with anchovies. But tonight she will settle for pepperoni and mushrooms and green pepper and pineapple and extra cheese so it will be thick the way she likes it. And he never says anything about her not being able to finish but half of the second slice before she wants to order her special dessert, the one she can only get here, the one that Mr. Luigi himself says would put anyone else but her in a coma. It's a cannoli with chunks of chocolate in the cream filling, but it also has some custard poured over the top and then some strawberries, and then some whipped cream. She once dipped her spoon into her father's zabaglione and topped her cannoli with it. A new dessert was born, which Mr. Luigi calls Alice's shortcake. It's Ned's favorite, too, although he would never ask for it himself. He had always just shrugged his shoulders and said nothing when their mother asked if he wanted any dessert. But then he'd kick her under the table and poke at her until she'd speak up and order it for the both of them.

She forgets all about the surprise her father promised. He asks her all about school and her friends and whether she likes it there. She says it's okay. But the kids are all kinda stuck-up. Like a lot of them who always have someone come pick them up after school make fun of those who take the special bus, but she's glad she takes the bus because it's more fun than having your parents pick you up. But not all of them are stuck-up. Some of them are okay, like Earl and Bobby and Davey are okay, and Bobby's sister Mary Elizabeth is okay most of the time except when she wants to spend the whole day talking on the phone. And Ruthie Zanger is okay, except sometimes Ruthie makes fun of her because she plays boys' games, but she knows Ruthie is just jealous because she has a crush on Bobby Conigham, but Bobby doesn't even know Ruthie exists, and besides, Ruthie spends all her time in the girls' room messing with her hair, but everyone knows it wasn't ever gonna be anything but kinky anyway.

She likes it when she makes her father laugh, which he does, although she doesn't know why, particularly. And she laughs too, and that somehow reminds her that he said he had a surprise.

"Well, Blossom, I think it's about time you and I took a vacation. What do you say? I thought we'd go out to California and see Disneyland and maybe go to one of the movie studios, and then we could drive up the coast and stay in a little hotel where we could watch the ocean and maybe see the seals out on the rocks. And then we'd drive up to San Francisco. Remember how much fun we had in San Francisco riding down that street that twisted back and forth down the hill? And then we'd go see your Aunt Claire in Seattle. What do you think?"

"This summer, you mean?"

"No, I thought we'd leave the day after tomorrow."

It's funny how sometimes you don't have to smash your finger or even run your head into something like Davey Wheeler to get that same feeling. All of a sudden you feel kinda like everything hurts but it doesn't, not really. It just feels like it in your stomach or in your head, like when you've just done something really dumb in front of a whole lot of people. That's how she feels. She doesn't know why except that she knows there is something very wrong.

"Is Ned going with us?"

"No, honey, Ned can't leave the hospital yet. He still isn't well enough. But I called the doctors this afternoon and they said we could go see him tomorrow. The both of us this time. So I thought that would be nice."

She cannot help it. She just begins to cry. She doesn't know why, she just does, and before she knows it, he has swept her up in his arms, and she holds onto his neck like when she was little, and he carries her to the car, where he smiles and asks, "Do you want to drive?"

He used to let her sit in his lap and steer as long as she didn't tell her mother, but that was only when they lived at Fishing Creek and there were lots of back roads. He never lets her do that in the city.

He tells her lots of things on the way home. She can't understand it all, but she knows he needs her not to argue with him. His voice kinda sounds like she feels, like maybe he feels sort of the same way, like something hurts him too. But what it all comes to is that she is going to live with Aunt Claire and Uncle Glenn and her cousins in Seattle, and it will only be for a few months while he takes care of some business that is going to keep him away from home a lot. No, she can't stay with Grandpa and Grandmother because they will be busy at the same time. But he promises he will come to see her as much as he can, almost every weekend. Besides, she's the lucky one, getting to live on that island and take the ferry to school and getting to sail whenever she wants, and she always has a good time with her cousin Julia, even if Glenn, Jr., and Sarah are older. Sarah is driving now, and he bets Sarah will drive her almost anywhere she wants. And after a few months, maybe they'll all be back together again. Maybe even Ned will be feeling better by then, and maybe they'll all just move out to Seattle and live there together.

When they get home she takes her bath without his even asking, and when she is ready for bed, he comes to her room and starts to tuck the covers around her. She doesn't say anything, but somehow he understands, and he lies down beside her while she tries to go to sleep. He hasn't done that for some time, not since the dreams started coming to her only once in a while. She's glad he decided to lie down with her: she is frightened that the dreams will come tonight for sure.

She doesn't know how long she had been asleep, but when she wakes up, he is not there beside her. The light is still on in the hall, and so she thinks it can't be that late. She hears some noise down-stairs. Strange noise, almost like someone is talking, but not quite. She goes to the top of the stairs and listens. It isn't the television, and it isn't someone talking. At least not any kind of talking she's ever heard. It's more a sort of low, broken voice murmuring some-thing. Like a crazy man, maybe. Like the robber who killed her mother maybe, and she is suddenly very frightened. She tiptoes to her father's room and opens the door, but he isn't there. She moves carefully back to the top of the stairs and begins to creep down them, taking each carpeted step carefully so as not to make any noise. At the bottom of the stairs, she hugs the wall until she can peek around the corner to the living room, where the sounds still come from. And she sees him, by the frail light of a single lamp, in his easy chair in the corner, slumped over himself, his head hung low between his arms resting on his knees, a cigarette glowing in one hand, a liquor bottle on the table beside him.

"Daddy?"

He looks up suddenly, and his eyes are red and frightened, and she knows he has been crying. She runs to him, and he grabs her, and he holds her, and for a very long time she just cries and cries while he tells her that everything will be all right. But she can tell he is just saying it. She can tell he isn't so sure.

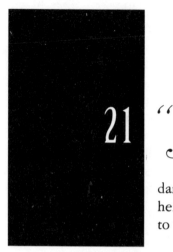

21

"*I*t's an interesting theory."

Christine takes her time with a sip of dark beer before an impish grin comes over her. "And you think there's something to it."

"Do I?"

Dr. Alan Mercle has never quite rid himself of old habits. Terminally bored with the academics and theoreticians with whom he spent most of his career, he several years ago left a tenured position at The George Washington University to work full-time with the FBI's Behavioral Sciences Unit at Quantico, Virginia. But in his manner and by his method of debate, he is still the professor of abnormal and criminal psychology who rarely answers a question directly, who prefers to lead his students to their own conclusions. Christine was, and remains still, his favorite, one of those rare students in whom the teacher sees reflected an idealized image of himself.

"Yes, you do," Christine answers. "Otherwise, you wouldn't have asked me to meet you here. You're curious, and you want to ask more questions before you let me know whatever it is you found."

They are seated by the front window of a small German restaurant on Washington's Capitol Hill. Mercle's full, round cheeks are a bright pink against his bushy white hair and moustache. The professor, as Christine still calls him, had walked the fifteen blocks from FBI headquarters, where he had spent the morning in meetings. If asked, he would say it was to save cab fare; but the truth, she knows, is that he could not resist a brisk walk on a sunny day, talking to himself about whatever for the moment has piqued his interest. He is obviously intrigued, and his large blue eyes, which never seem haunted by the dark subjects of his life's work, practically dance.

His expression reminds her of a child suddenly embarrassed. "Well, yes, I am curious," he says, "particularly about how you have come to be so definite in your conclusion. Given all the indicators you told me, the scene and the background and whatever, I agree your theory would fit. But there are a number of profiles that would fit here." He leans forward a bit, and his voice lowers as if he is about to impart something significant. "You know, I'm particularly intrigued with the cigarette butt on the vanity. That's an interesting observation, the possibility of a woman's involvement. I'd like to think I would have come up with that myself. You put that together with the method of killing, the neatness of it all, not just the use of the pillow to fire through but placing it over the victim's head afterward, not just tossing it aside; it does have a woman's touch, doesn't it? Almost like covering some unpleasantness she just doesn't want to deal with. But I wonder, too, whether that might also indicate that the killing itself wasn't the first or primary motive here, whether something might have happened after the killer entered the house that suddenly made the killing necessary. Wouldn't you think, given the time of death and the probability that the killer entered by stealth rather than breaking in, that if it was a planned assassination, the killing would have taken place in the victim's bedroom, while she slept?"

Christine raises her brows in speculative agreement as she takes a small bite of her hot potato salad. The professor, clearly enjoying himself, has barely touched his food.

"But, my dear, even so, it hardly eliminates the husband, now does it? I mean a man who exhibits the control you've talked about, and if the killing was more purposeful than passionate, wouldn't he have exercised the same control at the time? Might not we expect that he could, indeed would, carry it out as neatly as his plan allowed, given that he'd want to make it look like a break-in? The killing itself is neatly accomplished. This is, after all, if no longer his lover, at least the mother of his children, the mistress of the manor, and he is in his home. The ransacking to provide the cover comes afterward. And it does seem interesting that the most serious and destructive ransacking was with his things, his office, his computer, his artwork, or whatever. Other than the missing jewelry from the safe, the wife's area was virtually untouched, or at least undamaged, right?"

Christine nods. "Yes, it was moved around a bit, but no real tearing through it like in the husband's office."

"This is very interesting."

Christine leans forward, and speaks quietly. "Professor, please, eat some of your lunch. Edith will shoot me if you pass out again." At sixty-one years, the professor's blood sugar problems are no longer a matter he can afford to ignore; yet he does, often too preoccupied with his thoughts to bother with the meals he requires to avoid the sudden blackouts and the wrath of his wife, who has promised that if it happens again, she will stuff him in the trunk of their car and drive him to forced retirement at their waterfront cottage near St. Michaels.

He nods and takes an uninterested bite of schnitzel, then holds up his fork to emphasize his next thought. "But I disagree with your colleagues. This smoking thing implies just the opposite in my mind."

Christine has told him of the inferences Charlie Abbot and, to a lesser degree, Paul Wyzanski drew from Avery's claim to have stopped smoking when asked about the cigarette butt in the powder room, and later, his seemingly unconscious lighting of a cigarette when under the pressure of the interview in the county prosecutor's office.

"Yes, I—" Christine starts, but the professor presses on.

"It just doesn't fit, it seems to me. If the husband had been confronted with the odd fact of the cigarette butt in the powder room and questioned about it, and if it had any evidentiary relationship to him, he would be acutely aware of the implications. I think his smoking in the state's attorney's office implies just the opposite. That it didn't mean anything to him. But—"

Christine interrupts the professor with a nod toward his plate.

"Yes, of course. You know, you really shouldn't pay so much attention to Edith. She would have me in a sterile bubble if she could."

"How is she doing?"

"Fine. She's taken on two seminars at George Mason this semester. And she's still teaching that survey course. Won't give that up. And she complains about me not slowing down. Really, I don't understand her sometimes. But, you know, if there was a woman with him at the time—"

Christine again shakes her head. She is accustomed to Mercle's habits, his change of subjects in midsentence, his assumption that of course you are following the stream of his thoughts, a stream sometimes twisted and circuitous, but always clear and flowing toward a point.

"Just for a moment," he says, "let's hypothesize that perhaps this paramour from New York or some other woman was with him. I agree it's improbable, but just for the moment. He might not see her in the bathroom. Almost certainly would not. Would not be aware of the cigarette butt until questioned about it. But when confronted with it, he certainly would understand the implication of it as it would apply to his companion. He would be quite conscious of his actions in that regard. Wouldn't you think?" Christine shrugs. "No, I think the fact that he did smoke implies something quite the opposite from the position your colleagues have taken."

"You're really enjoying your work, aren't you?"

Mercle beams. "Best thing I ever did. All those years of teaching and writing and lecturing. All that unapplied theory. Well, that's spilt milk. I understand now what you've always said about the chase. Searching for the unknown instead of analyzing what's given to you. Yes, I'm really enjoying myself." He takes a big bite of schnitzel and then lowers his face, looking over the top of his wire-rimmed glasses at Christine. "But do not try to distract me. You still have not answered my question."

"What question is that?"

"Why you are so confident that the husband is not involved. I don't disagree with the other theories you posit, particularly this notion of a stalker. But you are far from being able to objectively eliminate the husband. Not on what you have now. Why are you so intent on that? Why so positive?"

She smiles broadly, and Alan Mercle sits back, waving his hand at her. "No, no, no. I won't listen to this. I won't let you do this."

"Professor, you know why you're getting so upset? Because you have something for me that makes you suspect I'm onto something, and it just drives you crazy to hear me say what you know I'm going to say. Aside from everything we've talked about, I just have a feeling."

He groans.

"I'm right, aren't I? You did find something and you just don't want to give it to me because you hate hunches. Right?"

"No, I don't hate hunches. It's just that there are more than enough people already who think our work nothing more than voodoo and speculation. I just hate to give them any more ammunition with talk about feelings."

"It's just you and me, Professor. So, what did you find for me?"

"Well, I don't know that I found anything. Well, that's not true. I found something. But I don't know that it means much. Well, I guess I think it does mean something. I mean the coincidence is there. But that may be all it is."

"What is it?"

"I found a record on Martin Lessing."

Christine sits up abruptly. She had spent hours accessing whatever record banks she could—state and local police, NCIC, motor vehicles—looking for some trace of the name that appeared on the note to Cooper Avery. After drawing a complete blank, she called the FBI Academy to ask her old friend for a favor. "Really? Tell me!"

"Well, it's really spare right now. But one Martin Lessing is listed as having been arrested by the FBI here in D.C. on May 18, 1952."

"1952? What else?"

"Very little. I didn't see the records myself. You can imagine being that old, that the only thing available is a few notations on computer files. But anyway, the fella that did the search for me says that there's no indication of a disposition. No conviction record or anything like that. Just the fact of the arrest. And . . ." he adds with a hint of something more significant, "a national security designation."

"What does that mean? 'A national security designation'?"

"It doesn't say what the charge was or what happened to the case, it just has a designation that whatever it was, it involved national security."

Christine's smile widens. "This is getting interesting. See, I always told you there was something to women's intuition."

He ignores her. "There're two more items. One, the file was what the fella called a 'Hoover file.' "

"A what?"

"A 'Hoover file.' The Director had a special taste for keeping special files, files that were not generally available within the Bureau: files, shall we say, that were particularly sensitive: national security information, or confidential informant or Special Intelligence Service information, or the really secret 'OC' files. 'Official/Confidential.' The political blackmail files. Nobody but Hoover was supposed to have access to them. Legend has it that those files were all destroyed after Hoover died. Anyway, the only trace of Lessing's file is an old code that indicates that it was sent to Hoover's office. In other words, forever gone, probably. My source said he wouldn't even know how to begin a search for it."

"But there is some record of what happened, if not the full file?"

"Well, like I said, there's the fact of the arrest *and*," he emphasizes, "a cross-reference to other case files. No names, just file numbers. But when he ran those numbers it came up blank. He says it most likely means there were codefendants or other targets, but he has no way of knowing where the files are, if they even exist anymore. They could have been Hoovered along with Lessing's."

"This is very interesting," she says, more to herself than to her informant. "You said there was a second item?"

"Well, you told me that Avery's father was in the FBI, right?"

"Yes, and you're going to tell me that his father had something to do with this Lessing case. Right?"

"No. At least, I don't know. I checked with Personnel, and they confirmed that the congressman was an agent at that time, but they didn't have any more without doing a trace for the files. They couldn't say where he was assigned or what he was doing at the time. Again, the actual files, if they even exist anymore, would be boxed up in some warehouse."

"What are the chances of getting any more information on whether the files really were destroyed or whether someone might know what the other file references were to or about Avery's assignment at the time of Lessing's arrest?"

"I don't know, and my man in Records doesn't either. He said an official inquiry upstairs might turn up something, but the request would have to go through official channels with a justification and all."

She smiles. "No problem. I'll have an official request on whoever's desk you say by tomorrow afternoon. Is there any way to speed things up?"

He reaches into his pocket and produces a slip of paper, which he hands to her. "Here's the address and a name to send the request to. And copy me. Then send me a separate inquiry asking for case assistance. I'll order the same stuff through my office. They'll respond quicker to an internal request."

"Thank you," she says, sitting back. For a moment she turns toward the window and her brow furrows, and she looks suddenly deflated, almost pained.

"What's wrong?" Mercle asks.

"I don't know." She shakes her head. "I should have seen this months ago. It was there, right in front of me, the whole time. Why didn't I see it?"

"My dear, you don't know yet that there is anything to see. This may be nothing. I think it's worth pursuing. Maybe the arrest was reported in the newspapers at the time. But whatever, don't get your hopes up. Keep your distance. You know better than I how these things usually turn into blind alleys. Particularly something this old. You're talking a long shot at best."

"I know, but somehow I just have this *feeling*."

■■■

The Library of Congress is a leisurely ten-minute walk from the restaurant. Taking Professor Mercle's directions, Christine follows Second Street toward the crest of the hill, passes the Hart Senate Office Building and the rear of the Supreme Court until she comes to Independence Avenue and the huge marble square known as the James Madison Building, the newest addition to the Library of Congress, where in the Newspaper and Current Periodicals Room the daily steps of history are stored on microfilm. Maybe the professor is right. Maybe Martin Lessing's arrest was reported.

She begins with *The Washington Post,* the day Lessing was arrested.

Sunday, May 18, 1952. Harry Truman predicted that the Democrats would win November's election on a "no-compromise fair-deal standard." A horse named Blue Man, which had finished third in the Kentucky Derby, came from dead last to win the Preakness by three and a half lengths. The Washington Senators were in second place in the American League, two and a half games behind Cleveland; Helen Gahagan Douglas, the former California congresswoman who had been drubbed by Richard Nixon in the 1950 senatorial campaign, was appearing onstage at the Gayety Theater in the musical comedy *First Lady;* a pamphlet published by "Freedom Clubs, Inc.," on whose advisory committee were such luminaries as Bing Crosby, Roscoe Pound and Senator Robert Taft, claimed that Senator Joseph McCarthy, then under investigation for financial improprieties, was the victim of "one of the most vicious smear campaigns in American history"; Mr. and Mrs. Edwin Fuller Parham announced the marriage of their daughter Margaret Pou Moran to Richard Erskine Clements, Jr., at the Church of the Holy Innocents; Woodward and Lothrop Department Stores were selling Palm Beach suits for $29.95; and the Glen Echo Amusement Park was advertising for two women, "White, Age 45–55," to be ticket-sellers. But there was not a hint of Martin Lessing.

On Monday, May 19, the *Post* reported on its front page that on Sunday, President and Mrs. Truman and their daughter Margaret had walked across Lafayette Park to St. John's Episcopal Church, where they heard the Reverend Dr. Charles W. Lowry offer a four-point program for meeting the Red challenge. "I've been preaching that myself for seven years," the President reportedly told the minister after the service. Several pages later, she saw it. The headline:

PROFESSOR ARRESTED IN SPY CASE, RADIO ANNOUNCER SOUGHT.

WASHINGTON, May 18—The FBI today announced the arrest of "a key figure" in a conspiracy to traffic in classified Defense Department documents. Martin Lessing, 32, an assistant professor of French literature at the University of Maryland, was arrested at Union Station as he was boarding a train for Baltimore. FBI spokesman Roger Hammel said in a prepared statement that Lessing was in possession of documents described as both "sensitive and highly classified."

Following Lessing's arrest, Hammel said, search warrants were executed at the Toledo Grove Apartments near the College Park campus where Lessing lives with his wife, and at Lessing's office on the third floor of the College of Arts and Sciences Building. The FBI would not comment on whether other classified documents were discovered at those locations.

At the time of Lessing's arrest, FBI agents in Baltimore were executing search warrants at the offices of radio station WMCR. Station officials said that they had been assured by the FBI that the station itself was not a target of the FBI's search. "We are cooperating fully with the authorities," station manager Harry Zorn said. Sources close to the investigation, however, revealed that the office and desk of veteran newscaster Byron Roth were searched. According to sources, Roth, 39, and a familiar voice to Baltimoreans for the past fifteen years, was not at the station at the time. Asked whether Roth's home was searched as well and whether an arrest warrant for the newscaster has been issued, Special Agent Hammel would say only that the FBI is trying to locate Roth "for questioning." Hammel did state that the arrest of Martin Lessing and the execution of the search warrants were the culmination of a year-long investigation into "an organization operating locally here in Washington and in several cities on the east coast." Asked to identify the organization, Hammel would say only that its purposes were "subversive in nature."

Friends and colleagues of Lessing have expressed "shock" at his arrest. Dean Richard Tydings of the University's College of Arts and Sciences described Lessing as a "quiet and unassuming fellow" who has been at the University of Maryland, both as a student and, since his discharge from the Army in 1946, as a teacher. Lessing, according to Dean Tydings, served in the infantry in France during the war and married a French national, the former Nicole Devereaux, shortly after the war in Europe ended. Mrs. Lessing is due to deliver the couple's first child "any day now," according to Dean Tydings. It is not known whether Mrs. Lessing was at home at the time the FBI searched their apartment. Special

Agent Hammel would not comment on Mrs. Lessing's whereabouts or whether she was a suspect in the case.

"I can't believe it," said Professor Henry Lyman, who has
known Lessing since his student days. "Martin was never
particularly interested in politics, no more than anyone else.
I certainly never knew him to express any views that were
disloyal. He and his wife were a very quiet couple. They
didn't socialize a great deal. This comes as a complete shock
to everyone who knows them."

The FBI would not comment on the connection between
Lessing and Byron Roth. Both Dean Tydings and Professor
Lyman said that they were unaware of any relationship between the two men or whether Lessing even knew Roth.
"I've never heard him mention the name," Dean Tydings
said. Officials at WMCR said they did not know Martin Lessing or whether there was any connection whatsoever to Roth.
"I wouldn't know him if I tripped over him," said station
manager Zorn, referring to Lessing.

Lessing is being held without bond at an undisclosed lo-
cation "for his own protection," according to Special Agent
Hammel. The FBI would not say whether Lessing is cooperating with federal authorities. No date has been set for
Lessing's arraignment in federal court, nor is it known
whether Lessing is represented by counsel. The FBI would
not comment on the specific charges they expect to be
brought against Lessing or whether they expect others, including Lessing's wife or Byron Roth, to be charged.

There were no other articles that week reporting Lessing's arraignment or Roth's arrest or "questioning," or what had become
of Lessing's wife. There were articles about playwright Clifford
Odets spending two days before the House Committee on Un-
American Activities offering his *mea culpa* for having once been a
Communist during the "horrendous days" of the Depression, and
explaining to the committee how liberals sometimes get confused
because the lines of leftism and liberalism "are constantly crossing
like the jangled chords of a piano"; and there was an article about
Lillian Hellman's refusal to apologize for herself or to testify about

others. But there was nothing about Lessing, not for the rest of that week.

On Thursday, May 22, *The Baltimore Sun* reported that Roth was still being sought by the FBI and had been fired by the radio station, and that the day before, May 21, Lessing's wife had given birth to a seven-pound, eight-ounce baby girl. That was the last reference to the case that Christine could find.

It is just after 9:30 P.M., and a librarian taps Christine on the shoulder and tells her that it is past closing time. Christine's head is pounding, and her back feels locked in pain. She has been at it for more than seven hours, screening every issue of every local paper she can find through March 1953.

Something is clearly wrong. It makes no sense that the case would suddenly and forever disappear from the public's eye. It makes no sense that the newspapers, having reported the initial arrest and searches, would not follow up with stories of the arraignment, or an indictment, or certainly a trial. It makes no sense that at least as to a public personality like Byron Roth, the newspapers would not have pressed the matter even if the Bureau somehow had lost interest. No, there is clearly more to this.

She is pleased with herself, as she stops for dinner at a small restaurant just a block or two from the library. She is certain that the information from Professor Mercle and the two articles she has found will be enough. The facts that the case suddenly disappeared from view and that the case file was "Hoovered" will be even more convincing. It might not yet be proof of her theory, but not even Charlie Abbot can ignore this. No, they will have to listen to her now.

22 O. B. Hardiman sits stiffly, his stare matching Christine's, their extended silence on the edge of being competitive. He is tapping the eraser end of a long pencil on the photocopy of the newspaper articles Christine has laid on his desk.

"Well?" she asks.

"Well, what? I don't understand what you think we should do with this."

She turns to Paul Wyzanski, whose expression is more quizzical than frowning. "I'm not sure I understand either."

She sits back and lets her head flop back to dramatize her frustration. "C'mon guys, don't play this game with me. Don't tell me you don't see the possibilities in this?"

Hardiman leans forward quickly, a sign that his patience is thinning. "Christine, I'm telling you I see a coincidence. I see that Cooper Avery got a sympathy card from someone named Martin Lessing."

"No," she says, "the card was from 'the friends of Martin Lessing.' "

"Whatever. And I see that some fella named Martin Lessing— and we have no idea that we're talking about the same man—was busted almost forty years ago for stealing government documents. But we don't know what ever came of that case or of this guy Lessing. Right?"

She nods, signaling that that should be enough.

"And not only do we not know whether there is any connection between the two Lessings, we don't know that there is any connection to Avery or his father or whether there is any significance to this sympathy card. All you can say is that when you and Paul first interviewed him six months ago, Avery mumbled something about not knowing what the return address was. What the hell is that supposed to mean? I mean I couldn't tell you off the top of my head what your address is and we've known each other for what, ten, twelve years?"

"But Captain—"

"No, no, just wait a minute. Now if you had come here and told me maybe that Avery or his wife or whoever had screwed over some guy named Lessing or that there was some demonstrable bad blood between them and that this same person or his friends or whoever were in fact the ones who sent the card, well, that's one thing. But you don't have any of that. Hell, you don't know that this Lessing character isn't one of the family's oldest and dearest friends, and Avery just didn't have a return address. Or, better yet, you don't know that the damn florist didn't send the wrong card to the wrong funeral. And based on that you want to stop everything we're doing and charge off in a new direction?"

Christine quickly assesses, then suppresses as too dangerous, her urge to reveal her conversation with Cooper Avery. She looks to Paul Wyzanski, who wears a pinched expression of embarrassment. It is obviously time to allow the captain and Christine some privacy. "If you don't mind," Paul says, "I think I'll get a cup of coffee." He rises, ignoring the fresh pot steaming in the corner, and leaves the office.

Hardiman watches the door slip shut and rises, going to the coffeepot and pouring himself a cup. He holds the pot up in an offer, but Christine shakes her head. It is a short, tense shake, as tense as her jaw muscles.

"Christine," Hardiman says, "you know how much I respect your abilities. But this time I gotta tell you I think—well, I think you've gone off the deep end here."

She remains still and tightly composed.

"I don't know why you decided so early on that Avery didn't do it. You've never given any reason except coming up with alternative theories for everything we've found. That's not bad. There's nothing wrong with alternatives. But honey—" He quickly stops himself. "I'm sorry. Anyway, the point I'm trying to make here is that there are times when suggesting alternatives is no longer helpful. I mean after a while, it just begins to sound like maybe you're not happy that the facts didn't lead us to the conclusions you were looking for. I mean it's almost beginning to sound like sour grapes—like ego."

Christine enunciates her words with some force. "You know that's not true."

"No, I don't know that. I'd like to think that's not true, but I don't know it. The real question is whether *you* know it's not true."

"It's not true."

"Listen, one of the things that's always set you apart around here, aside from brains, is that you've always been able to keep your distance. It was never personal, except that child porn case a few years back. But there you recognized it. You came to me and wanted off. I respected that. You were enough of a pro to cut yourself out. None of this macho crap. But there's something about this case. I don't know what, but for months you've been on this jag like this was personal. You've been fighting me and Paul and Charlie all along. Why?"

"Because I think you're wrong."

"But why? Give me a reason. Give me a fact. Give me some evidence."

"I've gone over it with you a hundred times."

"No, you've never given me evidence. You've given me theory, you've given me hunches. But you've never given me evidence."

"Baloney. Your whole case is circumstantial. It's all based on theory. But when I offer alternative circumstances, you suddenly won't be satisfied with anything less than an eyewitness. You tell me who's really being objective here. You tell me that there isn't some part of you and Paul and Charlie—and particularly that lean and hungry D.A.—you tell me that part of all this rush isn't the publicity and the pressure from the chief to close this out."

Hardiman stops his pacing.

"Look," she says in a retreating tone, knowing she has crossed the line, "I'm not saying there's any conscious cutting of corners here. I'm just asking you to tell me that all the hype around this case hasn't helped drive you all to accept the obvious."

He ignores her suggestion. "And the bottom line? Just what is it you think I oughta do here?"

"I think you should get Chasen to hold off on an indictment."

Hardiman's expression of surprise is more mocking than real. "Really? Based on this sympathy card?"

"Yes, and the fact that this Lessing was arrested on a spy charge of some kind at the same time Avery's father was in the Bureau and—"

"No! The fact is that *a* Martin Lessing was arrested, not *the* Martin Lessing. And we don't know that Avery's father had anything to do with that case. Christ, for all you know, he could have been assigned to Nome, Alaska, at the time."

"Don't you think—"

"Just wait a second. And more importantly, even assuming your premise, it wouldn't make any sense."

"But—"

"Just think about it. Let's assume that Avery's father was somehow involved with this Lessing thing. Assume he screwed him over royally. And assume that this guy Lessing is still around and been harboring a grudge all this time. He'd be what? Seventy, seventy-one, maybe? And suddenly, after all this time, he's out for revenge and so he pops who? Marian Avery? I mean, Jesus, think about it. How many times over the past thirty-five, forty years has he had an opportunity to go after old man Avery himself? I mean the guy was a congressman for Christ's sake. He was always out in public. And even if it were some—what'd the card say, 'friend' of Lessing?—that gets even more remote. And again, to go after the daughter-in-law? I mean not the congressman, or even his son, but the daughter-in-law? That makes sense to you?"

"Tell me something, Captain. Why is it that every time we go through this, everyone ignores every other clue except those that point to Avery?"

"What clues are you talking about?"

"What about the possibility of a stalker?"

"Oh, c'mon, Christine, we've been over that too many times. There's no evidence of it. Hell, you're the one who taught me the profile. Stalkers like signatures, some small sign that they've been there. Something taken, something left behind. We don't have that here."

"Yes, but—"

"Hell, even Avery said there was nothing to it. No signs at all. And if anyone would have jumped at the chance to add that meat to the stew, it would've been him."

"Maybe that ought to be your first clue that something's wrong here."

Hardiman stops and leans back against his desk, rubbing his eyes in a gesture of frustration. "I'm sorry, Sergeant, but I can't go to the D.A. with that. And I won't. At least not to tell him he can't indict. Now, I've got no problem with your going to him and telling him what you think. And let him make up his own mind."

"What about going to Avery and asking him about the card or whether he knows this Lessing, or asking his father the same thing?"

"Fine. But you're gonna have to go through his lawyer."

"You mean Layton?"

"No, Chasen says Avery's hired Jack Gabriel."

Christine smiles sourly. "Well, Avery finally wised up."

Hardiman nods. "Yeah, Gabriel's tough."

"And he's also not about to let me talk to his client."

Hardiman nods again.

"And you won't talk to the D.A."

"I told you. If you want to share your theory with Chasen, be my guest. And I also told you that you're free to follow whatever leads you think you should. But I'm also telling you that you're working this case, and that means you work with us, not against us. Okay?"

She does not answer, taking her time to absorb Hardiman's rigid expression. "Tell me something, Captain. Would you go out and arrest Avery on what you have now?"

"I think there's probable cause."

"No, that's not the question. The question is, based on everything you have right now, would you go out without a warrant and arrest Cooper Avery for the murder of his wife?"

"There's enough for a warrant."

"You don't need a warrant. And so, once again, I ask you. Would you, Orvis Beall Hardiman, given the evidence you've got right now and the legal authority to do so, would you go out and arrest Cooper Avery for the murder of his wife?"

He hesitates. "Makes no damn difference what I would or

wouldn't do. It's the grand jury and the D.A. who make those decisions."

"Captain, you and I both know you wouldn't arrest yet, even if
you were positive Avery did it. You'd wait. You'd want to know
first how this Lessing thing turned out. Wouldn't you?"

Hardiman offers no response, either by word or by gesture.

Christine's expression turns just short of a sneer. "My point,
Captain, is that if you're not certain enough yourself to make an
arrest, you ought to be willing to express those same reservations
to Chasen."

Hardiman looks out his window. "I have talked to him. He
knows how I feel, how circumstantial the case is."

"Have you told him if it were up to you alone, you wouldn't
arrest yet?"

"No. And I'm not as confident as you are about what I'd do.
The fact is there isn't anything that tells me that Avery didn't do
it, and there's a hell of a lot that says he did."

"I'm telling you he didn't do it."

Hardiman turns and shakes his head. "No, Sergeant, you're
telling me you've got a hunch he didn't do it. And as much as I
respect your talents, that's not enough."

■■■■

On Monday, April 8, shortly after nine o'clock in the morning,
while Cooper Avery and his daughter, Alice, are still asleep in a
small inn overlooking the ocean about twenty miles south of Car-
mel, California, Detectives Paul Wyzanski and Charlie Abbot appear at the offices of Thurston Construction. They had been to
Avery's house earlier, but the housekeeper reported that Avery
and his daughter were out of town. She did not know where they
had gone or when they would return. Mr. Avery had said only that
he expected to be gone for a week or ten days. That was last
Thursday and she had heard nothing since.

The detectives are ushered into the office of Edward Thurston,
who stands to greet them and offers each in turn a cup of coffee,
which each in turn declines. Thurston is older than they expected,
at least by his appearance. He is a man of medium height, with
narrow eyes set in a full, round face, a face that looks unnaturally
puffed and blotched with bright pink patches at the temples and

below the jaw line. His voice is steady, unlike his right hand, which shows a slight tremor, and he comes straight to the point.

"You here to arrest Cooper?"

Charlie Abbot and Paul Wyzanski exchange a brief glance, and Charlie says, "Yes, sir, I'm afraid we are."

Thurston shakes his head. "Nothing to be afraid of, Detective," he says. "I knew it. I never wanted to believe it, but I knew it all along."

"Sir?"

"I knew he did it." Thurston stops and pulls a handkerchief from his pocket, and the detectives watch in uncomfortable silence the difficulty with which his unsteady hand dabs at his eyes. "I know it sounds like an old cliché, but Cooper was like a son to me. He's brilliant. Aggressive. Had an eye for the future I admired. I gave him everything. I gave him this business. And he deserved it. He contributed. Worked hard, all the time. I mean really hard. I always thought he felt about this company the way I did. And I thought he and Marian were really a team. They worked well together. Same ambitions. They seemed to fit together really well. I couldn't believe it at first. But . . ."

"Yes sir."

"But the whole thing didn't make sense."

"No sir."

"No, not from the very beginning. No one would want to hurt Marian unless it was for money, or the stock. It never made sense that a burglar did that. Not that way, you know? And stealing the jewelry from the safe without even having to break in? I mean no stranger could have done that. I don't care how good a burglar he was. No, I knew it. I just knew it. And when I heard that Cooper had been whoring around with Sydney Lambert, it all made sense. That's why I went to the prosecutor. I didn't want to, but I had to let him know about the stock fight and all. Cooper just couldn't wait. I had talked to Marian. She was going to take back her voting rights. I know it. But what a thing to kill the mother of your children. My God! Even in his own right, he has more money than he could ever spend decently. Why would anyone do such a thing? And when you found her jewelry in the river . . ." Thurston again stops. Even holding the handkerchief pressed against his eyes, his hand continues to shake. "I'm sorry," he says weakly.

"We know this must be difficult for you," Paul offers. "Did you and Mr. Avery have any serious differences about the business?"

"I didn't think so," Thurston answers, suddenly sitting up straight as if he has now put his emotions aside. "Oh, there was that one time in the beginning of this Barth-Sanders business. But Cooper made it sound like he was looking after me."

"What do you mean?"

"Well, it wasn't much, but when we first learned that Barth-Sanders was about to make a run at us, Cooper and I talked about it, and he said he would understand completely if I decided to sell out. I would realize an immediate and substantial financial gain and at my age and all. He sounded so sincere. Just like he was willing to sacrifice himself if that's what I wanted."

"Wouldn't he have gained as well?"

"Oh, certainly. He'd be a very, very rich man, but he wouldn't have the business, which I'm not ashamed to say, if managed well, has an unlimited future. Our only problem is that we are very attractive to predators like Barth-Sanders. Broken up and sold off in pieces we could be worth substantially more than if everything is held together as it is now."

Paul is about to ask another question when Thurston changes directions abruptly.

"Well, gentlemen, I'm afraid Cooper's not here. And I'm sorry to say that I don't know where he is."

"Sir?"

Thurston turns to Charlie Abbot. "Yes, I'm afraid so. He called in last Thursday morning. Said he was going to take Alice—that's my granddaughter—he said he was going to take Alice up to see Ned. Damn strange, too, I thought. Since I thought that the doctors weren't allowing Alice to see Ned. But I thought, well, he wouldn't be taking her up there if the doctors hadn't said it'd be all right. I don't know that it was such a good idea. Alice is always fussing about wanting to see Ned. She's a headstrong little girl, that one. Just like her father. I guess that's why they seem to get along so well. I always thought he didn't pay enough attention to Ned. But that's another matter. Alice can be a handful. She'll sometimes even talk back to her grandmother about a thing as simple as wearing a dress to go out to dinner. And you know my daughter brought her up to know better than that."

"You haven't heard from them since last Thursday?"

"Not a word. Damn strange, now that I think about it. We don't bother them much on weekends. The relationship has been a little cool over the past few months. You can imagine."

Paul nods.

"You think he could have known he was about to be arrested?" Thurston asks.

"Perhaps. Do you have any idea where he might go?"

"No. His parents have a place down in Florida. And he has a sister in Seattle. But other than that, I don't know. I can't see Cooper running, though. He's not like that. But then I would never have thought him capable of harming my daughter either. My God, you just never know about people. You just never know what they're capable of, do you?"

■■■

Albert Chasen was barely able to control his rage. Armed with his indictment and certain that Avery would be available, Chasen had quietly alerted the press to be ready for a photo opportunity: Cooper Avery, son of the former congressman, prominent businessman and society don, in handcuffs and escorted into the county jail for processing and a bond hearing before a county commissioner. The prosecutor had donned his best suit and consulted his wife about which shirt and tie might best show him to advantage under the bright lights the film crews would bring to the press conference to follow. But Cooper Avery was nowhere to be found.

The press hounded Chasen's secretary while the state's attorney made repeated phone calls to the state police, only to be convinced finally that there would be no arrest that day. Trying to make the best of it, Chasen stood before the press and announced the indictment, saying also that he had agreement with defense counsel that Avery would voluntarily surrender.

Jack Gabriel agreed. "Yes, I spoke to Mr. Chasen about this. He assured me that he would notify me when an indictment was to be handed down and that my client could voluntarily appear in court. However, Mr. Chasen did not abide by his agreement. If he had, he could have avoided this little embarrassment. My client is on vacation and cannot be reached. No, I don't know where he is."

This literally was true. Gabriel had instructed Cooper not to tell him where he was going to be or how he could be reached other than by leaving a message with his sister. Cooper was to call in at a set time each day, but again, he was never to say where he was unless specifically asked by Gabriel or Lisa Paretti.

"But be assured that my client will appear voluntarily," Gabriel told the press. "Indeed he is quite anxious to get on with the trial. He has had these false rumors and suspicions hanging over his head ever since the tragic death of his wife. He wants the truth to come out. And anyone who knows me will tell you that I never make predictions in cases. But I will say this. We do not intend to simply show that the state does not have the evidence to establish my client's guilt; we intend to affirmatively prove that my client is absolutely innocent. We intend to prove that this crime was committed by someone else. That's all I have."

On the eleven o'clock news, Albert Chasen was seen but not heard, a voice-over describing the now public indictment. Jack Gabriel's entire statement was replayed.

Three days have passed, and Cooper Avery and Jack Gabriel sneak quietly into the courtroom of Stiles Newcomb. The county, unlike its more heavily populated neighbors which surround Washington and Baltimore to the north, has only one circuit court judge, and that judge is Stiles Newcomb. That makes Jack Gabriel's maneuverings easier.

Stiles Newcomb has been on the bench for twenty-two years and no one can recall an election in which he ran opposed. The local bar often refers to him as "His Majesty," although more with affection than derision. Secure in his position and power, Judge Newcomb is not known for slavish adherence to the procedural niceties. But neither is he sloppy. He is a man who likes matters in his courtroom, indeed in his courthouse, to proceed expeditiously, without the clutter of nonproductive arguments over form and procedure. And he loves a good courtroom fight. On both counts, he has long ago come to admire Jack Gabriel.

It is just two o'clock when Jack Gabriel and Cooper Avery walk into the courtroom, as Gabriel has alerted the judge's chambers they would, and Judge Newcomb orders his bailiff, "Call down to the state's attorney and get someone up here. And get someone from the clerk's office up here with a copy of the Avery indictment."

Five minutes later an assistant state's attorney, looking a bit confused, is handed a copy of the indictment. "Excuse me, Your Honor," the assistant says nervously, "but I think this is a matter Mr. Chasen would want to handle himself."

"Sir," Judge Newcomb addresses the young prosecutor, "I'm sure Mr. Chasen has better things to do than waste his time on a simple bond hearing."

"But Your Honor—"

"Sir, the state is present; we will proceed."

And they do. It takes less than five minutes for the court to release Cooper Avery on his personal recognizance.

"Your Honor—" the assistant prosecutor again protests.

"Sir, I understand that Mr. Chasen would want you to holler like a stuck pig. But let's not waste our time here. Mr. Avery was outside the jurisdiction when your boss decided to trump up some publicity with an arrest he had been assured by Mr. Gabriel was unnecessary. And Mr. Avery certainly has the financial resources that if he had wanted to, he could already be on some tropical island where he could probably live quite comfortably for the rest of his life. But he's not. He came here of his own accord because his counsel says he's going to prove you all wrong. That he is as he claims to be, innocent. And right now, this court, as the law commands, presumes that he is innocent. That's all, gentlemen. The defendant is released on his own recognizance."

Everyone agrees that round one has gone to the defense, even Albert Chasen, who vows a silent oath to avenge his embarrassment. But still, Chasen is worried. These statements by Gabriel about proving someone else did it are disturbing. It isn't like Gabriel. It isn't like any competent defense attorney to publicly promise affirmative proof. He wonders, and he feels the first stab of concern.

23 $\mathcal{I}$t is an uncertain day, too warm for winter, too cold for spring. The morning's drizzle has stopped, but the clouds retreat at a snail's pace, trailing behind a thick gray dank. Inside the diner, at the end of the counter, amid the clutter of conversations and the clank of heavy china against the worn Formica and the oily steam rising from the grill, Paul Wyzanski hunches over his coffee, the fingers of one hand curled around but not quite gripping the handle of the cup, unsure whether he really wants this second refill. He is unsure, too, how Christine can derive such apparent pleasure from the spectacle of Avery's lawyer smuggling his client into court and walking away with a release on personal recognizance while the state police were conducting a statewide manhunt and issuing teletypes throughout the country.

"I fail to see the humor in this," Paul says.

Christine sits erect on the stool beside him, her trench coat laid neatly across her lap, her coffee cup poised at her smile. She stops and looks at Paul. "You would if you'd take your own advice," she says, then sips.

"What's that supposed to mean?"

"You know, not taking these things personally? Don't get emotionally involved and all that?"

"You think this is personal?"

"I think it sure sounds like it. I mean you did your job. What do you care? Besides it wasn't you who got gamed. It was Chasen. And if he had been a tad more honorable and a tad less hungry for a headline, it wouldn't have been so easy for Avery and his lawyer to make a fool of him."

Paul sits up and looks straight at her. "*Us,* Christine. They made fools out of us."

Her smile leaves her, and her eyes narrow. "No, Paul, no one made a fool out of me."

Paul's back stiffens. He turns again to his coffee, which he sips in a long, silent draw. "You know," he says without looking up, "it's really beginning to bother me the way you keep talking about this case like we're on opposite sides."

"I wasn't aware that there were sides here."

"Oh yeah, Christine, there're sides. And you know it."

"No, I don't know that at all. What, you think this is some kind of contest we're in?"

"Yeah, whether you like it or not, the fact of the matter is that's exactly what we're in, a contest. And just because you might not like the play called doesn't give you the right to work against the team."

"Jesus, Paul, are you listening to yourself? The team? Calling plays? For God's sake, we're talking about charging a man with first-degree murder."

"Yeah, so? This isn't the first time that's ever happened. I mean that's what we do for a living, remember? We go after people who kill other people and we charge them with murder. This is just another case. Why're you turning it into such a damn crusade?"

"It's not a crusade," she snaps. "But just maybe it does bother me that you and everyone else thinks it's just another case." She stops to gather in her sudden anger. Her eyes scan the diner, and her words start slowly, almost as if they are directed to a different audience. "Maybe it bothers me that that's all we ever think about. 'It's just another case.' I mean do you ever stop to think about what we're doing to people? I don't mean just to someone like Avery, but to the families, to the kids. What happens to them? And what if you're wrong? What if a few months down the road you figure out that you were wrong? What are you and Charlie and Chasen going to do about it? I'll tell what you'll do. Nothing. Not a damn thing. Not even an apology. You'll just walk away, won't you? Won't give a second thought to what you've left behind. Just another case. Well, maybe I'm tired of watching that happen over and over.

Maybe I think we ought to make sure we're charging the right man for the right reason. Maybe I think we have some obligation to try to find the truth, not just probable cause. And it's for damn sure I don't think we ought to go along with indicting Cooper Avery just so Albert Chasen can prop up his political career."

"That's a real nice speech. I'll be sure and tell my kid to invite you to his school's career day." He shakes his head and turns his attention to his coffee cup. "Yeah, me, Charlie, the captain, Chasen, we're all idiots, right? Everyone but you. And none of us gives a damn about the truth, right? But not you. Not Joan of Arc." He turns back to her. "What's your secret, Christine? You've got some divine guidance, maybe? Maybe you're tuned in to the next life? Been talking to Marian Avery herself, have you? Got the inside scoop? Or maybe you were there, or maybe the killer sent you a videotape you haven't told us about? Tell me, what's your secret channel to the truth?"

Christine's face is rigid, and her eyes seem fixed on something she sees beyond him. She breaks her rigor to suddenly rummage through her purse for a five-dollar bill, which she tosses on the counter. "The secret, Detective, is that I deal with what is, not with what I want it to be." She spins off her stool and takes a step before stopping and turning back. "And it's Detective Sergeant. Don't you and your partner forget it."

She turns and is out the door without another word.

24 $\mathscr{C}$ooper Avery is leaning over a large map of the county, correlating various points with the two dozen aerial photographs which clutter the long conference table.

"This is Fishing Creek, and right at this point here is our property." He reaches for one of the photographs. "This is pretty close. Right here at the edge? That's the mouth of the river. You can't really tell from this photograph, but where the land ends right here? That's the bay." He takes his blue pencil to the map. "It would be this small area right here." He is not sure of the purpose of all this, but he is impressed by the detail of Jack Gabriel's preparation.

Gabriel turns to his young associate. "Carl, don't we have a better shot of this point, one with both the house and a wider view that shows the mouth of the river and the bay?"

The associate shuffles through the photographs. "Yeah, here's one."

Gabriel nods his approval. "Make a note to call the highway department. See if we can't get one of those high-altitude shots of the whole area. We need something that'll cover the area from above the Maryville bridge down past the mouth of the river, and maybe a mile or two north and south of the river along the bay shore."

Carl makes his note.

"And tell Eddie to track down this guy Barkin, the waterman who found the jewelry. Have him take a map and some of these photographs and see if he can't get the guy to point out exactly where the oyster beds are, exactly where he found the jewelry."

Carl notes the instructions he is to pass on to the private investigator hired to assist them.

Gabriel again looks at Cooper. They are speculating about the possible escape routes of the killer, accepting the government's theory that the escape was by water. "Now, let's say you're in something like your Boston Whaler, and you're here at the mouth of the river, north or south, where's the next creek or someplace where you could put in easily?"

Cooper shrugs and runs his finger along the map. "Well, going north there's really nothing for a good three or four miles. It's all shallows and sandbars along the shore there; most of them run fifty to seventy-five yards out. I suppose you could run up and wade in, or just beach a boat, but there're no docks or marinas in that area."

"What about roads close to shore?"

"Yeah, well, there's Muddy Bottom Road. It pretty much follows the shoreline. You can see it here," Cooper says, pointing to the map. "It runs north–south anywhere from about a hundred yards to maybe three-quarters of a mile from the water."

"What about houses, developments?"

"Not much. Mostly farms. Except around Muddy Bottom itself. It's an old squatters' community. There's a dock of sorts there. Pretty much falling apart. I don't know that anyone actually uses it and there're a bunch of small boats on moorings right off the beach. But no stranger's going to be able to put in and leave a boat without him or it being noticed. That's about it until you get as far up as Beall's Creek."

"Nothing else?"

"Not that I know about."

"What about this fella Johns? What's his place like?"

"Well, actually, I didn't think about that. He's got a small dock there, right around the point from our property. I don't know, I guess maybe it's a third of a mile or less from the mouth of the river. He's got a good three, four feet of water at low tide. But he raises bloody hell if anyone tries to use his dock or even anchors inside that point. The kids like to go swimming off their boats in there and he's always trying to run them off. But as far as his dock, that's off limits."

"And to the south?"

"Nothing, really. The cliffs start just south of the river and there's no place at all until you pass them and even beyond that I don't know of anything until you reach the Narrows, and that's way down here."

"And so if you had just killed your wife and you were going to escape by water, you wouldn't head toward the bay."

Gabriel and his client have quickly reached a level of comfort and understanding that allows Gabriel to ask such a question without hesitation or apology, and that allows Cooper similarly to answer.

"No, not at all. It'd be too hard to find your way around that shore at night, particularly if it was overcast or foggy or whatever."

"Which reminds me," Gabriel cuts in. "You said it was clear and sunny that day."

"Yes, at least when I got home that afternoon."

"What if the night before had been just as clear?"

"Well, you have to remember, that time of year, late October, November, the water's still warm and the air is turning cold. Often you'll get a pretty thick mist rising off the river. Anybody trying to navigate in the dark and probably in a fog, too, would have a hard time, even if he knew the area."

"Carl, contact the weather service. Get the weather conditions for that day, and for the day before, including temperature ranges. Highs and lows. Also, if the weather service doesn't have it, check with Natural Resources. See if they might have water temperatures for that area at the same time. Any reports of fog. And find someone who might be able to testify about fogs developing from the temperature differences. . . . Now, where were we?"

Cooper smiles. "Trying to beach a boat along the bay shore."

"Right, go on."

"Anyway, even if the air was clear, at night, trying to beach a boat somewhere close to where you'd have to leave a car or something? It'd be pretty dodgy. You'd really have to know that area well. Plus, just leaving a car along the side of the road down there would get anyone's curiosity up who saw it. No, I'd head back upriver. From my dock to town, it's only a few minutes' run in a whaler and there're two pretty good-sized marinas there. Hell, in the middle of the night, you'd have your pick of dozens of small boats you could steal and return without being seen. And there'd be enough cars around that one more wouldn't be noticed."

"Okay, assume you head up the river and toss the jewels somewhere along the way. How do you explain their showing up down past the mouth of the river, way down here, by the oyster beds?"

"Well, you said they were in a canvas bag, right?"

Gabriel nods.

"Well, the bag would have some flotation to it for a little time. I mean there'd be enough air in it to slow its sinking at least, and in the winter the current's pretty strong there, particularly with the tide going out. It wouldn't be unusual for something like that to be carried downstream quite a ways before it hit bottom. Hell, even after it hit bottom, with the tides and current, over a couple months' time it could easily have been rolled along the bottom awhile before it really settled in."

"I guess that's one explanation," Gabriel says, then looks at his associate. "Carl, tell Eddie also to ask this guy Barkin about all this, you know, access to the shore north and south of the river, navigating at night, if there was a fog, how strong the currents and tides are. Whatever. If he answers the right way, we can probably make some mileage on cross. But just in case, have Eddie dig up another waterman who can testify about the same thing. You know what we want."

Cooper leans wearily over the table, resting his forehead in his hand. "I'm not sure I understand why we're spending so much time figuring out what the killer might have done. Isn't that the prosecutor's job?"

"Look," Gabriel says, leaning back in his chair and propping his feet on the table, "we have to establish the physical improbability that you could have done this. The government's theory is you came and went by the river. We have to show how improbable that would be for you, at night, in a fog hopefully, having to get some other boat but your own, then dumping the jewels out in the bay and returning to New York unseen. No, we have to establish you couldn't have done that."

"But why do we need all that if Sydney Lambert's now willing to testify that I was with her the entire time? You did talk to her, right?"

"Yes, she's on board," Gabriel says, "but she's damaged goods.

She told the police a different tale. Which reminds me. Carl, draft a sort of nasty, whining letter to Albert Chasen asking him if he's made any statement or given any instructions to any witnesses, particularly Sydney Lambert, encouraging them not to speak to defense counsel."

Carl nods as Cooper frowns and says, "Wait a minute. I thought you just said you talked to Sydney."

"Relax, everything's under control," Gabriel says with a grin. "I want Chasen to think Sydney's not cooperating with us. It should make him feel more comfortable with her and encourage him to call her as his witness. It'll have more of an impact if it's one of his own witnesses who supports your alibi."

"And what about the issue of her being charged with perjury if she testifies differently than she did in the grand jury?"

"Cooper, that's not your concern. Besides, like I said, everything's under control. Now, where were we?"

"Still out on the water," Carl offers.

"Oh yes," Gabriel says to Cooper. "Now another thing I want to be clear on in my mind. I assume, of course, that you are not that familiar with the river and creeks and the shoreline in that area."

"Well—"

"I mean, you are a businessman, after all. And you work long hours, often six, seven days a week, and over the past few years you have had very little leisure time. And as far as your hunting, for example, you always used the blind right there in the marsh off your property, correct?"

"Well, yes, but—"

"And once in a while you'd go for an afternoon's sail or take the little boat out fishing in the river, but you certainly could not be considered knowledgeable of the area like, say, a local waterman or someone who'd lived there all his life. That's correct, isn't it?"

Cooper hesitates, and Gabriel adds, "You're certainly not knowledgeable enough to pick your way around these sandbars and shoals and small creeks or whatever in the dark, in the fog, correct?"

It suddenly dawns on Cooper that these matters are not being put to him as questions. He nods his agreement. "Yes, that's right."

"Good, yes, I thought that was the case." Gabriel hesitates with another thought. "Carl, let's check the county police records for say a two-week period, a week before and a week after that day. See if anyone reported a boat stolen or one found, particularly if anyone found a boat along the bay shore in that area." Carl nods and writes himself a note while Gabriel asks, "Next?"

"I've got a question," Cooper says. "What about this Lessing thing? You don't think we ought to follow up on that?"

Gabriel twists his mouth in consternation and leans his head against the back of his chair. "No, I think we should, to the extent we can," he says, but without much conviction, "but right now, that issue has to be given a pretty low priority. We don't have the luxury of time here. We have a trial to get ready for, and at best, that's a pretty thin thread to grab."

"You don't think there's anything to it?"

"I have no idea. I can see where it might have some possibilities. Those articles that, ah, what's her name, Detective Boland?"

Cooper nods.

"Those articles she sent you kind of pique my interest. But even if it's true, we're a long way from being able to do anything with it. Right now it's much too speculative for a jury to grab onto. One, it's too distant in time, and two, even if there is some connection between this Lessing and your father, for example, any relationship to your wife's death would seem too attenuated to get much mileage out of. Not yet anyway. Besides, we don't know that there really is a connection. Have you talked to your father about this yet?"

"Yes, some. But he had no idea what I was talking about. He's really slowed down. Mentally, I mean. He sometimes has trouble focusing on things. Last month, his former assistant came by for a visit and he didn't even recognize him."

"Well," Gabriel says, "maybe you can try again. Maybe something might spark his memory. You just never know what might be there. In the meantime, we need to find a better candidate for the murder, someone easier for the jury to replace you with, or if not replace you, at least see that the circumstances could as easily point to him."

Cooper rubs his temples and lets out a sigh that sounds almost like laughter. "Have you got a candidate?"

"What about this Oliver Johns?"

Cooper looks up, startled. "Are you serious?"

"Why not?"

"Well, I don't know. Ollie Johns? I mean you think anyone would believe he'd kill Marian because of some squabble over whether he kept his yard neat?"

"Cooper, you stole his land from him."

"Now wait a minute, I never stole anything. That deal was straight up and—"

"Cooper, listen to me. We're talking about a motive for murder. We're talking about what might be in the man's mind. You're the rich-boy son of a former congressman. You're married to the daughter of one of the wealthiest men in the state. But it's new money. Not like him. Not old family. Fifteen generations in the county and all that crap. And you stole his land and made a fortune developing it. You took and renovated and moved into the house he was probably born in. And where's he end up? A boozer living in a leftover tenant house on a spit of land where his great-grandfather probably kept the slaves. And to add insult to injury, your wife calls the county on him to tell him to clean up the pitiful piece of property that's left to him. Who knows? Things like that can work on a man's mind. Maybe things have turned even worse for him lately. Maybe he starts thinking you and your wife are the cause of all his troubles. One night he's drunk, or he's depressed, and he just snaps. And think about it. The man's lived around there all his life. Probably knows the river and the area around it like the back of his hand. Including your house. *And,* if you accept the police theory that the killer came and went by water and dropped the jewelry overboard on the way back, look at where those jewels were dropped." Gabriel moves to the map. "Now we've got to pinpoint this more precisely, but according to the police and what you've told us, those oyster beds are right about there," he says, pointing. "Pretty much on the line you'd travel if you were taking a small boat from your dock around the point and to where you say Johns lives. Right?"

Cooper stares at the map, his expression pinching to a frown before he says very quietly, "Right." He looks to Gabriel. "Do you really think he did it?"

"Do you have any reason to believe that he didn't?"

"I don't know. I just never gave him any serious thought. I mean, do you think we could prove something like that?"

"We don't have to prove it. We just have to raise a serious

question about it. Get the jury to start asking themselves why the police or the D.A. didn't check out that possibility. Start thinking that maybe the evidence against you is no stronger than it would be against Ollie Johns. That's some reasonable doubt they can sink their teeth into."

"And what about Johns?"

"What about him?"

"I don't know. I just—I don't know." Cooper looks away for a moment, considering his own question. He then moves on. "You think we should just forget this Lessing thing and Sergeant Boland?"

"No. I still want you to call and see if you can't push her to meet with me. Again, tell her that I'll guarantee all the confidentiality she wants, but I really want to talk with her in person. In the meantime, we have to operate as if this Lessing thing is a complete wash. Okay?"

Cooper shrugs his approval. "Okay."

25 Wedged between Route 395 and the
harbor's Northwest Branch is an accretion
of local bars and ethnic eateries, of merchants and mechanics and storefront lawyers, of the urban poor and the urban
pioneers who view their South Baltimore
neighborhood with eyes jaundiced and accepting and hopeful, with
a spirit as mixed as their backgrounds. Geographically centered on
the cross between Hanover and Covington is a Jewish deli offering
Southern fried chicken by the part, a grudging but quite profitable
nod to those who for years have been mistakenly drawn by the
implications of its name, Chic 'n' Jo's.

It is midafternoon, well after the lunchtime rush, and Christine
Boland signals the waitress to her booth.

"Check?" asks the young girl with soft Oriental eyes and a hard,
clipped voice.

"Yes, please," Christine answers. "Oh, and can you tell me, is
Mrs. Sapperstein here today?"

The girl looks at Christine suspiciously. "Uh, yeah. Why, sum-
pin' wrong?"

"No, not at all. I just have some business to see her about."

"Okay." The girl brightens, comforted that there is nothing for
which she is to be held liable. "I'll get her."

Christine thanks the waitress with instructions to keep the
change, and she sits back and takes the last sip of her coffee.

Almost at once a woman appears at Christine's booth carrying
a look of even deeper suspicion than that of the young waitress.

She is no more than five feet tall but stands erect, almost leaning back, while her hands wipe the soiled belly of her apron. "Can I help you?" she asks, raising the back of one hand to her forehead to wipe away a hint of perspiration and pushing aside a curl of black hair turning gray.

"Mrs. Sapperstein?"

"Yes."

"Mrs. Sapperstein, I'm Christine Boland. I'm a detective with the state police."

"Yes?"

"I was wondering if I might speak to you for a few minutes."

Mrs. Sapperstein glances toward a balding, narrow-faced man behind the counter, who puts down his carving knife and comes to the booth.

"Something wrong?" the man asks, as he moves just a bit closer to the booth than his wife.

"She's from the police," Mrs. Sapperstein says, and then to Christine, "This is my husband, Mr. Sapperstein."

Christine smiles. "Hello." The man nods but says nothing. "Please, there's no reason to be concerned. I'd simply like to ask you a few questions about Byron Roth."

The news does not relieve the woman's concern, but it does add curiosity to her expression. She looks at her husband.

"You are Mr. Roth's daughter, aren't you?" Christine asks.

"What is this? Whaddaya want with her father?"

"Mr. Sapperstein, really, there's nothing to be concerned about. No one's in trouble here, at least no one having to do with you or your family. I simply want to ask some questions about something that happened a long time ago; about some things having to do with a man named Martin Lessing."

Mrs. Sapperstein again looks at her husband, her frown deepening. Her husband leans closer to Christine. "What is that, you want to talk to an old man about something forty years ago?"

"I take it you recognize the name Martin Lessing?"

The couple exchange a look that concedes they are caught. The man says, "Yes, I know the name, but not the man. I never met him. Only from stories I've heard. But they're old stories no one wants to hear anymore. What is it you want from Mr. Roth?"

"I want to hear about Mr. Lessing. I want to know what happened to him." She stops, but neither Mr. or Mrs. Sapperstein responds to the silence. Christine goes on. "I know that this man Lessing was accused of stealing government documents back in 1952. I know there were some newspaper articles that suggested a connection between him and Mrs. Sapperstein's father, but that as far as I can find, Mr. Roth was never accused or charged with anything, except that he may have lost a very successful career in radio because of what happened to this Martin Lessing. A few days ago I learned that Lessing died in jail, shortly after he was arrested, so there was never a trial. He never had a chance to publicly defend himself. Apparently, neither did your father."

Mr. Sapperstein cuts through Christine's gaze at his wife. "Who told you to come here? Mr. Roth doesn't live here."

Christine keeps her attention directed at Mrs. Sapperstein. "Well, it's taken me a while, but it's no mystery. I started at the radio station where your father used to work. People know people who knew people and so forth. One person leads to another, and finally I was led here. No one seemed to know, or at least no one was willing to tell me, where your father is, but you and this deli are certainly well known."

"And so what do the police want to talk with Mr. Roth about?" Mr. Sapperstein asks.

Again, Christine focuses on the woman, who she guesses is in her mid-fifties, and very tired. "Well, like I said. It's about Martin Lessing and what happened back in 1952. You see, I think this Martin Lessing may have had some connection to the former congressman, Charles Avery. And if he did, there may be some connection to a matter that is under investigation now. I need to find out if that's true."

"Why, what's this got to do with us?" Mr. Sapperstein challenges, as his wife slides past him and into the booth opposite Christine, looking suddenly intent. "Does this have anything to do with that case down south?" the woman asks. "The wife who was murdered? Wasn't it the congressman's son who was charged?" She then looks at her husband, who signals his understanding with raised eyebrows as he, too, slides into the booth, next to his wife. Together they wait for an answer.

"Yes," Christine answers. "And yes, I think there may be a connection to whatever happened before. I don't really know, but that's what I'm trying to find out."

"But what could something almost forty years ago have to do with a man killing his wife today?"

"Well, Mrs. Sapperstein, we're not altogether sure that he did kill his wife. There is some evidence to suggest that the woman's death may have something to do with this thing with Martin Lessing."

"But the papers said the husband was charged. The police and everybody. Aren't you from the same police?"

"Yes, but—"

Mr. Sapperstein lets out a sneering sigh as he looks away with raised eyebrows. His wife puts her hand on his arm, and says, "Officer . . . Your name is what?"

"Boland, Detective Boland."

"And your first name?"

"Christine."

"Detective Christine Boland. Tell me, Detective Christine Boland," she says, leaning forward insistently, "do you think my father had something to do with this wife being killed?"

"No, not at all."

"Because my father is an old man. He hasn't had his health in fifteen years. He can't even come down here to the store on his own, if that's what you think. And I don't want you disturbing him about something that is none of our business. His heart is not good. He can't be upset like that. And none of us has any reason to want to help the congressman's son. We don't wish bad times on anyone, but we've got no reason to want to help Charles Avery."

Christine's eyes brighten and she concentrates on Mrs. Sapperstein. "So," she says softly, "there is a connection to Congressman Avery."

The couple exchange glances.

"Look," Christine says, "understand that I am not here to investigate your father. Without getting into all the details, whoever killed Mrs. Avery certainly was not an elderly man in failing health. I don't even know if the killing itself had anything to do with this Lessing. But right after the wife's death someone made a point of reminding the Averys of Martin Lessing, and I'm trying to find out why. And from what I'm hearing in talking to you, I suspect that you and your family are certainly not admirers of Congressman Avery, and that he may have had something to do with what happened to your father almost forty years ago. I know that the congressman used to be with the FBI. Maybe he was the one who arrested Lessing, or your father?"

"My father was never arrested."

"But he did have some connection with Avery, I mean before Avery was a congressman. Am I right? Back in 1952?"

The Sappersteins return Christine's stare, and she thinks it is time for the speech she has prepared.

"You know, we all think we know what it was like in the fifties, with McCarthy and J. Edgar Hoover and all that. But most people tend to forget, if they ever really understood. It's just something for the history books. I went back through a lot of old newspapers and even I was surprised how much of that craziness was going on." She stops and shakes her head. "I thought nothing surprised me anymore. But every week, even every few days, you could read another article about someone being called to testify before some committee, or people being fired because they exercised their rights or being called a Communist because they spoke up for someone else's rights—whatever. Maybe that's what happened to Martin Lessing . . . and to your father. Maybe they got caught up in a lot of hysteria, and maybe, just maybe, in a different way, that's what's happening right now to the congressman's son. Maybe the times and the reasons are all different, but maybe the bottom line is the same. What if Charles Avery's son is being railroaded because of who he is and not because of what he's done? The fact is, somebody, for some reason, made a point of connecting this back to Martin Lessing. I'm just trying to find out why, that's all."

Mr. Sapperstein squirms in his seat. "Do we have to talk to you? You have a warrant or subpoena or something?"

"No, you're not required to say anything."

"Because we have a business here. We can't just let our business go to talk forty years ago. We—"

"Chic," his wife says quietly, patting his forearm, "it's all right. Maybe this detective should hear the truth of what happened."

Mr. Sapperstein scowls at his wife, but she nods and says again, "It's all right. You take care of the counter. If I need you, I'll let you know."

He hesitates a moment, then leaves the booth. His wife calls after him, "And tell Ling to bring us some coffee."

■■■

I don't know everything. Only what I heard from my father and there were many things he wouldn't talk about, questions he wouldn't answer. I was just a young girl then. Only fourteen. I knew my husband even then. He was sweet on me but my parents said I was still too young. But I knew. He's a good man, my husband. It makes him angry still, everything that happened. But he's always been there for me *and* my father. It's not good that my father should be reminded again of all this. He's not a well man. The whole time Charles Avery was a congressman, you should have heard. It was bad enough when he was just a name we'd hear, but when he was a congressman. It was very hard on all of us, the way my father would get. But like my husband says, "Who could blame him?"

I don't know really what happened. I remember it was a Sunday, in the middle of the afternoon. My father wasn't there, and my mother came running upstairs and all of a sudden we were packing clothes, and my mother and my brother, Shel—Sheldon. He was only eleven then. He died a few years ago. But all of a sudden, my mother and my brother, we had all packed some bags and we were on a train to New York. We ended up staying there all summer. My brother and I missed the last month or so of school that year. That fall they let me take a test, but my brother ended up having to repeat the fifth grade. It killed him, the embarrassment. He wouldn't let anybody see it, though.

Anyway, when we went to New York, we stayed with my aunt and uncle in Queens. My father came, too, but later, and tried to find a job in the city. But he couldn't. And he wouldn't sell the house here in Baltimore for what people were offering. It was a nice house, with a big porch, up on Bolton Hill. He said everyone was trying to steal our house because of the trouble he was having, and he wouldn't let them do it. So that fall, we came back to Baltimore. But eventually, he did sell the house. He had to, he couldn't find work. Not for a long time. And so we moved in with my grandparents. My mother's parents.

But that didn't work out very well. My father's pride. He couldn't stand it. Living off my grandparents and my mother going out to work. He was very bitter. He couldn't let go of it. After a few years, my mother just couldn't take it anymore, and she divorced him. For a long time—I don't know, it was five, six years —we never saw him. I don't know what he did, and he won't talk about that time. But anyway, we didn't see him for a long time, not until after my mother got remarried. She was lucky. She found a nice man and the last twenty years of her life were happy. You could see her sadness whenever my father's name was mentioned, but otherwise she was happy. Lived happy, died happy . . .

I'm sorry, it just brings back so many things that we never talk about.

But my father? He was just never the same. When he came back to see us, Shel and me—my mother had just gotten remarried and they were fixing up their house—and Shel and me, we were still living with my grandparents, you know, until my mother's house was ready. Well, by then I was engaged to my husband, but Shel was still going to live with Mother, for a while anyway. Then he joined the service. My father never forgave him for that. He said the government didn't deserve his son.

Anyway, it was only a few months after my mother got remarried, it was a Sunday, I think, near the end of June, and my father just showed up, like he had just been gone for a few weeks. He came to see my brother and me. He even brought us presents, like we were still children. He didn't look the same at all. He was thin, and his face was drawn, and his clothes looked like what he was. He had a job then, selling Oldsmobiles out on the Ritchie Highway.

It took us a long time, but we got over it. We learned to be a family again. Even Frank. That was my mother's husband. He was such a good man. So patient. He even tried to help my father. But my father could be very stubborn and proud, and he was always on hard times, it seemed. But somehow, he managed to keep himself together. Until the past few years. He's been sick a lot. His heart and his circulation. But he has his own place. We help him as much as we can, and he manages. He has tapes of some of his old radio shows and he'll sit there for hours, playing them back, over and over and over.

I'm sorry.

What?

No, I never knew Martin Lessing. I met him, I think. I think he and his wife came to our house once. I remember my parents having a dinner for maybe a dozen people. I don't know what the occasion was. At that time they had a lot of friends and they had people to the house all the time. And after everything with the FBI, I don't remember anyone coming to the house for years. Anyway, after it all happened, I remember asking my father who Martin Lessing was, and he said that I had met him at this dinner party. But I really didn't remember him. But I can tell you that my father considered him a good friend and he was destroyed by what happened, my father, that is, by what happened to Lessing, his dying in jail. He was frightened, too, but he really never got over Lessing being arrested and dying in jail like he did. He tried to raise some money and to hire a lawyer for Lessing, but Lessing died before he could do anything. I don't know, but I think my father somehow always felt guilty about that.

No, I really don't know. All I can tell you is that my father to this day says it was all a lie. That the FBI lied about everything. He's always said that whatever papers Lessing had weren't even classified. He's always said that Charles Avery—he was the FBI man who arrested Lessing—he always said that Avery lied about everything, that if there really were secret papers, Avery planted them or whatever. And it was supposed to be all over some woman.

Oh yes, there was a woman involved. I don't know who she was. My father would never say her name. He always said that Avery had done enough to destroy her already and that speaking her name couldn't help anyone. I have no idea what that all means.

Yes, he did. Lessing's wife had a baby girl. She was born the day Lessing died. He never saw his daughter.

I don't know, really. I know his wife left the country shortly after Lessing died. I don't know where they went. I know my father and some friends got together some money for them, but I don't think it was much. And I know that even years later my father always tried to send them a little something. I only remember that because my mother and father would sometimes argue about it. It wasn't that Mother was opposed to him sending the money so much as it was that he really couldn't afford it. He was out of work for a very long time.

No, I have no idea what ever became of them. We don't ever talk about it anymore. It serves no purpose. No one cares.

I don't know. I'd have to think about it. Talk to my husband. I just don't see what good it would do to drag it all up with my father again. And I'm not sure that even he could remember everything today. His mind is not as strong as it was, and his memories are mixed with a lot of bitterness and anger and disappointment. You can imagine. All those lives ruined by a lie told by one man. You can imagine.

Oh yes, there was a woman. It was all about a woman.

26 lex has seen this before, several
times, and each time it has signaled some
eruption. But until tonight, the signs have
always been silent: her sudden, steady
withdrawal from conversation into a nervous, fidgeting quiet; the restive backing
into thoughts she irritably insists do not exist until the cage into
which she has crawled can no longer hold her, and she leaves, for
a day or two or three. Tonight, however, the fixation is anything
but silent.

"Hold it!" he yelps, as Christine sweeps his still full plate from
the table and heads for her kitchen, where she has already rinsed
her dish and put it in the dishwasher. "Do you mind if I finish my
dinner?"

Christine stops and looks back at him, confused. She then looks
at his plate and blushes. "Oh, sorry," she says, and again lays his
plate in front of him before continuing her pacing monologue.
"Don't you see? It's finally beginning to make some sense."

"But—"

"No, listen, think about it. She said there was a woman involved.
The whole thing was over some woman."

"But—"

"No, no. Listen!" She insists, almost like a child in the midst of
a tantrum.

Alex shakes his head slowly, retreating to his dinner as Christine
continues to pace.

"Avery's father somehow framed this man Martin Lessing and

Roth. Ruined them. Just think about it. Imagine the impact on their families. And however Avery did it, or why, whatever it was about, it was over some woman. Now Roth's daughter says even Roth would never mention this woman's name. He always said that Avery had already done her enough harm. And remember? Remember what I said right from the beginning? Remember I said that there was something about the scene that just smelled of a woman, something beyond just that cigarette butt on the vanity? There was just something about it. Even the professor said the same thing. When I told him about the scene, the use of the pillow, the way it had been placed over Marian Avery's head, he said it had the feel of a woman."

She stops and stares at him.

Alex looks up from his dinner and spreads his hands in question. "What? You're asking me?"

"Don't you see it?"

He shrugs. "Well, I understand the point you're making and I'm certainly no detective—"

"Just say it," she snaps impatiently.

"No, I don't see it. I'm not saying it's not there, I'm just saying that I think you're stretching things a bit. First, as I remember it, didn't you tell me that the little boy who was found in the kitchen had some feathers and blood on his hand? I mean, whatever the killer might have done with it, wouldn't that tell you that it was the boy who placed the pillow over his mother's head? I mean, wouldn't that make sense? That the boy wouldn't want to look at what had happened to his mother?"

Christine's eyes remain fixed on Alex, and she doesn't answer.

"And this stuff about a woman being behind all this or involved or whatever because of something Avery's father did. Boy, I don't know. I mean, you're talking about a lady who'd be what? In her seventies, probably? And waiting all this time to get revenge, and then not going after Avery senior, but his daughter-in-law? That just doesn't make any sense to me."

"But what about the card? 'From the friends of Martin Lessing.' What about that?"

Alex takes a deep breath. "Well, I tell you," he says, "I think everything you said and found about there being some people out there with a serious grudge against Avery's old man makes a lot of sense. And it sounds like these people have good reason to be bitter or whatever. But you're talking about something almost forty years ago. I mean, to wait all that time without doing anything and then to kill his daughter-in-law? No, I don't see it. Like I say, I'm no detective, but what makes a lot more sense to me is that there is someone out there who knows and remembers how Avery screwed over this guy Lessing. Maybe he read about the murder in the papers, and out of bitterness or whatever, he, she, whoever, sent the family that card. A reminder maybe that what goes around comes around: a subtle message that maybe the congressman deserves a little tragedy in his life." Alex shakes his head with a chuckle. "A little too subtle, though."

"What do you mean?"

"Well, if in fact someone really was trying to send a message with the card, the message was completely lost on the one who was supposed to get it."

Christine frowns, and Alex continues. "I mean, if you're right and there's any connection at all, or even if it's just what I said, you're the only one who seems to have put any of this together or shown any interest in it. Right?"

Her expression does not change.

"No one else seems to be paying any attention to this card about Lessing, not even Avery from what you've told me. I'll bet the congressman's never even heard about it. So, it looks like whoever sent the card was just wasting his time and a stamp. Right?"

Christine remains still a moment, then moves to the table and again lifts Alex's plate from in front of him. "I don't know," she says quietly, distracted by the thoughts that race through her head. She turns with the plate and walks to the kitchen.

"I guess I was finished anyway," he mumbles to himself.

"What?" she calls back.

Alex stands and follows her into the kitchen, where he takes her shoulders in his hands and begins to rub gently. "Look, I know you're convinced that this Cooper Avery didn't kill his wife, and I know you're looking for some logical motive that will lead you to who did. But you're not letting yourself get hooked on this Lessing theory the same way you say everyone else got hooked on the Avery theory, are you? I mean, is it possible that there's some of your own ego in this?"

Christine does not move or take her eyes from the window, which looks only to the street and to the line of red-brick buildings blocking her view of the harbor. "You think I'm wasting my time?"

Alex hesitates while his hands move up and down her arms. "No," he says finally, "not as long as you're certain you're doing what you're doing for the right reason." Again, he hesitates, and then asks, "Are you going to tell your people about what you found today, about this woman at the deli and everything she said?"

Christine shakes her head slowly, still not taking her eyes from the window. "I don't know. Maybe you're right. Maybe that'd be a waste of time. No one's paying any attention. They don't want to know. Somehow it needs to be spelled out in big block letters."

She turns suddenly toward him and cocks her head. "Dessert?"

PART *Three*

27 The Thomas Carroll Inn sits less than a five-minute walk from the county courthouse. Behind it, through a double set of French doors leading from a brick-floored pub called the Tack Room, is a patio where the defense team sits in the warmth of a bright mid-June morning. Their conversation is spare, only enough to interrupt the long silences with comments on the quality of the coffee and the fact that no one slept well the night before. They pick at their breakfasts as if their appetites have all been constricted by the nerves Cooper Avery thought only he felt. Cooper's trial is to start in less than an hour, and he suddenly needs to be as alone as he feels.

"If you will excuse me," he says, "I think I'll call my daughter."

Cooper has called Alice every morning since leaving her with his sister two months ago, waking her just as the sunlight first creeps across Puget Sound. And he will call her again tonight, as he has every night, just before each of them is ready for sleep. By this routine, Cooper manages to maintain his hold on the one essential thread that keeps him together.

"And then, I don't know. Maybe I'll take a walk. I'll meet you back here in the lobby at what? Nine-fifteen?"

Jack Gabriel nods and his partner, Lisa Paretti, looks up with a smile. "Remember," she warns, "everyone you see out there may be a potential juror, or a potential juror's brother or mother-in-law or whatever. So the less said the better. Humble and polite, but nothing to say. All right?"

He nods, accepting yet another set of instructions without comment or question. Each reduces him; imperceptibly, perhaps, but reduces him all the same. He is trying to hold firm to his own wisdom: when on dangerous and unfamiliar ground, hire the best talent you can find and trust them. He is and he has and he does. But still, it is hard to stand aside while others direct your life and contest your future.

They came here the evening before, and already Cooper feels closed in. It was his idea to rent the entire fourth floor of the inn. Gabriel and Lisa Paretti agreed that if Cooper did not mind the expense, having space they could use as an office and not having to commute the hour and a half from Baltimore each day would be an advantage. Their young associate, Carl McCullough, was not asked whether he minded leaving his bride of less than three months to live at the inn for the duration of the trial. And so they have turned one bedroom and an adjoining sitting room into a makeshift office and reserved the remaining four bedrooms for what little privacy each will be allowed.

Cooper returns to his room, where for several minutes he sits on the edge of his bed, absolutely still and staring at the phone. He envisions Alice curled in her bed, already awake and staring at her phone, waiting for his call. His sister, Claire, neither questioned nor objected to his installing a separate telephone line in the small room she prepared for Alice. He did not want his sunrise calls disturbing the rest of the house, he said. It was a small and harmless lie; and besides, Alice needed her own link to him.

"Daddy?"

Her voice is small and filled with sleep, and she sounds even more distant than the nearly three thousand miles that separate them. But she knows it is him even before he speaks, and for now, that is enough.

■

Mrs. Chalmer's fourth-grade class, that's what suddenly flashes through his mind as he turns the corner and sees the people gathered on the plaza in front of the courthouse. It is stage fright, like that which accompanied his first standing before the class to give a book report, the shiver of weakness in his legs, the back of his neck tingling with heat, and the rolling near-nausea in his stomach. It surprises him. He thought he was prepared.

They move toward what some might call a crowd. Still, it is not the frenzied movie-scene mob he has feared. Heads turn but no one crowds too close. Several reporters ask questions he does not answer, or indeed even listen to; but he does offer a patient if not apologetic smile. His lawyers move him forward. "Excuse us, please. Thank you, no. We have no comment. Thank you," and then they are in the courthouse climbing the open circular staircase leading to the second story, where a gray marble floor runs to the entrance of Stiles Newcomb's courtroom. Several uniformed deputies from the sheriff's department are talking, on the edge of arguing, with a crowd of people they are trying to move away from the heavy paneled door to the courtroom.

"I'm sorry, ma'am, we have to keep the seats open for the jury panel. Right now, the judge says only the press and the lawyers. I'm sorry, I don't make the rules here. You'll have to talk to the judge. Besides, ain't nothin' worthwhile seein' yet. They're gonna be spendin' the whole day, prob'ly, pickin' a jury."

The crowd's murmur quiets, and the deputy turns his head as Cooper and his lawyers approach. Jack Gabriel reaches for the door and then stops. He and Lisa Paretti look at one another, and both raise their eyebrows in a simultaneous change of expression. *"It's showtime!"* Lisa mouths, and the courtroom door swings open.

The state's attorney, Albert Chasen, is inside the well of the court, behind the long counsel table nearest the jury box. The table is laid with papers and files in neat order, and the two detectives, Paul Wyzanski and Charlie Abbot, are huddled in conversation with the prosecutor. All three turn to watch Cooper and his lawyers approaching. Chasen greets them with a silent nod, which Jack Gabriel acknowledges with a bright and smiling " 'Morning, Al. Detectives, how are you?"

"Gentlemen," Lisa Paretti chirps confidently.

The stage onto which they have stepped seems to have transformed his lawyers. Their posture, their movements, the tones of their voices, their expressions: they are no longer the serious, often humorless and worried debaters of factual details and legal tactics. They are something different, just as he has been told to expect.

Cooper has no idea how many hours he has spent with them over the past several months, often entire days, in their offices, in telephone conversations late into the night, a good deal of the time, he now knows, spent in nothing more productive than simply calming and reassuring him, trying to explain the inexplicable. For all its rules, they kept repeating, set out and defined and redefined and interpreted in the endless volumes that fill the endless shelves of so many law libraries, a criminal trial is still theater. And while scholars and theoreticians continue to apply accepted rules and precedents to given sets of facts to predict consistent results, any trial lawyer hardened by the wounds of experience knows that there is more art than science in the process.

To Cooper, it seems the theater of the absurd. It is beyond his experience. There are no numbers to crunch, no blueprints to follow, no contracts defining who will do what and when. He tried once to introduce some precision into the effort. A consulting firm in Seattle, composed of social psychologists and pollsters and computer experts, had offered to prepare a profile of the prospective pool of jurors by age and sex and occupation and marital and financial status and political preferences and social opinions, which profile, they said, could predict which jurors would or would not be favorably disposed given who Cooper was and the crime with which he was charged. How proud he was to have found this resource to offer his lawyers, at least until he presented it to them. They were openly amused, until they realized that he was serious, and were suddenly embarrassed that they might have embarrassed him.

"Tell me, Cooper," Jack Gabriel said, turning serious, "how many of those psychologists you think ever primed 'bacca?"

"Or ever heard of a skipjack or a bugeye or shaft-homing or a peeler?" Lisa Paretti added.

"I'm not sure I know what you mean."

"Look," Gabriel said, "we're going to trial in southern Maryland. Not in Seattle, not in New York, not even in Baltimore. I may be wrong"—which Cooper knew meant that he thought he was not—"but I suspect that it wouldn't sit too well with the local folk if they ever got word that we were taking polls to predict how they think. Now I certainly welcome any help that we can get, and I am not about to tell you how to spend your money, but if it'd make you feel more comfortable, and you really want to hire some jury experts, I'd suggest we hire a couple of the local boys who try cases in that courthouse every day."

"Have you tried cases there?"

Lisa Paretti answered for the suddenly uncomfortable Jack Gabriel, a man who never talked to a client about his past successes for fear that it might be considered a guarantee of the future. "We've both tried our share of cases down there. More importantly, Jack was born and raised on the Eastern Shore, and no matter what people might tell you, the only real difference between the two is that southern Maryland's never tried to secede from the state."

The issue was closed, and thereafter Cooper settled into his assigned role, more observer than participant. He likens his position to that of a man watching his own open-heart surgery. He has given over his life to others, he has no control, and it scares him as nothing else ever has, more than he would ever have imagined.

They move to the counsel table, all but the associate Carl McCullough. Carl settles in his spot on the first row of benches behind the rail, directly behind the counsel table. There has even been a debate about seating position and who should or should not be at the table. Cooper's lawyers were concerned that they not present too much of a show of force to a jury panel likely tinged with some distrust of wealth and power. They did not want to give away any of the natural sympathy that often exists for the defendant as underdog. Let Albert Chasen play the power role. And so Carl McCullough will sit unobtrusively in the spectators' section, his oversized litigation bag stuffed with memoranda and pleadings and documents that might prove useful, ready to run errands and make phone calls and do whatever research necessary, while Jack Gabriel and Lisa Paretti sit at the counsel table with little more than several manila folders and the ever-present yellow legal pads. They discussed, too, whether Lisa Paretti should be there at all, she having raised the issue of whether their case would play better with Jack Gabriel as the lone humble lawyer battling the power of the state. But Gabriel thought the presence of a woman defending Cooper would help.

"Do you really think juries even think about that kind of thing?" Cooper asked Lisa one evening, as they dined alone, and he tried to suppress thoughts brought on by the absence of any wedding or engagement ring on her finger and the pull of her good looks and the power of her intelligence.

She smiled. "Who knows? Every trial lawyer has his instincts. Some call them superstitions, but I prefer instincts. We tell everyone else it's experience. But in the end, who knows? Humor us, okay? It lets us feel like we at least thought of all the angles."

Cooper suspected, too, that whether the presence of a woman would have any impact at all, Jack Gabriel wanted his partner there, it being obvious that Gabriel respected her trial skills as much as he did his own.

Lisa Paretti looks up from the papers she has arranged on the table to smile and wave at the courtroom clerk, a middle-aged woman whose hair is set in tight gray curls. The woman smiles and waves back, as Jack Gabriel saunters across the well to say hello to her and to the court reporter who sits just below the witness box. All three share some joke, and Gabriel winks at the clerk as he turns to walk back to the counsel table.

Cooper is about to ask what the joke was when the dark oak door to the left and behind the bench swings open.

"All rise!"

Cooper stands, and a chill stiffens his back. *Oh, God. This isn't happening. Not really.*

28 *C*hristine reported to the prosecutor's office prepared for her day to be wasted. She was not disappointed. Albert Chasen, like every prosecutor about to start trial, was at his peak of neurotic fussiness, worrying over problems that did not exist. Were all the exhibits marked and ready? Were all the witnesses present and accounted for? If someone not scheduled to testify for days had not reported in, orders were given to check his whereabouts and to have a squad car ready to round him up if he didn't appear by such and such a time.

While the primary assignment of tummy-rubbing had fallen to Paul Wyzanski and Charlie Abbot—the silent rift between Christine and the rest of the prosecution team having widened with each passing day—her presence was required. As had the other detectives and witnesses, Christine made her brief appearance before the jury panel during voir dire, the process of introducing prospective jurors to the case and to certain general principles of law, to the parties involved and the witnesses expected to testify. So informed, potential jurors were questioned to determine whether there was any reason to strike them from the panel. Had any of them read or heard news accounts about the case, and if so, had they formed any opinion about the guilt or innocence of the accused? Did they understand and accept the principle of law that an accused is presumed innocent of the charges unless and until the state proves guilt beyond a reasonable doubt? Had any member of the panel or a relative or close personal friend been arrested, charged or convicted of a crime? If so, did that experience cause those who answered yes to form any opinion about the fairness of the police or of the judicial process? Did any member of the jury panel consider the testimony of a police officer more credible, or less credible, simply because he or she was a police officer? Did any member of the jury panel know any of the parties, the lawyers or the witnesses?

"Does any member of the jury panel know Ms. Christine Boland, either personally or in her capacity as a detective sergeant with the Maryland State Police?"

No one did, and so she was excused to return to the detectives' "war room," where she spent the rest of the day quietly and mostly by herself, reading a dog-eared copy of Camus's *The Fall,* while the questions and answers droned on in Courtroom Number One.

By midafternoon, she had run out of things to read, and out of boredom she agreed to play the third hand in a game of hearts. But the game could not distract her from her thoughts, and her impatience both with the enforced idleness and with Charlie Abbot's chain-smoking soon drove her to the hallways, where she paced until Chasen's secretary came down to report that they had been excused for the day. Paul invited her to join him and Charlie for a beer, but she declined. She had more important things to do.

Byron Roth's daughter had called the night before. She said she wanted to talk to Christine and asked if she could come by the delicatessen around seven o'clock the next night. Christine agreed readily.

She arrived at Chic 'n' Jo's shortly before seven, and by the tone of Mrs. Sapperstein's questions, she suspected that Byron Roth wanted to see her. Again assuring Mrs. Sapperstein that her father was not the object of any investigation, and that she would be sensitive to the need not to overexcite his weakened heart, Christine watched this cautious woman twist her mouth with the effort of decision. "I don't know," she said, "I hope I did the right thing in telling my father about you. I thought maybe it would be a good thing for him to finally get everything off his chest. He . . . he says he wants to talk to you. But you'll have to be patient. He sometimes confuses things. We never really knew how much of what he was saying was true and how much was just angry talk. But maybe you can help. Maybe you know about things that we don't and can tell the difference. I just hope it will help him let go of it all after all these years."

It takes a few minutes to walk around the corner from the delicatessen to the plain, flat-fronted building where Byron Roth lives in three small rooms on the second floor. As she follows Mrs. Sapperstein through the front door and down a brief and darkened hallway toward the living room, Christine is captured by the scent of a man who never leaves his rooms, the stale, musty air that is recycled, but never refreshed, as is his life, she suspects. In one corner of the living room, she sees a thin, sweatered man sitting in the shadows with his back to the window.

"Don't you want a light on, Poppa?" Mrs. Sapperstein asks, turning on a lamp without waiting for an answer.

The light exposes a gaunt, sunken face whose complexion almost matches the few wisps of gray-white hair that sweep back from a high forehead. One hand lightly waves away his daughter's question, and he murmurs something that is drowned out by the hum of the window air-conditioner.

"Poppa, this is—"

"I know who this is," Roth grumbles in a voice deepened by age and illness but which still carries a clear, smooth reminder of his better days. "So," he says, his dark eyes straining to focus through his thick-lensed glasses, "after all these years, the police say they want to hear the truth?"

"Yes sir, I—"

"Come closer."

"Sir?"

"Come closer. I want to look at you."

Christine moves to him and allows Roth to take her wrist in his soft, cool hand. He stares up at her for a moment until Mrs. Sapperstein says, "Poppa—"

"You look different," Roth says, ignoring his daughter.

Christine looks to his daughter, silently questioning, then turns back to Roth. "I'm sorry, I don't understand."

He shakes his head. "No, you look different."

"Poppa, this is the detective you said you wanted to see. Her name is Christine Boland."

"I know who she is," Roth says quietly, still holding Christine's wrist. "Josephine, would you mind getting your father and Miss Boland a cup of tea?" He looks to Christine. "Would you like some tea?"

"Yes, that would be nice, thank you."

"Josephine, would you mind?"

Mrs. Sapperstein shakes her head and turns toward the small kitchen off the living room.

"My daughter's name is Josephine," he says, shaking Christine's wrist in the rhythm of his speech, almost as if he is talking to a child, "but when she got married she decided she wanted everyone to call her Jo. She said that Josephine Sapperstein sounded like a children's rhyme." He chuckles at the thought. "It is a strange name for a little girl, I guess. Jo. But Josephine. I think it's a beautiful name. Don't you think so?"

"Yes, sir."

"My daughter has kept me alive all these years. I don't know why. I left her for a long time. Her mother, too. But maybe it was for the best. They made a better life for themselves than I did. I try to call her Jo if that makes her happy, but to me she is still Josephine."

"Poppa?" Josephine calls from the kitchen.

"I used to be in radio many years ago. Did you know that?"

"Yes, I know." Christine smiles. "That's how I came to locate you. You still have friends who remember those days."

"Friends?"

"Poppa?" Josephine again calls, this time leaning into the living room. "Did you hide the sugar again?"

He waves his free hand as if the question is a foolish one. "It's where it's always been, ever since you were a child. Next to the tea, next to the sugar, next to the coffee. Ever since you were a child."

Josephine takes a deep, silent breath and returns to her search.

He releases Christine's hand. "Please, sit down. Pull a chair close where I can see you. My eyes aren't so good anymore. Come close where we can talk."

Christine looks to a pair of straight-backed wooden chairs by a small table.

"No, no. Bring that chair over there," he says, nodding toward a worn upholstered chair next to a worn upholstered sofa. "We can't talk if you are squirming on an uncomfortable chair. Josephine?" he calls as Christine pulls the upholstered chair close to him. "Would you mind fixing us some tea?"

"Yes, Poppa," she calls back patiently. "It'll be ready in just a minute."

He nods. "She is just like her mother. Both of them better than any man deserves." He stops a moment. "So, you want to hear about Charles Vinson Avery, do you?"

"Yes, sir," Christine says. "I'm trying to find out what really happened to you and to Mr. Lessing."

"Why? Why do you want to know after all these years?"

"Well, I think it's important for people to hear the truth."

"The truth?"

"Yes, sir."

He shakes his head skeptically. "It's been so many years. The truth is hard to find after all this time. And if you find it, who will listen?"

Christine hesitates, and then she leans closer to him. "I will. I will listen."

He squints at her. "You're so young."

"Thank you. Sometimes I don't feel very young."

Again, he shakes his head. "Young people. Always trying to grow up before their time, and then one day you wake up to find that your time has passed. You are too young to be worrying about something that happened thirty-nine years and one month ago. That's how long it has been. Thirty-nine years, May eighteenth. Are you married?"

She shakes her head. "No."

"A pretty girl like you? You should be married. You shouldn't be here talking to an old man about some long-forgotten history. How old are you?"

Christine smiles. "I've heard it said that a woman who will tell her age will tell anything."

Roth sits back with a laugh and taps his hand on the arm of his chair. "Josephine," he calls out. "Come and listen to this. A woman . . . What was it?"

"I heard, Poppa," Josephine says, coming into the room carrying a tray laden with a pot and cups and milk and sugar. She sets down the tray and prepares her father's tea, adding a half-spoon of sugar and just a touch of milk. "Ms. Boland?"

"Thank you, just a little sugar."

"A woman will tell anything," Roth muses while his smile ebbs, and he takes a hesitant sip of tea, careful that the slight shake of his hand does not spill a drop.

Christine leans forward a bit. "I think you're wrong, Mr. Roth. I don't think what happened to you has been forgotten. I think what happened to you and Martin Lessing may be affecting what's going on today. That's why I need to hear from you the truth of what really happened. Not what the police or the FBI reports say, but what really happened."

He returns his cup to the saucer on the table beside him and looks directly at Christine, his face now pinched in serious thought. "It was all a lie. Everything, right from the beginning. All a lie."

Christine waits for Roth to go on, but he doesn't. His expression is stiff, almost vacant. "Please, Mr. Roth, I need to know. What really happened? To you. To Mr. Lessing. To your families. I want to know what Charles Avery did to you. Will you tell me?"

There is no response.

"Poppa?"

Roth looks to his daughter, and his eyes begin to tear.

"Oh, Poppa, it's all right, it's—"

"No," he says quietly to his daughter, reaching for a soiled handkerchief and lifting his glasses to dab his eyes. "It's been so long. No one ever wanted to know. It was easier for them not to know. But my family, Miss Boland, my daughter wanted to know. But how could I explain it? I couldn't prove anything, and what everybody said. How could I explain it? I was ruined and I didn't do anything about it. I ran. I thought I could protect my family and I ran. And I ruined them. My wife . . . I was so humiliated and so angry, and I just ran away from everything. But my daughter. My Josephine . . ." He stops, and in the long silence his daughter takes his hand.

"Poppa, please, you don't have to do this. It's not important anymore."

He shakes his head and pulls his hand back. "No, no, I want to tell you. You see, Miss Boland, how could anyone understand without proof? And against the FBI? The government? They said they had documents, and I had run away. I did not face them. Somewhere in your heart you have to wonder. I couldn't face that. I had no proof but my word. All I had was my anger, and it wasn't enough. I know that. Even now, you say you want to hear the truth. But why should you believe me?"

Christine looks away, to the window, which holds her stare until the silence feels uncomfortable. "I don't know, Mr. Roth. Maybe because after all these years you have no reason to lie. You have no need to defend yourself anymore. Maybe because all the pain your family could suffer they have suffered, and there is nothing left in you but the truth." Christine turns back to match Roth's stare. "Maybe because I think you want your daughter to know the truth. Because just maybe her father wasn't as bad a man as he thought he was."

Roth looks to his daughter, and after a long pause begins his tale.

■■■

I shouldn't have run, Josephine. That was the one mistake I couldn't recover from. I thought at the time if I just let things quiet down, if I could just buy some time. But running like I did, it changed everything.

I remember thinking of a quote from Salinger. J. D. Salinger? You remember? Of course you do. We used to read to one another all the time. You and Shel. Remember the contests to guess who the author was? Maybe I pushed you kids too much. We all thought we were such intellectuals at the time. Me and Sidney and Harold Ramsey and the others. And Lessing, of course. Martin was so intense about everything. He took everything so seriously, reading his poems and those short stories he was always trying to get published. But his work was always too political, too angry. He died before angry became fashionable. And poor Nicole. His wife. She was so young. She worshiped him, she really did. She'd just sit there listening, never saying a word, afraid her English wasn't good enough. All of us sitting around some smoky bar talking politics and books as if Gertrude Stein were looking over our shoulder. We were all so young. Not in years maybe, but you know what I mean.

Where was I?

Oh, yes, Salinger. What was my point?

A quote?

Yes, yes, I remember. I think it was Salinger who said, "The mark of the immature man is that he wants to die nobly for a cause, while the mark of a mature man is that he wants to live humbly for one." Do you remember that?

No? Well, I do. I remember being struck by it at the time. I remember thinking that I would be mature. What was the point of dying nobly? I would live for the cause. And so I ran. But the sad truth is I'm not sure that for me it was really a cause. I don't know, maybe it was a little adventure, maybe a little ego. Everyone knew my name from the radio. I was a celebrity of sorts and doing very well. Remember, Josephine? Remember the house on Bolton Hill? It was a beautiful house, wasn't it? And we had friends from all over. People others looked up to would come to our house. And then we had this little group. I'm not sure we were for anything so much as we were against things. McCarthy, mostly, and the people who all banded around that insanity, some out of fear, some just because they didn't know any better, most, I suppose, because it was the fashion.

But Martin was different. Oh yes, Martin Lessing was a believer. He and Harold Ramsey, particularly. It was hard to say what they really believed in, but what they were against, they were against with a passion. They weren't Communists. No, none of us were Communists. It was more that if someone like Joseph McCarthy was against the Communists, then the Communists must be doing something right, and they needed and deserved our protection.

I don't know why I smile. It wasn't at all funny.

How was it someone described the socialists, the liberals? Boy Scouts who insisted on helping little old ladies across the street even if they didn't want to go?

You laugh. Yes, I suppose that's right. I wish I could remember where I heard that. Remember, Josephine? Remember how I used to be able to quote chapter and verse? No more. Just as well. I guess I memorized quotations because I never had any thoughts of my own.

But whatever the reason, it was all very exciting. And who in good conscience, even then, could not hate Joseph McCarthy and all that that movement stood for? It was easy for me. And now?

Imagine it. What's there left to be against? No one believes in anything anymore. It's like our collective brain has been shot through with Novocain.

But Martin. Yes, he was a believer, and it is important that you understand that he never wanted to hurt our country. None of us did. We wanted to do something. We thought if we could discredit them, show what liars and hypocrites they were, people might really begin to understand. It had nothing to do with communism or socialism or liberalism or any other ism.

And being on the radio like I was, I had many people coming to me. I was very popular, wasn't I, Josey? Josephine remembers, don't you? We had a grand time there for a while. I still have some tape recordings. Would you like to hear? Josephine, get that tape on the top on the shelf there.

No, you're right. It's just . . . it's all I have left. No, no, don't. I know it sounds like self-pity, and well, maybe it is. But I like to remember that I was somebody once. I'm too old to be embarrassed by that.

No, you don't understand. I am not a fool yet. Maybe soon, but not yet. I know what is happening to me. I know sometimes I forget what day it is, or that my own daughter was here just this morning. But I remember what happened back then. I remember everything about that time. It's just that when I think of everything that happened . . . it's hard, that's all.

Ah, Josey, there was a time when you thought your father could do anything. And when you'd look at me that way, I thought I could too. And then you came to know better.

You see, Miss Boland? That's what I couldn't handle. What they did to me, maybe what I did to myself, it took that look from my children's eyes. You can't know what that feels like. No one can know until it happens to them. And it is something that you don't recover from. But now I look at my daughter as she once looked at me. I'm so sorry I ran, Josey. I wanted so much more for you. For Sheldon. You could have been anything you wanted. All the things I should have given you, all the things that were taken away. College. The chance to be whatever you wanted . . .

I'm sorry.

No, no, I'm all right. There's just so much to tell. Where do I start?

The government. Like those little fish. You know the ones? The little fish that can eat a pig in seconds?

Yes, that's it. Piranhas. That's the government. The FBI. They're like piranhas. Once they are on you, you can't escape. They are voracious, and even worse, they are lethargic and venal. They savor their mealtime. They gather around and pick and pick and pick, slowly nibbling away as if they almost relish your death and do not want to hurry through it. And after they have stripped you to the bones, they just move on to the next pig as if you never existed. There is nothing personal in it. It's just what they do.

You see? Now I've embarrassed my daughter. I cannot help it, Josephine. It is what I believe. I know who our guest is. Miss Boland knows, don't you? You are with them, and you know what I am saying, don't you?

Yes, you know. I cannot see much anymore, but I can see your eyes. You aren't offended, are you? You understand what I'm saying. Maybe that's why you have come here.

You see, Josephine? I am trying to tell you. For so long I thought no one would believe me, and whatever I said would only sound like an excuse. I was afraid you wouldn't believe me, Josey, and that maybe you would think even less of me because I was trying to excuse what I did. But Miss Boland is right. I am too old to be afraid anymore. At my age, what's the point? But back then? Yes, I was very frightened. It could have all been different if I had only stood up to them, but I didn't.

Martin Lessing wasn't afraid. I can't imagine what it was like for him those last few days, but somehow I just know that he wasn't afraid. I think in some ways he may even have relished it. He was always wanting to storm the walls. Do you know what I mean? And maybe that's what happened in the end. I often think of that. That maybe he brought it all on himself. I was always arguing that success would come in small steps. But Martin wanted to storm the walls.

You do not like your tea?

Josephine thinks I am taking up too much of your time with my rambling. She spent too much of her childhood listening to me lecture the world from the safety of our dining room table. I understand her impatience.

Perhaps some cookies. I have some Oreo cookies in the kitchen. I cannot help it. I love Oreo cookies. Josephine, would you mind?

. . . While she is in the kitchen, Miss Boland, you must tell me why you are here. Josey has told me you are investigating this murder case. And I read the papers. Oh yes, every day I read the paper from cover to cover. Everything. But I see you listening to me. I can't help thinking, I don't know, is there something more?

Wait, here she comes. We will talk later.

Thank you. Please, have a cookie. More tea?

Well, where to begin?

Yes, I suppose that's the place. It was a Sunday. Martin was in Washington. Harold Ramsey was supposed to be with him, but for some reason the plan changed. I don't know why. I never saw Harold afterwards. We talked on the phone months later, several times, but we were always afraid someone was listening. We agreed that we should not see each other for a while. It turned into forever.

But yes, Martin was in Washington. You see, we thought we had a chance to expose these people. Martin thought he had a way to show what liars and hypocrites they all were. A story I could use on the radio.

No, wait, I have to tell you something first. You see, there was this woman. Her name was Barbara Hoffman. She was beautiful. She had long, dark hair, and she never curled it like it was the style back then. She wore it long and straight. It was very striking. Maybe because it was so different for the times. Martin introduced her to the group. Nicole didn't like her at all. Maybe because she thought Martin paid too much attention to her. But maybe Nicole sensed something about Barbara that none of the rest of us saw, I don't know.

But anyway, Martin had met Barbara at the university. As I remember she was a teaching assistant or something, in a graduate program. But she was older. In her late twenties, at least. She had spent a few years working in Washington, on Capitol Hill. That's how it all came about. The fact that she had worked on the Hill.

Do you remember Oren Whittaker? He's dead now, but for many years he was a senator.

That's right! You do know. Yes, yes, that's right! Charles Avery went to work for him. You see, Josephine? You see the connection?

Yes, listen to me. That's what happened. No, please, don't tell me to calm down. How can I calm down? Listen to Miss Boland. She knows about Oren Whittaker and Avery.

Yes, all right, one step at a time.

Please, have some tea. Josephine, the tea is cold. No, I don't need any tea. Some brandy maybe?

Yes, Miss Boland, it was all about Barbara and Oren Whittaker and Avery. Oh, what a nest they turned out to be. How naïve we all were.

You see, Barbara Hoffman had worked in Oren Whittaker's office as some sort of assistant. Not a secretary. She was some sort of assistant. And Oren Whittaker, that . . . that . . . What do the kids say now? What is that word? Scumbag?

I'm sorry, Josephine, but it is such a wonderful word. *Scumbag!*

Yes, well, Oren Whittaker. How many bridges have been named after him? I tell you, I would swim a thousand rivers filled with a thousand alligators before I'd drive across a single bridge with that man's name. A *scumbag!* That's Oren Whittaker. As bad as Charles Vinson Avery. They are two of a kind.

Is your tea hot enough?

What?

Josey, maybe Miss Boland would like a little brandy for her tea. Yes, I would. I'm getting to the point. But maybe just a little touch of brandy would help. Miss Boland?

There, that's better.

Anyway, back to Oren Whittaker and Barbara Hoffman. You see? I remember everything, every detail, every name. And then sometimes I can't remember what day it is. Isn't that a strange thing?

A nutshell? You want me tell Miss Boland the whole story in a nutshell? How can I do that?

All right. A news report. Here's your lead. Martin Lessing died to protect the reputations of Charles Vinson Avery and Senator Oren Whittaker. There's your nutshell.

I'm sorry, Josephine, I'm not angry at you. It's just so hard not to get angry all over again. Even after all this time, it never goes away. And I don't want it to go away. I want to remember. People should know. You understand that, don't you, Miss Boland?

Do you mind? I've forgotten your name, your first name.

Christine. Yes, Christine. It's a pretty name. Was it your mother's name? No? Well, I always thought family names were important.

But where was I?

Yes, yes, Barbara Hoffman. She was a beautiful woman. She had worked for Oren Whittaker and well, as I heard it, she had had an affair with him. Of course, in those days, it was a much more serious matter to have an affair. It wasn't something that people just up and talked about. But somehow, we knew that Barbara had had an affair with Oren Whittaker. I think Martin told us that. Anyway, whatever happened between Barbara Hoffman and the senator, it turned out badly for Barbara. She had to leave her job. That's how she ended up going back to school, where she met Martin. And she was a bitter lady. Very sweet and intelligent in many ways, or so it seemed to us, but she hated Oren Whittaker, and she wasn't afraid to let us know it.

By that time things had started to change. Our little group started talking politics more than art, and more and more Martin and Harold Ramsey started arguing that talk meant nothing. We should take a stand. We should do something. But what could we do but talk and write pamphlets and whatever? But no one wanted to listen. Everyone seemed either afraid or just tried to ignore it.

Oh, there were those who spoke up. But who listened? I think it finally went away not because people were outraged, but maybe because people just got bored with it all. Maybe public boredom is the great antidote to political outrages. But what happens to the victims in the meantime? For them it lasts forever.

Yes? You agree, Miss Boland? Yes? Well, anyway, we are not here to debate that, are we?

Whatever, there were plenty of people who were outraged by McCarthy and Oren Whittaker. Oren Whittaker was no different. He was on the committees, he was right out there talking about the Red menace and publicly looking for scalps he could hold up at election time. Accusing writers and actors and whoever he could find of being Communist sympathizers. And newspeople! Anyone who criticized him at all. He was a powerful man, at least in this state.

But the time came when some of us started thinking about fighting fire with fire. We thought that maybe if we could give them a taste of their own medicine, expose them for what they were, then maybe more people would listen. We stopped meeting in bars. We stopped talking about books. We started talking about what we could do. We started meeting in secret, and I guess we got a little too full of ourselves. I believed that someone should be doing something, but at the same time I guess I saw that maybe I could be the one to break the big story. I was a bit frightened by it all, but still I admit that there was something in all that that excited me. Somehow I would be more than just another voice reading someone else's copy.

And like I said, Martin Lessing and Harold Ramsey, they incited each other. They made me nervous, I'll tell you, but still, there was something about them that made you a believer, too. Particularly Martin. He could write beautifully. His words could raise the hair on the back of your neck. And for him they weren't just words. I don't know how else to say it but that he *believed*. You could not help but listen to him. But at the same time, he could scare you, too. He could not temper his words. He could not find an audience except for people like us. No one would publish him, and his frustration was like a fire in him. And in the end, it killed him.

Miss Boland?

No, no, I thought . . .

But anyway, what happened?

I guess we all started to believe our own talk, but we really didn't know what was out there. We were all very, very naïve. We started meeting in secret and started talking about what we could do. That's when things started falling apart. Maybe it was just plain paranoia, maybe it was just that we wanted to believe that we were so important that the government had to be investigating us. But it was true that things happened that made us think someone must have been looking at us.

Martin had a cousin who worked in a bank. He had borrowed as much as they would let him to try and publish his own works. But then his cousin let Martin know that some government agent had been in to look at his loan files. And Harold, he ran a small bookstore over on Broadway, and his brother was a printer. Suddenly, the state tax people were all over him—Harold Ramsey, that is—auditing his books, and his brother was asked a lot of questions about some of Martin's pamphlets that he had printed. They were political tracts, very critical of the government, talking about the Communists as victims, arguing that the Communists had the same rights as everyone else. I make it sound so simple. But Martin's words were not simple. He presented wonderful arguments, but it was not the time for wonderful arguments. It was the time for silence. But he and Harold would take these pamphlets and leave them in bookstores and libraries and coffee shops and bars. That kind of thing. It was really harmless. Harold's brother denied knowing anything about it, printing the pamphlets, I mean. But it began to worry us, the fact that the government was asking all these questions. We started thinking that the government was listening to our phone calls, and maybe they were.

By that time, Barbara Hoffman was really part of the group. She would be there when Martin and I and Harold and sometimes that crazy Irishman, Danny Fitzgerald, would meet. It was Barbara who pushed us over the edge. It took her a while, until we all trusted and believed in her, but she was the one who really pushed us over the edge.

I remember one night we were all sitting in Harold Ramsey's kitchen. We had a big dinner, and probably too much to drink, and we were all talking about what a sonofabitch Oren Whittaker was. And then, all of a sudden, Barbara got real quiet, and then she said that she had once seen a file that could prove that when Oren Whittaker had been U.S. attorney for Maryland, long before he was senator, that he had taken a bribe to squelch an investigation of Free State Steel. Everyone knew about Free State's battles with the unions. It had gone on for years. And everyone remembered when there had been an explosion at the plant down near Sparrows Point. Thirteen people were killed. The explosion was blamed on the union, but according to Barbara, it had been the company that sabotaged its own plant. I don't remember all the background, but whatever happened, I remember that there had been an investigation of the company. We had gotten wind of it at the station, but we could never get confirmation for a story.

Anyway, that was all Martin had to hear. He became obsessed with somehow getting a hold of that file. And I admit, I wanted to get it, too. What a story for me to break. Anyway, that went on for months. Martin just kept pushing Barbara, over and over, but she just kept saying that she was trying to convince whoever it was who had the file to give it to us. Even Harold told Martin that he was pushing Barbara too hard. We kept telling him that it could be dangerous for her. But he was so intent. Barbara never said who it was who had this file or how she could get it, and I began wondering if there really was such a person or file. I began to wonder whether she had just made it up because she wanted to belong so badly. That's how she seemed to me. And I wondered if she had just made up the story because she knew how we all felt about Oren Whittaker. Or whether maybe she had some other reason.

No, I'm fine. I'm just thinking. Maybe a little more brandy.

I should have known to stop it. But there was that part of me that wanted to believe as much as Martin Lessing. For different reasons maybe. But I too wanted that file to exist and to get my hands on it. I never thought we were doing anything illegal. Sneaky, just like they were, but not that there would be anything illegal in it.

But right at the end there, I should have seen it coming.

No, no, I mean that. I should have known. It was all right there in front of our faces, but we didn't want to see it. We only wanted to prove our point. Maybe in that way we were no different than the people we were always accusing. I think of that, too.

What happened? I'll tell you what happened.

The last time I saw Martin Lessing, the very last time—Harold Ramsey, too—it was a Friday. Harold called me at the station. It was right after I finished the evening news. He said I had to meet him and that Martin was coming too. That's all he would say. We met at Jacob's. Remember, Josey? Remember Jacob's? It was a wonderful little restaurant. Remember how you and your mother would meet me there? No more, though. It's a shame, but it's gone now.

Anyway, we met at Jacob's, and the three of us sat at our table near the back. I thought at the time that I'd never been so nervous. If we'd had any idea . . .

But anyway, Harold had this news. I don't know to this day how he had found out. He wouldn't say, at least not to me, but he told us that Barbara Hoffman was having an affair with Charles Vinson Avery. Who was Charles Vinson Avery? I mean, back then he was nothing. Not a congressman, nothing. A young, nobody FBI agent. But an FBI agent? Can you imagine? An FBI agent? We had spent all that time talking in front of a woman who was sleeping with an FBI agent? I tell you, I was never so scared.

But Martin! My God, Martin. He scared me, too. Oh, he never raised his voice. But the look in his eyes. You could see it. The rage. The betrayal. The look in his eyes scared me almost as much as what Harold had said.

Both of us, Harold and me, both of us told Martin not to do anything. But Martin wanted to confront Barbara. He said we couldn't just let it go. He wanted to tell her that we knew, tell her that we would expose what she and Avery were doing. Avery was married, and Martin wanted to expose him and Barbara and everything. He couldn't control his anger. He was certain that Barbara had been sent to spy on us. And, yes, I thought the same thing. But we said to him, don't tell Barbara we know. We just stop what we're doing. Don't talk with her.

I never saw Martin again. Harold either.

The next two weeks, ten days, I don't know what went on. We said we should not meet for a while. Not even talk. Except, three, maybe four days . . . No, it was a Thursday. Yes, three days before he was arrested, Martin called me at the station, but he wouldn't talk. He said that I should go to a phone booth and call him back. Imagine that. We were like children playing a game all of a sudden. But I did as he asked, and when I called him back, he asked me. He said, "Byron, tell me the truth. If I get the file on Oren Whittaker, will you use it? Will you promise to use it on the air?" I said, "Martin, what are you doing? What has happened?" He said, "Byron, just tell me. If I get the Whittaker file to you, will you report it? Will you do that?"

I said I would. If we were certain the file was legitimate and it proved what Barbara had said, yes, I would use it. But I kept asking what he was doing. What had happened with Barbara. But he wouldn't say. He just said, "I have your word?" And I said yes.

You see, Josephine? I am to blame, too. I wasn't all that innocent. I should have told him no. I knew how impetuous Martin could be. I should have known better. It was crazy. How could we have been so stupid? But I wanted that file, too. I wasn't willing to go out and take the chances like Martin, but I wanted that file. What a scoop I would have.

Harold? Oh yes, I called him. And it was the same craziness. He went to a phone booth, I went to a phone booth, we all went to phone booths like we were real spies, like we really knew what we were doing. So Harold told me. He said Martin had confronted Barbara and that Barbara denied spying on us. She cried and cried,

Harold said, and she admitted that she had an affair with Avery. But she would never spy on us. She said she believed in us and that Avery knew nothing about what we were doing. She said that Avery was just a young man in a bad marriage. And she loved him, she said, but she never told Avery anything. *And,* she said, she wanted to prove to Martin that she was no spy. She wanted to prove herself. I thought, is Martin crazy? I said to Harold, "Is Martin crazy?"

Harold said he told Martin to be careful. "Be careful?" I said. Were they both crazy? But I didn't tell Harold what I should have. I should have said to him, "You get a hold of Martin and the two of you listen to me. This is crazy. Don't listen to this girl. No, I won't report this file even if you get it." That's what I should have said. But I didn't. I didn't because even as crazy as it was, I wanted that file too.

Then it was Saturday night, and Martin called me. It was late, maybe ten o'clock, and again the phone calls and going to phone booths. He was sick, had a terrible cold. But at the same time he was very excited. He sounded like a kid or something. He just told me where to meet him on Sunday, at two o'clock. To wait at a phone booth at the train station. To be there at two o'clock and he would either be there or he would call. He wouldn't listen. He said Harold would be with him but only when he got the file. They would split up then. I told him. I said that I didn't think it was such a good idea. I told him that it didn't sound right to me, but he just said, "Do I still have your word? You will report this if I get the file?"

And I said yes.

I said yes, and the rest . . . Well, you know the rest. You know what happened.

What?

Ah, Josephine, you don't know how happy you make me that you do not know. You are still like we were then. You cannot imagine how people really are. But our guest knows, don't you? You know. You are one of them, and you understand, don't you?

. . . Miss Boland?

29 "*H*e was set up, I take it."

The night is still warm, and Alex has moved a cushion out onto his fire escape, where they sit, looking not at each other but out across the rooftops. He gives her a moment, but she does not answer.

"But there's something I don't understand. If they arrested Lessing with these documents about the senator, wouldn't the senator have been exposed anyway? I mean, how did Avery finesse that?"

Christine's answer comes slowly, and in a voice that is flat and removed. "No, Avery wouldn't have used the documents on Whittaker, if they ever even existed. He'd have gotten the woman, Hoffman, he would have gotten her to say that Lessing and the others had been asking for defense information. And they'd just get some old military records that were harmless but still classified."

"They could do that?"

She looks at him, her expression challenging the naïveté of his question.

"But what about all the other agents? All the searches and all that?"

"Look," she says, "the Bureau probably was investigating Lessing and Roth and the others. Avery was using the woman as a source. When Lessing threatened to expose his affair with this Hoffman woman, Avery just comes up with a story that this imaginary Communist was pressuring Barbara Hoffman to use her contacts on the Hill to get defense information. Everyone jumps on board. They get some file from the Defense Department, and no one but Avery and the woman and maybe the good senator is any the wiser. Avery gets credit for a big bust, the senator is covered and later hires Avery as a favor in return. The rest is history."

"But why wasn't Roth and this other guy, Ramsey—why weren't they ever arrested? I mean why wouldn't they have been charged, I don't know, with conspiracy or whatever?"

"I don't know. I suspect that when Lessing was arrested, he probably told them what he was really after. He wouldn't have said anything about the others, but he probably told them he thought he was getting documents to prove an illegal bribe. Avery could pass it off as just another wild story made up by a man trying to save his skin. But maybe the whole thing started to smell. Maybe the affair with Barbara Hoffman came out and the Bureau began to question what was really going on. Then Lessing dies, Hoover and his boys don't want to take a chance of looking bad, so they let the case die as quietly as possible. The whole thing gets buried in Hoover's files. Hoover's owed another favor by a powerful senator, and he's got Avery on the hook forever. Maybe they tell Avery that it'd be best if he left the Bureau, and the ever-grateful Oren Whittaker takes him under his wing. Everybody's happy. Everybody important, anyway. And Roth, the others? They're too scared to say anything. Besides, what could they say?"

"Jesus," Alex says softly.

Christine shudders. "Oh, Alex, you should have seen him. Roth, I mean. If you could have been there. He looked, I don't know, he looked like his whole life had been sucked out of him."

Alex takes a sip from his glass of vodka and looks at her. One of her hands is locked on the neck of a bottle of wine—she had refused a glass—and her face is lifted to the sky. "I know," he says.

She shakes her head quickly. "No, you don't. No one can know what it is like unless it happens to them."

"I suppose."

"All those years. Imagine all those years, living with the disgrace, and no one knew or cared about what really happened. Roth, his family. And Martin Lessing. What happened to them, to Lessing's family."

"What did happen?"

"To Lessing's family?"

"Yes, did Roth say?"

"Yes. He said Lessing's wife went back home to France. They had a daughter, born the day Lessing died. But Lessing's wife couldn't handle the pressure, I guess. Imagine. You've only been in this country for a few years, and your only friends are your husband's friends, and suddenly everything collapses around you. Your husband dies in jail while you're giving birth, you're in debt up to your ears, and you and the few people you know are being accused of spying or whatever. What do you do? What could you do but run? Roth got together some money, as much as he could, I guess, and he gave her the money to return to France.

"The daughter—Roth remembered that she was named Marielle. Marielle Devereaux. That was Nicole's maiden name, Devereaux. She was afraid to give her little girl her own father's name. The child was just two months old when they left. They had nothing but what little Lessing had in a checking account and whatever Roth could give them, and they left."

"Did Roth know whatever became of them?"

Christine shakes her head. "Not really. Roth's daughter told me that for years he had tried to send them little gifts at Christmas, birthdays, things like that, but I don't think he ever really knew what happened to them. I asked him, but he became so emotional, he couldn't talk about it anymore. He just wanted to tell his daughter about what he had done when he left them. After his wife divorced him, Roth disappeared for a long time, and he wanted to tell his daughter what had happened to him. What he had done. He kept insisting, and she was crying, and I . . . I just thought I should leave them alone."

Alex turns toward Christine. She looks as tired and drawn as she has described Byron Roth. He reaches over and gently sweeps her hair from her face and touches his fingers to her cheek, but she does not react to his touch.

"It all makes sense, doesn't it?" Her eyes, wide and questioning, flit back and forth as if she is computing the clues like a column of figures. "I mean you can see how someone close to Lessing or these people could harbor a real anger over a long period of time. How it could turn to an obsessive anger. What Avery did to these people, to all of them. Someone wants Charles Avery to know what he did to these people, to think about what it was like for them. Maybe wants everyone to know what he did. Maybe make him suffer the same way." She pauses a moment and then says, "He asked me to come see him."

"Who? Roth?"

"Yes. As I was leaving, he stopped me. He stopped me and asked if I'd come to see him again. Just imagine what he must have gone through, what they all must have gone through."

30 $\mathscr{I}$t is all moving so slowly, and not at all as Cooper hoped; and if the solemnness of their expressions and the cryptic nature of their conversation are any indication, neither is it going as Jack Gabriel and Lisa Paretti hoped.

Throughout the long weeks of preparation, through all the endless hours of planning, of readjusting to new facts and refining their theories and tactics, Cooper had come to expect dramatic moments. He had expected to see the state's case, like an ornate but fragile sand castle, disassembled in large observable chunks by the relentless tide of their defense. What he did not expect, what he was not prepared for, is the reality of this trial: a process that seems to inch along like a conversation spoken in half-sentences to a jury overwhelmed by indifference.

He wants to see the jury react. He expects them to react. How many times had he watched courtroom dramas on television, seen them in movies, read about them in books? Juries always react, don't they? The sudden awakening of comprehension, the undercurrent of murmurs, a long, dramatic glance at their fellows, a stare at the offending witness: isn't that what happens? But here the jurors seem unaware of their moments, moments which pass them by like a single car in a long line of traffic.

Like the afternoon before. Detective Abbot described in detail his investigation of the weapon the state would have the jury believe killed Marian Avery: how he searched through the state's weapons registry for the Smith & Wesson .38 Cooper had reported stolen more than a year before Marian's death; how he traced backward to determine when and in what job lot that weapon had been manufactured; how they took the slug recovered from Marian's brain and compared its rifling marks with those of a bullet test-fired from a Smith & Wesson .38 manufactured in that same job lot; and how the rifling marks on the slug matched the land and groove and twist patterns of the test-fire—implying, of course, that Cooper's gun was the murder weapon. And then, on cross-examination, Jack Gabriel drew the detective through a long, slow series of questions to establish that the land, groove and twist patterns of the gun Cooper had reported stolen were no different from those of any other Smith & Wesson .38 manufactured at the same time, and that at the time of Marian's death, the Smith & Wesson .38 was a standard-issue revolver for state police detectives.

"In fact, Detective, is it not true that even aside from law enforcement officers, the Smith and Wesson .38 was a very popular weapon among private individuals?"

"I guess that's true."

"And it is true also, is it not, that the land and groove and twist pattern is precisely the same with all weapons produced by a single manufacturer in a particular job lot."

"Well, I suppose—"

"You suppose?" Jack Gabriel straightened up, then leaned toward Detective Abbot. "Detective, I would ask that you not suppose, but state whether you do or do not know the answer to my question."

"Could you repeat the question?"

"My question is whether or not it is true that all thirty-eight-caliber revolvers manufactured by the same company in the same job lot have the same rifling characteristics, that is, land and groove and twist patterns?"

Detective Abbot hesitated with a frown, allowing Albert Chasen to object.

"I'll allow it," Judge Newcomb ruled.

Jack Gabriel looked to the witness. "Detective?"

"Yes, sir, I understand your question. Yes, every weapons manufacturer has its own rifling design or pattern."

"Now, sir," Gabriel continued, "is it not also true that each individual weapon leaves its own distinct markings on a bullet fired through its barrel, markings in addition to land and groove and twist patterns that are unique to that particular weapon?"

"Yes."

"And the only way to determine if one particular weapon fired one particular bullet would be to compare the questioned bullet or slug with a test-fire from that same weapon? Isn't that true?"

"Yes, sir, that's true. But in this case we never found Mr. Avery's gun."

"Precisely. And so you did not make such a comparison, did you?"

"No, sir, but—"

"Sir, the question is whether you made any such comparison between the bullet recovered from Marian Avery with the gun that Mr. Avery had reported stolen over a year before his wife's death."

"No."

"I'm sorry, Detective, I couldn't hear you."

"*No!*"

"But you could have investigated which if any Smith and Wesson .38s which were owned and registered by any number of private individuals, or even to any number of law enforcement officers, may have been manufactured in the same job lot as the revolver stolen from my client, is that correct?"

"Well, I don't know, you know, you're dealing with a whole lot of guns and—"

"Sir, excuse me. The question is whether you could have researched those guns listed or registered with various law enforcement agencies to determine which, if any, had been manufactured in the same job lot as the weapon whose rifling characteristics matched those on the slug recovered from Marian Avery."

"You gotta understand, Counsel—"

"Sir, could you have done that?"

Judge Newcomb turned to Abbot and in an even voice said, "Just answer the questions, Detective."

"I suppose we coulda done that."

"Did you do that?"

"No."

"And you could have identified those weapons manufactured in the same job lot and then tested each one to see if it matched the unique identifying marks found on the bullet that killed Marian Avery, isn't that correct?"

"Well, I don't know. That would've taken . . . I don't know whether we coulda done that or not."

"Did you try?"

"No."

"Did you even think about it?"

"Like I said, Counsel, you're dealing there with a whole lotta guns. God knows how long something like that coulda took."

"Exactly. And it would have been a burdensome task, would it not?"

"Yes, of course."

"Very time-consuming?"

"Yes."

"And that didn't fit your schedule, did it?"

"I beg your pardon?"

"Your schedule, Detective. To do that kind of investigation, to actually try to find the specific weapon that fired the specific bullet that killed Marian Avery, would have taken a great deal of time, and you had already determined in your own mind that my client was guilty."

"Well, I—"

"And you were only interested in looking for evidence that might fit a theory you had already settled on."

"Your Honor!" Albert Chasen protested.

"Overruled. Answer the question, Detective."

"Well, you know, it was just one of those circumstances."

"And is it not also one of those 'circumstances' that the actual murder weapon might have been one of the many guns you did not investigate or test?"

"Well . . ."

"And is it not also a 'circumstance' that your investigation establishes that it is no more likely that the gun reported stolen by my client a year before his wife's death is the murder weapon than perhaps it is one of hundreds or even thousands of other identical weapons?"

"I can't testify to that."

"And you can't testify either whether one of the weapons that you could have tested might have been the actual murder weapon, can you?"

"Well—"

"Because you didn't care, did you, Detective? The truth didn't matter, did it? You were only—"

"*I object!*" shouted Chasen.

"Of course you do," Gabriel shot back.

"Your Honor, can I—" Abbot tried.

"*Quiet!* All of you," Judge Newcomb interrupted. "Counsel, come to the bench."

Jack Gabriel stalked to the bench as Chasen rushed up behind him. Cooper glanced at Lisa Paretti to catch her reaction and saw her jaw clenched to suppress a grin of delight.

But the jury showed no reaction at all. Cooper watched for it, but saw not a hint, not a twitch, not a nod, not a rolled eye. All twelve of them—seven men and five women, and the alternates, two men and two women—sat expressionless and impassive, almost bored: like juror number eight, a woman in her mid-fifties, who appeared to welcome the interruption of the bench conference as an opportunity to add a row or two to the small patch of knitting that occupied her at every break in the proceedings.

Did they understand? Did they care?

And now it is another day, with another witness, and another point to be made or attempted by yet another tactic. Cooper understands, he thinks, but he is not altogether certain. It has all been explained to him, but it all seems too subtle. It all seems too much a lawyer's game, the proverbial chess match that only they, the lawyers, appreciate. It reminds him of Professor Conti, who once returned a test paper he had filled with verbiage to mask the fact that he knew little or nothing of the subject. "Too much sugar coating, not enough pill," the old man had written. Cooper wants desperately to see the pill, to see it fed to the jury and to see them react. But there is no way of telling whether they are listening; or if they are listening, whether they understand; or if they understand, whether they even care.

Do something! Even if it's only to smile, or frown, or shake your head in disgust. But let me see something of what you see. Anything!

They have reassembled after the lunch recess, and the large, oak-paneled courtroom falls silent as Judge Newcomb, a trim man whose salt-and-pepper hair recedes from a round, almost cherubic face, sweeps into the room from a door to the rear and left of the bench. "Remain seated," he says with a wave of his hand. The jury files in through a door to the right, each in line to take his or her assigned seat. Juror number two turns and says something to juror number three. Both women laugh.

Jack Gabriel is tapping the end of his pen on a yellow pad that contains not a single note, not even a doodle. He still seems disturbed. Over lunch, he and Lisa Paretti were unusually quiet and self-absorbed, their conversation with Cooper designed more to avoid his questions than to answer them. They denied their concern, but they were hardly convincing.

Detective Paul Wyzanski had completed his direct testimony just before lunch. It was a meticulously ordered presentation of the events of the morning Marian's body was found: exactly what was done, what was searched, what was found; complete with photographs, physical evidence and inventory lists. But Wyzanski and the prosecutor failed to perform as Gabriel and Paretti had expected, or as they had hoped. Albert Chasen tried none of the gambits they had expected. Everything was surgically clean and by the book, and that disturbed the defense strategy.

They had expected, even planned on Albert Chasen's trying to elicit from the detective the inferences to be drawn from the evidence: for example, that the shards of glass found overlaying the muddy bootprints on the kitchen floor meant that the killer had entered the house with a key and had broken the glass in the door after leaving to make it appear to have been a burglary; or that the lack of any marks of force on the opened safe in the master bathroom indicated that the killer knew the combination. The rules, of course, prohibited such opinions being offered by a witness, but the rules never prevent lawyers from trying. And they would not object if Chasen tried, hoping that the state would commit itself to such theory and supposition. It would then be their right on cross-examination to challenge the state's thesis with their own suppositions, and thereby begin to introduce their "other man" theory to the jury: the man they would imply had an equal if not greater opportunity and motive to kill Marian Avery.

But Albert Chasen did not bite. Perhaps he was more clever and controlled than they had expected. He was not the zealot they had hoped for, and except for a rare burst of pique, in front of the jury he remained what they did not want him to be, a quiet, meticulous prosecutor confident of his evidence and disdainful of the histrionics of his more desperate adversary. It appeared to Cooper that Albert Chasen was playing Jack Gabriel, and that Jack Gabriel did not like it.

"I remind you, Detective, that you are still under oath," Judge Newcomb says, as Paul Wyzanski resumes the stand.

"Good afternoon, Detective," Gabriel begins with a weak smile, resting one hand on the jury rail while the other absently scratches the tip of his earlobe.

"Counsel," Wyzanski nods in return.

"Detective, you spent quite some time this morning—a bit over two hours, I believe it was—going over all the bits and pieces of evidence you and your people found at the house on the morning Mrs. Avery's body was discovered."

"Yes, sir."

"And by all those exhibits, the photographs and all that—I can't remember how many we were shown here."

"I believe we left off at exhibit number 112."

"Yes, thank you, Detective. Now, by all these exhibits, I would say that you and your colleagues conducted a very thorough search of the house and the surrounding area, is that right?"

"I think we did, yes, sir."

"In fact—let me see here—yes, here it is. Exhibit 52. This is a rather lengthy inventory of all the items found and recovered in the master bedroom, is that right?"

"Yes, sir."

"And exhibit 52(a), that's an inventory listing everything that was found or observed in the master bedroom but was not taken as evidence or for examination, is that right?"

"Yes, sir."

"Now, I see on this list, ah, 52(a), that you—excuse me, were you the person who prepared these lists, exhibits 52 and 52(a)?"

"Yes, sir. Myself, along with Crime Scene Technician Bettis."

"Yes, all right. Now, I see on this list, that is 52(a), that you even listed odd bits and pieces of paper that you saw in, for example, Marian Avery's drawer, the one in her dressing table."

"Yes, sir."

"Including, I see here, notations about a dry-cleaning ticket and what looks like a discount coupon for some cosmetic product, is that right?"

"Yes, sir, there are paper items on both lists. We recovered a sample of paper items to try to recover fingerprints, and left others there that seemed to have no evidentiary value. But we made a note of everything."

"And I take it that if you had found anything, even an odd slip of paper, that might even remotely have been of value, you would have recovered it or at least listed it here?"

"Yes, sir. Even if something appeared to have no value at all, we at least listed it."

"Very thorough, Detective. Very professional indeed. Thank you, I have no further questions."

A sudden hot flash races up Cooper's spine and grips his throat, where his questions stick unuttered. *What? That's it?*

"Call your next witness," the court directs Albert Chasen, as Jack Gabriel starts back to the counsel table.

Cooper wants to shout. *Wait! Hold on! I want my lawyer to ask some more questions.*

"The state calls Edward Thurston."

No, no, wait! Cooper's expression says as he feels Lisa Paretti's hand grip his forearm firmly to remind him of their repeated instructions: Never speak out. Never show surprise or anger. Stay calm, no matter what happens. Write us a note if you must, but never show the jury that you disagree with us.

But there's no time for notes. What about all the things we talked about? What about all the questions of whether Ned or Ellen Haley or even all the police officers who were walking about the house could have kicked some of the glass shards over the bootprints? What about all those questions about whether they had investigated Oliver Johns? What about how the oyster beds are right along the route Johns would have taken between our dock and his? What about . . . ?

"It's all right," Lisa whispers to Cooper, who is obviously straining at the silence imposed on him. She tightens her grip on his arm and then releases him to turn back for a file offered up by Carl McCullough, the young associate who sits silently behind them, producing files and papers before his bosses ever ask for them.

Jack Gabriel sits down and releases a breath sounding of fatigue.

He rubs his eyes a moment, and without looking up or at Cooper, says in a quiet voice, "Relax. We'll talk about it later."

It sounds to Cooper like his father speaking, a man who never seemed to have time for his son's questions. *We'll talk about it later.* A tiredness sweeps over Cooper, a tiredness that numbs his back and legs, a tiredness that lets him feel the chill of his own perspiration. There is no one he can talk to, no one to hear his protests, to share his fear or his anger, no one for him to hold on to, if just for a moment. There is only this courtroom filled with strangers debating his life, a debate over which he has no control. He has no decisions to make. His life, their decision. He wants to simply stand up and walk out. But he can't stand up, and he can't leave, not even to take a few moments to pace the hallways and smoke a cigarette. The rules require him to be there at every moment. They can do nothing without him, but they want nothing more of him than to just sit and watch and listen.

He watches his father-in-law take the oath, but he does not listen. Edward Thurston looks smaller and more worn than Cooper remembers. He has not seen or spoken to his father-in-law since taking Alice to Seattle. Cooper has spent little time at his office since the indictment, and what little time he has spent, he has spent alone. His and Ed Thurston's offices are on separate floors, and what contact they have required of each other has been accomplished by initialed memoranda and cryptic phone messages taken by their secretaries, nothing more. For reasons he feels but cannot really explain, Cooper knows that Edward Thurston will wait for the jury's verdict to do what he cannot bring himself to do directly, to remove Cooper from his business and from his life.

Cooper thinks of Alice. He wishes he could just sweep her up with her laughter and feel her hold on to him. She would listen to him, but what can he say to her? She must never know what they have accused him of, what he is going through. He fears her constant questions, the curiosity that can never be satisfied. He fears that she already knows, that she has read a newspaper or seen a television report or overheard some hushed conversation or a slip of the tongue; or that she simply knows because she knows him.

This weekend. Maybe he can get out there for the weekend. He concentrates on that: How long to get to the airport? He could catch a late flight. Would she be awake when he arrived? Maybe they could go for a sail on Puget Sound, just her and him. No one else. His mind drifts with the vision of Alice begging to take the tiller until he lets her. He sees her thinly muscled arms struggling to hold it against the wind and water, pulling it higher and higher as the boat heels and the lee rail dips toward the rush of water, while her eyes widen with nervous delight.

They will have dinner at that place on the water, out on the deck overlooking the Pacific. They will order lobster. No, better than that, king crab, lots of it, plates piled high with crab legs, and they will drool butter on their paper bibs while watching the sun set, and Alice will tell of her adventures, and she will make him laugh.

Sunday they will take everyone out for breakfast, and Alice will order a stack of pancakes with strawberries and whipped cream and a side of bacon, and she will eat barely a third of it, nibbling sporadically while she chatters on. And Sunday night he will leave her with promises: that everything is fine, that they will be back together soon, that Ned will better, that she will never be too old to be called Little Alice Apple Blossom. He will tell her again not to cry, and maybe this time she won't. But still, in one small corner of his heart he hopes that she will, if just a little. He needs her to miss him.

And then he will board the red-eye back. Will he have time to make it to court on Monday morning? A gift. He must remember to get her a gift. Maybe tonight, right after court, he will walk down to one of those shops—

"No further questions."

Cooper looks up, startled. Albert Chasen has finished questioning Edward Thurston, and he has heard none of it. It was just noise. *Jesus Christ, get a hold of yourself!*

Lisa Paretti stands and reaches for her yellow pad filled with notes. She hesitates for a moment, then replaces the pad on the table and walks slowly to the lectern. It is a gesture, Cooper supposes, to communicate that she does not need her lawyer's script.

This woman fascinates him: a woman who speaks her mind, who sugar-coats nothing, except by the soft, even tones of her voice. He feels constantly disarmed by her, never quite able to place her in one of the various neat categories in which he most often places women. She is not the tightly strung businesswoman in the dark jacketed suits; she is not the cocktail-party hostess who asks questions only to give you an opportunity to speak; she seems completely self-contained; she accompanies no one; she is no one's lover, or wife or mother, or sister or daughter, or at least not that she will tell you or let you see. He wants to know her, but somehow he knows better than to ask.

Unlike the other lawyers, Jack Gabriel and Albert Chasen, who ignore the lectern and its microphone to throw their voices from their ever-changing positions in the well of the court, Lisa Paretti stands erect at the podium, speaking into the microphone, which magnifies the impact of her quiet questions.

Edward Thurston looks uneasy, and his eyes drift toward a glass of water set on the side rail of the witness box.

She does not miss the signal and offers with a slight smile, "Please, Mr. Thurston, have a sip of water, if you'd like."

He nods and takes the glass in a slightly tremulous hand.

She does not move while he takes a sip. Her hands are folded on the lectern, and she keeps her body still in its straight black skirt and white silk blouse.

"Thank you," Ed Thurston whispers into his own microphone as he replaces the glass on the rail.

"Now, Mr. Thurston, you have described in some detail the profits that Mr. Avery might have realized if your company had been bought out by Barth-Sanders Industries, is that correct?"

"Yes."

"And you have also described how your daughter had signed over to Mr. Avery the voting rights to her stock in the company."

"Yes, that's right."

"Your daughter owned almost eleven percent of the outstanding stock, is that right?"

"Yes."

"And that eleven percent of the stock, if voted contrary to your wishes, might have meant that Barth-Sanders could have succeeded in its attempt to take over your company."

"Oh, yes, her stock could have easily controlled the result."

"Now, sir, before your daughter signed over to her husband the voting rights to her stock, did you consult with her as to how she should vote on issues that arose?"

"Oh, she always asked my advice on such things."

"And was it not shortly after Cooper had been named president of your company that she signed over the voting rights to him?"

"Yes, I guess it was about that time."

"Did she discuss that decision with you?"

"Well, not really. But things had changed when this Barth-Sanders thing started."

"Did you talk to your daughter about her taking back the voting rights?"

"Yes."

"But she didn't do that, did she?"

"No."

"Did you ever discuss with Mr. Avery her taking back her voting rights?"

"That was just between me and my daughter."

"I see. Now, you also have explained to the jury how adamant you have been that Barth-Sanders not succeed in their attempt to take over your company, correct?"

"Yes, I've been against that all along."

"Now, did my client, Mr. Avery, ever indicate to you that he was in favor of Thurston Construction selling out to Barth-Sanders?"

"Not in so many words."

"Well, if you could tell the ladies and gentlemen of the jury exactly what Mr. Avery said to you on the subject."

"Well, as I said, he came to me right at the beginning of all this and talked about how much the stock might be worth to Barth-Sanders."

"Did he also discuss with you how much a sale to Barth-Sanders might have meant to you personally?"

"He didn't have to tell me that. I know what the figures are."

"And do those figures indicate that if Barth-Sanders actually succeeded in taking over your company, your personal net worth would more than double?"

"The money means nothing to me."

"But your personal net worth would more than double, would it not?"

"I imagine so, yes."

"I don't mean to be impolite, Mr. Thurston, but could you tell us how old you are?"

"I'm seventy-nine years old."

"And you had started your business, Thurston Construction, almost fifty years ago, is that correct?"

"Fifty-four years, to be exact."

"And during that time, you worked very hard building a small construction company into a highly successful corporation with business interests throughout the United States and in Europe, is that right?"

"I worked seven days a week, year in and year out, to build the company, yes."

"You are rightfully proud of what you and the company have accomplished, isn't that correct?"

He nods.

Judge Newcomb leans over. "Sir, you'll have to answer yes or no. The court reporter can't take down a nod."

Ed Thurston leans toward the microphone. "Yes."

"Now, sir, it was just about eight years ago, was it not, that Mr. Avery was named president of the company?"

Again, Thurston nods, and then he catches himself. "Yes."

"And even before he became president, Mr. Avery and yourself worked very closely together."

"Yes."

"In fact, even before Mr. Avery joined your company, he had been quite successful as a real estate developer on his own."

"Yes, I never said Cooper wasn't smart. He's brilliant, in fact. He worked as hard as I did, and I—I thought he and I wanted the same thing. I never—I just never thought . . ." He stops himself and takes a deep breath.

"You just never thought what, Mr. Thurston?" It is not a challenge. Lisa Paretti's voice remains quietly sympathetic as she finishes the thought Ed Thurston has left hanging. "You never thought, perhaps, that Cooper would ever do anything to hurt you?"

"I never thought he'd do anything like this. Never. Not ever."

"In fact, when Cooper first came to you about the Barth-Sanders bid, didn't he tell you that he would understand if you wanted to sell out?"

"Well, yes, but he knew I'd never want to do that."

"But he did tell you that he would understand, didn't he?"

Thurston does not answer.

"He told you, did he not, that he would understand because given the shares of stock you own and the differential in the value when he acquired his stock, you could have made a profit perhaps as much as ten times what Mr. Avery would realize?"

"I don't know the exact figure, but I suppose that's right."

"And at that time, you had given over the daily running of the business to your son-in-law, and you were acting primarily as an adviser and spending less time with the business. Isn't that correct?"

"I guess."

"You were able to spend more time with your wife and family, isn't that true? You were able to rest if you chose so that you and your wife could enjoy the well-deserved fruits of your labor, correct?"

"I didn't need a rest."

"But Cooper did tell you, did he not, that he'd understand if you made your own decision to take a rest?"

"Yes, I guess you could say that."

"But when you told him you wanted to fight the takeover, he spent many months traveling constantly, negotiating with banks and institutional lenders, and doing whatever he could to fight Barth-Sanders' takeover bid, didn't he?"

"Well, that's what he said he was doing. That's what I thought he was doing, but . . ." Thurston stops and looks away.

Lisa Paretti gives him a moment before asking in a near whisper, "But you think he was doing something else, don't you?"

"I know he was up to something else."

"And what you know is that Cooper had an affair with a Ms. Sydney Lambert."

He does not answer.

"And you know that Sydney Lambert is general counsel for Barth-Sanders Industries, isn't that correct?"

"I never would have believed it. He was like a son to me. I couldn't believe it."

"That hurt you a great deal, didn't it, Mr. Thurston?"

"Yes," he whispers, as he reaches for a handkerchief, with which he dabs his eyes.

"Mr. Thurston, how did you learn of Cooper's affair with Sydney Lambert?"

He hesitates for a long moment, and Lisa Paretti presses him. "Mr. Thurston, could you tell us, please, how you came to learn of Mr. Avery's affair with Sydney Lambert?"

"Phil Layton told me."

Judge Newcomb looks up sharply.

"Is that the same Phillip Layton whose law firm represents both your family and your business?"

He hesitates. "Yes."

"Mr. Layton also represented my client, Cooper Avery, at that time, didn't he?"

"Yes."

"When did Mr. Layton tell you of Cooper's affair with Ms. Lambert?"

"It was right after Marian, my daughter, was murdered. It was maybe a week later. I don't remember exactly the day."

"And Cooper had gone to Mr. Layton for advice, as his lawyer, and Mr. Layton reported to you what Cooper had said?"

Thurston frowns and looks to the judge, who hesitates briefly before ruling. "Just answer the question."

"Yes."

"Did Mr. Layton also tell you that Cooper had said that he had nothing whatsoever to do with the death of your daughter?"

"Your Honor," Albert Chasen interrupts. "The question calls for hearsay—"

Lisa Paretti interrupts him. "Your Honor, we're not concerned here with the truth of the matter asserted, but only to determine the witness's mind state of mind at the time. The issue—"

"That's all right, Counsel, I'll allow it."

"Thank you, Your Honor. Mr. Thurston, do you recall the question?"

"Yes, Phil told me that Cooper said he had nothing to do with Marian's death."

"But you didn't believe that, did you?"

"I beg your pardon?"

"You didn't believe that Cooper had nothing to do with your daughter's death, did you?"

"I don't know what I believed then."

"You were very hurt by the news of Cooper's affair, weren't you?"

"Yes, I just couldn't believe he would have done that to Marian and the children. To me, to my wife."

"And you were angry, as well, weren't you?"

"Yes, I was. Very angry."

"But you never said anything to Cooper about your conversation with Phillip Layton, did you?"

"No. I thought that was something for the police to deal with."

"Did you go to the police with this information about Cooper's affair with Ms. Lambert?"

"Well, not to the police, exactly." He stops with a shrug.

"In fact, Mr. Thurston, you went to Mr. Chasen, didn't you, the prosecutor in charge of the investigation? Isn't that right?"

"Yes, I did. I thought he should know about it."

"Because you thought that Cooper's affair with Ms. Lambert had a great deal to do with the possible motive for your daughter's murder, didn't you?"

"Yes, I did," Thurston says with conviction.

"Because, even before you heard about the affair, you had suspected Cooper, hadn't you?"

"What?"

"Isn't it a fact, Mr. Thurston, that right from the first, you saw some things that made you suspect that your son-in-law had killed your daughter?"

"Well . . . I don't know."

"Mr. Thurston, weren't there things you heard from the police and saw yourself in your daughter's bedroom that made you suspicious?"

"Yes, all right, there were things."

"Like the fact that the safe had been opened without any evidence of force or tampering, isn't that right?"

"Yes, that's right. I knew about the safe, and I know that Marian had never even told the children about it. And no one but Cooper and Marian had the combination. No one. And I know it was a very expensive safe, and that it had all kinds of burglar-proof features about it."

"And so you knew that without the combination, it would have been almost impossible for someone to get into the safe without damaging it in some way."

"That's right."

"And you knew that only Cooper and Marian had the combination, didn't you?"

"Yes, that's absolutely right."

"And as painful as it was for you to think it, as horrible a prospect as it seemed to you, you began to suspect that Cooper might have murdered his wife, your daughter."

His hand is shaking, and he again dabs at his eye.

"I know this is difficult, Mr. Thurston. Please take whatever time you need."

Judge Newcomb leans over. "Would you like for us to take a brief recess?"

"No," Thurston says. "I'm all right." He looks up at Lisa Paretti. "Yes, ma'am. As much as I didn't want to believe it, that's what I thought. And that's what I think today."

"And given these suspicions, as much as they hurt you, when you heard of Cooper's affair with Sydney Lambert, you convinced yourself that Cooper was involved in your daughter's death, didn't you?"

"Well, it certainly made me think something was wrong."

"And the pain that caused was almost unbearable, wasn't it?"

"Oh yes. Yes, you can't imagine."

"And you were angry."

"Yes, I was angry. Wouldn't you be?"

"And so you went to the district attorney and told him about the affair."

"Yes."

"And you told him your thoughts about the safe."

"Yes."

"And you told him all about Barth-Sanders's attempt to take over your company, and who Sydney Lambert was, and all about how you had been talking to your daughter about her taking back from Cooper the voting rights to her stock, but how you were convinced that Cooper had talked your daughter out of that so that he could keep control himself, didn't you?"

"Yes, I did. I wasn't trying to take anything away from Cooper. It was just that it was her stock, and I thought she should be the one to vote it, that's all. But Cooper wouldn't let go of it. He convinced Marian to let him keep the voting rights."

"That's what you believed, isn't it?"

"It's the truth."

"And when you told all of this to the district attorney, the police then had a motive to work with, didn't they?"

"Well—I don't know what they had."

"Did Mr. Chasen seem interested in what you had to tell him?"

"Yes."

"Did he take notes?"

"Oh, yes. We talked for a long time, and I explained everything to him. About the stock and how Cooper could have engineered the takeover if he were able to vote my daughter's stock the way this Lambert woman and Barth-Sanders wanted."

"And so now the police have their motive."

Chasen is on his feet. "I object to that."

"Withdrawn," Lisa says.

The judge frowns at this needless interruption and waves his hand to signal them to go on.

Lisa Paretti waits a moment, then asks, "Mr. Thurston, Marian was your only child, was she not?"

"Yes."

"And of course you loved her very much."

"She was everything to us. We love our grandchildren, of course, but Marian—she was everything to us. Everything."

"And like every loving parent, you were always there for her, helping her in any way you could?"

"Yes."

"Perhaps even at times spoiling her a bit?" Lisa allows herself a small, shy smile, and Thurston shrugs just as shyly.

"Yes, I guess we did."

"And even though your daughter herself could afford to buy whatever she needed, you and your wife would give her small gifts even when there was no specific occasion, such as a birthday or Christmas, is that correct?"

"Yes, sometimes."

"In fact, when Cooper and your daughter moved into their new house in Fishing Creek, you gave her a gold bracelet, is that right?"

"Yes."

"A gold identification bracelet?"

"Yes."

Lisa Paretti walks to the prosecution table and whispers something to Albert Chasen, and the two of them take a moment to rummage through the box of exhibits before she turns to approach the witness.

"May I, Your Honor?"

Judge Newcomb nods.

"Mr. Thurston, I am showing you what has been marked as state's exhibit number 27. Do you recognize that?"

"Yes."

"What is it?"

Thurston takes a deep breath. "It's the bracelet my wife and I gave Marian."

"For the record, Your Honor, exhibit 27 is the bracelet Marian Avery was wearing at the time of her death." The judge nods. "Now, Mr. Thurston, I note that the bracelet has some engravings, is that correct?"

"Yes."

"Your daughter's initials are engraved in script on the top of the ID plate?"

"Yes."

"And on the back of the plate is engraved her address in Fishing Creek and her telephone number, is that correct?"

"Yes."

"Did you have that information engraved, sir?"

"My wife did."

"This was not the first identification bracelet you and your wife had given to your daughter, was it?"

"No."

"In fact, ever since your daughter was a little girl, every time she moved to a new address or got a new telephone number, you and your wife would give her a new bracelet with the new information engraved on the back, isn't that correct?"

"Yes, I guess we did."

"Now, your daughter was a college graduate, was she not?"

"Yes, she graduated from Sweet Briar."

"She was a fine arts major, is that right?"

"Yes—"

"Your Honor," Chasen says, "I fail to see the relevance of this line, and it is well beyond the scope of direct examination."

Judge Newcomb sits forward and peers down at Lisa Paretti. "Counsel, I trust that there is a point to all this."

"Yes, Your Honor."

"Well, let's see if we can't get to it," the judge says, looking at the wall clock ticking toward 3:00 P.M.

"Yes, Your Honor. Mr. Thurston, again, your daughter was a fine arts major?"

"Yes, she was. She was a very good student."

"And she showed a great deal of talent for painting and design and things of that nature."

"Yes, she was very talented. Friends were always asking her advice about decorating their homes. Things like that. In fact, she helped design our offices. She could have been a professional if she had wanted."

"But there were some areas of her studies where she did have some problems, isn't that correct?"

"Well . . ."

"Isn't it true that your daughter had a problem with mathematics?"

"A little, I guess. Mathematics wasn't her strongest subject."

"In fact, Mr. Thurston, isn't it true that your daughter had a great deal of trouble with mathematics?"

"Well, I don't know that I'd say that."

"Isn't it true, sir, that throughout her schooling, including college, she required tutors to help her get through even the basic math courses?"

"Marian wasn't stupid, if that's what you mean."

"No, sir, not at all. In fact, her problem with mathematics had nothing to do with her intelligence, did it? In fact, it was not until her senior year in college that she was tested and it was discovered that she had a form of dyslexia, isn't that right?"

Thurston does not answer.

"Isn't it true, sir, that it was discovered that your daughter's problem was not her intelligence but that when it came to numbers, particularly strings of numbers, her brain would for some reason record those numbers in a different order than they appeared?"

"Yes, I guess so. The doctors said it was something about the way she'd see the numbers differently, get them mixed up. She just couldn't see them the right way."

"And because of this problem that had nothing to do with her intelligence, she couldn't remember numbers?"

"Well, that's what they said."

"She would even have problems remembering her correct street address or telephone number."

"Well, it wasn't really a problem. She would carry a little address book with her. Things like that."

"And isn't that why from the time she was a little girl, and even when she was an adult and married and had children of her own, she always wore a gold identification bracelet that would have her address and telephone number inscribed on it?"

"Yes."

"Now, sir, did you know the combination to the safe located in your daughter's master bathroom?"

"No."

"Would it surprise you—"

"Your Honor, I object," Chasen says. "What would or would not surprise this witness—"

"Overruled. I'll allow this line of questioning."

Lisa Paretti retrieves a slip of paper from her skirt pocket and leans forward to pull the microphone just a bit closer to her lips. "Sir," she asks quietly, holding up the slip of paper, "would it surprise you to learn that the combination to that safe contained five double-digit numbers, and that each number required a different number of turns in a different direction?"

Chasen is on his feet, his voice agitated. "Your Honor, Counsel is now testifying, there's nothing in evidence—"

"Overruled."

"Mr. Thurston—" Lisa Paretti begins.

"I never knew the combination."

"Sir, the question is whether it would surprise you to learn that the combination to that safe was four turns to the right and stop at sixteen, five turns to the left and stop at thirty-two, one turn to the right and stop at thirty-two again, two turns to the left and stop at forty-seven, one final turn to the right and stop at nineteen?"

"As I said, I never knew anything about the combination to that safe. It was none of my business."

"Assume, sir, that the combination was as I described it. Would you say that that is not a simple series of numbers to memorize?"

"I don't know."

"Knowing your daughter as you did, sir, knowing that not for any lack of intelligence, but because she had this form of dyslexia that often caused her to confuse her own street address and telephone number, would you say that she could have memorized the complex combination of numbers and turns that I have just described?"

Chasen leaps to his feet. "Your Honor, I must object. Counsel is asking this witness to speculate—"

Lisa Paretti turns sharply toward Chasen. "Your Honor, the state's entire case is based upon the speculations of this witness."

"*Counsel!* Both of you. Come to the bench."

Cooper watches the huddled conversation at the bench. The lawyers' arguments drift out as garbled whispers as they compete to be heard, and the judge waves his finger at both of them. Cooper looks over to see that for the first time, juror number eight has not taken up her knitting, but sits like the others, staring at the bench, waiting for the punch line. Ed Thurston looks tired, his shoulders droop forward, and his head bows a bit as if it is suddenly too heavy. The lawyers turn from the bench and Chasen's jaw seems clenched with exasperation as he returns to his seat, and Lisa Paretti resumes her stance at the podium.

"Mr. Thurston," Lisa says. "I ask you again. Knowing your daughter as you did, particularly knowing her problem with this form of dyslexia and her inability to remember even her street address and telephone number, could she have memorized the combination to the safe that I have described?"

He shakes his head slowly. "No, I don't think she could have."

"Now, in order for her to have been able to get into that safe whenever she needed, she would have had to have the combination written down somewhere, isn't that correct?"

"Yes, I suppose."

Lisa Paretti walks quickly to the prosecutor's table to retrieve a sheaf of papers stapled together. "Sir, I am going to show you what have been previously marked as exhibits 52 and 52(a)." She hands Thurston the police inventory of items observed in Marian Avery's bedroom. "Have you seen these exhibits before?"

"Yes."

"When did you see those documents?"

"The police let me look through all these things to see if I thought there might be something I knew about that they missed."

"Did you find anything that they missed?"

"Not that I could see."

"But you know this to be a listing of all the items they observed in your daughter's bedroom?"

"Yes."

"And do you see there, I believe on the third and fourth pages of exhibit 52, and on the third page of exhibit 52(a), listings of items found in the drawer of your daughter's dressing table?"

He takes a moment to look at the pages. "Yes."

"And among the items found or observed are such insignificant things as a dry-cleaning slip and handwritten notes about a cocktail party that had been arranged?"

He looks again. "Yes."

"There is even a handwritten note that says 'Connie, November third,' and a telephone number. Is that right?"

"Yes."

Again, Lisa Paretti goes to the box on the prosecution table, and after a brief search retrieves a sheet of notepaper. She turns to Ed Thurston. "Sir, I am showing you what has been previously marked as exhibit 52(a)-16, indicating a note that was found in the drawer of your daughter's dressing table. Is that note in your daughter's handwriting?"

"Yes," he says, and draws a quick, audible breath.

"Do you know who Connie is?"

"Yes, Connie is—*was* one of Marian's oldest friends. They talked almost every day. She and Marian were friends all the way back to grade school."

"And the telephone number, do you recognize it?"

His words stumble. "Yes, well, I think . . . Yes, that's Connie's number. I—my wife and I know the Neals. We see them—but not really since this all happened—but, yes, that's Connie's number."

"So it appears, does it not, that your daughter had even written down the telephone number of one of her oldest friends, someone she talked to almost every day?"

"Yes."

"Mr. Thurston, I would ask you to look carefully at both exhibits

52 and 52(a), all twenty-one pages, and tell us whether you see any notation of any piece of paper that contained any numbers that might have been the combination to the safe in the master bathroom."

Thurston dabs his eyes with his handkerchief and takes a deep breath before concentrating on the exhibits. It takes several minutes, while the courtroom remains still, except for the electric clock, which whirs and clicks with each passing minute. He then looks up. "No, I don't see anything like that."

"Mr. Thurston, don't you think that if a burglar were rummaging through your daughter's dressing table looking for valuables and came upon—"

"*I object!*" Chasen erupts in a shout. "This is the grossest form of speculation."

Judge Newcomb snaps forward with a finger pointing at Chasen. "Counsel, I have already ruled on this matter. You will *not* object again to this line of questioning." He turns to Lisa Paretti. "Proceed, Counsel."

She waits a moment, then looks up slowly at Ed Thurston, who has an almost frightened expression on his face. "Mr. Thurston, when you decided that Cooper had killed your daughter because the safe had been opened without any marks of force or damage, you didn't stop to think that the killer might have rummaged through your daughter's drawer and come across the combination written down on some piece of paper, did you?"

There is no answer.

"Nor did you stop to think that if the killer had seen what would appear to be a combination, that he would start looking for a safe, did you?"

"I . . . I don't know what happened."

"Nor did you stop to think that when the killer found the safe in the bathroom, he could have opened it as easily as your daughter, or even you or I, for that matter, if we had that same piece of paper. Isn't that true?"

Thurston is staring at her, but he says nothing.

"And so when you went to the district attorney with your suspicions and told him about your son-in-law's affair with Ms. Lambert and about the stock fight, what you told him was colored by your belief that Cooper was guilty of killing your daughter, isn't that right?"

She waits a moment, but again there is no answer.

"And because of your suspicions about your son-in-law, you never stopped to think that perhaps Cooper wasn't trying to control the voting rights to your daughter's stock, but that perhaps your daughter, because of her problem with numbers and mathematics, simply did not want to deal with those issues, did you?"

He is shaking visibly now. "It was her stock. I . . . I would have helped her. But it was her stock, not his."

"And the suspicions you told the district attorney, about Cooper trying to manipulate the stock, were driven by your suspicions about the condition of the safe. And it was the condition of the safe that made you suspect that Cooper had murdered your daughter, isn't that right?"

"I . . . yes, but I never . . ." He stops himself, his face contorted with confusion.

"But somehow you never told the police or the prosecutors that Marian would have had the combination written down on a piece of paper that the burglar—the real murderer—"

Chasen is on his feet. "Objection to counsel's assumption about who the 'real murderer'—"

"Sustained. The jury will disregard that remark."

"Mr. Thurston," Lisa Paretti continues, undisturbed, "you never told the police or the district attorney that Marian would have had the combination written down, did you?"

"I didn't think . . ." He stops and looks at Cooper.

"And so all your suspicions, all you told the police, and all you've told this jury about what you thought were Cooper Avery's motives, was based upon a mistake, wasn't it?"

"I don't know. He was the only one who could have opened the safe. I didn't want to believe it, but when I saw . . . I, I don't know."

"In fact, Mr. Thurston, you understand now, don't you, that Cooper wasn't the only other person who could have opened that safe without damaging it? It was an easy mistake to make, but one with *terrible* consequences."

"Objection!"

"Sustained." Judge Newcomb raises a finger of warning to Lisa Paretti. "Counsel, I would caution you against such remarks."

Lisa says nothing but stares at Edward Thurston, who rocks in his seat a bit, his expression one of stunned confusion. She steps aside so that Thurston can look directly at Cooper. His eyes fix on his son-in-law, and they appear to be filling.

"No further questions."

 **31** Christine sits in the corner of Albert Chasen's office with her legs folded under her, her attention focused on the plastic cup of yogurt she is exploring for its bottom layer of gelatinous fruit.

Paul Wyzanski is slouched in one chair with his long legs stretched to rest on another. "How bad was it?" he asks.

Chasen answers with a cock of his head and eyebrows raised more in question than concern. "Well, she scored some points," he says, referring to Lisa Paretti's cross-examination of Edward Thurston. "And they obviously have the judge interested in this other man theory. He gave Paretti a pretty free rein, but the bottom line here is that's all they have, theory. We just have to make sure the jury understands that, and that what we have is facts." He turns toward Christine but is interrupted by Charlie Abbot entering the office with a notepad in one hand.

"Well," Detective Abbot says, "I checked with the clerk's office. Last night the defense served a subpoena on a Mrs. Joanna Albertson. She's one of the neighbors in Fishing Creek Estates. I just talked to her on the phone and made an appointment to go see her in about an hour, but what she says is that about a month ago she was contacted by that defense investigator that's been all over the county asking questions. And then Jack Gabriel came down to see her, took her to lunch and was asking all kinds of questions about this guy Ollie Johns."

Paul Wyzanski sits up a bit. "That the guy who went broke and lost his land to Avery, the same guy Neavitt was talking about?" he asks, referring to the deputy sheriff who alerted them to Cooper's purchase of the new camouflage hunting outfit, and who has since kept them apprised of local rumors and, to the extent that he knows, of people who have been contacted by any defense investigators.

"Yeah, that's him," Chasen says. "Ollie's sort of a dark legend around here. The family's been in the county for generations. Very wealthy until Ollie took over. If I remember, he's the last of the line. An only son. He's had problems with booze and gambling, went through a few marriages, dissipated what was left of the money and let the farm go to hell. I never really knew much about what happened except that somehow Avery and his partners managed to pick up that land dirt cheap. For back taxes and maybe a little extra. But except for Ollie being picked up a few times for drunk driving, I haven't heard much about him for years."

Paul asks Charlie Abbot, "What were they talking about with this lady Albertson?"

"Well, I didn't get into a lot of detail, but apparently she was in the community association with Marian Avery, the board of directors, or whatever they call it. Some time ago, Marian Avery and this guy Johns got into a real battle royal over whether Johns was violating some county codes about the way he kept his property. I didn't understand exactly what she was talking about, but apparently there was some bad blood between the two of them—between Johns and Marian Avery."

Albert Chasen smiles. "So that's their straw man? Ollie Johns?"

"Sounds like it," Abbot says.

Chasen turns to an aerial photograph showing the area around Fishing Creek that is tacked to an easel in the corner behind his desk. He muses for a moment and then goes to the easel. "If I remember right, this is where Johns lives. Right here, right around the point from the Avery house. Let's check that out to be sure. Call the deputy, Neavitt. But I think I'm right."

Paul Wyzanski stands and approaches the easel.

"Look at this," Chasen says to him, pointing a finger. "If I'm right that this is where Johns lives, lookit here. That's where Earl Barkin found the jewels. Those oyster beds are right in line between the Avery place and where Johns lives, right? So what if their theory is that Johns could've come around the point by water, killed Marian Avery in the house he used to own, and then left the same way, dumping the jewels on the way back to his place?"

Paul nods his agreement. "And since Johns used to live there, in Avery's house, they might try to say he would've known some way to get in without a key and then maybe he broke the window in the kitchen door on the way out to fake the burglary. Not bad."

"But that don't make no sense," Charlie Abbot protests. "First, the house was completely renovated, right? Which means all new locks and keys and all that. What? They think this guy Johns had some secret passage or something? And another thing, if this guy Johns is so down and out, why would he dump the jewels? That don't make no sense. I mean, what's this guy's motive?"

"That's what we have to find out," Chasen says. "But it sounds like whatever the dispute was, they're going to argue bad blood, not killing for money. And I suppose they'll say this dispute was just the tail of the dragon. You know, Johns loses his house, his land and all that. He turns bitter. Been harboring a grudge against the Averys for years. Particularly against Marian, since she's not only stolen his land and is living in his house, but she sics the county on him for some kind of code violations. Maybe it's revenge. Maybe he does go over there just to steal. Marian confronts him and he kills her. He panics, starts worrying about getting caught with the jewels and he tosses them. It's not a bad theory."

"But can they prove it?" Paul asks.

Chasen smiles and shakes his head. "They don't have to prove it. All they have to do is make the jury wonder. Make them think it's a possibility, and they've got an argument for reasonable doubt."

"This is bullshit," Charlie says, "this Johns stuff."

Christine puts her yogurt aside and speaks up for the first time. "Charlie's right. It doesn't make sense, and I think we're getting sidetracked here."

Chasen turns toward her with exaggerated surprise. "Don't tell me, Sergeant. You mean you've finally come to agree with us that Avery did it? That the other man theory is bullshit?"

"No, I'm telling you that this Ollie Johns stuff is bullshit."

"Bullshit or not, we've got to cover ourselves on this. Charlie, I want you—"

"Wait a minute," Christine interrupts. "Just wait a minute. What if that's not where they're going? Don't you think that if they're really going to try and come up with an alternative killer, a real person with real motives, don't you think they'd go after this Martin Lessing business? Don't you think that makes a lot more sense? Don't you think—"

The strain of impatience takes over the expressions of all three men. "Sergeant," Chasen says, "for Christ's sake, we're not gonna go through that again. I've listened to you on this over and over again. And it's nonsense. Okay? And even if Gabriel and Paretti know about that stuff—which we've got no reason to believe they do, right? But even if they are aware of it, they must think it's nonsense, too. They haven't even hinted at anything like that. As far as we know, they've never even approached what's-his-name—Roth? They haven't talked to him, they haven't subpoenaed him. It's nothing, it's ancient history no one gives a good goddamn about. I don't want to hear it anymore. It's crazy, so just give it a fucking rest. All right?"

Christine sits frozen, her eyes wide and her face flushed a sudden deep red. She stands quickly, and Paul says, "Chris, let's talk about this later."

"No," Chasen says, "we haven't got time for hand-holding right now."

Christine reaches for her purse and starts for the door. "Gentlemen, I trust you don't need anything further from me." She turns back to Chasen with narrowed, angry eyes. "And nobody," she growls through clenched teeth, "and I mean *nobody* needs to hold my hand."

Christine stalks out of the office, and Chasen murmurs, "I don't need that shit!"

"You were a little rough, don't you think?" Paul says.

"Forget it!" Chasen says abruptly. "We've got work to do. Charlie, I want you to get a hold of the deputy, Simon Neavitt. Have him meet you after you talk to this woman Abramson, Albertson, whatever her name is. Check out exactly where Ollie Johns lives. Find out anything you can on Johns. Go see him if you have to. Find out if we can establish an alibi for him on the night of the killing. Paul, I want you to track down the oysterman, Barkin. I want to talk to him. Tonight. Whenever you can find him and get him in here. I never asked him about Johns. We need to pin him down on where those oyster beds are in relation to Johns's property, and I want to make sure he's ready for any of these theory questions Gabriel might toss at him.

"Next, I want to reschedule some witnesses. I think maybe I'll wipe some of Paretti's points off the board with the county nurse and Ellen Haley. You know, let the jury know how the kid reacted to the hunting clothes and his own father. And the shrink from the hospital up in Pennsylvania, Dr. Storrs. Paul, give her a call and see if she can't be here tomorrow morning. Tell her I'll guarantee that she'll be on and off the stand tomorrow if she can be here by say, eleven o'clock. If she can make it, I'll work the others around her."

"What about Sydney Lambert?" Paul asks. "You had her scheduled for the morning. I called the hotel, and she checked in this afternoon."

"Did you talk to her?"

"I tried, but she just said the same thing all over. She wasn't talking to anybody. She said she's complied with the subpoena and that's all she's required to do. Just to let her know when to be in court."

"What a bitch," Chasen murmurs.

"Al, I don't trust this lady. I'd be real careful with her."

"I understand that. But we don't have to trust her. I only need her to answer two questions. Did she have an affair with Avery, and was he with her on the night his wife was murdered?"

"But what if she comes up with some of that same crap she did in the grand jury? You know, Avery couldn't have killed his wife and all that?"

"No, even this judge isn't going to let her get into her opinions like that. And too, I don't care if she comes across as a bitch. In fact, I hope she does. The less the jury likes her, the less they'll sympathize with Avery. Besides, she can't hurt us. What can she say? In the grand jury she adopted the statement she gave you guys. She's not gonna get up and perjure herself and suddenly claim Avery was with her, right? She hasn't got a choice. Besides, it looks like she's not cooperating with the defense any more than she is with us. Remember that bitchy letter from Gabriel? The one asking if we had instructed her not to talk to them? No, she doesn't want to help anyone. She just doesn't want to be here at all. But she's stuck. No problem."

"I don't know, man," Paul says, "there's something about her that just makes me nervous."

32 "Are you going to tell me what happened today?"

Christine does not answer.

"Aren't you going to eat anything?"

Her eyes are upon him, but she is looking past him, her dinner untouched.

"Look, I may be a lousy cook, but it's hard even for me to screw up steak and baked potato."

Alex allows some time before taking a final bite of his steak. He then sits back and tosses his fork, which lands on his plate with a rattle that draws her attention.

"No, it's fine. I'm just not hungry."

"What is it? Tell me. You're always hungry."

Christine does not move, and the tone of her voice is as flat as her expression. "They think I'm crazy. All of them. Even Paul. They think I'm nuts. Everybody. Even the defense."

"What're you talking about?"

"And what's *really* crazy," she says with sudden animation, "is that everything that Avery set in motion—Cooper's father—everything he set in motion forty years ago just keeps rolling on. It just keeps sweeping people up, and no one cares. It's like some dark, evil machine that he created to grind a few people up to protect himself, and after all these years, it's still grinding. No one knows why, no one even bothers to ask why: it just seems easier to keep feeding it than to try to understand it, or even to turn it off."

Alex frowns with the effort to understand. "I'm sorry, I'm not sure I—"

"Do you know what's happened?"

Alex shakes his head.

"They're covering for the old man. The defense attorneys are ready to sacrifice another victim to protect the old man. What is it about him? What do I have to do?"

"Chris, back up a minute, you've lost me. What happened today?"

Christine's voice sounds more perplexed than angry as she details the discussion in Albert Chasen's office concerning Oliver Johns, the defense subpoena to the neighbor, Joanna Albertson, and what that implies as to where they think the defense is headed.

Alex gives himself time to absorb what Christine has said and then suggests, "Maybe the defense has some evidence that really points to this guy Johns."

"No, they don't."

"How can you be so sure?"

"Because I am! There's no evidence there. They're just coming up with some patchwork of theories to offer up a scapegoat. They're doing exactly what they keep complaining about the government doing. They're basing their case on a bunch of gratuitous assumptions. They don't give a damn for the truth. They don't want the truth to come out. And they don't care who gets hurt in the process."

"Well—" Alex hesitates, unsure whether this is the time to offer his opinion. Then he does. "I'm no lawyer, but it seems to me that a defense attorney isn't obligated to stick to the truth. His job is to defend his man. Isn't that right?"

She stares at him.

"Isn't that what he's supposed to do, the defense attorney, I mean? If he can feed the jury some other suspect that'll help get his client off, isn't that what he should do? He's not the prosecutor. I don't know, but it seems to me there's a big difference there, you know, between what's required of a prosecutor and a defense attorney. I mean they have a whole different set of obligations, isn't that right? Whether you call it legal or ethical or whatever, it just—"

She shuts him off with a violent shake of her head. "Just stop! You're not listening to me. Why is it no one wants to listen? Why is it no one gives a damn about what really happened here?"

Alex's patience begins to unravel. "Just hold on a minute. I understand what you think happened, and up to a point, your theory makes a lot of sense. But, Christine, for God's sake, it's still just a theory. Just like the D.A. has his theory and Avery's lawyers have their theory. But right now, there's a trial. A murder trial. And I suspect no one, particularly not the defense attorneys, has any time for theories that don't work for them. The only truth they're worried about is whether their client gets tagged for killing his wife. Right?"

She does not answer him.

"Right?" he asks again.

Christine offers a smile so strained as to look painful. "I think I'd better go."

"Oh, for Christ's sake—"

"No, no," she says softly, "I'm not angry. I'm just tired. Maybe you're right. I don't know. But right now I don't want to argue about it. I don't want to argue with you."

"I'm not arguing, but—"

"No, that's all right. I'm just tired. And I ought to go home anyway. My place is a mess, and I need to clean, and maybe I just need—I don't know, maybe I just need to chill out a bit."

"Chris, listen, at least eat some of your dinner. Don't go off angry."

"No, I'm not. I'm just tired. I just need to go home. I just have this sudden urge to clean." She gets up from the table and looks around for her purse. "I'm sure there's all kinds of dark psychological significance to that but . . ."

Alex laughs a bit and walks over to her, taking her shoulders in his hands. "Listen, tomorrow's Friday. Why don't I take off and drive down and meet you at the courthouse, maybe sit and watch a few minutes of the trial. Whatever. And when you're through, we'll go have dinner. There're a bunch of good restaurants on the water near there. Maybe we'll even spend the night."

Christine nods, but not convincingly.

"How does that sound?" he asks. "Could you ride down in the morning with the other detectives?"

She nods again.

"You sure?"

"Yes, that's fine."

"Fine? That's fine?"

"Yes!" she answers irritably.

"You're sure? You don't look—"

"No. How many times do I have to say it? It's fine, it's okay, it's hunky-dory. All right?"

He does not answer, and she turns to find her purse, and she goes to the door.

"I'm sorry. I just need to take care of things . . . by myself. I'll see you tomorrow, all right?"

She waits at the open door a moment, staring back at him. He nods, and she slips out without another word.

33 $\mathscr{A}$lbert Chasen rocks back in his chair, its slight squeak covered by the sounds of the jurors settling in their seats and the rustle of paper as the reporters and courtroom artists open their notebooks and sketchpads to record another day. Judge Newcomb concludes a whispered conference with the bailiff and looks toward the jury.

"Good morning, ladies and gentlemen," he says.

"Good morning," the jury mumbles in unison.

"Counsel? Both sides ready?"

Jack Gabriel barely rises from his chair. "Yes, Your Honor."

Chasen is on his feet, and with a sigh, says, "Yes, Your Honor."

"Call your next witness, Mr. Chasen."

"The state calls Ms. Sydney Lambert."

Nerves are part of the game, Chasen knows, and it is often said among trial lawyers that when the day comes that you no longer feel the butterflies, that is the day to start looking for another line of work. You have lost the edge. But this morning the butterflies crowd his stomach, and he feels the thumping of his heart. Detective Wyzanski's warning of the night before did not concern him until this morning and his brief meeting with Sydney Lambert. It was their first and only meeting since her grand jury appearance months before. It was not that she was unpleasant, particularly, it was just that she made a point of not volunteering anything that was not legally required of her. No, she saw no need to go over the questions she would be asked. Yes, she understood the nature of the testimony she would be asked to give. Yes, she would take the time to once again read over the typewritten report of Detective Wyzanski and Abbot's interview of her last December. "You need not be concerned, Mr. Chasen," she had said. "I understand very well the law of perjury, and I have no intention of saying anything but the truth." Somehow, her assurances had unsettled more than comforted him.

He had been careful during his opening statement to the jury. He did not elaborate beyond the essentials. He said only that on the night of Friday, October 26, and through midday Saturday, October 27, at some point during which time Marian Avery had been murdered, Cooper Avery claimed to have been in New York City and in the company of Ms. Sydney Lambert. "You will hear evidence, ladies and gentlemen, that that statement was untrue." That was all he said, and that was all that needed to be said. While it might have been nice to be able to draw from this witness a more lurid tale of Cooper's infidelity, sometimes less is more. Often a jury's imagination may be more damning than the facts, and so he will give this witness little or no room to elaborate, to explain, to excuse, to offer any opinion. He will treat this witness as she treated him, and go straight to the point.

All heads turn as Sydney Lambert walks directly to the witness box. She stands tall and erect as the oath is administered, her light gray suit showing not a wrinkle, her brightly patterned silk blouse emphasizing a fair complexion accented by carefully understated makeup. She is everything one might expect of a wealthy New York lawyer or businesswoman, and Chasen wonders whether this jury will admire or resent her high fashion and her demeanor. He hopes the latter.

"Please state your name."

"Sydney Burke Lambert."

The court reporter asks her to spell her name, which she does.

"Are you married, Ms. Lambert?"

"Yes. My husband is Victor Rais. That's R-A-I-S. But I go by my maiden name, Lambert, for professional reasons."

"Where do you live, Ms. Lambert?"

"New York City."

"How long have you lived in New York?"

She stops to think. "Twenty-one, almost twenty-two years."

"Do you have any other residences?"

"Yes. My husband and I have an apartment in Brussels, Belgium. My husband's business requires him to be there a great deal of the time. We also have a house in Grindelwald. That's in Switzerland. But except when I am visiting my husband in Europe, I live in New York. That's our home."

"Are you employed, Ms. Lambert?"

"Yes."

"How are you employed?"

"I am general counsel for Barth-Sanders Industries."

"How long have you held that position?"

"Four years."

"Ms. Lambert, do you know the defendant, Cooper Avery?"

"Yes."

"Could you point him out to the ladies and gentlemen of the jury?"

Jack Gabriel rises quickly, and he says in a tired, almost annoyed tone, "Your Honor, we'll stipulate that my client is the Cooper Avery known to this witness."

"Thank you," Chasen says. "Now, Ms. Lambert, when did you first meet the defendant, Cooper Avery?"

"I don't recall the date exactly, but I have known him for many years. There were any number of occasions when our paths crossed through mutual business acquaintances, meetings, things of that nature."

"Did there come a time when you became personally involved with Mr. Avery?"

She draws a quick, barely perceptible breath. "Yes, for a short period of time we—Mr. Avery and I had I'd guess you'd say a personal relationship."

"I don't mean to be indelicate, Ms. Lambert, but just how personal was your relationship?"

"Well, I don't know how you could call that question 'delicate' "—a light snicker rolls through the courtroom, and the jury joins in a collective grin—"but yes, for a short time, Mr. Avery and I had an affair."

"You were lovers?"

She hesitates slightly, as if she objects to the word, but says, "Yes."

"Could you tell us the time frame during which you and Mr. Avery were lovers?"

She raises her eyes in thought. "It was sometime in mid-November 1989 until October 1990."

October? Chasen frowns a bit, thinking to himself, *October?*

"We saw each other irregularly, sometimes once, sometimes two or three times a month during that period."

Chasen stops the thoughts racing through his mind, and goes on. "Are you familiar with a hotel in New York City called the Albemarle House?"

"Yes. Mr. Avery and I often met there—stayed there together."

Chasen is surprised that she is volunteering complete answers. He should be pleased, but somehow alarm signals keep ringing in his head.

"How often did you and Mr. Avery stay together at the Albemarle House?"

"I can't truthfully answer that. I'm sure you must have the hotel records."

"Ms. Lambert, would those hotel records reflect either your name or the name Cooper Avery on the register of guests?"

"No, not when we stayed there together. Mr. Avery always registered under another name."

"And what name did he use when registering?"

"I think it was Belkindas. George Belkindas."

"Do you know why he used that particular name?"

"No."

"Did you ever ask?"

"No. I don't know whether it was a real name or one that he made up. But obviously neither of us wanted to register in our own name."

"Why was that?"

"You mean aside from the obvious reason that we were both married at the time?"

"Yes."

"Well, there was the additional concern about our respective jobs, particularly when it became known that Barth-Sanders was attempting to gain control of a majority share of Thurston Construction stock."

"Did you and Mr. Avery discuss that potential takeover?"

"No, sir, we did not. Except that when I became aware of my company's interest in Thurston Construction, Cooper and I discussed the problem that presented as far as our personal relationship. We began to see each other less and less, and the few times we did see each other, we abided by a hard and fast rule not to discuss anything having to do with our business at all."

"Was either your company or anyone at Thurston Construction aware of your relationship with Mr. Avery?"

"I don't know what the people at Thurston Construction knew or didn't know, but I have never said anything to my people about it."

"Ms. Lambert—"

"If I can say one thing, Mr. Chasen. I did not tell my company because I know that I never did a single thing to compromise my company's interests or to assist Cooper Avery in any way. I gave him no information or suggestions, nor did I discuss the matter with him in any way. Nor did Mr. Avery ever ask me to divulge any information, nor did he talk to me about Thurston Construction. I took no active part in the work associated with Barth-Sanders's bid to take over Thurston. Any work that was required of the general counsel's office I assigned to one of my assistants, and except for reviewing their work, I took no part in that process. But I do know that after today, after all these reporters write their stories and give their newscasts, I will certainly be fired by Barth-Sanders." She turns to the jury. "You are watching the end of my career, and probably my marriage."

"And yet you have come to testify—"

"Mr. Chasen, I am here under subpoena, as you well know. I have no other choice but to testify and to tell the truth."

Chasen stops himself. The alarm bells grow louder. He decides to cut through the preliminaries.

"Ms. Lambert, I am now showing you what has been previously marked and introduced as state's exhibit 138."

"Yes."

"This is a registration card for the Albemarle House Hotel in New York City, is it not?"

"Yes."

"And what is the date of that registration card?"

"October twenty-sixth. It doesn't give a year."

"And what name is on that registration card?"

"George Belkindas."

"Is that the same name you have previously indicated Mr. Avery used when registering at that hotel?"

"Yes."

"Does the card indicate how many people were in Mr. Belkindas's, or Mr. Avery's, party?"

"It doesn't say."

"Ms. Lambert, on the afternoon or evening of Friday, October 26, 1990, did you meet or stay with Mr. Avery at the Albemarle House Hotel in New York City?"

"No, I did not."

The alarm bells go silent. Chasen's relief is palpable, flowing over him like a cool shower.

"At any time, ma'am, on the evening of Friday, October twenty-sixth, did you see or meet with Cooper Avery in New York City?"

"Yes."

The first time he experienced the sensation, he was twelve years old and playing second base for Calverton Buick in the county Little League. Ricky Sandstrom had hit a hard ground ball that took a bad bounce and caught him square between the eyes. He'd never forget that first flash, before the pain came, that sudden, stunning sensation that he could taste and smell, even before he had any idea how bad the pain to follow would be.

He slows the pace of his thoughts. *Don't panic. You know what you have to do.*

He takes his time, staring at Sydney Lambert, then reaches for the file on the counsel table, from which he extracts the statement she gave Detectives Wyzanski and Abbot. He holds the statement up, contemplating it and allowing her to see what is coming.

"Ms. Lambert, I ask you again, at any time on the afternoon or evening of Friday, October 26, 1990, did you see or meet Cooper Avery in New York City?"

"Yes, I did."

"I remind you, Ms. Lambert, that you are testifying under penalty of perjury."

Jack Gabriel is on his feet. "*I object!* Counsel is trying to intimidate the witness because he doesn't want to hear the truth."

"*Your Honor,*" Chasen shouts, "this witness—"

"*Counsel!* Both of you. Come to the bench," Judge Newcomb orders. He then turns to Sydney Lambert. "Step down, Ms. Lambert."

At the bench, Judge Newcomb wears a bemused grin, as if he enjoys the prospect of a heated argument; an opportunity, Chasen suspects, to relieve the boredom and frustration of the trial lawyer turned judge, forever relegated to the role of passive observer rather than active participant.

"So, Mr. Chasen, it would appear that your witness has jumped ship." The judge then turns to Jack Gabriel. "Counsel, you, of course, had no idea this was coming, did you? Never mind, you don't have to answer that."

Gabriel does not need to answer the question. His reticent smile answers for him, as well as the fact that he has come to the bench with a copy of Sydney Lambert's grand jury testimony.

"Mr. Chasen, talk to me," the judge says.

"Your Honor, first let me say that this witness's answer to the last question comes as a complete surprise to me. Secondly, if she persists in that answer and continues to say that she was with Cooper Avery in New York on that Friday night and Saturday morning, October twenty-sixth and twenty-seventh, she will be committing perjury. She already has committed perjury by her last answer, and if she is allowed to continue unadvised—"

"Excuse me, Your Honor," Gabriel starts.

"No, no, let Mr. Chasen finish."

"Your Honor, I submit that this witness be advised by the court of her obligations and of the penalties for perjury. Moreover, even aside from however the rest of my examination goes, to allow the defense to pursue this line in order to elicit testimony that this witness was with the defendant on the twenty-sixth and twenty-seventh would be inviting more perjury. And I don't think that can be done without advising her of her rights."

"Your Honor—"

"Excuse me, Mr. Gabriel, I haven't finished. Secondly, Your Honor, I'm claiming surprise."

"So I gather," Judge Newcomb says impishly.

"And therefore, Your Honor, I'm asking that the court allow me to impeach this witness with her prior statement to the police and her testimony to the grand jury. I'm also asking that the court declare her a hostile witness and that I be allowed to cross-examine."

"What is it about these prior statements, Mr. Chasen, that makes you think she's lying now?"

"Your Honor, this witness gave a lengthy statement to Detectives Wyzanski and Abbot last December in which she categorically denied that she saw or met or was with Cooper Avery on the night of the twenty-sixth or during the day on the twenty-seventh. Not in New York, not anywhere. She adopted that statement in the grand jury. Now, for the first time, and for reasons I can only imagine"—Chasen looks to Gabriel, whose expression remains irritatingly amused—"she is saying that she was with Avery at that time."

The judge turns to Jack Gabriel. "Well, Counsel?"

"Your Honor, Mr. Chasen is absolutely correct that the witness gave a statement to the police. And he is absolutely correct that the statement says what he said it says. And he is correct that the witness testified in the grand jury that she had given the statement to the police. But she has not yet given any perjured testimony, neither here nor in the grand jury, nor do I expect that she will perjure herself."

"I'm not sure I understand your point, Counsel, but I'm certain you're about to enlighten both me and Mr. Chasen, is that right? Is that the grand jury testimony?"

"Yes, Your Honor. It seems that this witness is more versed in the legal arts than Mr. Chasen had given her credit for. As I said, she did give the statement to the police denying that she had been with Cooper Avery on the night of the twenty-sixth and on the twenty-seventh during the day. And in the grand jury she did testify that she had given that statement to the police. But what she did not say, and more particularly what was not asked of her, was whether that statement to the police was true. Mr. Chasen read her police statement into the record in front of the grand jury, and you can see from the transcript that Ms. Lambert and Mr. Chasen got into a bit of a word game with each other. But the bottom line here is that in the grand jury Ms. Lambert was asked not whether the statement she gave to the police was true, but only whether the typed report of the police interview accurately summarized what she had told them. Now it is clear that at the time, Ms. Lambert was not pleased with being hauled before the grand jury, and was not of a mind to help anyone. But all she ever said in the grand jury was 'Yes, that's what I told the police,' not 'Yes, what I told the police was true.' Now it is my understanding that this witness will readily concede that she lied to the police about not being with Cooper Avery. And she can give her own explanations for that on the stand. But it is a fact that she never testified in the grand jury that she was not with Cooper Avery on the days in question." He pauses, looks briefly at Chasen, and lets his grin widen. "The bottom line here is that it appears that Mr. Chasen got distracted by all the sparring that was going on in the grand jury and missed asking the one crucial question of Ms. Lambert. 'Was your statement to the police true or false?' "

Judge Newcomb sits back in his chair, shaking his head slightly, trying to suppress a grin that sparkles in his bright brown eyes. He turns to the jury. "Ladies and gentlemen, we're going to take a brief recess while the court reviews some documents. Again, as I have cautioned you before, do not discuss this case with anyone, not even among yourselves, until you have heard all the evidence and received the court's instructions. Bailiff, if you'll escort jury."

And then to the lawyers. "Gentlemen, let me have the police statement and the grand jury transcript. I'm going to take a little time to read these over a cup of coffee and a doughnut. All right, I'll see you back here at ten-thirty."

Chasen shakes his head. There is no need for the recess. He knows already what the court's ruling will be and what will happen next. He's been had, but what he cannot understand is how he missed it. He can understand how he missed asking the question in the grand jury. He allowed Sydney Lambert to irritate him, and then to play on that irritation and on his impatience. But his failure to pick up the mistake later angers him. He read over the grand jury transcript, several times, he thinks; but obviously he did not read it carefully. He wasn't looking for it. It was one of those mistakes so obvious that you just don't see it.

And so he will go for a cup of coffee himself, then return to hear the judge rule that the grand jury transcript reflects exactly what Jack Gabriel had described. And when Sydney Lambert testifies here in court that Cooper Avery was with her on the dates in question, it will not be perjury, any more than was her testimony in the grand jury. It is the classic example of the answer that is literally true but factually misleading. But, he knows, the judge will also rule that he has a legitimate claim of surprise, and thus he will be able to cross-examine her and impeach her with her own statement. He also knows, however, that Sydney Lambert's statement to the police cannot now be used as substantive evidence. In other words, as a matter of law, the jury cannot consider the substance of the statement, but may only consider it as a prior inconsistency to be used in judging her credibility. But the legal niceties of such rules have more meaning to law professors and appellate judges than impact on the realities of a trial. In the final analysis, Chasen knows that Sydney Lambert's statement to the police will be heard by the jury, and it will be remembered by them. And while it cannot have the same impact that it would had he been able to argue that statement as fact, those jurors disposed to convict Avery will silently use it to support their conviction. Those jurors disposed to acquit will abide by the court's instructions. He hopes that Sydney Lambert's demeanor, and the obvious fact that she lied to the police and played a lawyer's game to turn on the prosecution, will lead the jury to the conclusion that she is lying now. And in the end, if the jury thinks Sydney Lambert a liar, her eleventh-hour claim that Cooper Avery was with her on the night of October 26 may well hurt the defense more than it hurts the prosecution.

And so it happens just as Albert Chasen knew it would. The judge rules as expected and Sydney Lambert returns to the stand. Although it takes some time and bantering to get through it, Chasen impeaches Sydney Lambert with her prior statement to Detectives Wyzanski and Abbot and turns her over to the defense. She does not resist Jack Gabriel as she did him, and Chasen is glad for it. It helps cement his grounds for later arguing that her current story is a fabrication. But yes, she does say that Cooper Avery was with her on Friday night, October 26, and through midday on the twenty-seventh, when she drove him to the airport for his return home. Yes, she lied to the police when they first confronted her. She had been upset by their visit and questions, and she had been concerned about the consequences her affair with Cooper Avery might visit on her career. And yes, she was also angry at Cooper, angry that his life was suddenly having such a devastating impact on her own. And she just didn't stop to think about the impact her lies would have on him. After all, she says, she could not imagine anyone believing Cooper capable of killing his wife; the detectives had said that Cooper was not being accused or charged, that they were simply "covering all the bases," she thought their words had been, and maybe her lie would end their interest in her. Maybe her lie would prevent the fact of her affair from ever becoming public, and maybe, just maybe, her career and her marriage need not be ruined.

Albert Chasen barely looks at Sydney Lambert during Jack Gabriel's examination. He keeps his eyes on the jury while the jury's gaze is riveted on Sydney Lambert and Jack Gabriel. They show no reaction beyond their unwavering attention. They seem as interested in Jack Gabriel as they do in the witness, maybe more. He wonders how they view Gabriel and what might appear to be his lawyer's games, and is pleased that he has reserved for redirect examination his last and most important questions.

"Ms. Lambert, today is not the first time you have met or talked with Mr. Gabriel or his staff, is it?"

She hesitates too long before answering, "No."

"And before you came to court today, you told the defense what you would say, didn't you?"

"Yes."

"But until you took the stand this morning, you never told me that you had lied to the police, did you?"

"No."

"Even this morning, before court, when I asked you about your testimony, you didn't tell me, did you? In fact, you wouldn't talk to me at all about your testimony, would you?"

"I told you that I would tell the truth."

"But you did not say that your current version of the truth was diametrically opposed to what you had led us to believe previously, did you?"

"I said I would tell the truth."

"And until you took the stand this morning, you had never told the police you had lied to them, did you?"

"No."

"And you never told the grand jury what your current version of the truth was, did you?"

"I . . . I never wanted to be involved. I didn't want to have to testify at all. I wanted to avoid all this. I just didn't want to be involved."

"But the fact is that you were always involved, weren't you?"

She lets her head droop a bit. "Yes, unfortunately."

"You were *involved* with Mr. Avery, weren't you?"

"Yes."

"And you became *involved* with the defense of Mr. Avery, through his lawyers, didn't you?"

"Well . . ."

"You volunteered to Mr. Gabriel the story you are telling now, isn't that right?"

"Yes, I suppose you could say that."

"But until you took the stand this morning, you chose not to be *involved* with the police, with the grand jury, with the prosecution, by telling any of us your current story, did you?"

"I wasn't . . . I had no obligation."

"No, Ms. Lambert, that's legally correct. And apparently the only obligation you felt was to consult with the defense team and to hold back so you could spring your grand secret at just the right time—"

"*I object!*" Gabriel shouted.

Chasen does not bother to respond. "*Your* witness," he emphasizes, and sits down, satisfied that perhaps Jack Gabriel has fallen victim to his own game.

34 *I*t is shortly after 1:00 P.M., and, not knowing where else to look, Alex has come to the offices of the state's attorney. It takes a moment for the receptionist, a young, dark-eyed girl whose nose has the mottled appearance of a recovering sunburn, to look up from her book of astrology and the notes she is making.

"Oh, hi," she says. "Can I help you?"

"Yes, I was wondering if you could tell me where I might find the detectives who are working on the Avery trial."

"Are you a witness?"

"No, I'm just looking for a friend. Are they here in this building?"

"Gee, I'm not sure, a whole bunch of them went out with Mr. Chasen for lunch. It was a little while ago, but you can probably catch them. They're usually over to Barney's. The hot food's not much to write home about, but the sandwiches are pretty good. If you go out the front door and take a left, it's about halfway down the next block, on the other side of the street."

"Do you know if Detective Boland was with them? The ones who went to lunch."

"Which one's he?"

Alex smiles. "She. She's a lady detective."

The young girl brightens. "Oh, you mean Christine? Is she your friend?" She does not wait for an answer. "She's real nice. She always stops by to say hello. I've only been working here about a month, but she always stops to say hello. I guessed right away that she was either a Taurus or Gemini and it turns out she was born right on the cusp, on May twenty-first. Isn't that interesting? I mean Taurus being kinda the stubborn, real organized type, and Geminis being sort of split personalities, real idealists and all. And then she ends up being a murder detective. That's kinda wild, idn't it?"

"Well, yes, I guess it is. Did you say she went with the others to lunch?"

The young girl looks at Alex with a sudden curious squint. "Are you the friend that does, you know, statues and things?"

"I beg your pardon?"

"The artist? Are you the one that does statues?"

Alex blushes. "Well, yes, I guess you'd call them that."

"Oh, she told me all about you." The girl leans across the desk and offers Alex her hand. "Hi, I'm Sandra. Sandra Kopecki. I've never met a real artist before."

"Alex Trigorin, and thanks for the compliment."

"I beg your pardon?"

"For calling me a real artist."

"Oh, no, Christine told me all about you. They sell your statues in galleries and everything. That makes you a real artist in my mind. Heck, around here, they think an artist is anyone who can paint a water line on a crab boat."

"Well, by that standard, I'm not sure I'd qualify"—the girl laughs—"but did you say that Christine went with the others to lunch?"

"Gosh, you know, I really didn't notice. They're always running around in such a rush. I'm not sure. But they oughta be back here pretty soon. I mean court starts up again at one-thirty. Are you gonna watch the trial?"

"Well, I thought I might."

"Isn't it something? I mean all these reporters and TV cameras and all? It's the biggest thing that's hit this town in a long time. There's people waiting in line every day just to get in to watch the trial. I'll bet they're lined up already for this afternoon."

"You think I'll have a problem?"

Sandra Kopecki scrunches her peeling nose in thought. "Wait here," she says. "I'll go back and see if I can't get you one of the special passes. At least it ought to get you to the head of the line. But if you want to get a quick bite, you ought to try the Dog House across the street. It's just a counter, no place to sit down or anything, but the hot dogs are great. I like 'em with everything on 'em. But you wait here a minute. Let me see if I can't get you a pass."

Armed with a pass in its plastic clip-on case, Alex wanders up to the second floor and joins the crowd of hopeful spectators gathered in a loosely formed line in front of the courtroom door. The conversations are hushed but the opinions are not.

"Ol' Earl really gave it to that defense attorney, didn't he?"

"Whaddaya you talkin' 'bout? He just told it like it was."

"No, I mean when that fella Gabriel kept pushin' Earl to say that Ollie Johns musta dropped the jewels out by the oyster beds and then Earl just reared back and said, 'No, Ollie woulda never done that.'"

"Yeah, and then that lawyer was dumb enough to ask why not and Earl says what any waterman 'round here'd know. Hell, Ollie woulda know'd that with all the folks workin' those beds, somebody sooner or later woulda pulled them jewels up."

"Yeah? But since when did Earl Barkin get to be such a friend to Ollie Johns?"

"It got nothin' to do with being friends. He's just telling what everybody knows. Ollie's been livin' on that point all his life. If he was tryin' to get rid of the evidence, he'da never dropped them around those oyster beds."

"Man, how can you say that? Any man who'd kill a lady outta spite like that ain't thinkin' right anyway. He coulda just as easily been outta his head, you know, scared or drunk or just not thinkin' right."

"You sayin' you think Ollie mighta done it?"

"I'm sayin' everybody knows there's been bad blood between him and the Averys. Hell, Ollie ain't done nothin' for ten years but sit around gettin' drunk and grousin' 'bout how he got cheated outta his land, and just bein' generally mean-spirited."

"Shoot, man, Ollie ain't nothin' but talk. Weren't ever nothin' but talk and drink and livin' off his ol' man's money."

"Yeah, but what about that time they hauled him down to court for hittin' on his ol' lady before she up and left him?"

"Man, where'd you ever hear that? I never heard nothin' like that. You're just fillin' in a story to make it sound like he mighta done it. 'Sides, it wouldn't make sense for Ollie to throw them jewels away, as down and out as he's always makin' out to be. Now, Avery, that's a whole different story. A man like that, as rich's he is, he'd throw 'em away in a blink of an eye. He could buy some more without ever missin' the money. Now that makes more sense to me."

"And his girlfriend? That woman from New York? You see her? The way she sat there, just as tough as nails. Man, how'd you like to come home to that every night? She was lyin' for sure."

Alex wonders whether the debate in the hallway, unfettered as it is by any rule of law or evidence, is any different from that going on in the minds of the jurors; and for him, that question alone sheds new light upon the frustrations Christine has been voicing ever more angrily over the past few months. The truth of what did or did not happen in one cold, dark kitchen on one cold, dark morning some eight months before seems to have been reduced almost to irrelevance. What consumes the audience is the debate itself. Fact and theory, assumption and opinion, sympathy and prejudice, relevance and irrelevance, are all gathered and joined and molded to form some collective statement that becomes the truth. As with his art, what matters is not what is expressed, but how the expression is interpreted. But here a man's life hangs in the balance.

He returns to the first floor, where Sandra Kopecki reports that the other detectives have returned from lunch but that Christine was not with them. "I'll be sure to tell her that you're here whenever I see her," the receptionist says.

"Thanks. Just tell her that I'm going to take your recommendation for one of those hot dogs with everything on it, then I'll go up to the courtroom."

It takes some time after Alex returns from the Dog House before the deputy sheriff standing guard at the courtroom door allows him in, pointing to a single seat at the end of the fourth row in the spectators' section. The courtroom is quiet, except for the mumblings rising from the bench, where the attorneys seem by their exaggerated and impatient body movements to be in a heated discussion with the judge, of whom little can be seen except for his hands, which keep gesturing for the lawyers to tone down their remarks. In the well of the court are three televisions on wheeled stands. One is stationed directly in front of the jury and faces them. The second faces back toward the judge's bench, the court reporter and a woman seated in the witness chair, whose tortoiseshell glasses exaggerate her stolid expression. The third television is turned so as to be visible to the attorneys and the gallery behind them. The judge leans back and says to the woman on the witness stand, "Dr. Storrs, would you mind coming to the bench for a moment?"

The witness does, and her small, trim figure is quickly surrounded and engulfed by the lawyers, as if their competitive closeness might influence whatever answers she will offer to the court's questions. Minutes pass with everyone in the courtroom but the participants at the bench remaining still and quiet. Alex thinks of asking the woman to his left what is going on, but her expression tells him not to. She is a middle-aged woman in a navy dress who holds her purse in her lap, her hands folded primly on top of it. She stares straight ahead with the reverence of a churchgoer. The lawyers then turn from the bench and walk toward the counsel tables, while the witness returns to the stand and Judge Newcomb leans forward.

"Once again for the record, the defense motion for the court to reconsider its previous ruling on the videotape is denied. Proceed, Counsel."

"Thank you, Your Honor," Albert Chasen begins before the judge raises his hand.

"Just a moment, Counsel, before you begin. Ladies and gentlemen, to everyone in the audience here, without making any comment on what you are about to see in this videotape, I want to make absolutely clear that the court will tolerate no outbursts of any kind." He hesitates briefly. "All right, proceed."

"Thank you, Your Honor," the prosecutor repeats. "Now, Dr. Storrs, once again, will you explain to the jury the circumstances under which the videotape we are about to see was made?"

"Well, as I explained, we had been treating Ned—Mr. Avery's son—for a little more than two months, and . . . Do you want me to go over again the clinical diagnosis of his condition at that time?"

"No, Doctor, just describe how this videotape came about."

"Well, when we were contacted by the police—it was Detective Boland who called me. Christine Boland. We had a long discussion about the possible connection between Ned's reaction to the neighbor, Mr. Haley, and the fact that he had been wearing military fatigues. And, of course, whether there was any connection or association Ned might have made to his father being a hunter. Detective Boland had obviously been trained in psychology and seemed quite knowledgeable and articulate. Anyway, we had a long discussion about whether it might be appropriate to show Ned these hunting clothes to see if they, in and of themselves, might have stimulated his acute and negative reaction. After that, I conferred with several other staff and consulting psychiatrists at the clinic, and with Dr. Eckert, the medical director, and it was our unanimous opinion *medically*—and I want to emphasize that: our decision was purely a medical one. In any event we decided to go forward with the procedure."

"And by 'procedure,' what do you mean?"

"To present Ned with these hunting clothes in as nonthreatening or nonstressful a manner as possible and to see what if any reaction he might have. And if there was a reaction, we thought it might be one means of perhaps refocusing our treatment."

"And did you videotape this procedure?"

"Yes, we did."

"Why did you videotape it?"

"We often videotape our patients, particularly during diagnostic tests and procedures, particularly when we may be introducing a new treatment. We have found that no matter how complete and accurate written and verbal reports might be, in consulting with other physicians, it is always helpful if they can see the patient's reactions as close to firsthand as possible."

"Does the patient know he is being videotaped?"

"No. The camera is set up behind a one-way glass. The patient is unaware that he is being observed or videotaped."

"Did you consult with Mr. Avery before performing this procedure?"

"Yes. I called him personally. He agreed to the procedure. He said that we should do anything that we felt would help his son. He seemed very concerned for his son's welfare."

"Now, Doctor, you have previously testified as to how this 'procedure' was set up. That is, how and why you planned to have an attendant come into the room in normal clothing and then introduce the hunting clothes to Ned as if they were his own, the attendant's, that is."

"Yes."

"Now, the videotape we are about to see is of that procedure, correct?"

"Yes."

"Was this tape edited in any way since it was first recorded?"

"No, this is the entire, unedited tape."

"Now tell us, please, exactly when during the process this videotape begins."

"It starts approximately one minute before either I or the attendant enters the room. Ned is in the room alone, except for a nurse who is reading to him. And it continues until the end, until Ned is finally restrained . . . and medicated, as I testified earlier."

"Your Honor?" Chasen asks.

The judge nods. "Proceed."

The courtroom falls silent as the televisions flick on and there is a moment of two of scratching, static noise and the jumbled sight of the tape reeling forward, until there comes into focus the vision of a small boy sitting at a small table in a large, colorful room, and the low, rhythmic tones of a nurse reading to him, her voice translated by the hidden microphones into a hollow, distant sound.

Alex feels his heart quicken. He knows what is coming. He remembers Christine telling him about the first time she saw Ned on the day his mother's body had been discovered, and how Ned had dug his fingers into her breast and had locked his teeth onto her blouse until he had to be torn from her, and he remembers how she broke down and wept from the experience. He recalls, too, her description of the "procedure" at the clinic—although she did not call it that; she called it an "experiment"—when she had watched the boy through the glass painted with bright green hills and blue skies and white, puffy clouds and large, gaily colored balloons, and how her description was so cold and clinical, as if she could not have handled the memory any other way.

This is not what he has come to see. He is not at all sure he wants to see Ned's torture introduced like any other piece of evidence to be played back and discussed and argued over. But still he is drawn to the television screen, as is everyone else in the courtroom; everyone else, that is, except Cooper Avery, the father, the accused, who sits between his lawyers, hunched over with his head in his hands, refusing, or perhaps unable, to watch.

The tension grows more palpable as the tape rolls on, the dead silence of its audience accentuating the eerily cheerful voices of its players. The camera lens draws the viewers closer to Ned, framing his vacant stare until they see his first flicker of curious recognition and the quickening of his breathing as he looks at the orderly donning the hunting jacket, then quickly at Dr. Storrs and back at the orderly, and Ned's eyes snap wide in an instant, all-consuming fear, and he breaks. The violence of Ned's reaction and his desperate, clawing attempt to cover Dr. Storrs's face and head draw almost simultaneous gasps throughout the courtroom.

"Oh dear God," the woman next to Alex whispers, and she looks down, her fingers tightening around the strap of her purse. Alex looks over as the woman whispers, "That poor child." She looks up at Alex, a tear beginning to trail down her cheek, and she speaks softly. "I used to work for the family until a few years ago. Ned was always a strange, nervous child. I don't know why I came here. I just can't believe Mr. Avery could do such a thing. I just can't believe it."

Alex is suddenly startled by a whispered voice to his right.

"Alex? Alex Trigorin?"

He turns to see a man crouched beside him, and he nods.

"Alex, I'm Paul Wyzanski. We've talked a few times on the phone. I work with Christine. Could I talk to you for a moment, you know, outside?"

Alex looks up to see that the videotape has ended, and he nods again and rises slowly to follow the detective to the hallway outside the courtroom.

"I'm sorry to pull you away from the trial," Detective Wyzanski says, "but the girl down at the reception desk told me you were here."

"No, that's all right," Alex says. "I'm almost sorry I was here to see that."

"The tape of the boy? Yeah, that's tough to watch."

"What's happened to him? I mean since—you know."

"Well, actually, the doctor says that he's doing better. They have him talking some. He's not making any sense, apparently, just talking in random words that don't seem to mean anything, but at least they have him talking. He's still up at the clinic. The doctor says they're more optimistic than they were a few months ago. But who knows whether he'll ever be, I don't know, normal."

Alex shakes his head slowly.

Paul looks a bit uneasy as he asks, "The receptionist said you were looking for Christine?"

Alex frowns. "Yes, I was. Is anything wrong? Is she all right?"

"Well, actually, that's what I wanted to ask you."

"Why, what's happened?"

"Nothing, actually, it's just that she didn't show up today, and I called her apartment, but there was no answer. Did she say anything to you about taking the day off?"

The question stops him, and he does not answer.

"Look," Paul says, "I don't mean to be stepping into something that's none of my business. It's just that I was getting a little concerned. I thought maybe she might have had some reason she decided to take off."

"You mean what happened yesterday?"

"Did she tell you?"

"A little."

Paul looks up and down the empty hallway as if he is unsure what else to do. "It's just that it's, you know, pretty unusual for her not to call in or anything."

"I don't know," Alex says, "maybe I got the signals crossed. I thought we were going to meet here and have dinner after she finished work. I just took the afternoon off and thought I'd see some of the trial."

"She said she was going to meet you here?"

"Yes, that's what I thought. But tell me something, what did happen yesterday?"

Paul again looks away. "Look, like I said, it may not be any of my business, but would you mind if we talked a bit? Maybe we could go down to the war room where we could have a little privacy."

Alex agrees and follows Paul down to the first floor, where he is led to a small, windowless office crowded with three desks, two phones, stacks of paper, photographs and charts, a well-worn pack of playing cards, a half-dozen opened and empty soda cans and an overflowing ashtray. He is introduced to Charlie Abbot, who slides his feet off one of the desks and rises to shake Alex's hand.

"Nice to meetja," Charlie says with a wide smile. "I heard a lot about you. You're the artist, right?"

Alex nods while Paul says, "Charlie, you mind giving us a coupla minutes?"

"Sure," Charlie says, and then stops. "Is everything okay? With Christine, I mean?"

"Yeah, it's fine. Just give us a few minutes."

"Sure," Charlie says again, and he picks up a pack of cigarettes to leave. "I'll be down the other office if anything comes up."

The door closes, and Paul pulls out a chair for Alex to sit in. "Can I get you some coffee, a Coke or anything?"

Alex shakes his head.

"Look, stop me if I'm outta line here, but, you know, Chris and I have worked together a long time. Got to be pretty good friends and all."

"I know," Alex says, and Paul's discomfort is sudden and obvious. "Look, it's okay. I know you and Christine were together for a while. But you said something happened yesterday?"

"Well, yeah. She seemed pretty upset when she left." Paul proceeds to detail the conversation in Chasen's office the evening before, and ends with, "Chasen was a little outta line. He didn't have to come down on her like that, not in front of us. But everybody knows the man's on edge. That's part of the game. We've all been through that shit before. These lawyers always take winning and losing personally. You just gotta pamper them. She knows that."

Several stacks of eight-by-eleven color photographs sit on the desk in front of Alex, and he absently begins to look through them as he speaks. "Look," he says, "you know Christine. She takes a lot of pride in her work. It's not easy for her to just shrug off someone calling her crazy because he doesn't agree with her theories."

Paul sits forward with a jolt, as if he is offended. "Who's called her crazy? No one's calling her crazy."

"Well, I suppose that's overstating it. Those are my words, not hers. But I think she feels like everyone thinks she's gone off the deep end over this Martin Lessing business."

"She's talked to you about that?"

"Well, some. There's nothing wrong with that, is there?"

"No, no. I was just thinking, that's all."

"And I think she feels pretty strongly that she's right, and she doesn't appreciate being blown off like she was nuts or something."

"I don't think she's nuts. I think she's wrong, but I don't think she's nuts. And no one else does either. It's just that somehow, I don't know, maybe it's just that she's turned so stubborn on this one. It's almost like she's working against us. It's not like her. I know her. And I can tell you that she's the best I've ever worked with. I really mean that. For picking up things no one else sees, and thinking through and analyzing a case, no one's better. And I don't know anyone that doesn't think about the same. But this time . . . I don't know. Right from the beginning, there was something different about her, something about this case that turned her stubborn."

"And you think she's wrong."

"Yeah, I do. I'm sure Avery did it. I think all this stuff about the friends of Martin Lessing and all, it's an interesting coincidence. But I don't think for a minute that some friend of a guy who was arrested by Avery's father some forty years ago is gonna up and decide to kill the old man's daughter-in-law. I mean, that's a real stretch, and besides that one sympathy card, there's no evidence at all. And there's no way of knowing if the card was real, or something sent to the wrong funeral by mistake, or even if it wasn't a mistake, whether it was just somebody who remembered the old days and had the bad taste to send a card like that. Put that against all the evidence that says Avery did do it, and I don't think it's close. I wouldn't be sitting here if I thought otherwise."

Alex seems distracted by several of the photographs on the desk in front of him, and his words sound separated from his thoughts. "What—but what if you're wrong? What if this crazy theory of Christine's is right?"

"No, she's wrong. I mean I hope to God she's wrong, given we're in the middle of this trial. But if she's right, I'll be the first to tell her so, and I'll do whatever she says to help her prove it. She ought to know that."

Alex does not answer, and Paul picks up on his obvious curiosity about the photographs.

"That stack's the jewels that were never recovered. Those are the photographs from the insurance company files. The photos they took when they wrote the policy. The other pictures are of the jewelry that was fished out by the oysterman." Again, Alex says nothing, and after a pause, Paul fills in the silence. "You ever see so many diamonds in one necklace?"

Alex looks up. "What? I'm sorry, what were you saying?"

"I was just saying, you know, about the jewelry. I mean, can you imagine some burglar killing a woman to steal jewelry like that and then just dumping it in the river?"

"No, I guess not. Anyway, we were talking about Christine. Is there, ah, some real problem about her not showing up today?"

"No, not really. Charlie and I have everything covered. And like I said, I hope I'm not out of line here. I mean, hell, I'm not about to question what my boss does. I mean, she does outrank us. It's just after yesterday, you know, I was a little concerned. Maybe I'm just letting the line between friendship and work get a little fuzzy here."

"I understand. I don't know, but if I were to take a guess, I'd bet she woke up this morning fixed on some idea she had to follow up. Probably whatever was said yesterday made her even more determined to prove her point."

"Yeah, you're probably right. When she gets hold of an idea, she doesn't give it up easily. Look, I'm sorry I pulled you out of the trial. If you want to, I'll take you back up and make sure you get in."

"No, thanks. Watching that videotape was enough for me. I think I might just wander around town for a while." Alex again focuses on one of the photographs. "I'll, ah, I'll check back later to see if Christine shows up or calls in. If she does, just tell her I'll be back, what, around five?"

"That should be fine. Just come back to Chasen's office and knock on the door. We usually sit around for a while and do a postmortem on the day and what we gotta do for tomorrow. But just come back to office, and if Chasen's secretary's not there, just knock and poke your head in."

Alex nods, then picks up one of the photographs. "You're right. It's hard to imagine . . . you know, someone just tossing jewelry like this in the river."

35 *I*t is the thirtieth of June, and already the summer has settled on the west coast of Florida with the hot, heavy feel of late August. The air is still, and the waters of the Gulf of Mexico neither curl nor crash upon the shores of Sanibel Island, but sit like a placid pond seared by a lowering sun. The house sits back from the beach, shaded on three sides by a grove of pine and casuarinas. The fourth side, composed of a large screened lanai set on stilts, opens to the beach and to the sunset, which is reproduced by the thousands on the racks of postcards found in the village shops less than a mile away.

Martha Avery steps out onto the lanai and leans over to kiss her husband on the cheek. "You'll be all right?" she asks. "I do wish you'd stop being so stubborn about these things. It would do you good to get out and see some people once in a while."

"Have you seen the boat? I can't find it here. Did you take it?"

Martha lets go a sigh. "Charles, you finished that one yesterday. This is a new one, remember? This is the one of the Alps."

Charles Avery stops and sits back in his chair. "Yes, of course. I was thinking of something else." On the large card table in front of him are the thousand jumbled pieces of a jigsaw puzzle he is about to begin, just another in a long series of puzzles that have become his obsession over the past six months.

"You know, it would be a whole lot easier if you'd keep the box top here so you could see what the picture is supposed to look like."

"That's not the point. I just thought there was a boat. I'll be all right. You go on."

"I wish you'd come with me. The Hartmans will be disappointed."

"It's too hot, and besides, I need to wait here for Cooper to call. I need to talk to him."

"Sweetheart, Cooper went to see Alice this weekend. Remember? He's—"

"No, he's going to call. I need to talk to him."

"Well . . . Do you want me to turn on the fan? It's boiling out here."

"No, no, I'm fine."

"Well, at least take off your robe. Look at you, you're sitting there all bundled up and sweating. You know, you simply cannot spend the rest of your life sitting around in your pajamas and robe doing crossword puzzles."

"They're jigsaws, Martha, jigsaws. And there's a lot more to this than meets the eye. I'm all right. You just go ahead and have a good time. I have to talk to Cooper."

"Well, then, I should be back by eleven. Nancy is here if you need anything."

Nancy is the part-time nurse hired not so much to answer any of the former congressman's medical needs as to guard against a repetition of what he has done twice in the past month: wandered off down the beach to a point where he has become confused and unable to find his way home.

"Hmmph. That woman needs a hearing aid. She never hears the phone." Charles Avery separates a dozen or more pieces from the rest of the puzzle and begins to arrange them into even smaller groupings. "I don't know how many calls we've missed because she's too stubborn to admit her hearing's not what it used to be."

"Dear, the portable phone's right there if anyone calls. Just remember that you have to push the button—"

"Martha! I am not a child."

"I didn't mean that, dear. And you don't need to raise your voice. Do you want the whole island to hear you?"

He turns back to the puzzle and focuses on a single piece, which he begins to move around with his finger, looking for its mate.

Martha Avery allows herself a brief shiver of exasperation. "Anyway, I should be home by eleven."

She turns, and as she leaves flips the switch to the overhead fan, which begins slowly to move the stagnant air.

It has been some time since the Averys stopped entertaining in their home, the former congressman having made plain his peevish disinterest in—and over the past year, his ever-waning facility for—social intercourse and the politic manners that were the cornerstone of his career. After their retirement from Congress, the Averys enjoyed several years of activity before the social and political invitations came less and less often, before Charles Avery's speaking engagements ceased entirely, and before the corporation on whose board he sat allowed his term to run without nominating him to another. They—actually, more Martha than Charles—decided to sell their home on the Severn River near Annapolis and to move here, to the house Cooper found for his parents and helped them to buy a little more than six years ago. Thankfully, Cooper also guided his mother in their investments, so that they can now live, if not extravagantly, at least comfortably.

Martha Avery found the transition easy, indeed she welcomed it, but her husband, forever in his mind the former congressman, reacted not unlike a child who refuses to play unless he is captain: he took his ball and went home. Whether Charles Avery's self-imposed isolation is deliberate, or whether it is symptomatic of some developing mental or emotional disorder, the doctors will not speculate. They simply nod thoughtfully and say that the congressman "does display certain characteristics that are not unlike those one might see in the early stages of dementia." But beyond the rations of pills that seesaw his blood pressure with their ever-changing type and dosage, the doctors do little more than offer Martha a smile and another appointment every month or two.

Cooper's mother, however, has refused to join her husband's isolation, and she regularly accepts the invitations of friends good enough to acknowledge Charles Avery's condition by ignoring it. "How's Charles?" they will ask politely at every greeting, and Martha will say, "Oh, he's just fine," and it is left at that. The circle of friends has grown smaller since Cooper's indictment and trial have become the subject of headlines in *The Baltimore Sun* and both *The*

Washington Post and the *Times,* which some of the Averys' friends have mailed to them daily. But that is to be expected. It isn't so much that people are judging Cooper, Martha thinks, but simply that to some, the subject must be both unavoidable and uncomfortable. She can understand that. Before going through it herself, she certainly would not have known what to say to a mother whose son was charged with the murder of his own wife. But still, there are a few good friends, like the Hartmans and the Sturgesses and Millie Peckman and, of course, Bitsy Lyons, whom she has known since high school and who followed the Averys to Sanibel after her husband's death. They all offer their encouragement and their prayers and whatever else is available to maintain the genteel camaraderie they have developed over the years. But it isn't easy.

Martha is disappointed that Cooper did not bring Alice to stay with them after the indictment, rather than with his sister. Claire can be so obstinate. Over the past few years, Claire has found one excuse after another not to visit her parents' home, although she regularly suggests that *they*—although she implies Martha alone— come visit "whenever." For whatever reason, Claire will not forgive her father over some dispute which Claire will not explain and Charles will not acknowledge. Unlike his daughter, who holds firm to her grudges, Charles Avery chooses simply to ignore them, and anything else, for that matter, which he thinks could reflect unfavorably upon him or his family. Although he has readily accepted the fact of Marian's death, to this day he speaks of his son as if Cooper had never been indicted or put on trial for her murder.

Martha is disappointed too that she cannot be with Cooper during this awful time. But Cooper, as he has in every other aspect of his life, has been staunchly insistent that he handle this problem on his own. And her husband certainly could not have traveled back to Maryland, and could not have helped if he had, and she certainly could not have left him alone, not for several weeks or months, not in his condition. So it is best, she thinks, that she simply carry on. What else can she do?

■

The hours have passed into a dark, moonless night, and the lanai is lit by a single goosenecked lamp that focuses on the card table and the jumble of jigsaw pieces, of which less than a score have been matched and joined together. The house is quiet but for the faint echo of television voices and canned laughter that comes from the den, where the nurse nods, hastened toward sleep by boredom and a tall bourbon and Coke.

"So much snow," Charles Avery murmurs, as he contemplates a piece that he has named Upper Michigan. He is searching for northern Wisconsin or southern Ontario. He thinks he hears a chirp from the telephone, but there is no ring. He hesitates and then lifts the portable phone and fumbles with the buttons and pulls out the antenna.

"Hello?"

There is no answer.

He fiddles again with the buttons, but still there is no sound, not even a dial tone. "Damn fool contraption." He sets the phone aside and returns to his puzzle.

"The cat," he whispers, referring to yet another piece he thinks might well curl around Michigan's Upper Peninsula. "What did I do with the cat?"

It takes some time for him to pick slowly through the pieces looking for the shape of a cat with an arched back and rigid legs. He finds it and tries it, but it does not fit, and he places it in the corner, where he has separated all the other pieces he has tried unsuccessfully to fit with the emerging section of snow and its rim of evergreen.

He sits back and glances again at the phone. "Nancy?" he calls to the nurse without looking up. "Did you get that? Was that for me?"

There is no answer. A few moments pass.

"*Nancy!*" he calls again, this time over his shoulder with an impatience that borders on anger; but again there is no answer, only the sounds of the television two rooms away. "Damn that woman."

He pushes his chair back and starts to rise, but he is stopped by the flap of his thin cotton robe, which has caught between the chair's seat and arm. He gives it a yank, and it pulls free with a rip that leaves a bit of the cloth behind. "Damn that woman!"

He turns and is startled to see a figure standing in the doorway, a figure whose face is shadowed by the faint light from the living room behind. The lamp on the card table focuses only on the puzzle, and it exaggerates the surrounding darkness.

"Look what you made me do," he says, holding up the tear in his robe.

"Sit down, Mr. Avery," the figure says.

"Nancy, I asked you if that was for me. Did you answer the phone?"

"I said sit down, Mr. Avery."

The voice confuses him. It is low and even and sexless and like no other voice he might recognize. He squints for a better look. "What?"

The figure steps forward and grabs the front of his pajama top and pushes him back into his chair. The violence startles more than frightens him, and as he falls backward, his arm sweeps dozens of pieces of the puzzle to the floor. "What are you doing?" he demands, and looks at the floor, confused, the cloth of his pajama top still bunched in the hand at his chest. He tries weakly to stand.

"I told you to *sit down!*" the voice barks, and the hand punches him back into his seat as it lets go of his pajamas. It is a woman's voice, but there is nothing soft in it, nor in the force of the hand he felt. His confusion is spiked by a sudden fear, and the thoughts run through him like a fever. He wonders if this is one of those dreams Martha says he has been having more and more. But he is angry, too.

"Look—look what you've done," he stammers. "You've knocked the pieces to the floor. You're ruining it."

He leans forward a bit, and quickly this figure, which stands so tall that its dark, featureless face seems lost in the night, again pushes him back and grabs the lamp from the card table and twists its gooseneck so that its heat and light are only inches from his face. He can see nothing but the light now, and his fear is complete. "I thought it was Cooper. He's going to call."

"*Quiet!* Don't say anything." The voice is controlled, but barely so. It is certainly a woman's voice, and he thinks he recognizes an odd but somehow familiar scent. Canvas? Yes, it is canvas that he smells, and a light perfumed fragrance. It is the familiar scent of late afternoon, before their cocktails, when Martha emerges from her shower to lie in the hammock. It is a sweet, lazy scent, and he knows this must be one of those dreams Martha will later tell him he has had.

He feels himself smiling at his own foolishness. What else can he do? He moves slowly with one hand to close the robe about his chest, while with the other he reaches for the pieces of the puzzle, and turns his face to avoid the light. It is so bright and so hot, so close to his face. He can see one arm reaching across the table, and he recognizes the shaded greens and browns of the light canvas. It is camouflage. The table suddenly jumps as the hand slams down on it, arresting his thoughts, and in one sweeping motion, it scatters all but a few pieces to the floor.

"*No!*" he protests, straining to lean back from the light. "You're ruining everything. Get out of here. You can't come in here. *Get out!*"

The woman grabs the neck of the lamp and pushes the light to his face so that the rim of the metal shade cuts at his brow and the bulb burns the tip of his nose. He can smell the heat, and his lungs strain for more air.

"I told you to be *quiet!*" The quiver of her hand resonates in the lamp against his face, but before he can move, she pulls the lamp back and sets it on the table, again adjusting the light to bear down on him. He tries to block the light with one shaking hand while the other feels the stinging cut on his brow and the quickly blistering scald on his nose.

There is a long silence, and he begins to wonder again whether his pain and his fear are real, whether he should just get up and move away from this awful light, whether he should get a glass of water and maybe one of his pills. Martha always leaves the pills on the counter next to the sink. Maybe a drink of water and one of his pills . . .

"So, Congressman," the woman says, the suddenness of her voice coming like a pinprick, "is this what you do now? Is this what so occupies you that you cannot be bothered with the fact that your son is on trial for murder? You sit here with a child's puzzle? A game?"

This is no dream. He is almost certain. But he will not say anything to Martha. He cannot bear to hear again the sigh of impatience, the chuckle that is meant to make light of it all but only makes light of him. No, he will not say anything about this. But the heat, the pain in his chest, the dryness in his throat. This seems so real. His hand reaches out slowly, searching for the alarm button beneath the desk in an office he has not seen for ten years. How did this person get in here? "Please, you cannot come in here. You don't have an appointment. You cannot come in here without an appointment. Please, I am waiting for my son to call. You must leave."

But there is no button, and he realizes there is no desk or office or staff or security, and he raises his arms to cross in front of his face.

"Put your arms down. I want to see your face."

He refuses as if he has not heard, and he keeps his eyes closed tight. "No, you don't understand. You must leave."

He feels the cloth belt being pulled from his robe. Why doesn't he just get up? Why doesn't he stop her? Why can't he move his legs?

One arm is suddenly jerked from his face, and he yelps with the pain of it being twisted behind him. He feels her hand grab his other wrist as the combination of fear and confusion strips him of any will to resist. She ties his hands to the back of the chair, and he keeps his eyes closed while his ankles are bound to the legs of the chair, with what he does not know.

"Now look at me."

He refuses again, and presses his chin tight against his chest, straining to keep his eyes closed.

"*Look at me!*"

He can feel her words as much as hear them, and he raises and twists his head and opens his eyes to a squint, but all he can see is the light. She is no more than a faint outline, a shadow, the penumbra between absolute light and absolute dark.

"My son," he pleads, "My son will be calling. You should talk to him. He will be calling any minute now. But you must leave. You are not allowed in here."

She does not answer, and a long silence settles between them, a stillness so complete that the television is no longer a faint, garbled noise, but is now a clear conversation, the banter of women and the audience's laughter. He hears the occasional rush of a car passing down the road, and each time thinks it might be Martha. But the cars neither slow nor stop; they simply fade away, and he wonders if anyone remembers that he is here.

The nurse? Did Martha say Nancy was here? Is this . . . ? No, Nancy is short and gray, and she knows not to disturb him when he is working.

He listens to the distant, rhythmic ripple of the gulf upon the sand, the lazy chirping of the crickets, the absolute stillness all around him, and he wonders if he will say anything to anybody about this.

His eyes water, but he squints less. Despite the pain, his eyes are adjusting to the light, and he feels oddly drawn to it. It is all he can see now.

"Tell me, Congressman—" The voice starts so softly it seems to him that they must have been talking for a very long time. The fright has faded into something else, something close to resignation. He blinks slowly and looks to the light and listens for the voice. "—what will your son tell me when he calls? Will he tell me that his wife died because of you?"

He hears the words but they make no sense. His question comes as softly as hers. "What?"

"Will he tell me that he is on trial for murder because you have never had the courage or the honor to tell the truth?"

"Who are you? What are you talking about?"

"Does your son even know? Does he know how many people you sacrificed, how many lives you ruined for your *whore?*"

That word. *Whore.* It strikes him like a word he has never heard, it being so divorced from the context of his thoughts. He hesitates and cocks his head to one side. He is suddenly more curious than confused, but still, he has no time for this. "Please, if you will come back later."

The light comes closer to his face so that its heat tingles against his cheeks, and the smell of it mixes with that of the perfume and the canvas camouflage jacket, which he can hear rustle with movement, and he can feel the puff of her words. "Does your son even know about your *whore?*"

He has no answer. He can only sit until he feels the light drawn back a bit.

"Tell me, *Special Agent* Avery"—the title is spoken with contemptuous emphasis, and the sound of it tightens his flesh—"when my father died alone in his jail cell, were you fucking your whore? When my mother lay in the hospital, frightened into near madness by your lies, and giving birth to me and not knowing if she even had a home left where she could take me, whether she would even be allowed to keep me, were you fucking your whore? Were the two of you celebrating your victory, celebrating your lies, celebrating the fact that you had killed my father, that you had driven Byron Roth and his family into hiding and ruined his career, ruined his life? Were you celebrating, Special Agent Avery? Were you *fucking* Barbara Hoffman to celebrate how you had *fucked* everyone else?"

Avery's head falls back as if his neck muscles have been severed. His mouth is open, and his eyes are wide, and suddenly, he can see her. The long brown hair so dark it is almost black. The hair that she wouldn't curl, that fell straight and to the middle of her back, and covered them like a tent as he lay on his back looking up at her. And he sees her face, pale and smeared with the makeup that is being wiped by the tears, the blood-red eyes, her expression contorting between hurt and rage. How could she not understand? He had a wife and children. What did she expect? His lips can barely form around the name. "Barbara?"

The voice softens to a slower rhythm. "Yes, Barbara Hoffman, your little whore. You do remember, don't you? You really thought no one would ever know, didn't you? You thought that you could simply walk away from it, that it would never come back to you?"

He does not answer. His jaw hangs slack and his mouth gapes.

"You really did, didn't you? You believed it. You thought you were safe because the only people who knew what you had done and who had any power or authority had hands as dirty as yours. You could go on as if none of it mattered, and all the innocent people you walked on and all the lives you ruined were nothing. They were just clumps of dirt to be scraped from your shoes after you tramped all over them. And you were right, weren't you? For years you had all the power and money and reputation anyone could have asked for. Anyone, that is, except my father or Byron Roth or Harold Ramsey or people like that, people who didn't matter. Isn't that right? And the whole time you thought no one would know how you concocted your lies, how you engineered my father's arrest just to protect some thieving senator who could do you favors, and so you could keep sneaking around fucking your whores and trashing people's lives whenever and however you pleased. You thought it was all forgotten, didn't you? Well, you were wrong. Some things people cannot forget. And there are people still who remember. *I* remember."

The piercing heat and light of the lamp draw a tear, but he does not blink, his expression stiffened by a sudden cognizant fear that chills him. "Barbara? Is that you?"

The woman grabs the lamp and places it under her chin, the light contorting her face with fearsome shadows like some grotesque Halloween mask. "Oh no, Special Agent Avery, I am not your whore. I am the daughter Martin Lessing never saw because you killed him. I am the daughter who could not have her father's name because of the fear you put in my mother. I am the daughter who watched Martin Lessing's wife, my mother, die a slow death every day, trading favors with strangers to keep us both alive, never able to love any man but the one you killed. I am the daughter who watched her mother die so poor neighbors had to take up a collection to bury her. Look at me. I am Marielle Devereaux. I am the daughter of Martin Lessing and Nicole Devereaux, and I have come to give you back all the pain you gave so many people for so many years."

His mouth barely moves and the words gurgle up like vomit. "My God."

Again she pushes the lamp to his face, and he jerks his head back. Her voice sneers at him. "Look at you, sitting here in your pajamas, playing with a child's puzzle. Everyone probably feeling sorry for this babbling old fool, this harmless, babbling old fool. But you and I know better, don't we? We know how dangerous you are, how dangerous you have always been. Only now, you don't have to do anything to destroy yet another life, do you? You accomplish the same thing just sitting here, keeping it all to yourself, playing your child's game while your own son suffers the consequences."

"Cooper? You know Cooper?"

"Oh yes, it's beginning to dawn on you, isn't it? You're beginning to put it together, aren't you? You're wondering what the connection is, but you're beginning to see that there is some connection, aren't you? Yes, Mr. *Congressman,* Mr. *Special Agent* Avery. Yes, Marian died because of you, and now your son will be convicted of her murder, and all you can do is sit here in your pajamas playing with your puzzles."

"Marian?"

"You sound just like her, all your pompous, stupid blathering about making appointments, about how I don't belong here, as if you can just dismiss me. She was the same way. She just couldn't shut up, she just wouldn't listen, prattling on about mud on her floor, and holding that stupid pillow in front of her as if I weren't good enough to look at her, too busy begging and threatening to listen. It didn't have to be that way. No, it didn't. How many times had I been in that house? Watching your son and her sleeping in the comfort of wealth and power. I saw it all. I saw what you created. I saw all your profits from selling off my father's life. Oh, I could have killed them at any time. All of them. But it was you I wanted to see. Not her, not that stupid, whining woman. If she had just stayed in her room, if she had just *stopped talking!*"

He can hear the effort she makes to slow her breathing.

"But, no, she couldn't do that. She had to just keep talking, never listening. Crying and begging, then yelling and giving orders, telling me you weren't there. She wouldn't listen. Standing there holding that stupid pillow in front of her and threatening me? Telling *me* that Martin Lessing's life meant nothing to her. *Nothing?* It meant *nothing?*"

She lurches forward and again presses the lamp to his face. "But we know better, don't we, *Congressman?*"

"Oh God, please, no."

"Oh God, yes, Congressman."

He can feel her anger vibrating in the metal lampshade against his forehead and cheekbone. Then, in an instant, she pulls the light back, and her voice again calms.

"Yes, we both know better, don't we? We know that everything you did, everything you have, everything you ever had, you owe to my father. You killed more than a man. You know that, don't you. You know what he was. You know what he could have been. His writing, the beauty of his writing, his thoughts, his genius. All of that you killed. For what? Your whore?"

"I . . . I don't understand you. What else could we do?"

She laughs. "What else? You set my father up and let him die in jail for something he never did to protect you and your whore, and some thieving senator, and you ask what else could you do?" She laughs again, then stops herself. "Do you know—do you know that when my father died alone in his cell, not even a lawyer had seen him? His own wife, my mother, wasn't allowed to see him. Do you know that when my father died, he did not even know that I had been born? Did you know that?"

"I don't understand. You said Cooper . . . I don't understand."

"Oh, I think you do. I think it's finally coming home to you. You didn't even let my father live long enough to learn that he had a daughter, to ever see me, to even know I existed. But I've always known him. He has been with me every day of my life, and I finally know the truth. I know everything, everything you did to him. And now your son will know what you did. Your wife will know, your daughter will know. Everyone will finally know the truth. And they will know who Martin Lessing was, and they will remember him."

"Please, what do you want?"

"What do I want? Money, how about money? You have plenty of that, don't you? After all, once you had killed my father, and Byron Roth had been driven underground, you had everything you ever wanted and more, didn't you? While my mother lived on the edge of madness, with poverty and fear and loneliness, because of what you and your whore had done. And Byron Roth. You took his career, you took his family, and left him nothing. Why don't you just offer us all some money? Maybe that will make it all go away."

Avery struggles for an answer, but none comes. He rolls his head back and forth like a blind man who has no visual reference.

"It was all a lie, wasn't it?" she asks quietly. "God only knows what happened to the rest. To Harold Ramsey and the others. Even to Barbara Hoffman."

"Barbara?"

"Do you even know what happened to her, where she is now?"

Avery twists his face to one side, as much to escape the heat of the lamp as to evade her question.

"It was all a lie, wasn't it?"

He neither answers nor moves, keeping his face turned away and his eyes shut.

She grabs his face and he can feel the smooth leather of her gloved hand. *"Damn you!* Look at me. Look straight at me and tell me it was all a lie. The papers, the so-called military secrets, it was all a lie, wasn't it?"

"I don't know what you want. I—"

Her gloved fingers tighten painfully on his lower jaw. "Before you die, damn you, just once tell the truth. It was all a lie, wasn't it?"

It takes a moment, but finally Avery tries to nod against the resistance of her hand. She releases him. "Say it," she orders.

Avery drops his chin, and he takes several deep breaths. He then looks directly into the light and says, "Yes."

She stands erect and backs into the darkness. "Yes," she repeats in a whisper.

"Now, after all these years, you understand. You know now why Marian died and why your son will be convicted of her murder. Because of what you did. Because of everything you set in motion. You see that now, don't you? The rest of them, they don't see it. They don't want to see it. Not even your son's lawyers. They're still trying to protect you, for God's sake. They're all the same. They just go along chewing up lives like birds following a trail of seeds, their heads down, not looking or caring where they're headed, just consuming one seed at a time, one life at a time. My father, my mother, Byron Roth, and now, even this man Ollie Johns. This pathetic man who made the fatal mistake of believing he had a right to live however he wanted on that little spit of land left him, and apparently the effrontery to say so to Marian Avery. Besides, he's such a convenient tool for yet another Avery to use. Why not? It's worked so well before. So now he'll be chewed up like all the rest. They're all the same to people like you: my father, Roth, Ollie Johns, they're all fungible, aren't they? Faceless fodder. Just a few more innocents along the trail."

Charles Avery stares into the light with a sudden attentiveness. His body rocks ever so slightly against his bindings. "Marian?" he says in a parched voice. "Cooper didn't kill Marian?"

She lets go a snort of disgust. "Your own son. You believed your own son killed his wife. What, were you embarrassed? Is that why you just abandoned him? Is that why you never told his lawyers about Martin Lessing? They asked you, didn't they? And you just lied so no one would bother you while you sat here in your pajamas playing with a puzzle. Your own son."

Avery no longer feels his bindings, nor the cuts and burns on his face, nor the heat of the lamp. But he feels her. She is no longer a voice beyond the light, no longer a sporadic thrust of pain. She is suddenly real and present, like the past that is forming a picture in his mind. A cooling tingle crawls down his spine until his whole body is captured by it, and he is taken by a sudden, single shake of understanding. He cannot speak.

"No, Mr. *Congressman,* your son did not kill Marian. You did. No, you weren't there, you didn't pull the trigger. You didn't have to. But you killed her all the same, and you put your son on trial for her murder. The day you concocted your little scheme to frame Martin Lessing, the moment you decided to sacrifice all those people to hide your whoring and protect Oren Whittaker, you loaded the gun that killed Marian Avery."

"Oh my God, why are you doing this? Why now? After all this time. I never knew what happened to you. I didn't know."

"How does it feel? To watch your whole family destroyed? To see your world torn apart and the pieces scattered to the wind? To have absolutely no control, to have no defense? How does it feel?

"My mother knew how it felt. My father knew, and Byron Roth and his family, they all know. And now you know, and if now you can feel only one small minute of the horror you inflicted on them, on all of them, on me, it will have been worth it."

His voice rasps at the words. "But why? I didn't know he was your father. Lessing and the rest, they—they were Communists. It was my job. You know that. You know it was just my job."

"No," she says evenly. "They weren't Communists. God, how stupid it all sounds now. Communists. No, they weren't Communists. You know it now like you knew it then. But people like you didn't want people who believed in something different to speak their minds. My father . . ." She stops herself. "That doesn't matter. Communists or not, what you did had nothing to do with politics or national security. They found out about you, and they found out about Oren Whittaker. That's why you did it. Not because they were Communists. You did it to cover up for yourself, and you did it to protect Oren Whittaker, and the hell with anybody you had to destroy to do that. And worse, you gladly collected a bounty on all our heads. You were rewarded for your lies and treachery. A special assistant's job, then administrative assistant, then a seat in Congress and all that came with it. And now, finally, here you are, getting the reward you deserved all along. How does it feel?"

He feels nothing. "Are you going to kill me?" he asks, almost passively.

She hesitates before answering with almost the same passivity. She sounds now like a teacher considering her lesson plan. "I should. I suppose it would be the merciful thing to do." She stops, collecting her thoughts. "But I can't. It's important that you live on knowing what you have done and knowing that now everyone will know." Her voice quickens and grows more urgent and angry. "You will have to live with that. All that is left for me is to make sure you can't keep the lie going anymore. You would like to pretend that you know nothing about why this has happened. You would like to perpetuate the lie like you have all these years. But that's not going to happen. Everyone must know. You must be alive to see all their faces when the truth is finally so apparent that they cannot ignore it. Yes, you must see everyone look at you when they learn the truth, a truth even you won't be able to erase."

There is a long, silent moment, before he hears the woman come forward, and he can feel her closeness, her quick, short breath against his face, and the scent of her perfume mixed with perspiration. The lamp is pulled from his face, but its light remains burned in his eyes while he feels its heat now on his chest. The woman's hands grab onto and rip open his pajama top.

"Oh God, please . . . Barbara? I'm sorry."

36 *A*lex cannot remember exactly the minute or the hour or even the day of her leaving, but he can recall with absolute clarity all that he has seen and heard and touched since. He can recall, too, his thoughts, thoughts he has gathered like individual stones and piled one on top of another until they form a wall around his mind, separating him from sleep.

This is his third, maybe fourth, cup of coffee, each laced with a taste of Cointreau, since he arose from his bed and took from the darkened corner of half-formed projects the twisted figure he deformed with his fist the night Christine told him of her encounter with Ned Avery and of the child's terror-induced psychosis. The figure sits on his workstand, spotlighted in the otherwise darkened room, but he does not touch it. He can only stare at it, and study it, and think perhaps that he can save it. But even that hope is evaporating, as the night crawls toward morning, and the first sounds of another day approach.

From the street below, the voices of the Ferrante brothers sound their ritual argument over the recalcitrant lock on the front door of the bakery. Soon the warm breath of fresh-baked pastries will rise through the building; and soon after that, a delivery truck will squeak to a halt in front of the building and drop a thick stack of newspapers on the sidewalk. The sun will first appear with an almost hesitant glow, and then it will fill the street and become part of it. The neighbors will step out for their papers, and the tradesmen will sweep the walks in front of their shops, and most will wave or speak or nod to one another. And if it does not rain, and if he has not died, Mr. Spyropoulos, who lives on the corner in a single room on the second floor, will struggle down the stairs with his beach chair and settle at the edge of the sidewalk, where he will read the newspaper over and over and pretend to ignore all those who mumble some greeting as they pass him by.

But for Alex the day's routine will not include him. Whether it's today or tomorrow or the day after that, he knows that the end is inevitable, and there is nothing for him to do but wait.

An hour or more passes before the sun fills his loft, and he calls down to the bakery. Ciro answers the phone and tells him yes, the first batch of pastries is ready, as is the vat of coffee, and Alex says that he will be right down.

It is a few minutes before the bakery is to open, and Alex is sitting at a small table in the corner, sharing a pastry and some conversation with Anita, the Ferrantes' seventeen-year-old cousin, who seems perpetually happy despite the fact that her entire family is perpetually angry at her dropping out of school.

Ciro appears from the back carrying a large tray of pastries, which he slides into the display case. "Anita," he barks, "it's time to open," and Anita answers, "Okay, okay," as she gets up to unlock the front door.

"So, Alex," Ciro says, walking to the table and reaching into his shirt pocket beneath the long white apron dusted with flour and powdered sugar, "look at these. Four tickets, third row, right behind first base." The Red Sox are in town.

Ciro was once given a tryout with one of Boston's farm teams, but he was never signed. Still, it was more than was ever offered to any of his friends in either of the two summer leagues in which he plays, and his loyalty to the one team that gave him a chance is unshakable. "How 'bout you and me, we take Carla and Christine tonight. Roger Clemens is pitching," he adds as a further inducement.

"I wish I could," Alex says, "but tonight's bad for me. Maybe next time, but I appreciate the offer."

"No problem," Ciro says, as his attention is suddenly drawn to the sidewalk outside, and he frowns.

Alex follows Ciro's stare, and he sees Detective Wyzanski standing next to his police cruiser, looking up at the building as if he is checking the address against the information in a notepad he is holding. Wyzanski then looks to the window of the bakery and sees Alex, and he starts toward the door. Alex feels a tingle of apprehension which must show in his expression.

Ciro asks, "You know him?"

"Yeah," Alex says, "he works with Christine."

Paul Wyzanski steps inside, and Alex introduces him to Ciro. The two men shake hands, and Ciro calls back, "Anita, how 'bout some coffee here for Alex and his friend?" He turns back to the two men. "Nice meetin' ya, Detective."

Paul looks nervous and uncomfortable. He remains silent while Anita brings them both a cup of coffee and asks if either would like a pastry, which both decline.

"Something's wrong," Alex says as Anita turns away, and Paul takes a deep breath.

"I hope not, but yeah, maybe."

"Have you heard from Christine?"

Paul shakes his head. "No, but I'm hoping you have. That's why I'm here."

Alex, too, shakes his head, but he says nothing.

"Alex, we need to talk. Is there someplace else?"

Alex hesitates, thinking that maybe the comfort of the bakery with its warm odors of coffee and pastries and the company of the customers who are trickling in will soften, if not ward off, the news he suspects is coming. "No, we can talk here. Tell me, is this visit official? I mean are you here as a friend or a detective?"

Paul frowns. "I hope it's as a friend, but I have to ask you some questions, officially."

"What is it? What's happened?"

"You haven't heard from Christine?"

"No, not since I saw you. Why don't you just tell me what's going on? Aren't you supposed to be down at the trial this morning?"

"It's being postponed, at least for today. You sure you don't want to go someplace a little more private?"

"No, and unless you tell me what's going on, I don't think I want to continue this conversation."

Paul leans forward. "Look, I've been trying all weekend to find Christine. Frankly, we're a little worried."

"We?"

"Well, up until about three o'clock this morning, it was me. But now *we're* worried. The state police, that is. It's turned official."

"Why? What's happened?" Alex asks more urgently.

Paul takes his time, looking about the shop and taking a sip of coffee. "Okay, last night, sometime between seven and maybe eleven, eleven-thirty, someone broke into Congressman Avery's house down in Florida. The congressman was there alone except for a nurse. His wife was at a dinner party or something. Anyway, when the wife came home, she found the nurse. She had been knocked out with chloroform—or at least they think that's what it was—and bound. And . . . she found the congressman."

Alex's expression stiffens, and the color drains from his face. "What do you mean, she 'found' the congressman?"

"He had been, I don't know, I guess the word is terrorized. Assaulted, but in a very scary way."

"Is he alive?"

Paul nods.

"And the nurse?"

"She's all right. Nothing serious."

"Exactly what do you mean that the congressman was 'assaulted'?"

"Well, his hands and feet were tied to a chair. He had some cuts and bruises and burn marks like someone had pressed a hot lamp to his face, and he had been tattooed."

"What?"

"Yeah, tattooed. Whoever it was had taken some kind of indelible ink, like a fabric marker or something, we're not sure yet, and had written a message on his chest. Then she took a sharp blade—a razor, maybe, or a penknife, whatever—and, ah, she sliced his skin along the lines of the letters in the message so that the ink would get under the skin and leave a permanent tattoo."

Alex feels his throat close and his stomach turn, and the words "My God" barely escape. He sits back and takes several deep breaths to compose himself.

"What do you mean, 'she'? Did he know . . . Did he say who it was?"

"Well, the local police say he was just babbling and didn't make any sense. About the only thing they could understand was that he kept saying the name Barbara, over and over. They don't know who or even what he was talking about."

Alex waits for a chilling wave of dizziness to pass, and after another deep breath asks, "But why are you so concerned about Christine? You don't think she had anything to do with this, do you?"

"Alex, listen, the message left on the man's chest said, 'Remember Martin Lessing.' "

"And?"

"And there were a couple of things left behind. Obviously on purpose. Obviously as a message to us. There was a jacket and a pair of pants. A camouflage hunting outfit. Something that would fit either a small man or a woman. I know you know enough about the Cooper Avery case to know what that means."

Alex pauses. "Yeah, well, I guess it may mean that Christine was right all along. The same person who killed Marian Avery and sent that card or whatever to the family, did this, trying to give everyone the message that he or she wanted to give when Marian Avery was killed."

"Maybe. Maybe it is the same person. But I need to find Christine. Do you know where she is?"

Alex stops to gather his thoughts. "Barbara? . . . You know, Christine told me about her talk with Byron Roth. I assume you know about that?"

"Yeah."

"Didn't Roth tell her that the woman who the congressman had an affair with, you know, back when that whole Lessing thing happened—wasn't her name Barbara? Barbara Hoffman?"

"Yeah, I thought about that. And I've got somebody trying to track that down, but this Barbara Hoffman would have to be at least in her late sixties, maybe early seventies. This wasn't the work of an old woman."

Alex remains silent.

"Where's Christine?" Paul asks again.

"Oh man, you can't really believe Chris would do something like that. You *can't* believe that."

Paul looks at him stiffly. "Alex, we need to find Christine."

"You're telling me that the police think Christine had something to do with this?"

"No one's saying that, but . . ."

"But what?"

"But there's something I need to ask you. Friday, when we were talking down at the courthouse, you kept staring at those photographs of Marian Avery's jewelry. I mean, I couldn't help but notice that you were fixed on one in particular. The photograph of the necklace, the diamond necklace that hadn't been recovered . . . until now."

"What do you mean?"

"Whoever did this to the congressman left something else behind. She left a diamond necklace draped around his neck."

"Marian Avery's necklace?"

"It looks that way. Right now we're only dealing with what the police down there have told us, but the way they described the necklace they have, it sure sounds like the same one. By the end of the day, we should know for sure."

Paul waits for a response, but Alex says nothing. Finally, Paul says, "I need you to tell me why you were so interested in the photograph of that necklace. I mean, it seemed to me that there was something about it that really struck you."

Again, Alex says nothing.

"I'm asking you, Alex, was there something about that particular necklace that caught your attention? Did you recognize it for any reason?"

Alex takes a long time before answering. "No," he says finally. And then, shaking his head, "Jesus, you people are really something."

"What do you mean?"

"Why don't you just come out and tell me what you're thinking?"

"What is it that you think I'm thinking?"

Alex looks away, his face twisted with disgust. "Man, I'm not going to get into word games with you."

Paul presses forward a bit more. "Look, this thing with the congressman fits Christine's theory like a glove. If anyone should be working this, it ought to be her. Right?"

"But that's not why you're looking for her, is it?"

"Alex, listen to me. Christine hasn't been in her apartment all weekend. I've been checking, first because I was worried and I wanted to talk to her. But this morning, after I got called about this Florida thing, I thought I'd better do some checking myself, before the whole department goes off the deep end."

"You're telling me the police do think she had something to do with it."

"No one's said anything yet, and nobody wants to, but obviously some people are getting nervous. Particularly Captain Hardiman. I've never seen him so upset, and so worried. He feels like I do, I guess. Caught between concern for a friend and, well, what we have to do officially. But the questions are there. Where is she? Is she missing? Is she all right? Has something happened to her? That's the talk now. But there're people wondering if we should go into her apartment. I mean no one wants to get a warrant for obvious reasons, but they're getting itchy to go inside her apartment to see if she's okay and all that. And yeah, they want to look around." He pauses. "She hasn't been there, Alex. I know because I talked with her neighbor, Mrs. Braverman, not more than a half hour ago. She hasn't been there all weekend. The only one who has been in that apartment is you. You were there Saturday, for about an hour. And again yesterday. Mrs. Braverman said you looked worried."

"Yeah, I am. But only because the last time I saw Chris she was upset. I told you that last Friday. You know what she was upset about. I was just checking to see if she was okay. But she wasn't there. She probably just took the weekend to get away."

Paul looks away for a moment, and he shakes his head at Anita, who has asked if they need more coffee. He turns back. "You haven't answered my question about the necklace."

"Yes, I have. I said no, I didn't recognize the necklace in the photograph. I was just curious, that's all. I can't give you any more help than that."

Paul sighs. "Okay, I understand. Look, I've got to be at the airport in less than an hour. I'm going down to Florida to talk to the congressman and all that." He stops a moment, then says, "Listen to me, Alex. I haven't said anything to anyone else about you and this necklace business. But the longer it goes without hearing from Christine, the harder it's going to be to keep it to myself. Understand?"

"I understand."

"And I swear to God I hope all this stuff rattling around my head is just 'cause I haven't had much sleep and I'm not thinking straight. I hope Chris is on her way down to the courthouse and that in a couple of hours I'm going to be really embarrassed and owe her a big apology. But if you hear from her, will you let me know? All you have to do is call the office and tell them who you are and ask them to get through to me. I'll make sure they know what to do. All right?"

Alex nods. "And you'll let me know if you hear from her?"

"The minute I hear, I promise."

■■■

Alex watches Paul Wyzanski drive off before he walks the two blocks to the nearest phone booth, where he calls Christine's apartment. There is no answer. He calls his boss to say he will not be in, and then turns toward the harbor and starts walking. An hour or more passes before he is even conscious of the distance he has traveled or where he is, and he thinks suddenly that he should get back to his apartment and stay by the phone. It takes him some time to find a cab, and by the time he returns to his building, his nerves have numbed his hands and feet and so tightened his back that he feels barely able to reach the fourth floor and his apartment. He is drained of all feeling, and when he opens his door and sees her there, he shows no surprise.

Christine is curled on his bed. She clutches her purse to her stomach like a child holding a teddy bear. She sits up quickly and crosses her legs in front of her. She tries to smile, but the expression is more pained and frightened than anything else. Her face looks almost skeletal. Her eyes, darkened by lack of sleep, are sad and sunken, and her hair looks as if she has not bathed in a week.

"Hi," she says softly.

"Hi?"

"I've done it again, haven't I? You're angry."

He does not move.

"I'm sorry. But that's what I always say, isn't it?" She pulls her purse tighter to her stomach, and she begins to rock slowly on the bed. Her eyes dart about the room, avoiding him, and her voice is nervous and uneven. "I had to get away. But this time, I don't know, it was different. I wanted to think about us. Do you remember a couple of months ago? Do you remember that you said that no matter what happened, you'd always have a hot meal and a warm bed for me? Do you remember that?"

He nods.

"And you made me laugh. You said they'd never take us alive, and I laughed. Do you remember?"

"Yes, I remember."

"And you said that you loved me and that you wanted me to be here when you woke up in the morning. Do you remember that?"

"Christine—"

"Well, I know that I haven't made it easy for you, but you've always been there for me. You're the only one who has always been there for me, and I've been thinking a lot, and I want to be the one who's there for you for a change. I want us to get married, and I want us to go away somewhere. I want you not to have to work on anything but your art, and I'll have babies and it'll be all right."

"Christine, I want you to come with me."

"No, it'll be all right. I know it will. I've saved a lot of money. I have. I have lots of money, and I'm going to quit the police, and then we'll have my retirement money, and—"

"Christine, please, listen to me. We need to get you someplace where you can be helped. We need—"

"No, I'm fine. I really am. I have plenty of money saved, and you won't have to work down at the docks anymore. We can get a place in the country somewhere. Or maybe even Europe. I've always thought of us going back to Europe someday. I think France would be nice. They would love your sculptures in France. We could be married, and you could work on your art, and I will have babies, or if you don't want babies, that will be all right. We just need to be together, that's all."

"Babe, please, I want to call Professor Mercle. I want you and me to go see him. Today. Right now. He'll know what to do. He'll know where we can go to get help. You trust him. I know you do. He's been like a father to you."

"I remember a lot of my French from high school, so we'll be all right. And you know Spanish. Maybe we should think about Spain. I might really like Spain. I've never been there, but I re-member when I was a child, I had this huge atlas that was filled with all these wonderful pictures, and I always thought that Spain would be a wonderful place. Down south, where it's always warm. But I don't want to go to Germany. I never liked Germany."

"Please, babe, come with me. We can talk about that later. But right now, I want you to come with me to see the professor. Please."

Suddenly her eyes stop their wandering and her body its rocking, and she stares at him coldly. "Why should I? Because Paul says so. I saw you talking with him. I saw the two of you together. What, just because I take a day off, he thinks I'm crazy? You think I'm crazy? Did the two of you have a good time comparing notes about how crazy I am? Did you exchange your little boys' locker room jokes?"

"No, Chris, we didn't talk about that. He's looking for you. Everyone's looking for you. He told me what happened in Florida. Sweetheart, we need—"

She stops him with a shake of her head, and turns to look out the window for a moment. "God, you take one day off. What can they do? Dock me a day's pay? So what? I'm quitting anyway. I have quit. I don't want to do that anymore." She turns back to him, her eyes wide and childlike. "Oh, Alex, it's going to be so much better from now on, it really will. We can get married, and you'll have your own studio, and I'll go to the market every day and buy fresh fruits and vegetables and bread. I can learn to cook. Not just cook, I mean I want to learn to prepare really elegant meals. I want to bake cakes. I remember once having a birthday cake that had white icing with flecks of orange all over it. It was wonderful. I think it was the best cake I ever had. I want to learn to cook like that. Do you know what I mean? Oh, you'll get so fat, but I won't care, and maybe . . . maybe when the children are old enough, we can—"

"*Stop it!* Please, just stop and listen to me."

"You don't want to marry me?"

Alex lowers his head. "Oh God, I've wanted that for so long. But now . . . babe, I don't know who you are."

She laughs and again starts her rocking. "Oh, don't be ridiculous. I've just been giving this a lot of thought, that's all. And I know what I want now. All that other stuff is behind us. We're going to be a family now. We're going to be happy. I'm not going to be a detective anymore. Not for one more minute. I know what I want.

For the first time in my life, I know exactly what I want. And I want you and me to be together. And I know you want that, too. It's going to be grand. It really is. Just think of it. We'll find a house. It doesn't have to be too big a house because we'll build you a separate studio, and all around your studio I'll plant flowers and there'll be all these trees and you'll have your own studio in the middle of a wonderful garden, and I won't let anybody bother you. It'll be perfect."

It feels to him as if all the air has been sucked from the room, and he takes several deep breaths to steady himself as he walks over to sit on the edge of the bed. "Christine, please don't say anything for just a minute. Please. Just listen. Sweetheart, you need to get help. You need to come with me to see Professor Mercle. I know he will help us."

"What in the world are you talking about? I don't need to see the professor. I told you, I'm not going to do that work anymore."

Alex reaches for her hand, but she frowns and clutches her purse even tighter to her stomach. "Babe, I know about Marielle. I know who she is."

"But of course you do. I told you about her. But that has nothing to do with us. You're not listening to me. That's all over now. The case, the job. It's all behind me now. It's done, it's all settled. We can be together now without all that nonsense getting between us. Don't you see?"

"Babe, I saw the photographs of Marian Avery's jewelry. I saw the picture of the necklace."

"What are you talking about? Alex, you aren't listening to me."

"Last Friday, remember? We were supposed to meet after you were through with court and go to dinner?"

"Oh, I know, I'm sorry, but—"

"No, wait . . . just wait. When you didn't show up at the courthouse, Paul was worried about you, and he asked me if I knew where you were. And he and I were talking in that room, whatever you call it. The war room? Anyway, while I was talking with him, I saw the picture of the necklace."

Christine looks away quickly and directs her question to a far corner of the room. "What necklace?"

"*The* necklace, babe. The necklace that you wore the night of my opening."

She turns back to him, and begins to shake, and her voice turns weak and pleading. "You saw my mother's necklace?"

"God help me, babe, I didn't want to believe it. But when I saw the photograph, I don't know, everything just got crazy in my mind. And when you didn't show up at the courthouse, and I couldn't find you anywhere, everything that's happened just started rolling over in my head. I didn't know what to think. And then Saturday, I went to your apartment. You never answered your phone, and I felt like I just had to see you, I had to talk to you. So I went to your apartment, and I'm sorry, I just couldn't help myself. I started looking around. I guess I wanted to see that necklace and know that it really wasn't the same one. But it wasn't there."

"My mother's necklace?"

"No, sweetheart, it wasn't your mother's necklace. It was Marian Avery's necklace. I know now what you went through. I know now why—"

"You were going to take my mother's necklace?"

"I couldn't find it. I looked everywhere. But I found your box. And I found all those letters to your mother, and I found the photographs of your father and mother together, before he died. He was still in the Army. He looked so young in his uniform, and he was smiling, and he had his arm around your mother. She was beautiful, wasn't she? And I saw the photograph of you and her together, when you were just a little girl. You couldn't have been more than seven or eight, but I knew it was you. You look so much like your mother. Except the eyes. I think you must have your father's eyes. And I finally understood." His tears come in a sudden rush as Christine pushes quickly to the far side of the bed and presses herself into the corner. "God, what did they do to you?"

Christine's eyes are wide and frightened, and her voice turns hard. "You took my papers? You took Mother's necklace?"

"Christine. It was not your mother's necklace. You put the necklace around Avery's neck so that everyone would know what you had been trying to tell them. Your parents didn't die in an automobile accident. You never had a brother. As much as you want to believe that, it's not you. Not the real you. You're Marielle, you're the woman you've been tracking, and I know that whatever you did, you did so that everyone would finally know what Avery had done to your father, to Martin Lessing, and to your mother, and even to you. But that's over now. Everyone knows now. You did what you had to do. But now it's time to take care of you. You need help, babe. Please, let me take you to see Professor Mercle. Let us help you before it's too late."

Christine's body has turned rigid. Nothing moves but her eyes, which are narrowed and angry. Her voice comes in a slow, menacing cadence. "How dare you tell me that I need help. I don't need anybody. And to think she was ready to marry you. You've ruined it, because you're weak, like she was. But that's not me. I don't need your help. I don't need anything from you. *Nothing!* You, all of you, you're all the same. Just like Marian Avery, just like the mighty congressman, the almighty FBI agent. Whining and begging. They stole everything they ever had. They killed my father, they drove my mother mad, and Byron Roth and all the others. Oh, I saw how they lived. As if they could stop me, as if they could lock me out. Hah! It was so easy. I was in that house a half-dozen times, and not once did they ever know. *Not once!* They still don't know, and they never will. There is nothing they can do to me. Except . . ."

Christine breaks her stare, and her eyes search the room. "You stole my papers? Where are they? Did you tell them about those papers?"

"I have them here. No one has seen them, and I haven't told anybody about them. I put them under the bench. But right now that's not—"

"That's right! No one will ever see them. And without them, no one will ever know." Christine's head falls back and she lets out a moan as her eyes begin to tear. "Oh, Alex, we can be so happy. You and I. We can just go away. It's all over now, don't you see? We don't need to fight anymore. I promise you that we'll be happy. We don't have to go to France if you don't want. We can find someplace else. We can go anywhere we like."

Alex begins to reach toward her, and Christine shouts, "*Stop!*" and her feet scramble to push her hard against the headboard, and her eyes flash with fear. "Stay away from me. Don't come near me." She fumbles quickly with her purse, and she pulls out her revolver and points it at him. "*Damn you!* You've ruined everything."

Alex doesn't move, but he keeps his hand out to her. "It's over, babe. We're going to put an end to all of it. You and I are going to see Professor Mercle."

She cocks the pistol, and her expression has turned from fear to anger. "No, we're not going anywhere. I don't need your help. I don't need the professor. I know exactly what I am doing. I always have. I don't need anyone to play with my mind, trying to turn me into what they want me to be. I'm not sorry. Do you understand? I'm not sorry. I gave them only what they deserved. I let him experience just one small speck of the pain he caused. Someone had to let him know. All those years, it was like he was being rewarded for what he did. I only gave him one small helping of what he deserved to have done to him. Why can't you understand that?"

Alex takes a long breath, and he asks very softly, "Did the boy deserve what happened to him?"

She does not move, and her expression shows no reaction at all, and Alex asks again, more urgently, "Did he? Did that ten-year-old boy deserve what happened to him?"

Still she remains absolutely rigid, showing no reaction, and she does not answer.

"*Did he?*" Alex shouts, and she winces.

Her eyes scan the room rapidly, but focus on nothing.

"Don't you see? You—"

"Stop it," she says, as if she were shooing away a small annoyance.

"No, I can't. You must understand—"

"Stop it. You don't know what you're saying. The boy wasn't there. There was no one else there. *They* did that to him."

"No, Christine, he was there. The boy—"

"*Stop it!*"

"Or what, you'll shoot me? Is that what happens next? And then what? Do you think shooting me will stop your pain? Think, babe. Please, it's time to put an end to all this. It's time to get help."

Christine is breathing hard, and her hands tremble slightly as she continues to hold the gun stiff-armed, pointing it at him.

"Listen to me, Christine. Please. The boy was there. Don't you see? Don't you see that you let it get away from you? You let it turn you into a mirror image of everything that happened to you. Everything—"

"No, you don't understand. There was no one else there."

"He was there, Christine. He saw what you did. He—"

"Stop!"

"He saw you. He—"

"No!"

Alex sees the flash, but before he hears the report, the bullet slams into his chest. He has no sensation of being thrown backward or of falling. There is only that brief instant when he feels the fire deep inside, and he looks up from the floor, searching for her and trying for a breath that will not come. And that is all.

37 *S*tepping from the thick August heat into the reception area of the William T. Packard Clinic, Paul Wyzanski feels a quick chill trickle down his spine. Whether it is the air-conditioning or the immediate memory of that cold, dank day he and Christine came to observe Ned Avery, he does not know nor even care to speculate. Today the foyer is bright with the midmorning sun, and the receptionist looks up from her desk with a smile to match.

"Can I help you?"

"Yes, my name is Paul Wyzanski. I'm here to see Mr. Avery. I believe he said he would be with Dr. Eckert or Dr. Storrs."

"Ah, yes," the receptionist says in a slow tone of recognition. She picks up her phone and dials three digits. "Polly? Yes, there's a—I'm sorry"—she turns to Paul—"your name again?"

"Detective Wyzanski."

"Yes, Polly, I'm sorry, there's a Detective Wyzanski here. He has an appointment to see Mr. Avery? . . . Yes, all right." She cups her hand over the mouthpiece, and smiles silently as the message is passed on.

Two months before, as Cooper Avery was leaving the court-room, the state having dismissed all charges against him, and before the reporters could swarm around in a futile attempt to extract a comment from him, Cooper approached Paul with a simple request.

"Do you know where she is? What's happened to her?"

"No, sir, not yet," Paul replied, struck by the unexpected tone of Avery's voice and the questioning look in his eyes. If Cooper Avery felt any of the anger or accusation that was his due, he did not show it. His look was one of stunned confusion and a deep, almost painful curiosity, almost as if he was not yet convinced that the game was over and that he had survived it.

"Will you let me know when you do find out?"

"Yes, sir," Paul promised and set about his search, as much for the truth of what had happened as for Christine herself.

Cooper has spent the intervening time living in a small rented cottage near the clinic, seeing Ned as often as the doctors allow and patiently following their every suggestion. Paul has spent the time in an obsessive but constantly frustrated search for answers. Except for one long interview in which Cooper detailed his conversations with Christine, the two men have not spoken until two days ago, when Cooper called. He was leaving the area permanently, he said, and he simply wondered what, if anything, the police had learned. The answers could easily have been given over the phone, but for his own reasons, Paul wanted to see Cooper, to talk to him face to face. It took some gentle prodding, but finally and reluctantly, Cooper agreed to meet with him this morning, at the clinic.

"Yes?" the receptionist says suddenly. "Yes, all right." She turns to Paul. "Detective, won't you come with me?"

Paul follows the woman down the familiar hall to Dr. Eckert's office, where she opens the door and motions him in. Cooper Avery is seated across the room, and he makes no motion to rise or greet the detective. Dr. Eckert steps out from behind his desk to shake Paul's hand and to offer his best professional smile. "Good to see you again, Detective," he says. "Well, I'm sure you gentlemen have much to talk about, and I have several things to take care of myself, so I'll just leave you alone. Make yourselves comfortable." And then, as an aside to Cooper, "Ah, Dr. Storrs will be down shortly. My secretary will buzz you when they're ready."

Cooper nods, and both he and Paul watch the doctor slip out the back door of his office. There is a long silence as Cooper remains seated, looking unsure of his reaction to seeing the detective again and in this setting. Cooper is even thinner than Paul remembers. A freshly laundered pair of blue jeans and a faded pink golf shirt look oversized on him; but the darkness has left his eyes and his complexion hints at time spent in the sun. Paul starts to slip his hands into his pockets, but stops, not knowing quite where to start.

"Thank you for seeing me," he says. "I had thought a number of times before of coming to see you, but to be honest, now that I'm here, I'm at a bit of a loss for what to say."

Cooper looks directly at the detective. "Well, I'll be honest as well. This isn't particularly easy for me either. I mean, I've always understood that you and your people had a job to do, but still . . ." Cooper stops, but keeps his stare fixed on Paul.

"Yes, sir, I understand. It's true, we had a job to do and we tried to do it as best we knew how. Still are, for that matter. But the fact remains that . . . well, we were wrong, and I'm sorry. For everything. I just thought I owed you that much. You know, to tell you that in person."

Cooper waits a moment, his eyes still steady, as if he is taking Paul's measure, and perhaps his own. "I guess I still don't understand it all. But frankly, I'm not sure anymore that I even want to. I only want to put it behind me. There's nothing left for me and my children but to move on."

"Mr. Avery . . . Do you mind if I sit down?"

Cooper nods, and then asks, "You haven't found her?"

"No, sir, not a trace. At least not as to where she might have gone."

"Or who she really is . . . or was?"

"Well, the fact is that's hard to say. We're certain that she must have been Martin Lessing's daughter, or at least someone very close to him or his family, but that's theory, not fact. We've traced every record and lead we could find but they don't tell us much, or at least not enough. It's almost as if she didn't exist before she came to the University of Maryland. We know she entered as a junior, as a transfer from the university's campus in Munich. How she got to Munich, we're not sure. Her application and student transcripts say she was a student there, but we can't find anyone who actually remembers her. We're sure those records were falsified. There's no record of her at the high school she listed. The Defense Department has no record of her father, who she listed as a colonel in the Air Force, or of her brother, who was supposed to have been in the service. There's no record of a passport being issued until she was here in the States, so we don't know how she came into the country. Her Social Security number wasn't issued until she got to College

Park. The few people we've found who knew her in college all say that she was, you know, well liked and all, but when we asked who her close friends were, no one could say. They all remember her as being a bit of a loner, never joined anything, no clubs, sororities or anything like that. She just seemed to be someone everybody liked but no one really knew. She was very bright, always at the top of her class. The records say she was fluent in French and German, which is something we never knew. I mean no one who worked with her ever knew that. She never gave any hint of it. It's really odd, but it feels like I'm tracking a complete stranger."

Cooper slouches forward, resting his elbows on his knees, and without lifting his eyes from the floor, asks, "You were close to her, weren't you? I mean more than just working together?"

"Yes, sir, we were close."

Cooper nods to himself, then looks up. "Do you understand it, why this all happened? I mean, even if you accept this revenge theory, even if you accept that maybe she was this Martin Lessing's daughter, and"—he hesitates—"and my father did everything they say he did, it still doesn't make sense to me. It doesn't tell me why. It doesn't explain killing Marian, or why she would then have tried to help me. I mean, it seems like she was out to prove her own involvement. That just doesn't make sense."

Cooper stands suddenly and moves to the window looking out onto the broad expanse of lawn leading to the river. He continues to stare into the distance while his voice goes on quietly, almost as if he were speaking to some other audience. "I don't know. I keep thinking about my father. I understand that he's barely coherent and no one can make any sense of what he's said, but still, the only name he keeps repeating is this Barbara person."

"Well," Paul begins, but Cooper cuts him off.

"You know, in a strange way I was really taken by her. I really believed she wanted to help. I really believed that she wanted the truth to come out, and still, even now, there's this one part of me that wonders if maybe it wasn't really her. That maybe there's something out there that we still don't know. That there's more to the story." He turns back to Paul. "Is that possible?"

Paul shakes his head. "No. As much as I'd like to believe that, I don't think it's possible. Look, I've spent almost every day over the past couple of months trying to piece it together. I've spent a lot of time with a psychologist down at the FBI, Dr. Mercle, who probably knew Christine longer and better than anyone. He was her professor and adviser when she was doing graduate work at George Washington. And I've tried to talk to Byron Roth and track down Barbara Hoffman, but Roth won't talk to us. It's almost as if Christine was his own daughter."

"And the boyfriend, the one she shot? Did you ever find out—?"

Paul stops the question with a shake of his head. "No, we'll never really know what happened there. But I did talk to Roth's daughter, and she told me the story Roth told Christine. When you piece everything together against the background of that story, the revenge theory makes a lot of sense."

"But why Marian? She had nothing to do with whatever my father had done."

"Well, we don't think Christine intended to kill your wife, or at least that she didn't go to the house to do that. At least that's what Dr. Mercle thinks, and I guess we all agree with him. I'm not sure that I understand or can explain all the medical and psychological jargon, but basically Mercle thinks this obsession of hers, this fixation on her father and what had happened to her family and the others, was something she was able to control or suppress for long periods, years even, and in every other respect she seemed to be . . . well, normal. But something happened. Maybe it was something recent or maybe it had been building for years, but something happened to bring out those ghosts or demons or whatever. Whatever it was, it just took over, and she had to do something to get it out of her system. And Mercle suspects that this wasn't a single isolated instance. He said he wouldn't be surprised if she had been to your house before. Maybe several times." Paul pauses and shakes his head. "You know she even told us that. Christine said that the killer had probably been stalking your house."

Cooper nods. "She told me the same thing."

"Anyway, Dr. Mercle thinks that for whatever reason she went there, it most likely was not to kill you or your wife. But something unexpected happened, a confrontation, maybe, between her and your wife, something that so angered her or even frightened her, that . . . you know, she shot her. And afterwards, Christine's rational side had to make the killing mean something. She had to give it some purpose. Everything about the scene, Mercle said, everything points to the fact that she hadn't planned for that to happen. The way she made the burglary look so obviously faked. And after finding the combination to the safe, making it so clear that whoever broke into it had the combination. And only vandalizing your things. Even the cigarette butt, trying to show that a woman was involved. These were really random and mixed clues, some of them blatant, some of them, like the cigarette butt, subtle. Almost too subtle. The kind of clue that only she would look for. Her mind was racing to try to create a trail. But she wasn't thinking clearly. She was rushed, maybe even panicked. Dr. Mercle says that if she had really planned it out, she would have left that note—the Martin Lessing note?—she would have left something like that on the scene so that there would have been no doubt about the motive. But it didn't occur to her until later.

"And the fact is, she really was trying to help you. It was her way of proving her theory, of trying to bring out this whole business about your father. But when no one paid any attention, and when she saw your lawyers start pointing a finger toward Ollie Johns, who Mercle says she would have seen as another victim, she just snapped. She had to do something direct. Anyway, that's the professor's theory."

Cooper turns back to the window and remains silent for some time, his hands stuffed in his pockets. "You know," he says finally, "it's the oddest thing. I can't really explain it, except that I have such a vivid memory of when she and I met . . . and talked— everything about her. Somehow I just can't put that woman together with what she's supposed to have done. And as much as I should hate her, still, there was just something about her, something that keeps some small part of me wondering if all of you might be wrong . . . again. Isn't that odd?"

"No," Paul says, lowering his eyes. "I can understand that."

Cooper is again staring out the window when the quiet is suddenly interrupted by the buzz of the intercom. Cooper picks up the phone and listens. He then turns to Paul. "I'm sorry, Detective, but I'll have to cut this short. They're bringing my son to me."

Paul stands quickly. "He's better, then?"

"Yes, much. He's a long way from being well, but today we're leaving, the three of us, together. In a few hours, we'll all be on a plane to Seattle, to start over."

"I'm glad the boy's able to come home."

"Well, not entirely. He'll be staying at a residential treatment center out there. I don't know for how long, but I think he's past the worst of it. And we'll be together. Dr. Storrs is going to accompany us out there to help introduce him to his new setting. It's a start."

Paul nods. "I'll be going, then. I appreciate your seeing me. I just wanted to say . . . you know."

Cooper nods and offers his hand, which Paul shakes. "You have no idea where she's gone?"

"Not a trace," Paul says. "There're lot of theories floating around, and we've sent inquiries and teletypes all over, but so far, she seems to have disappeared the same way she came, into the ether."

Cooper has opened the door to the hallway and is about to say something when he hears his daughter's voice. "Daddy?"

Paul follows Cooper out into the hallway and sees Dr. Storrs walking toward them. She is smiling, holding on to Ned's hand. Alice walks beside them holding her brother's other hand.

"Daddy, I think Ned wants to go swimming," Alice announces. "Will we have time to go swimming before we leave for the plane?"

Ned walks easily between Dr. Storrs and his sister, but his face offers no expression, and he shows no sign that he is part of, or even hears, the conversation. Cooper kneels down as Dr. Storrs and Alice let go of Ned's hands. He takes his son in his arms and stands up, hugging the boy to him. Ned's arms fall around his father's shoulders. He does not hold on, but neither does he resist his father's touch. Cooper looks back at Paul for an instant before Alice diverts his attention.

"Can we, Daddy? Go swimming, just for a little bit?"

"No, Blossom, we won't have time today."

Dr. Storrs says something about the van being packed and ready, and Cooper turns and starts walking toward the sunlight streaming through the front door, his son in his arms, his daughter at his side, chatting on.

"Well, can we stop for some french fries or something? Ned's hungry, and I've got three dollars and fifty cents, so maybe we should stop and get something to eat. But y'know, since we've gotta go to Bal'mer—"

"Bal'mer?"

Alice scrunches up her face with exasperation. "Since we gotta go to Bal-ti-more to get the plane, maybe we oughta go to Mr. Luigi's and have a pizza first, and Ned and me could have our dessert, but we could still get some french fries and maybe some ice cream 'cause . . ."

The front door closes behind them, shutting Paul off from their conversation. For several moments he does not move. He simply stands there, alone in the empty hallway.

38 *T*he late September air slides down from the north and carries with it the first crisp feel of autumn's approach. Still, the sun is bright, and it warms the polished surface of the headstone before which she kneels, and her fingers reach out to trace the carved inscription. "Roland Michaud, 1911–1983."

"*Est-ce que tu es étonné, Monsieur, de me voir après toutes ces années?* I'm surprised myself, to be here. I'm sorry, my French, it feels so awkward. *Est-ce que ça te dérange si je parle en anglais? J'ai tellement de choses à te dire. Ça serait plus simple si je parlais en anglais.* Yes, I know you can understand me, even in English. I suppose I don't have to speak at all. I imagine that you can hear my thoughts. *Tu entends ce qui se passe dans mon coeur, non?*

"There is so much to tell you, how do I start? *Est-ce que je parle avec un accent américain?* I cannot hear it anymore. It has been so long. *Cela fait si longtemps.* Remember what a good student I was? How hard I worked practicing my English, to speak like the Americans spoke. Maman had taught me so much, but I needed to speak just like the Americans. I knew I had to go there. I . . . *Non, non, je dois garder le fil de mes pensées,* I must tell you what happened, *en anglais.*

"Oh, Monsieur, I did not mean to leave you like I did. You and Madame and Gagnon, I didn't know you were coming for me, I didn't know what else to do after the funeral.

"I saw Maman's grave, just over the hill there. Thank you for doing that. It's a beautiful stone. She would have liked it. She always liked pretty things. She deserved better, she really did. But it's over now, it's all settled, and she has her peace.

"But still, I had to come and tell you why I left. It wasn't your fault. I loved you, *Monsieur, et Madame également.* You were so kind to me, always. And Gagnon, too. It was just that I knew it was time for me to leave Strasbourg, and after the funeral it was as if Maman spoke to me, telling me to move on.

"Oh, Monsieur, she tried. She really did try. I know you never believed that. I know you did not like her, but you did not really know her. You did not understand what she had been through. She just was not as strong as you or I. There were so many times she would make me angry, too. The drinking and sometimes the men. And whenever I'd get angry, she would try to tell me, to explain why she was so lonely and hurt and how things would have been so different if they had not killed my father. And she would tell me about him, how gentle he was; a poet, she said, but also how much fire there was in his thoughts, and how his words could excite people so. But still I didn't really understand.

"But later, I did. Yes, I came to understand what it was like for her. You see, Maman could never forget what had happened. She could not escape the anger and the pain, and I think, too, the fear. You should not judge her too harshly.

"You see, I was much the same. I wanted to forget, too. When I finally got to America, I tried to put it all away. At first it seemed so easy to forget, to pretend that it never happened. I could make up a whole new life.

"Do you remember how Sister Berthe said my English was better than hers? Well, by the time I left Strasbourg, my English was good enough to get a job at the American college in Munich, in the registrar's office. I worked there for almost two years, and all day long I would speak nothing but English, and I would listen so carefully to how they spoke, listening to the accents and the little phrases that only the Americans used when they spoke to one another. And when I was ready, when people told me I was speaking English with an American accent, all I had to do was make up a whole new file for myself.

"I know, I shouldn't laugh, but it did seem funny at the time. There I was, in charge of filing student records and answering inquiries for transcripts and all, and when I decided to go to America,

I just made up my own records. I applied to the University of Maryland, and when they asked for the records and transcripts, I was the one to answer them. It was so easy. I became this whole new person with a history I created myself.

"I had so much practice at that, didn't I? Sometimes, I'd even embarrass myself. I could tell you and Madame knew I was making up stories, but you enjoyed them, too. Wasn't that true? Yes, I think so. Sometimes I would tell those stories as much to entertain you as for myself. How easy it was for me to fly away, to be somewhere else, to be someone else, if only for a little while. But it's all so different now.

"Do you remember the atlas you and Madame and Gagnon gave me? It was my eleventh birthday. Remember? How I treasured that book. I called it my book of dreams. *Mon livre des rêves.* I picked out all the places I would see one day. I remember that birthday. You and Madame, and Gagnon, and the cake with the flakes of orange peel? What a wonderful birthday you and Madame gave me. I remember every minute of it to this day. I can see Gagnon now, walking across the street with the atlas wrapped in bright red paper. I tried so hard not to want things because I didn't want to be disappointed. Maman tried, she really did, but we had no money. But you, Monsieur, you and Madame, you never disappointed me. Gagnon either.

"I went looking for Gagnon today, but, well, you know. I was sorry that he too had died. Did you know he sold his shop? Oh yes, many years ago. But I did see Madame Gagnon. She remembered me, and we talked for a long time, and we cried a little. She told me where you were and that Madame is now with your niece and her husband in Nancy. But your shop is gone. Not the building, it's still there; but the shop is a restaurant now. It's a very nice restaurant with white tablecloths and flowers. But still, it made me sad not to see all the fruits and vegetables in the stands. I wanted to steal another orange from you and let you catch me. But I was too late, wasn't I? Like you and Gagnon were that day, the day of the funeral. Just a few minutes' difference and you would have found me, and maybe everything would have been different. Maybe . . . *tout aurait été différent.*

"Oh yes, I learned what happened from Monsieur Roth just a

few months ago. Do you remember Monsieur Roth? Do you remember writing to him in Baltimore? He told me about your letters.
The Christmas card he sent me that year, after Maman died, and I
had left for Munich, the postman must have brought it to you. I
was just sixteen. And you wrote to Roth to tell him what had
happened and asked him to let you know if he heard from me. Do
you remember? And then, all the letters you and he sent one another, he kept them all. He showed them to me. It made me feel
so sad to see your letters.

"Oh, Monsieur, I'm so sorry. I didn't know you and Madame
were looking for me. Not until just a few months ago. And this
morning, when I found Madame Gagnon, she told me as well. I
didn't mean to hurt you and Madame. You were so kind to me.
And Gagnon, too. I just never understood. *Je n'ai jamais compris,
c'est tout.*

"I thought I could leave it all behind me. Start all over. To be
a completely different person. And I was. For many years, I was
who I wanted to be. I did well, Monsieur. You would have been
proud of me. You always said I could be whatever I wanted, and
I believed you. Except, I don't know, that history was part of me.
But, at the same time, it was something apart, almost like the stories
I had made up for myself. It was as if I had become the story, and
the real me was a dream.

"But that's all over. I just needed to tell you that I didn't run
away from you. I just had to get away for myself. But I couldn't.
Not forever. It just kept coming back. *Comme la fièvre, comme la
malaria.* That's how I thought of it. Do you know how malaria
keeps coming back? How once you are infected there are these
little bugs in your system that can lie dormant for long periods, and
suddenly they wake up and begin to secrete their poison, and it
just overtakes you? That's what it was like.

"I'd see his name in the paper, or on television or whatever.
Congressman Charles Avery! And I'd think of my mother and father
and what we could have been and I'd get so angry. I wanted to tell
everyone who this man was, to tell them everything he had done,
what Maman had told me, but I couldn't. I couldn't say anything,
because I wasn't that same person anymore. Sometimes it would
be days before the feeling would go away. But I learned how to

deal with it, and for a very long time I found it easy to do. I always knew I could lose myself in my work or, sometimes, with other people—with men. Like Maman.

"Please, don't say anything. If you could have only known what it was like for us. If you had really known Maman, you would have understood her, understood us. Oh, I know what people said, what they thought she was. *Une prostituée,* they said. *Une pute!* I always knew. Maybe not when I was a little girl, but later, I learned. I came to understand how sometimes she just needed to pretend that the pain wasn't there. That maybe for those few moments she could believe that it never was there.

"I was no different. No, Monsieur, I was no different at all, except that I had no need for their money, and I could choose who *I* wanted, whenever or wherever *I* wanted. Do I embarrass you? Don't be embarrassed. You must understand that like Maman, I, too, sometimes needed to just get away from all those thoughts, from the fever. How easy it was to escape, how easy it was to convince a man of whatever you wanted him to believe; and somehow, for a while, he might help you believe it yourself. One way or another, doesn't everyone do that?

"But they just couldn't let things be. Maybe Maman knew better than I. Maybe her way was best. With me, I always seemed to let them stay too long, and then they'd start to want more. To know more than they had a right to know. Why are men so, I don't know, suspicious? Do you know what I mean? They're always asking questions as if what you are, what they see, isn't enough for them. I think they want to hear the lies that will make them feel better about themselves, as if they need to turn you into whatever they want to believe you are, as if your life began with them. They can be such children. And sometimes they'd just keep pressing, trying to get so close, like they wanted to burrow in and take over, as if they couldn't feel complete unless they took something away from me, and I'd have to get away. I'd have to leave.

"But Alex, Alex was different. Oh, yes, Monsieur, you would have liked Alex very much. He was an artist, a wonderful artist, and we loved each other very much, we really did. But he died. Yes, it was very sad. But we really loved each other, and at least I have that.

"But there was this one time, just about a year ago, when it all started up again. I remember Alex telling me about his father, and how his mother had run off when he was a child, and how his father had turned so bitter, and how he died, and Alex seemed so—how can I say it? So accepting. It sounded like he was talking about a stranger, about someone who had no connection with his life. I don't know why, but it made me angry. He talked as if he had chosen his own life, and what his mother did and how his father lived had no impact on who he was.

"I guess I was angry for him, because he refused to be. I kept thinking of what they had done and how his life could have been so different. But it also made me start thinking again about my father. How my mother's life could have been so different, and Monsieur, it took me over. The fever just took over. It was a fever that would not let me go, and I knew I had to do something. I had to let these people know what they had done. People like Avery, Monsieur, they never look back; they never want to know what they have really done to others. I had to teach him, to make him understand. But . . . it wasn't at all like I planned. No, I didn't mean for things to turn out as they did. I don't know, suddenly everything just seemed to spin out of control.

"But that's not what I wanted to tell you. That's all over now. The fever is gone, forever. No, I wanted to tell you that I was sorry that I left you and Madame the way I did. I just didn't know. I couldn't think of anything else to do but to get away. To start over. Can you understand? It's been so long, and so much has happened. But I'm better now. *Je vais mieux maintenant, ne penses-tu pas?*

"Suddenly, I am so tired. It seems like it has taken me so long to get here, and there is so much to say, *mais je suis fatiguée, tellement, tellement fatiguée.* I thought of going to Nancy to see Madame, but I am afraid it will only make her sad. And I am so tired . . . and hungry, too. I feel like some ice cream, before the sun gets too low and it gets too cold. Maybe I will go down to the park and get an ice cream cone. *Ou du sorbet. Oui, du sorbet à l'orange, c'est exactement ce dont j'ai besoin.*

"*Tu ris?* You laugh? Ah, yes, I still love orange. Some things never change."

▬

At the edge of the city there is a park, and through it a wide gravel path leads toward the lowering sun and dissects a stand of chestnuts whose limbs hover over children playing the games only they can understand. Christine's pace is slow, and she stops to give way to a small boy rushing toward her on a bright blue bicycle with bright white tires of silent rubber kept upright by noisy plastic training wheels. She smiles at the child, whose blue jean cuffs are rolled above his bright red socks, which fall over what were once but are no longer bright white sneakers. The sneakers are scuffed and dirty, as the shoes of all small boys should be. The child acknowledges her with a cock of his head and a shout that comes like a laugh as he speeds past.

"Jean-Paul!" a woman seated on a nearby bench shouts after him. The boy skids to a halt and looks back to receive a rebuke from his mother or his nanny—Christine cannot tell which. The boy turns and begins to speed back down the path, this time giving her the wide berth that apparently is expected of him. *"Je regrette,"* the woman says a bit sheepishly, but Christine shakes her head and smiles that she is conceding the path to the children.

She moves off and sits on the grass, leaning back against the trunk of a tree and enjoying her sorbet as she watches the children, listening to their voices call up traces of her memories: a hot summer morning, by the canal, the boys playing football.

But that was so long ago. And now?

Well, for the moment, she is satisfied to have nowhere to go and no time to be there.

Limping up the path, a young man with a single crutch leads a small, stubborn pony carrying a little girl who Christine imagines is riding a great white stallion over the endless prairies of the park. The pony's head bucks at the squeal of another child who is dancing in the path ahead, arms spread to corral the wind-blown leaves, which ignore the child's reach and carry on down the path. The child, whose tousled hair and rumpled play clothes give no hint of its gender, reminds her of Alex: this is how he would see the child, as just that, a pure child who needs no further definition.

She stops herself, quickly painting over the thought of him, erasing it, if only for the moment. It is over, a useless memory, only a reminder that this day too will end, and that tomorrow will be different.

For the children, the days never end until they do, and then with no regrets, because each tomorrow brings the same, until that tomorrow comes when they learn to forget the afternoons when imagination was reality and reality was momentary and their souls were the souls of dreamers; when they were not yet embarrassed by their imaginings or their realities, or their laughter or their pain, or their grand adventures aboard a small bike, or the crisis of a scraped knee or the cooing solace of a mother's hug.

Christine looks up and to the dappled light coming through the trees. There is something different, she thinks, and special about the autumn and its sun. It is lower and softer and more comfortably warm against the cooling air. Its shadows are longer, not so defined, and the air is filled with the color of leaves whose drying and falling at their grandest moment begins that slow, soft slide into winter's night. It is nature's cocktail hour.

Tomorrow, it will be different, but for now, all she can see and feel and hear is soft and sweet and quiet. And so it is time.

She curls back against the tree, and from her pocket takes a small vial and empties its contents into her lap. Two and three at a time, she swallows the pills, each swallow helped along by the sweet, cool taste of the sorbet. It does not take long before the first warm rush sweeps over her, and quickly her eyes feel leaden and her chest constricted. She does not feel her hand drop, but she sees the cone and its last drool of orange fall to her skirt. She tries to brush it away, but her hand seems to have lost its will to move. She stares at the stain and then smiles. For the first time, she just doesn't care.

EPILOGUE

*I*t is almost dusk before Paul Wyzanski finds the unmarked address north of Cockeysville, and turns down the long dirt drive to a small farmhouse shaded by a single red oak. A large moving truck and a brightly painted van sit next to the house and point to a small barn in back, where Paul can see and hear the racket of men working. Hammers pound on the roof while men unload the truck, and one voice rises above the others.

"Will you *puleeze* be more careful? These are not stones we're moving. Honestly!"

Nicky Kane pulls a handkerchief from his pocket and mops his brow as he turns toward Paul's approach. "Can you believe this? I mean, where are we? It's a bloody wilderness. I mean what is he thinking?" Nicky suddenly realizes that he is talking to a stranger. "I'm sorry. Have we met?"

"I'm looking for Alex Trigorin."

"Are you a friend?"

"Well, sort of," Paul says as he offers his hand. "I'm Paul Wyzanski."

"Nicholas Kane. It's a pleasure."

"Is Alex here?"

"Alex? Well, Alex is off playing in the dirt. There behind the house. I mean, really, he hasn't been out of the hospital a month, and he's off playing in the dirt. Maybe you can talk some sense into him. Are you a friend from work?"

"No, I'm, ah, with the state police."

Nicky's back straightens, and his expression turns wooden. "The police?"

"Yes. I met Alex before, you know, before he was shot."

"You knew Christine?"

"Yes."

"Is it about her?"

"I think I should talk to Alex."

"Oh my God," Nicky murmurs. "You have news, don't you? You have news of Christine."

"I just need to talk to him."

Nicky's eyes widen, and he holds his handkerchief nervously to his mouth. "Is she all right? Have you found her? She didn't mean it. I know she didn't. She loved Alex. She would have done anything for him. Please, he won't talk about it. Can't you leave him alone? She was just—"

"I know," Paul interrupts quietly.

Nicky hesitates before he asks, "Is she all right?"

Paul shakes his head.

"Oh God. I'll go with you."

"No, I think I should talk to him alone."

"I'm going with you!" Nicky insists.

They walk down the drive and to the back of the house, where Paul can see Alex on his knees in a large patch of freshly turned earth. A score of small bushes and flowering plants still in their pots rim the patch, and Alex is digging in the dirt with his hands, ignoring the tools which lie on the ground near him. He looks up to see them coming and stiffens reflexively, then quickly settles back on his haunches.

There is a long silence and Alex's eyes narrow to a squint. He then turns back to his work. "She's dead, isn't she?"

"I'm sorry," Paul answers.

"It's all right, Nicky," Alex says, his eyes fixed rigidly on his hands working the soil almost to a fine powder. "We'll talk about it later."

"Alex?"

"It's okay, Nicky. Really. We'll talk later."

Nicky lets go a long, sad sigh, and he turns to walk back toward the barn.

"Suicide?"

Paul nods. "Pills. Dilaudid, we think. She was found in a park, lying against a tree." He stops a moment, and then adds, "She had been eating an ice cream cone."

Alex releases his breath with a brief smile, and he shakes his head. "Somehow I just knew she'd end it her own way. She'd never . . ." He stops himself, and again there is a long silence. Finally, he sits back and looks up at Paul. "Did she go home? To France?"

"Yes, to Strasbourg. The French authorities notified us early this morning. She was still carrying her badge. That's how they knew to contact us."

"Yes," Alex says, nodding, "she would want you to know. She didn't like loose ends."

Paul nods too. "Yes, I guess that's right. Look, I'm sorry, Alex, I really am. I wish we could have found her. Stopped her before . . . well, you know."

Alex takes a moment, studying Paul with a frown. "Why?"

Paul is taken aback. "Why? Well . . . because, you know."

"What? So she could spend the rest of her life in prison or in some mental institution? No, Paul, if you have any feelings left for her, be glad that she was able to end it as she did, in her own way. For her, I have to believe that this was best. She . . ." Alex stops and looks away. "Ah, well, it doesn't matter. It's ended."

Paul waits a moment, and then asks, "Did you know?"

"Know what?"

"You know, what had happened. Who she really was. I mean, I remember when I asked you about the necklace, I thought maybe you had some idea then."

Alex does not move, except that his brow furrows in a pained expression, and he does not speak.

"Is that what happened? There at the end, did you—"

"Paul." Alex stops him, his face clearing itself of any hint of his emotions, his words quiet and even. "Please, I told you, over and over, it was an accident. If there was any fault, it was mine. There's nothing more to say." Again, Alex turns his eyes away.

He asks Paul about Cooper Avery and about the boy, and Paul tells him of his meeting and of the apparent progress Ned has made.

"That's good," Alex says.

"Well," Paul says a bit uncomfortably, "I guess there's nothing else. I'm sorry, Alex, I really am. And if there's anything I can do."

Alex picks up a clump of dirt and turns it over in his hand. "Well, there is one thing. Do you know if there's been a funeral? What they've done with her, with the body?"

"I don't know. I just didn't think to ask."

"Well, if you get the chance, if you could find out who I might call or if there's anything I can do to make sure she gets a decent burial, I'd appreciate it."

"Sure, I'll see what I can find out."

Alex nods, and then turns away, as if he is considering which bush to plant first. It takes several moments before Paul understands that there is nothing more to say, and he turns to leave.

"Paul?"

The detective stops and looks back over his shoulder. "Yeah?"

"Thank you. Really. I appreciate your coming out here to tell me yourself. She . . ." Alex stops himself with a shake of his head.

Paul nods and then turns away as Alex leans forward and buries his hands in the dirt. His thick fingers clench the earth and hold on as he presses his eyes closed and strains to block out everything but the sounds of the workmen's hammers, and of Nicky Kane shouting at the movers, ordering them not to touch the finished sculpture of a woman rising from one knee, her head turned and looking back, her right arm reaching forward, the fragile fingers pointing toward something she cannot see.